Red Snow

by

Sean Ryan Stuart

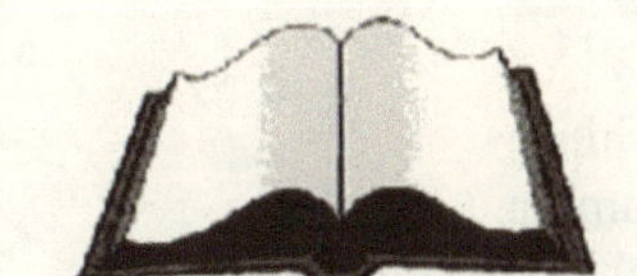

CCB Publishing
British Columbia, Canada

Red Snow

ISBN-13 978-1-926585-47-5
Third Edition

Library and Archives Canada Cataloguing in Publication
Stuart, Sean Ryan, 1948-
Red snow / written by Sean Ryan Stuart – 3rd ed.
ISBN 978-1-926585-47-5
I. Title.
PS3619.T8325R44 2009 813'.6 C2009-904860-4

Publisher: CCB Publishing
British Columbia, Canada
www.ccbpublishing.com

This book is dedicated to all members of the United States Armed Forces past and present, and especially to my son, SGT Justin Hood, currently serving in the US Army. Also my best friends, MG Peter Gravett, Colonel Brian Barlow, U.S.A, Special Forces (ret), and Colonel David Baldwin, currently serving in California.

Contents

Prologue to War

Afghanistan and the Mujahidin

Night comes to Afghanistan with a vengeance. Her majestic mountain peaks are glowing with vestiges of a setting sun. It appears as if the earth is radiating with pools of blood and demands revenge. This is a land of contrasting beauty and natural realism. A land of lunar-like landscapes, arid deserts and towering mountain passes. A land full of clashing colors, terrain and personalities. A region full of contrast and diversity. Strong Islamic fundamentalist influences seem to be setting the current fashion statements, and fewer women are wearing Western style clothing.

This is a country so beautiful and mysterious it demands passion and respect from its more than twenty different ethnic tribes. Rudyard Kipling once wrote, "A place where terrible things always happen to people." A country successfully invaded only twice, Alexander the Great did it in 400 B.C. and the Mongol hordes a thousand years later. Kipling's fictionalized accounts of the Northwest Frontier, Khyber Pass and the great mountain ranges made for interesting reading, but never truly honored these magnificent Afghani warriors. Unlike traditional guerrilla fighters of the twentieth century, the mujahidin (Muhahedin, Mujahedeen) are not inhibited by modern military techniques and equipment. If they had to move from point A to point B, they simply used whatever means were available to get there, walking, donkeys, mules, horses, and occasionally a vehicle. Using these primitive methods, they were able to successfully defeat a modern and well-equipped Soviet army. Varying sources estimate that between 17,000 and 24,000 Soviet soldiers were killed and over 100,000 wounded in their conflict with the mujahidin. Some CIA sources estimate an even higher death toll. It is also estimated that over one million Afghans were also killed; five million refugees took up residence in neighboring Pakistan and Iran.

Strangely enough the entire Afghanistan conflict began around 1973, when a family quarrel turned in to a blood bath. Muhammud Daoud, who was the first cousin and brother-in-law of Zahir Shah, decided to overthrow his cousin, the shah. Daoud's first action was to eliminate the monarchy and immediately proclaimed himself President of Afghanistan. Five years later, the Afghan Communist Party killed him and all members of his family in a sudden and vengeful act, and assumed power. ***Quid Pro Quo***.

Afghan politics during this time period assumed a television "soap opera" scenario, when Prime Minister Hafizullah Amir, had his superior killed by having him smothered with a pillow. These events obviously caused a great deal of concern to the big "Bear" of the North, the Soviet Union. In view of the seemingly chaotic situation in this satellite of the Soviet state, the Soviet Politburo, under the guidance and control of Leonid Brezhnev, launched the invasion of Afghanistan.

The Soviets then brought in one of their puppet leaders and appointed him as ruler. Babrak Karmal, an exiled Afghan leader, never really successfully controlled his own destiny. Although he had nominal power, his awkward leadership style made him an unpopular leader. Additionally, he was never able to manage the ever-present political turmoil within his government.

His political failures were even surpassed by a long series of military defeats against the mujahidin. At no time, was the Kabul-led Afghan communist army a match for the mujahidin; unlike the mujahidin, the Kabul soldiers were unwilling draftees who had no desire to die for the glory of Kabul and its leaders. To the contrary, many of the Kabul soldiers were members of the upper class. Their fathers were middle-level government employees, wealthy businessmen and high-ranking officers. Kabul soldiers showed no desire to die for this corrupt government.

The Soviets deployed over 145,000 soldiers, but could never control the mujahidin. The Soviet army was ground down in a political and military morass; reminiscent of Napoleon's invasion of Russia in the nineteenth century. The Soviets once again interfered and replaced the dreaded Karmal with another despot, Dr. Najibullah, the former head of the secret police. Despite all of these changes both the Soviets and Kabul communists could not control their own political destiny. Although the Kabul communists hung on until April of 1992, their faith was predestined the day the mighty Soviet army invaded their country. Some remnants of their rag-tag forces are probably still fighting somewhere today in a desperate attempt to stave off their annihilation. Radical Pro-Islamic students have forced them out of Kabul and in to the mountains. Since the war officially ended with the Former Soviet Union (FSU), a continual vicious civil war has raged between all participants and it is very difficult to sort out who is now in power. However, radical Muslim fundamentalists have taken over Kabul and are now attempting to regain as much territory as possible.

Unlike other third-world countries, the Afghan people were never colonized by anyone. Consequently, they did not develop any of the usual third-world prejudices and fears toward Westerners. They still did not trust everyone they met, but judged every stranger individually. They usually allowed most Westerners the opportunity to prove themselves, one way or the other. Afghanistan was a country forgotten by time until the 1979 Soviet invasion. A land never recently conquered or subjugated. The British colonial empire fought three major wars and never successfully subdued this stubbornly independent nation. In 1842, the British Empire fought a series of engagements with the Afghani tribesmen and were thoroughly defeated. In one famous engagement only one man survived out of 4,500 British troops evacuating the city of Kabul.

The Afghani tribesmen were ruthless and merciless when dealing with invading powers. The courage, stamina and physical prowess of the Afghan fighter was legendary. No one had ever so successfully resisted the British colonial empire and lived to tell about it. These extremely hardy people could go long periods of time without food or water. Their stamina was legendary; their goat-like agility and strength were unmatched by any soldiers in the world. The origins of the Afghan people remain a mystery to this date. Some believe, they were descended from the Greek troops of Alexander the Great, who passed through Afghanistan in the fourth century B.C. Some believe that they are descendants from the original Indian tribesmen. Others would have you believe that they are long-lost cousins of an ancient Hebrew tribe, and others would swear that they are an Aryan people called the White Huns. There are as many theories as there are stars in the sky. Legends tell of ancestral roots dating to the time of Israelite kings, mystical Babylonian emperors and other ancient tribes of "Holy" genealogy. Regardless of their roots, they learned to fight at an early age, and were successful in defeating the Soviets. No one will ever satisfactorily solve the mysterious origin of this land and its people. One thing is certain, most of them embraced the Muslim religion, and used its teaching to overthrow the Soviet army.

It is of these hearty and brave warriors that we will tell you about, the mujahidin, Northern Alliance and its war against the "Mighty Evil Empire," as President Reagan once called the Soviet Union.

It is obvious that the events of 9/11/2001 changed our world forever. We can no longer sit at home and feel as secure as we did on that horrible morning. There are more than three thousand souls that have convinced us that we must fight terrorism whenever and wherever we can. Some of our former allies turned against us, and some are now fighting along side of us.

Although this book was initially written during that hectic period of 9/11/2001, the same enemy exists. The United States, NATO, and the UN face a similar enemy in the Taliban. However, their sphere of influence spills over into Pakistan, and we must be weary of a nuclear Pakistan.

Chapter 1

The Camp

Among the scraggly odd pine trees, sprinkled with cacti and thorns, a small band of men climb rock-strewn slopes. Ten strenuous days of hard walking, mostly at night to avoid the ever present danger of Soviet Hind (helicopter gunships), brought this band of fighters to the outskirts of the Spinghar district. This plateau was protected on three sides by nearly insurmountable peaks and fast- moving rivers. For centuries this region had been a sanctuary for roving bands of outlaws; it now offered perfect protection from the prying eyes of the Soviet military. The headquarters of this band of guerrilla fighters, more commonly known as mujahidin (soldiers of God), was strewn haphazardly across the wide plateau overlooking the Kabul-Jalalabad highway. Small groups of mujahidin were huddled close to their still glowing campfires. It was a feeble attempt on their part to glean the last vestiges of warmth, before the strong rain soaked their tired bodies. They now knew that the Soviets were reduced to occasional air raids with high-flying TU 16s (tactical fighter/bombers) or daytime raids with helicopters. A few years ago, they never would have dared to have open campfires, but now it was quite evident that the Soviets were conserving forces in preparation for their departure. They were all aware that discussions were going on in Geneva, and hoped that this miserable war would be over in a few months.

A few hours earlier the valley floor cooked in a cauldron of heat and dust. Shimmering heat waves dancing in the distance like exotic belly dancers. Everyone had sought shelter from the burning sun. The mujahidin crowded around the few remaining shade trees like cattle on a hot Texas prairie. Now a late fall shower soaked their bodies, and robbed them of their remaining strength.

From this position, like birds of prey, the mujahidin could observe the highway and monitor all Soviet movement along the strategic road.

Their important location was cleverly blended and camouflaged into the rocky hillside. Their small shelters were similar in color to the existing scrub pines and bushes. Their camouflage techniques were vastly superior to the unsuccessful Soviet attempt at concealment.

At times, it seemed as if the Soviets thought they were invincible, neglecting to practice even minimal concealment, and camouflage. The Soviets were arrogant, and at the same time ignorant of their adversary. They were sometimes even more colonialistically inclined than the once glorious and mighty British Empire. They treated all Afghans in a less than compassionate fashion and were surprised to find out that the Afghan freedom fighters had no respect or fear of the Soviet war machine. They knew that they had a just cause and eventually Allah (God) would prevail. There was an air of confidence in this camp. An almost insolent atmosphere permeated the area. Nine years of resistance against the supposedly invincible Soviet army, had hardened these guerrilla fighters into a band of well-trained and extremely cagey freedom fighters. In fact, they had a secure defensive perimeter which would rival that of any modern army in the world. The camp was heavily fortified and included a captured Soviet heavy machine-gun of the ZSU-23-4 (SHILKA, usually mounted on a modified PT-76 Tank chassis, 4X23mm AA guns) type as well as one “Strela 1” launcher (AKA SA9) antiaircraft missile, not as effective as the newly acquired American Stinger missiles, but dangerous nonetheless for any low-flying Soviet aircraft.

They were fortunate indeed to have captured this complete SA9 air-defense system on a previous raid along the Pakistani-Afghan border. Their enemies had been so surprised by this raid that several communist Kabul soldiers had willingly defected, and now proudly manned this air-defense system for the mujahidin. The ZSU-23-4 was normally used as an antiaircraft weapon system, but could be devastating when used against lightly armored vehicles or ground personnel. It provided the mujahidin with a certain feeling of security and confidence. These two weapon systems were highly compatible to each other, and could be extremely devastating against low-flying aircraft.

Chapter 2

The Company Man and Flashback to Another War April 3, 1988

Jeremy Grant, the local CIA operative, had arranged for a shipment of American-made Stinger missiles. Grant was a veteran of the Afghanistan campaign. He had spent nearly three years hiking up and down the entire country. His reputation had grown by leaps and bound among the mujahidin because of his phenomenal strength and stature. His exploits were so remarkable that even the Soviets admired his great courage and had posted a reward of forty thousand rubles for his capture, dead or alive. By mujahidin standards, he was a giant, six-foot-five and 220 pounds of raw muscle and power. However, his nearly three years in-country had caused him to slim down from his usual 240 pounds to his current weight. Weekly bouts with dysentery and meager donkey rations had inevitably reduced his bulk.

Jeremy reflected on his current state of health and his slim new figure. He had unsuccessfully tried every known diet to man, but never lost those extra twenty pounds. He couldn't help but laugh aloud, as he had the perfect new formula for instant weight loss, a cup of impure Afghan water and a slice of tired and overworked donkey meat. Jeremy laughingly thought of the many commercial possibilities of his new and effective weight-loss plan. As he laughed, before and after photos flashed through his head. Jeremy still resembled a professional football player. His physique hard and sinewy despite nearly twenty years of covert operations. His many years of martial arts training had assisted him in maintaining his trim figure, and also greatly enhanced his reputation with the muhajidin.

Grant had in fact, been an All-American football star at West Point. Had the Vietnam War not interrupted his plans, he very well could have been a pro-football player. However, two tours in Vietnam, one of which as a member of the Phoenix Program (CIA-sponsored infrastructure re-adjustment program for the VC), ended his dream of professional football.

His involvement with the CIA was due in part to the CIA's interest in expanding its role in Southeast Asia. The need to expand the "Agency's" (CIA) role in Vietnam had caused a great deal of consternation in Washington. Most politicians in power there were convinced that the military was capable of handling the Vietcong. It was felt that perhaps the CIA should restrict itself to collecting and producing good intelligence products and stay out of paramilitary operations. However, by mid-1967, the CIA had over one thousand agents in Southeast Asia and became actively involved in military operations.

This was Jeremy's introduction to the real world of intelligence and war. As a Special Forces officer, he was given the opportunity to work closely with the CIA, and was actively involved in this phase. South Vietnamese Special Forces were trained to carry out missions for the CIA. Their objective was to locate and root out the entire Vietcong infrastructure and eliminate its leaders through "extreme prejudice." Unfortunately, many South Vietnamese officials used this U.S.-led operation to settle personal scores and eliminate personal as well as political rivals. Many Vietcong leaders were killed, however, many innocent civilians were also exterminated by the South Vietnamese forces. Their ultimate goal was quite often unclear, and eventually led to their failure.

Jeremy was actively involved in the training of these "Special South Vietnamese cadres" and participated in several confirmed assassinations. It was during one of these raids that Grant's pro-football and military careers vanished into thin air. He nearly lost his life when he was captured by the Vietcong during one of these raids. His team had been betrayed by a renegade South Vietnamese (ARVN) officer; his entire five-man team had been ambushed and taken captive. He was kept prisoner for ninety-seven days, under the harshest possible conditions. His fellow captives had been hideously tortured and beheaded. Their genitals were cut off and stuffed in their mouths; their heads were then speared on bamboo stakes and left near American forces as a sign of contempt, and as a reminder of their disregard for human lives.

It was during this ordeal in Vietnam that Grant developed an intense sense of survival that would help him twenty years later in Afghanistan.

Jeremy sat on the ground in front of his small tent and reviewed his current situation. Here he was on a high plateau in the mountains of Afghanistan trying to convince a bunch of fanatical Muslims to accept his help. Ten days of stressful evasion from the Soviets had worn his body down. The situation was both mentally and physically as exhausting as his capture by the Vietcong. His thoughts flashing back to a similar debilitating fatigue he'd endured during his escape from the VC, and of a sadistic little VC major two decades earlier.

His current sheer physical exhaustion and mental fatigue overpowered him and he promptly fell asleep. Although his memories of Vietnam were not pleasant ones, his mind seemed to force him to recall this episode in his life. Within a few seconds he was there, back in the stinking rice paddies and jungles of Vietnam.

His sleep was deep, yet restless. Throughout his ordeal as a P.O.W. in Vietnam, Jeremy was segregated from the rest of the prisoners, and only learned of the atrocities perpetrated against his fellow team-members from a verbose guard. Upon hearing of these atrocities, Jeremy was horrified and shocked at the monstrous hate of his enemies. He reflected on a very "apropos" quotation that he had learned while at West Point, *"**Communism has nothing to do with love. Communism is an excellent hammer which we use to destroy our enemy (Mao Tse Tung).**"* The VC soldiers who had committed these atrocities were mere instruments in the overall communist strategy. Jeremy's dream continued. Although, Grant was now fast asleep on the ground in Afghanistan, his thoughts were far away in Vietnam.

Still dreaming, Grant relived his entire Vietnam capture. While in this deep sleep, Grant began to realize that his life was only valuable as long the VC needed him. When his usefulness ended, so would his life. He was but a pawn in their propaganda campaign and he feared for his well-being. The Vietcong were particularly proud of the fact that they had captured an intelligence officer, even worse, a possible

CIA-sponsored "Phoenix" team member. The local VC commander, a foul-mouthed dwarf named Van Trang Dong, considered Grant his personal property, and was determined to march him up and down the entire country to prove his merit as a tactical commander. Although the vicious little major had nothing to do with their capture, he went around bragging of his cunning and stealth in capturing these vicious "Imperialistic American Dogs."

Grant often wondered why major Dong had such a particular dislike for Caucasian officers, especially intelligence officers. One month into his captivity, major Dong called Jeremy into his rundown office for another one of his torture and questioning sessions. The slimy little major began to interrogate him.

"Grant, you will talk now!"

"You will tell me everything you know; I am tired of hearing your excuses, CPT Grant."

*"**The Vietnamese people deeply love independence, freedom and peace. But in the face of United States aggression, they have risen up, united as one man.**"* "Do you know who said this?" Major Dong asked, his voice increasing in pitch.

"Of course not, you wouldn't," shouted the small major. "Our great leader, Ho Chi Minh. I feel the same way," screamed Dong, in a hysterical manner, his small dark eyes bulging like a small bulldog giving birth to a St. Bernard.

"Your negative attitude has forced me to pursue a course of questioning, which you will long remember."

"Major Dong, you already have all the information you want. You know I can't tell you anything else, even if you kill me," Jeremy stated.

"Oh, no! Death is too easy for you, I guarantee you will talk and you will suffer." Major Dong's eyes had a habit of bulging out of his head when he got excited.

Major Dong suddenly began screaming French, German and Arab obscenities at him.

"Espese de con," "Salopar," "Enculez," "Aschloch," and "Anta keebir haloof, "Zub anta", in Arabic, (Asshole, bastard, faggot, big pig, up your ass).

Grant looked at major Dong in total amazement, not understanding, nor knowing what was said to him. Jeremy waited patiently not comprehending, and awaited an explanation. Dong finally calmed down long enough to blurt out, his lips quivering with hate, "You filthy white trash."

"I will show you what real pain is! You think you are invincible, don't you?" Dong screamed.

Still dreaming, Jeremy slowly looked up and pondered whether or not he should challenge this madman. While reflecting on his delicate, and dangerous situation, Grant's thoughts once again wandered in a desperate attempt to escape this horrible predicament, a dream within a dream. These experiences had been so traumatic that he was able to escape the horrors by shutting off reality. His favorite means of doing this was closing his eyes, and drifting off the planet. Escaping the reality within a dream by falling asleep in his dream and escaping his torturer.

Once again his eyes slowly closed, as he inwardly shuddered at the thought of this little maniac. Jeremy desperately wanted to forget his current circumstance. He forced himself to recall another of the many famous quotes his history professor had taught him at West Point. It was, as usual, a very good quote. His history professor had forced the entire class to memorize dozens of these small gems, and perhaps now it would keep him alive. Remembering these often antagonistic quotes kept him from losing his sanity. Grant was fascinated by the fact that after all these years he was still able to recite these quotations by heart.

"A communist is a like a crocodile, when it opens its mouth you cannot tell whether it is trying to smile or preparing to eat you up." (Winston Churchill).

One of Major Dong's sudden outbursts brought Jeremy back to reality. Nah, he thought, this guy is too crazy and he didn't feel like ending up in the soup pan for dinner.

"Well, everyone talks eventually, and you will, too," Dong shouted.

"CPT Grant, you probably think you have been mistreated? Don't you?" shouted Dong.

"You now will suffer, the way the French made me suffer. The

French tried to break me! Oh how they tried!" He whimpered.

Major Dong seemed to lose control of his body and slowly sank to his knees. His face was twisted in a hideous mask of pain and grief. The entire room was shocked by this display of weakness. Twenty seconds slowly ticked away, before the small major quietly regained his composure and resumed his ferocious attack on Jeremy.

"Yes, I fought the French at Dien Bien Phu. You, like them, will lose this war! You do not have the spirit or strength for your cause. You cannot defeat our people," ranted Dong, only pausing for breath.

"I was captured by members of the 5th Parachute Regiment of the French Foreign Legion," shouted Major Dong.

"I was leading a small reconnaissance patrol near one of their outposts, when members of the "**Green Frogs**" (nickname of the French Legionnaire Parachutist Regiment) savagely attacked our unit, killing everyone, but me."

Major Dong spoke slowly and deliberately, as if trying to recall every detail; his evil little face contorting like a hideous mask.

"General Ho Chi Minh, our great leader, had entrusted me with this important mission and sent my patrol to scout the main runway at Dien Bien Phu," continued Dong with menace in his voice.

The little major spoke as if he had an audience of attentive school children; his gnome-like features creased in anticipation of applause from his invisible audience. The major continued in a barely audible whisper.

"All French Legionnaires were worthless scum, they mistreated and abused my people and all Vietminh!" "Ha!" shouted Major Dong.

"I got my revenge, and they still remember me, *"**Sal maudit Legionnaire,**"* (Dirty cursed—), he continued with fervor.

"Insolent and stubborn, at first. But, even their Germanic pride was no match for me. Did you know, CPT Grant, that many of these legionnaires, were, in fact, former SS soldiers?" He asked, the still silent Jeremy.

"But I showed them how to crawl and beg for mercy. At the end, they all begged for mercy," screamed Dong.

He seemed to slip in and out of consciousness and reverted back and forth between French and English, his lips contorting and twitching. His eyes were glazed and dark. He suddenly shouted: "Those Legionnaires were foreign mercenaries fighting for an imperialistic power. They fought in Morocco and Algeria and developed many interesting torture techniques. You are lucky, CPT Grant, I will personally introduce you to some of the more enjoyable Ones!" leered Dong, at the stoic Grant.

Although Jeremy was dreaming, his entire Vietnam experience unfurled within his now sleeping brain.

Major Dong's threats had Jeremy suddenly feeling a cold chill throughout his body, and he visibly shrank into a tight ball. Grant didn't really care about Major Dong's sad experience with the French Foreign Legion. He only hoped that he could survive this new form of torture. Grant's only wish was to get his hands around Dong's throat and squeeze until all of his rotten beetle-juice-stained teeth popped out.

Jeremy was then paraded from camp to camp throughout Vietnam. However, Grant noted that the VC always seem to be heading in a northerly direction, and he had no intention of ending up a P.O.W. in North Vietnam.

After the strange episode, Major Dong took particular pleasure in torturing and abusing Grant. Dong felt as if he had shamed himself in front of his men and blamed Jeremy for his Faux-pas (mistake). He took singular delight in running a six-foot length of bamboo behind Grant's back, and tying Grant's hands in such a fashion that any downward movement would cause excruciating pain. Dong would then fasten another rope around his neck and ankles causing him to choke whenever he fell. Jeremy had endured this abuse for over three months; his mind was becoming a blur of green hell, pain and agony. Grant knew that if he allowed his mind to wander too much, he would never escape this inferno. At this point, Jeremy did not know which part of his dream he was in. The violent thoughts rolled into each other in his hapless brain. His torment continued as he relived his capture by Major Dong.

One remote VC camp after another became a nightmare of renewed hell and abuse. Grant tried in vain to maintain his sanity by using every trick in the book. Focusing on one subject, he had found, helped his concentration. He repeatedly recited poetry or verses, and found that a poignant verse he had written during his first tour caused him to temporarily forget the pain.

Grant's mind wandered. His thoughts drifted like a butterfly on LSD. His soul floated between the stark realism of Vietnam, and the pleasant thoughts of a long-lost past, and the current events in Afghanistan. His dreams switched between the reality of his existing situation, and events which occurred over twenty years ago. During this particularly troublesome situation, Jeremy had difficulty in sorting out his dreams. His restless spirit would stray between dreams, and he seemed to lose touch with reality.

Although he was asleep, he continuously tried to focus on events and occurrences that were of particular significance to him. His mind was being continually torn apart by conflicting emotions and feelings. Even in his sleep, he was so confused that he was usually unable to achieve a deep REM state. After many hours of troubling dreams, finally succumbing to mental exhaustion, he fell into a deep REM sleep. His mind drifted into a semi-hypnotic trance.

Jeremy gradually escaped his torturer, and began dreaming and focusing on a training class that he had taken at Ft. Bragg, years earlier as a young second lieutenant. For some unknown reason his entire mental capacity was now concentrated on this event which took place so many years ago. Pleasant experiences were replacing the traumatic ones with Major Dong.

His Escape and Evasion class (E&E) had started routinely enough, but one idea clearly stuck in Grant's mind, "**S.U.R.V.I.V.A.L.** and Repetition." Grant's sole thought was now concentrated on his former instructor, and what he had taught him.

"One of the paramount experiences that hundreds of servicemen learned during WWII and Korea was that SURVIVAL was a matter of mental outlook. If you had the will to survive, you would do so! Another valuable tool was repetition and concentration. Be obstinate and more determined than the enemy and you will win the battle of wills!"

His instructor, Sergeant First Class (SFC) Donald Glenn Murchison, AKA "DG" (Dead Guy), a second-generation Scotsman from Dumfries, Scotland, had instructed his students to attempt and focus on one subject, and keep repeating this thought over and over and over. SFC Murchison had drummed into their heads that every soldier might experience emotional problems resulting from fear, anxiety, loneliness and boredom. Not only would they experience these mental problems, but they might also be subject to hunger, pain, severe wounds, and thirst. This combination of mental and physical torture could possibly overcome their strongest intentions. The words SURVIVAL and REPETITION kept appearing in Jeremy's thoughts. Jeremy kept hearing SFC Murchison scream at them, "SURVIVAL is spelled:

S ize up the situation
U ndue haste makes waste
R emember where you are
V anquish fear and panic
I mprovise
V alue living
A ct like the natives
L earn basic skills

"You will forget the, ***"New Testament,"*** and memorize the Department of the Army Field Manual, FM 21-76, SURVIVAL. Is that understood, gentlemen?" Jeremy's dreams were so realistic that he was transported back over and over again to Fort Bragg.

Grant's memories of SFC Murchison were always full of great esteem and respect. His time spent there now appeared like stories in a DC Comic book, short stories full of action and adventure. Jeremy's exhausted mind played tricks on him. Just when things were getting good or bad, the story line would shift. After a series of flashbacks his dream finally settled into an epic adventure.

"DG's" war stories were almost like an act of contrition. A price had to be paid in time, beer and hangovers. Jeremy fondly remembered their last encounter in the Senior NCO Club at Ft. Bragg.

Another senior NCO had also been present at their table, and he loudly proclaimed that "DG" had to be the greatest escape artist in the history of the United States Army.

"Hey, lieutenant, how in the hell were you allowed in this club? We don't allow no Shavetails in here!" proclaimed Sergeant Major (SGM), Richard "Bunny" Howard, a close colleague of "DG's."

"Well, huhh, you know, I was invited by "DG" to come along, and I hope I am not offending anyone," Grant said, hoping not to piss-off the drunken Sergeant Major.

"Naahh, that's okay, lieutenant, any friend of "DG's" is a friend of mine. Did you know why he was called "DG"? Huh?" stuttered "Bunny."

"No, I didn't, but I am sure if I buy you another beer you just might tell me! Right?" replied the young second lieutenant.

"Your damn right I will, but it's going to take more than just a little beer to get me to talk about 'DG.' How much time do you have, LT.? All night I hope, because I feel like getting drunk!" SGM Howard proclaimed in a loud voice. With that last remark he started rattling off like an out of control M-60 machinegun.

"'DG' Murchison is a highly-decorated combat veteran of both W.W. II and Korea. 'DG' has the distinct fame of having been taken prisoner in both wars, and therefore is an expert on the subject of escape and evasion. 'DG' got his nickname during the Battle of the Bulge. His position was overrun by the hard-charging 5th SS Panzer Division of Oberst (Colonel/later General) Joachim Peiper. Peiper was the former commander of Hitler's own 1st Leibstandarte Panzer Regiment and led the spearhead during the Battle of the Bulge. He was also responsible for the Malmedy massacre, in which unarmed American soldiers were shot down in cold blood.

'DG' was severely wounded and left for dead by his comrades. SGM Howard blurted out that last paragraph with hardly a breath between words. He continued after slowly taking a long swig of beer.

"Even his parents received a telegram from the Department of the Army, listing him as 'Missing in Action' (MIA). They were, of course, both surprised and elated when he turned up a few months later alive and kicking. His younger brother, Frank, had exclaimed, 'Hey, you're suppose to be a Dead-Guy.'

"Are you listening to me, LT?" "Bunny" barked!

"Yes, I am Sergeant Major. Please continue," Grant replied, his youthful voice breaking at the harsh bark of the drunken Sergeant Major.

"Well, the nickname stuck, from then on it became 'DG', replied Howard in a matter-of-fact voice." Twenty-six beers had finally taken their toll on the drunken soldier. His head hit the table with a loud '*Thonk*' and Jeremy knew the story was over for tonight.

The next day both Jeremy, the Sergeant Major and DG had a terrible hangover. But, from then on, Jeremy was more prone to paying attention to SFC Murchison. Although 'DG' continually yelled obscenities at his class of less than enthusiastic young second lieutenants. Jeremy Grant was one of the few avidly taking notes and listening to this grizzled combat veteran. Jeremy hoped that he would never need to know any of this stuff, but he felt it might come in handy one day.

Although Jeremy was dreaming, these vivid memories of a distant past life reinforced his determination to survive at all costs. In his dream and in reality, CPT Jeremy Grant had formulated a plan to defeat any attempts at coercion and torture. Repetition, hypnotic repetition! Grant snapped back to reality in his dream, and realized that he was now sitting on his muddy cell floor, in a rotten little corner of Vietnam. A sudden feeling of anguish and loneliness seized his heart, and he abruptly felt very alone and vulnerable. His mind willed him to be strong, but his soul was aching for companionship.

At various times during the night, Jeremy woke to find himself sitting in front of his tent in Afghanistan. This added to the confusion. At times he was unable to tell the difference between reality, Vietnam or Afghanistan. Flashbacks of another war kept muddying the dreams. Jeremy had never used drugs, but he was sure that this must be what all the veterans called "flashbacks."

As the night progressed back in Afghanistan, Jeremy crawled inside his tent and immediately fell fast asleep. It was as if his mind was pre-programmed for certain channels, and he wanted to continue watching the Vietnam Horror Channel (VHC). As soon as his head hit the rolled-up prayer blanket, Jeremy was back in Vietnam in his cell.

Jeremy dreamt that a green millipede slowly crawled across the floor. The creature scurried as fast as its tiny legs could propel it. He curiously watched the hundreds of little black legs wriggle in unison in a fascinating snakelike motion. Jeremy slowly reached out with his right hand and picked up the still-moving insect; carefully observed the strange colored markings on its belly and popped it in his mouth without further thought. **Survival** was one of the words that 'DG' had pounded in his head, and by God he was going to survive!

The deeper his sleep got the more vivid the memories were of Vietnam. In his dream, he was determined to maintain his sanity, and win the mind game with Major Dong. However, his protein starved and exhausted body kept shifting into the hibernation mode. Although his mind attempted to fight the urge, his physical collapse forced him to continually drift in and out of reality. In both his conscious and unconscious dream his exhausted body longed for sleep. No matter how hard he tried, his battered frame floated into deeper sleep. Once again, Jeremy slowly drifted into a state of hibernation. At first, his tortured thoughts screamed with despair and agony, but eventually his dreams became less violent in nature, and they quietly focused on his first visit to San Francisco. Jeremy felt himself transported thousand of miles, and thousands of hours away. He was suddenly there, landing at the airport, his memories and consciousness virtually alive. It later seemed to him like a child's dream of flying, floating in the air, but not really flying or touching the ground. He was aware of the floating sensation, but somewhere in the deep recesses of his brain he longed for *terra firma.*

Chapter 3

"Frisco" in My Dreams

As the night progressed, his dreams were becoming so realistic that he could almost swear he could feel San Francisco's cold moisture wetting the back of his shirt. Jeremy awoke in his tent, high on a plateau in Afghanistan, only to find out that a sudden squall had ripped the top off his tent and the rain was pouring in. Jeremy jumped up, got his bearings and realized that he was still in Afghanistan, wet and miserable. Luckily he had a piece of waterproof canvass, and duct-tape and he was able to quickly repair the damage. He changed the position of his bed and within minutes was fast asleep and had resumed his dream.

There he was at the San Francisco airport hailing a cab. Jeremy was visibly upset, as he had heard so many nasty stories of war protesters, and there they were, blocking traffic, screaming and yelling obscenities at him, and all other military personnel coming home from Vietnam. His cab driver, a WW II Navy veteran was not intimidated by the angry crowd, and drove past them, mouthing obscenities at them as he drove through the crowd at a high rate of speed.

Jeremy had always been extremely patriotic. After all, this was his first tour, and he was shocked at the spectacle that greeted him in San Francisco upon his return home. He had grownup in an All-American tradition and could not believe the vile and hateful creatures that spat upon his uniform in San Francisco. Jeremy was so furious at these sub-humans, that he swore never to set foot again in the "City by the Bay." These memorable events were causing him to stir restlessly on his sleeping bag. These incidents bothered him very much and he was unable to track his thoughts, either in his dreams or in his conscious moments. He drifted in and out of reality.

Although not all of his memories were fond ones, the city had a magical appeal and sparkle to it. Although his first impressions were negative ones, he still felt a strange attraction to San Francisco. The incredible sights and interesting landscapes attracted him to this unique city it was a city of mixed emotions, cultures and feelings; yet irresistible. Jeremy's thoughts drifted to the bumpy cab ride on his rip to the Presidio of San Francisco. At the time it seemed like an oasis a warm and friendly "firebase," where lonely soldiers could stop at the "O" Club (Officers Club) on the hill and consume "firewater" with the natives. He couldn't help but fondly remember getting plastered at the Officers Club. Jeremy always felt secure among fellow soldiers, and these comforting thoughts were probably the catalyst of his current dreams.

It was here, in this friendly milieu that he first recited his verse to fellow officers. Here among fellow warriors, he was able to let down his guard, and just relax. General Mac Arthur once said, "**Old soldiers never die, they just fade away.**" In this environment, Grant's soul opened up to his compatriots, and his poem on Vietnam just came shooting out of his mouth like a .50 caliber M-2 machine gun. At first they all stared at him not knowing what to say. Here among "old soldiers" Jeremy felt like "fading away."

The entire bar became silent, as during the minute before an attack. Everyone listened closely, and they were so moved that many of them openly cried. Even a hardened USMC combat veteran, LT/Col Anthony "Glorious" Barnum, wept like a baby, and kept saying "Semper Fi, Mac." Jeremy did not consider himself a poet, but the political upheaval and his experiences had inspired him to write his one and only poem. He always kept it in his wallet, and brought it out at appropriate times. This had been such an occasion.

LT/Col Barnum sat at the bar nursing a double rum and Coke. His eyes glazed, and his mouth was blabbering filthy obscenities at anyone within earshot. "Glorious" was a Marine Corps legend, his combat exploits were only surpassed by his John Wayne story. "Glorious" Barnum had the singular pleasure to have had his picture taken with the "Duke" in Vietnam. The "Duke" had visited Vietnam and posed with LT/Col Barnum. "Glorious" carried his tattered photo every where he went, and always relished the opportunity to show his well-worn photo, plus it also bought him a lot of free drinks.

Grant remembered the night at the Presidio and wished he could now be there drinking rum and Coke with "Glorious." His thoughts wandered in and out of consciousness. He never quite knew whether he was dreaming or just wishing he was back in San Francisco. At times, both dreams merged into one confusing and terribly scary one. Jeremy was unable to differentiate between his Afghanistan experience and Vietnam. His thoughts and emotions flashed across the time spectrum at the speed of light. However, one thought kept appearing over and over, the words to his poem. Jeremy knew the effect that this poem had on him; it gave him strength, honor, determination and stamina to carry on his lonely battle against solitude and despair either in Afghanistan or Vietnam.

In his dream, he slowly regained consciousness, and began sobbing uncontrollably. The finality of his position gripped his heart, and he felt vulnerable and afraid. Yet, his subconscious kept sending out disjointed "Frag-Orders," such as "**don't give in, keep it up**," repetition, SURVIVAL! Jeremy jerked his head up and began shouting silent screams.

Vietnam

Valiant are the few who fought and died,
Vanquished are the masses who fled and lied,
Victims are the mothers who stayed and cried,
Vanished are the many to whom we said good-bye,
Victory belongs to those who cared and tried,
Valor was common, but they still all died,
Vermin are those who crawled and cringed,
Verify, they cried! But, they never lied?
Vengeance some cried, but others were pacified,
Verdict we demanded, but now they are elected,
Vietnam, Vietminh, Vietcong, are still all wrong,
Valiant are the few who fought and died,
Victorious are we who cared and tried.

Jeremy's current dream had, in fact, been a dream within a nightmare and he was back in Vietnam. His confused thoughts drifted between Vietnam and Afghanistan. Jeremy's subconscious had taken over and he was back in his cell in Vietnam.

His hysterical outburst caught the prison guards by surprise, and they came running over to investigate. They had never seen the crazy American act in this fashion, and they were shocked by his screaming and ranting. The only word they could understand was Vietnam. He kept repeating these words over and over and over. They laughed at him and thought he had finally gone off the deep end. Jeremy continued in this manner for hours; until his voice finally gave out.

At times he too doubted his sanity. Pictures of Fort Bragg, 'DG,' San Francisco kept flashing in front of his eyes. These kaleidoscopic visions only seemed to confuse him. After a while, he then just sat in the corner of his cell, and whispered his poem over and over and over. His desperate outburst had somehow calmed him down. These desperate mental attempts at escape were possibly indicative of his current situation in Afghanistan. His vivid dream continued, and he now began recalling his escape from Vietnam.

Grant had patiently waited for his chance to escape. Early one morning, God granted him his wish, and the area erupted in a mass of flames and thunder. The entire horizon exploded into a mass of shaking, quivering earth. Mounds of earth, trees, bodies and huts were violently flung in the air. Jeremy had been sleeping, and he awoke believing he had died and was now on the threshold of hell. He was blinded by the intense heat, smoke and concussions of the explosions. He had no way of knowing that his camp had been targeted by high-flying B-52 bombers. Each bomber carried up to seventy-thousand pounds of HE (High Explosive) bombs; destined to liberate or kill him. It seemed like the bombing lasted for hours, but in fact had only been for approximately nine minutes. These high-flying bombers had come all the way from either Udapao, Thailand or Guam. The first and second wave of B-52s had wiped out the entire camp and eight square miles of stinking Vietnam jungle. Human remains were scattered around gaping mounds of earth, up to fifty feet deep and one hundred feet across. The entire area was covered with a thick veil of smoke and many trees were still burning. Heavily forested jungles were turned into a burning inferno. The whole area took on a lunar-like landscape. The violence and suddenness of the attack had caught the VC by surprise. Even the survivors were so shocked by the attack that they aimlessly wandered throughout the area, not knowing what had happened.

They were still licking their wounds when Grant managed to escape. The entire camp, along with its supporting bunkers, tunnels and buildings, was completely destroyed. Jeremy was slowly able to regain his sanity and analyzed his situation. The walls to his cage were completely blown away and the devastation was complete. Jeremy knew that he would need a few things if he expected to survive in the jungle. He glanced around and saw that the kitchen hut was on fire, but still standing. Jeremy ran over and poked around the ashes. He was able to find a partially cooked piglet, some rice and two canteens of water. *Eureka*! *he thought, I'll be able to last two weeks with all this food.* His thoughts now drifted to searching for a weapon. None was around, but he spotted an old machete lying under a burning mound of earth a few feet away. Jeremy walked over and started to pull on the machete, only to realize that the burning mound of earth had once been a human being. Jeremy gingerly removed the machete from the burning corpse and ran toward the nearest jungle. On his way out of the camp, Grant spotted Major Dong staggering around, half covered in dirt and completely dazed. Grant walked up to Dong,

"We meet again, Major Dong," Jeremy shouted.

His hearing gone and severely stunned, the little major looked up slowly and tried to focus his eyes on the giant standing over him. Jeremy glanced down at the once feared little major and laughed. The flames had completely burned away most of his clothes and Jeremy saw the evidence of Major Dong's hatred for the French Foreign Legion. His manhood had been severed, and in its place a small scarred stump remained. Jeremy felt no compassion or mercy for this little snake, because he knew that Major Dong was capable of similar acts. In fact, the little major had performed them on many of his colleagues, and unlucky Legionnaires.

"Who are you? Speak up, I can't hear you!" shouted Dong.

"It doesn't really matter, you worm, I am going to slowly squeeze the life out of you," whispered Grant.

Grant leaned over Dong, reached out and with his right arm, gradually squeezed Dong's scrawny throat until all signs of life wheezed out of his lungs. Grant had gotten his wish, he had managed to kill Major Dong with his one good hand, and had been thrilled at the sight of the little worm gasping for breath. Jeremy also took this opportunity to take Major Dong's AK-47 assault-rifle, ammo pouches and another canteen. Grant knew that his chances for survival were almost non-existent, but he was convinced that he would rather die in the jungle than in that stinking POW camp. Jeremy left the area as soon as possible and headed in a southeasterly direction. He realized his only hope for survival was to travel at night and lie low during daylight hours. However, today he had to put as much distance between the camp and himself as possible. Jeremy was positive it would take them at least two hours before they realized he was gone, or had any resources to send after him. This was his only advantage and he was determined to get away. Jeremy found a small stream and followed it southward for about two hours. He then felt confident enough to travel inland and resume his southeasterly course. Darkness was slowly beginning to fall and Jeremy knew that he had to find a spot away from prying eyes. He continued down a well-worn trail, figuring his signs would blend in with the many others tracks, until he found an ideal hiding spot. Before him, loomed a giant tree; its roots and base were at least twenty feet in diameter. It was leaning against a large rocky outcropping which was part of a very steep hill. Halfway up the tree, about fifty feet above ground level, there appeared to be a small opening in the hillside. It was only accessible from the tree and it was barely visible, unless one stood directly under the tree and looked up in that direction. Grant gathered his belongings into a bundle, slung them over his back and did his best imitation of Cheetah, the movie chimpanzee.

The large tree had many handholds and small hanging vines. Jeremy was able to climb up the tree with relative ease until he reached the cave entrance level. The opening appeared to be large enough for a man, but not much else. Jeremy crawled across a branch and pushed aside some heavy brush and wriggled his way into the cave. Well actually, "cave" was a misnomer, *hole* would be more appropriate. Grant immediately noticed a rather strong odor emanating from the hole. If he didn't know any better, he could have sworn that it smelled like a cat's litter box, but he didn't know of any domesticated cats living up a tree in a hole in Vietnam. Anyway, he was so damn tired and hungry he didn't really care if he shared a hole with a cat or not. Jeremy packed all of his belongings at the front of the hole and covered them with nearby bushes. He promptly fell into a long and almost comatose sleep. He had been so tired that he had forgotten to eat and drink. His restless sleep had eventually been interrupted by a loud and gnawing rumble coming from his stomach. Jeremy opened his eyes and quickly tried to raise himself. Forgetting where he was, he hit his forehead hard enough on the ceiling to draw blood.

"Oh, shit! Oh, shit!" He exclaimed, blood streaming from his face.

A loud, piercing, blood-curdling scream came from the back of the cave, and Jeremy froze in fear. He had no idea what type of animal or thing had suddenly screamed, but it sounded very close and annoyed. He suddenly noticed a large pool of warm and wet liquid oozing from his crotch. He had pissed on himself! *Oh, great,* he thought, *I have to take control of the situation, now!* Another, equally frightening scream, pierced the evening calm. Jeremy slowly regained his composure and realized that whatever was in the cave with him couldn't be very big. Just then, a blinding pain reminded him that this creature could be small in stature, but extremely vicious. Jeremy's anguished yell was as loud and startling as the creature's. *Enough is enough*, Jeremy thought, *I have to kill whatever that thing is, now*!

Grant rolled over on his side, grabbed the old machete, and tried to slash at the darkness beyond his feet. His pathetic attempts only angered the animal and it continued to bite and scratch his foot. The animal screamed hysterically and only appeared to be getting angrier. Jeremy finally managed to drag his leg outside the small hole and turn around head first. He grabbed the machete in the right hand and slowly crawled back in the hole; his right arm making a ninety-degree sweep as he moved forward. The animal suddenly grew quiet, and Jeremy was petrified it would make a mad dash for freedom. Just then, he could feel the machete strike something fleshy and bony. The machete had struck something and was now imbedded in the animal. Jeremy yanked with all his might and managed to pull the weapon free. An audible hiss was heard and the unmistakable smell of blood was present. Jeremy knew that he had killed his adversary, but was still too scared to reach in the darkness and pull out the corpse. *Oh, well,* he thought, *I'll just wait until daylight*. The rest of the night was spent in a semi-conscious state, not trusting himself to fall asleep completely.

The noise of someone walking on the trail had him instantly alert and ready for action. He slowly raised his AK-47 and pointed it down the trail, instantly forgetting about the dead animal in the cave. Jeremy spotted what appeared to be a squad of Vietcong heavily burdened with weapons, mortars, supplies, etc. They did not appear to be looking for him, but in fact were part of a supply column marching through the area. He quickly realized that his cave was in the middle of a major Vietcong re-supply route and he would have to move when it got dark. His thoughts once again turned to the un-welcomed visitor at the end of the cave. He carefully turned around, making sure not to expose any parts of his body, and reached down toward the back of cave. After a few tentative sweeps of the hand, his right index finger felt a soft and furry animal. He gingerly grasped what fur was available and pulled it forward. The animal had already begun to stiffen and smell. After what seemed like an hour, he managed to drag the carcass past the rest of his body, he discovered that his vicious enemy had been a small monkey. However, this small monkey had created more fear and horror than anything the now departed Major Dong ever did. One good thing the dead monkey had done was to add a substantial amount of red meat to Jeremy's diet for the next two days.

Grant continued to wander around the jungle for seven days, day and night blending into a green hell of musty smells, foul water and strange and eerie noises. CPT Grant had completely lost all track of time and motion. His water and food long since exhausted, he continued going southeast. Although he had never used any drugs, he perceived his current dilemma as bad as a bad LSD trip.

Jeremy had almost given up all hope when he heard the sweetest music in the world, the heavy "whirl-whirl/chop/chop" of a helicopter. Jeremy tried to concentrate on the sound and run toward it. He frantically thought of ways to attract the chopper. Grant ran toward a clearing and energetically waved his black pajama top in the hope of being seen. The American U.S.A.F. HH-53B ***Jolly Green Giant*** helicopter (a U.S. Air Force Rescue Helicopter) slowly cruised the area and attempted to pick up an emergency frequency signal from another downed pilot. Grant's rescue had been miraculous. He had, in fact, been on the verge of dying from exposure, malnutrition and the ravages of fever.

The ***PJ*** (Air Force Para-Rescuemen) had been looking for another downed pilot, when he glanced downward and saw this strange looking individual waving a ragged black pajama top at him. The PJ immediately knew that it had to be an American, because he had never seen a six-foot-five VC before. The second PJ nervously scanned the thick foliage for any sign of the enemy, his Gatling gun sweeping the area in anxious anticipation of combat. The crew chief, Tsgt Ray B. Stone, manned the other gun, and kept whispering, "Hurry up, hurry up, I got a bad feeling."

One of the PJ's, SGT. Anthony "Tony" De Grazia, shouted to the pilot, "CPT Brown, at three o'clock, there is a guy waving at me, come around, come around now!"

CPT Brown brought his aircraft around and also spotted the ragged looking individual. CPT Brown, a cagey Vietnam veteran, was concerned about the sudden appearance of this ghost-like creature in the middle of the clearing. Suspecting a Vietcong trap, CPT Brown picked up his radio transmitter and depressed the talk key.

"Bird Dog 1, this is Spooky 7, over."

"Spooky 7, this Bird Dog Leader, what can I do for you?" The voice was heavily accented in a deep southern Texas drawl.

"Bird Dog Leader, we are going in on an attempt pick-up however, I feel real hinky and I suspect a trap, can you provide some cover?"

"***No problema, amigo***, that's Spanish for friend, you understand. We are six-clicks (kilometers) north of Elephant Valley, near the river, and we will be there in about four mikes (minutes)," answered Major

Sam Houston Dennis, the flight leader and detachment commander of the 50th TFW (Tactical Fighter Wing) out of Da Nang.

"Bird Dog Leader to all my puppies, follow me, we got a mission just south of here." Major Dennis shoved his stick to the firewall and kicked in his afterburners. The F-4 Phantom screamed and trembled as the afterburners shot it forward at more than Mach 1. The three other planes in his flight followed right behind him, like a pack of hunting dogs following a raccoon scent.

Three minutes and forty seconds later, Major Dennis spotted the slow-flying HH-53B. Bird Dog Leader buzzed the Jolly Green Giant to let CPT Brown know that the hound dogs were around. CPT Brown sighed a breath of relief and called SGT De Grazia on the intercom.

"Tony, you be careful out there. Any sign of trouble, shoot first and we'll **Didi Mao** (Vietnamese GI slang for scram) out of here," CPT Brown yelled in the microphone.

"Bird Dog Leader, from Spooky 7, my PJ is going in on the penetrator, keep your eyes open, over." CPT Brown said, hoping and praying that they would not be needed.

SGT De Grazia nervously scanned the area, but not seeing any obvious enemy signs, he slowly lowered himself down the winch. Tsgt Byron, the crew chief, provided cover with the mini-gun. SGT De Grazia nervously covered the area with his M-16. The tall, but scraggly looking man staggered toward him. Although Tony recognized the tall apparition as a Caucasian white male, the tall man had somehow picked up a greenish tint to his skin and was covered with open sores.

Slipping as he walked, Jeremy made slow progress toward the nervous SGT De Grazia. Every step seemed to take an eternity. He noticed the nervousness in the young airman's eyes and tried to smile at him. However, his lips were so parched that it only caused him pain, and he frowned instead. He eventually reached Tony and stammered.

"Thank God! Thank God!" Jeremy's voice cracking with joy.

"Who are you?" Screamed De Grazia.

"CPT Grant, CPT Grant, US Army, Special Forces, I was captured over three months ago, and just recently escaped."

"Well, welcome aboard, you are a lucky man, we were looking for someone else and just stumbled into you." SGT De Grazia clipped his microphone and informed CPT Brown of his rescue. SGT De Grazia secured Jeremy to the metal penetrator and yelled in the mike, "Get us out of here, pronto."

"CPT Brown get, us up, and the hell away from here."

Just as the aircraft began its slow upward flight, the surrounding jungle erupted in a staccato of small arms and machine-gun fire. Clearly visible green tracers curved slowly upward towards the slow-moving aircraft. The speed of the bullets seemed to increase as they got closer to the aircraft. Hidden Vietcong positions opened up with everything they had. Jeremy had somehow managed to walk into a Vietcong battalion headquarters and not be observed until the helicopter circled the area. The VC commander decided to spring the trap at the moment of the rescue. However, he did not count on the four Phantoms.

CPT Brown pushed his stick to starboard, and raced for Da Nang. It seemed that his helicopter was being pelted by a huge storm of marbles and angry giant wasps. Round after round hit the sturdy Jolly Green Giant, but CPT Brown managed to keep her flying toward Da Nang. Just as it seemed they were going to get away without even a single casualty, several 12.3 mm heavy machine-gun rounds hit the aircraft. The aircraft seem to shudder in mid-air and a small fire started in one of the auxiliary generators. Tony was able to put out the fire and CPT Brown was able to keep the aircraft flying. However, the first round struck the crew chief, Tsgt James O. Byron, in the chest. The round made a gaping four-inch exit hole in his back, and Tsgt Byron dropped to the floor without even uttering a single groan or word. Jeremy and SGT De Grazia stared in horror as the rounds continued hitting the aircraft. *How ironic* Jeremy thought, *I am going to die in this copter after being saved by them.* Just then, the aircraft began stuttering again and blowing dark and oily smoke all over the sky. It seemed that they were going to crash. Jeremy hung on to the nearest hand hold and began saying a "Hail Mary" to himself.

CPT Brown struggled and somehow managed to regain control of the aircraft and slowly nursed it back to Da Nang, his aircraft trailing and belching smoke the whole way. The numerous large holes in the fuselage made such a racket that both Jeremy and the rest of the remaining crew had to hold their hands over their ears. Jeremy was amazed that any aircraft could still fly after such a beating. Some of the holes in the fuselage were as large as a dinner plate, but somehow the amazing flying skills of CPT Brown kept them flying. Jeremy made a mental note to himself to buy the whole crew several drinks at the club, if they ever got back.

As a parting gesture to the still hidden Vietcong positions, CPT Brown did manage to vector the F-4's into the area and they smothered the entire jungle canopy with napalm, Willie Petes (white phosphorous) and cannon fire. As the helicopter slowly pulled away from the area, a fiery greasy hell was observed by all who had participated in the rescue. As quickly as it had started, an eerie silence covered the battlefield. Where once an entire battalion of the enemy had lived, now there was nothing but charred remains and stench.

CPT Brown had sent a message asking that a second-53B be sent to the general area to search for the original pilot they had been looking for. CPT Brown was now convinced that no living thing could have survived that inferno, and he called to thank Major Dennis.

"Bird Dog Leader, this is Spooky 7, thanks for the assist, it was hot and heavy down there, old buddy."

"Hey, Spooky 7, anytime. If you want me and my boys to barbecue anymore chili for you, just give me the word, hombre," Major Dennis answered with his now recognizable twang. Just to make sure that you get home all right, me and my puppies will escort you, amigo!

"Hey Bird Dog Leader, this is Spooky 7, thanks a lot and muchas gracias to "you all." We sure can use an escort home," replied CPT Brown, his voice breaking with emotion.

Upon landing at Da Nang, the crew examined the aircraft and counted over seventy-eight holes in the HH-53B. SGT De Grazia was so impressed with the sturdiness of this helicopter that he decided right then and there to write a testimonial to the manufacturer and thank them for their quality construction.

Grant was gingerly carried from the aircraft by a team of caring nurses. He was transported to the base hospital at Da Nang for treatment, prior to stateside evacuation. The corpse of Tsgt Byron was also removed from the helicopter and transported to the morgue, where it would remain until transportation could be arranged for the remains to be shipped back to the U.S.A. The grisly reality of war hit Jeremy right between his eyes. *How unfair, he thought, this poor man died trying to save my life.* Grant decided to write a thank-you letter to the family of Tsgt Byron.

The physical carnage had been too much for Jeremy's system. He was examined, probed and prodded for seven days prior to being returned to California. It would take nearly four months to recover from his wounds and tropical parasites he had picked up in the jungles of Vietnam. His entire body had a strange green tinge to it. He had quarter size, puss-infected sores throughout most of his body. His right shoulder had been partially dislocated by Major Dong and Jeremy suffered from malaria, amebic dysentery and a number of other jungle diseases. Jeremy was amazed that his body could even function after such punishment.

All of these dreams about Vietnam, and San Francisco reinforced his longing for a quieter life. He could not get his mind off San Francisco and Loretta, his one true love. Just when Jeremy began to doze off again, Khalil came to his tent and woke him up.

"Hey Jeremy! What is wrong with you? Are you okay?" asked Khalil, the leader of all mujahidin forces in this neighborhood.

"My men tell me that you have been screaming and talking all night." Are you having flashbacks?" asked a concerned Khalil.

"Yes, you might say that. I am having a dream within a dream, and I am having a difficult time focusing on reality. Thank you for your concern, Khalil," replied a now awake Jeremy Grant.

"Well, maybe you should tell me what happened from the point I awakened you. It might relieve the pressure on your brain," smiled a gracious Khalil.

"Okay, why don't you come in and share some coffee with me, and I'll try to explain what was causing all those dreams."

Both men sat down, and Jeremy began recounting his San Francisco experience.

Chapter 4

Return to Frisco

Jeremy crossed his legs, and began telling Khalil that his return to San Francisco had not been a pleasant one and it held many strong memories. With a little prodding from Khalil, Jeremy began to recount his tale. Jeremy started his story from the day he found himself sitting in his hospital room.

Jeremy still had strong feelings about this city and wondered whether or not he could endure many months of solitude at the Presidio. Jeremy's arrival this time around was less confrontational than his first stay, but somehow he missed the excitement. He pensively recalled the last four months since his capture and escape. His mind wandered between the horror of confinement and the thrill of escape and freedom. The whole thing had a surrealistic feeling to it. His body told him, you are sitting in a nice comfortable chair; gazing out at San Francisco Bay. His mind however, said, you are still sitting in that rotten little cell, watching the green millipede slowly crawling across the dirt floor.

Grant was suddenly awakened by his doctor, CPT Loretta Q. DeFaut, USA MC. Loretta DeFaut, a stunning brunette from Baton Rouge, Louisiana, was concerned about this rather quiet and withdrawn soldier. She went out of her way to spend time visiting him every day.

"Good morning, CPT Grant, "How are you this fine morning?" Loretta asked with concern in her voice.

Jeremy slowly turned his head toward the sound of the voice and said, "Uh, uh, good morning, doctor. I guess, okay, thanks."

"How is that shoulder? Feeling better?" CPT De Faut asked, as she walked over and gingerly examined his still bruised and swollen shoulder.

"Yeah, I guess so. Hey, Doc, how long do I have to stay in this cage? I am feeling a little confined, and would love to get out of here and get plastered at the 'O club.', I have some old buddies to look up," Jeremy blurted out.

"Oh my, you must be feeling better, but I can't honestly release you for at least two more weeks."

"You got to be kidding; I will go crazy in this place," shouted Jeremy!

"I am honestly disappointed, captain. You survived over three months under the worst possible conditions and can't last a few comfortable weeks in my care," CPT De Faut chided him.

Jeremy was slightly embarrassed, and sheepishly looked away; trying to recover his composure.

"Uh, excuse me, doctor. I am sorry, this has nothing to do with you. I am restless and need to get out among people," Jeremy answered

"Okay, okay, I'll compromise; I'll see if I can get you a three-day pass next week," CPT De Faut promised with a smile.

Loretta was amazed at her strong feelings for Jeremy, but he never seemed to care or pick up on the strong animal magnetism she was transmitting. Loretta came from Baton Rouge, Louisiana, and still had a rather cute Cajun accent. Her physical attributes were stunning, to say the least. God and "Mother Nature" had blessed her with a rather voluptuous figure. At five-feet-eight and one hundred and forty pounds, she wasn't one of those skinny looking model types. She was extremely proud of the fact that she strongly resembled the sexy 40s-50s screen siren Jane Russell, Howard Hughes's ex-femme fatale. To the dismay of her colleagues and superiors she knowingly wore rather provocative hospital gowns and revealing uniforms. Loretta firmly believed that "a little bit of femininity was the only thing those poor wounded returning veterans needed. "I am determined to do my patriotic duty," she would teasingly whisper to her shocked fellow doctors. She had won the "Miss Baton Rouge" and "Miss Louisiana" contests, and was bound and determined to proudly display her ribbons, trophies and many attributes. It was easy to see why she was the most popular doctor in the hospital.

She realized that her interest in the young Special Forces captain was not just professional courtesy and patriotic duty. Jeremy reminded her of a long-lost boyfriend she once had. He had also been a quiet, sulking and solitude seeking individual. Major Beauregard "Beau" Armstrong Lee, had been a hot-shot Air Force pilot with 89 missions under his belt. At twenty-eight years old, he had been one of the youngest fighter aces in Vietnam. Unfortunately, his luck ran out, and he was shot down over North Vietnam and never heard from again. Like so many other *M.I.A.* (Missing in Action) families, Lorretta had hoped that someday, her "Beau" would be found safe in some POW camp, but as the months turned into years, she slowly accepted the fact that he would never be coming home.

Her professional training told her that this young soldier needed more than just medical care. She sensed an air of desperation and loneliness in this quiet and withdrawn human being. Although she tried every trick in the book, CPT Jeremy Grant totally ignored her advances. She realized that he was suffering from a variety of both mental and physical stresses, but he refused to cooperate with her demands to see one of the psychiatric counselors.

Well, she thought, *If he's too stupid to get the hint, maybe I'll make him walk and exercise himself back to reality.*

She informed him that he needed physical therapy, and recommended long walks and exercise. The abundant pathways that surrounded Letterman Hospital were ideally suited for someone seeking solitude and exercise. Jeremy spent many lonely hours hiking among the pines and oaks that abound in the Presidio. His daily exercise routine became an important part of his rehabilitation. Jeremy was convinced that he could only regain his health and mental stability, if he adhered to a stringent exercise program. He awoke every morning at 05:00 hours to the sorrowful sounds of the foghorns. The foghorns were very audible in the inner bay area, and each had a distinct, yet comforting sound to them, their mournful wails echoing like ancient creatures calling for help. Jeremy would often fantasize of a long ago past when prehistoric dinosaurs roamed this angelic location; bellowing love messages across the bay. The foghorns were simultaneously melodious, hypnotic, alluring and also annoying.

Grant walked and exercised along the many paths for two hours, before returning to his quarters. His route would take him down from the hospital, along the seashore by Crissy Field, and up to the Golden Gate exit and back. Grant had come to like the solitude and regularly visited the military cemetery. He was fascinated by the tombstones and almost came to wish he could also be buried among the trees overlooking this magnificent bay. If one had to die, this had to be the spot that funeral directors dreamed of. Jeremy was envious of the soldiers who were stationed here on a permanent basis. *What a cushy duty*, he thought to himself.

He made it a point to try and find new and interesting trails. Jeremy was particularly fond of the solitude, stillness and awesome beauty. Grant was always amazed by the diverse and changing weather patterns in San Francisco. The city had air quality that no other city of the world could match. The fog would suddenly and silently roll in from the west side of the Golden Gate Bridge and smother everyone into its fold. Just as suddenly the fog would blow away, and the entire bay would be covered with a brilliant sunshine. This almost daily routine was part of the San Francisco charm that he had grown to love. He was not always fond of its citizens, but the city's charm could overpower just about any negative feelings he encountered. It was this strange and ever-changing environment that attracted so many tourists to this city by the Bay. However, many of the unsuspecting tourists were often caught unprepared by the city's fickle weather patterns.

Jeremy had been following this strict and regimented program for over ten days when he received a request from CPT De Faut to come in for a check up. CPT Grant showed up punctually and knocked on her office door.

"Come in," she said.

"Good morning, CPT Grant. Well, captain, how do you feel?" questioned CPT De Faut.

"Well Doc, I feel pretty good, as a matter of fact, I am ready to leave this 'puzzle palace' and get back to real soldiering," CPT Grant answered, his voice rising in excitement.

"Well, CPT Grant. I am thoroughly disappointed that you can't wait to get out of here, and abandon me to these damn Yankees! CPT

De Faut, shot back, her eyes wide in mock horror. But as you know, your system suffered an immense shock, and I am afraid your days of soldiering are probably over," CPT De Faut stated.

"What do you mean, over? Like discharge, maybe?" CPT Grant inquired.

"I am afraid so, captain, your shoulder will probably never get better again, and you would greatly benefit from a long home R&R (Rest and Recuperation) leave. You currently have over a dozen rare and potentially dangerous intestinal parasites, malaria, scurvy, etc. Not to mention your shoulder, and foot damage. I am going to recommend you for an immediate Physical Evaluation Board (PEB) hearing, and if they concur, a Medical Evaluation Board (MEB) hearing with a medical discharge," stated CPT De Faut with emphasis.

Jeremy looked at her in silence, too stunned to reply.

"You may think that you are healthy, but you have a long way to go. Additionally, you need to be among people and restore human contact with our society, but most important of all, you need to get laid," Loretta said with a sexy smile.

Grant's initial reaction was one of shock and amazement. Never in his wildest dreams had he contemplated leaving the Army. He was shocked and disappointed. He was so stunned in fact that he didn't even hear her "laid" remark. He developed a temporary, but intense dislike for Loretta, and blamed her for his current woes. He was somewhat amazed at her direct line of questioning.

Loretta purposely stared at him, trying to assess his reaction to this new development. Jeremy stared back, and carefully analyzed the situation and after a few minutes of clear thinking he came to the conclusion that he could not possibly blame CPT De Faut for his bad luck. *Shit happens*, he thought.

"You also need to be among people and get laid," CPT De Faut repeated, her eyes boldly staring at him with anticipation, hoping that the young captain would finally get the hint.

Jeremy was initially shocked by her statement, but quickly grasped the meaning of her direct line of questioning.

"Laid, did you say?" Grant asked, his eyebrows raising in mocked horror.

"You heard me, captain. You are so uptight, and frustrated by L.O.P.s, that you are about to pop your cork," Loretta said in a firm, but insistent voice.

"L.O.P.s? What in the hell is that?" Jeremy asked, not wanting to appear too stupid.

"Why, I declare, CPT Grant, a world traveler like yourself doesn't even know what L.O.P. stands for," smirked Loretta, her lips grinning from ear to ear.

"Lack of pussy, you dummy. Oh, dear me, you do know what that is, don't you?" Her eyes rolling in feigned amazement.

"And here I thought you were a southern belle, a fine lady. Maybe you are right, doctor! Any takers?" answered Jeremy in his best Rhett Butler imitation.

Although the thought of leaving his beloved Army made him sick, the idea of being a mere civilian again made him gasp in repulsion. He had devoted eight long years to the service of his country, and had never even thought of someday taking a civilian job. What would he do? Where would he go? All of these thoughts whizzed through his head like a runaway freight train. The thought of going home suddenly became a pleasant memory.

"Hey, yo! Hellllooo, I am here," yelled Loretta from across the room.

Jeremy slowly looked up and carefully admired this beautiful woman. He began to realize that Loretta was flirting with him. For the first time, he couldn't help but notice that the beautiful captain was openly coming on to him. He glanced up at her and admired her two greatest points of interests. It was the first time in months that he noticed a visible stirring in his loins. The harder he stared at her breasts, the more excited he got.

She finally said, "Well one thing's for sure, your eyesight hasn't suffered any."

Jeremy actually felt himself blush and was forced to look away.

"I am sorry, ma'am, he said in his best Rhett Butler imitation again, I didn't know you were a lady in distress. However, I must confess that I am one of those damn Yankees you are referring to" Jeremy answered, a wide grin smeared across his face.

"You mean to tell me that you are from the northern half of our glorious country? I could have sworn you were a southern gentleman," she mockingly yelled at him.

"Yup, that's me, guilty as sin," Grant laughed

"Doesn't the name Grant have a familiar ring to it? You guessed it, my great-great-great grandfather was General Ulysses S. Grant."

Jeremy wasn't sure whether he should mention this fact to Loretta.

CPT De Faut suddenly stood up, and glared at Jeremy in mock shock and disbelief.

"You mean, I've been treating the great-grandson of that butcher and murderer? Well, I guess I am going have to take some radical action and correct this mistake," Loretta stated.

"You think you're up for a hot date this weekend, CPT Grant? I am approving a three-day pass for you, and just to make sure that you enjoy yourself I am to go along with you."

"OK, sure," stuttered Jeremy. I don't know what to say, do you have any particular plans?" He asked sheepishly.

"Yep, don't you worry about honey, this little Cajun girl is going to take good care of you. Putain alors, tu vas avoir un beau temp" (Shit, you are going to have a good time), she slowly said in French, and smiled at him.

Jeremy wasn't sure of what she said, but he assumed it was very nasty and he was going to have a good ole time with this Southern Belle. Loretta told him to be ready at 18:30 hours. He returned to his room, and nervously paced the floor until CPT De Faut came by to pick him up. At exactly 18:35 hours, she knocked on his door. Jeremy excitedly rushed to the door and opened it. Miss Loretta Q. De Faut stood before Grant, wearing a spectacular low-cut gown showing a healthy amount of cleavage and long, lovely legs.

"Mama Mia," he whispered.

"You sure are a sight for sore eyes, ma'am," he blurted out like a young country boy on his first date.

For the first time, Loretta blushed slightly and looked into his eyes and said, "You don't look so bad yourself, Jeremy. I am ready to show you the town, so just sit back and let me do the driving."

"Okay, ma'am, let's move out and have some fun," Jeremy

answered, not knowing what he was getting himself into.

Loretta led Jeremy to the parking lot. Standing in the red No Parking Zone, was an equally "Ferrari" red Mustang convertible. The car glistened; every piece of chrome sparkled like a diamond necklace.

"Wow, you really know how to make a guy feel good. Where did you pick up this beauty?" Grant stammered.

Loretta suddenly grew silent, and looked down, her eyes tearing up.

"Oh, it belonged to a man who no longer needs it, and I'd rather not talk about it anymore, so let's get out of here and party," Loretta answered, her voice breaking with sorrow.

Jeremy realized that he had accidentally blundered, and decided not to push the subject until a more appropriate time. He opened the door for her, and once again admired her incredible body from a more strategic position.

"A tit man, are you, CPT Grant?" she suddenly blurted out.

Jeremy was caught by surprise; he honestly thought that she hadn't noticed his piercing and lecherous glance.

"Guilty, as charged, ma'am! I am one of those damn Yankees who preys upon helpless 'Southern Belles.' I am sorry, Loretta, I haven't been near or thought about women in months. I guess my eyes are guilty as charged. Please forgive my bad manners," Jeremy replied with a lecherous smile.

"Now, now, there is no need to apologize, I would be disappointed if you didn't stare. Hey, you don't think I spent two hours squeezing into this corset for nothing, do you? I strongly believe that it is the duty of all men to stare at and enjoy ladies bosoms," Loretta shot back at Jeremy.

Loretta's beautiful Mustang slowly wound its way through the busy San Francisco traffic. San Francisco's traffic is nearly always heavy, but Friday night has a way of bringing out even the most aggressive and crazed driver. Jeremy admired her agile handling of the beautiful little red Mustang. Loretta showed traces of driving habits which were extraordinary for anyone; especially for a young and beautiful doctor.

"I am impressed, where did you learn how to drive like that?"

shouted Jeremy over the din of traffic.

"What do you mean, monsieur? I always drive like this," Loretta replied.

"I believe you, but how do still have your driver's license?" Grant laughed.

"My, monsieur, are we always so critical on the first date? I am a very good driver, n'est-ce pas, cheri? (Isn't that so, darling)"

"Okay, okay, spoil sport, if you must really know. I spent a year as an exchange student in Paris, France, studying at the Sorbonne, prior to medical school. My French lover, Henri LeClerc Toussaint, taught me how to drive, and make love French style," Loretta answered with a smirk.

"Well ma'am, if your lovemaking capabilities are half as good as your driving style, I am in for a real treat," Jeremy answered, laughingly.

"Please, answer one thing for me, where are we going in such a hurry?" Jeremy wanted to know.

"Hang on, Jeremy. We are going after treasure, on Treasure Island. Haven't you ever been on Treasure Island, cheri?"

"Nope," answered Jeremy.

"Well, there is this beautiful island, right in the middle of San Francisco Bay, and it is called Treasure Island. It has the most beautiful view of San Francisco, and it's cheap, even if we have the admiral suite at the Bachelors Officer Quarters (BOQ)."

"Huh, what do you mean, admiral's suite?" asked Grant suspiciously.

"Don't you worry, mon cher (my dear), Loretta will take care of 'The general'."

"Hold on there, sweetie, what general, who, what are you talking about?" Jeremy asked.

"Haven't you heard, mon cher? You have been promoted to Brigadier General. Therefore, you deserve an admiral's suite, okay, oui?"

"Look, cheri, darling, sweetness, I don't mind a little fun in the hay, but I don't want to end up in Leavenworth for impersonating a General officer!" stated Jeremy.

"Alors, (And) this is the way you thank me for getting you the best suite in the city? You are worrying too much about going to the **Bastille** for a few years," she said, her Cajun blood beginning to show signs of cooking.

"I promise you, mon cher, everything will be just fine" Loretta replied, her voice beginning to take on a slightly irritated pitch to it. *Patience, patience* she thought, *after all, he is only an* "homme" *(man).*

"Well, I hope so. I am not really the confinement type, if you know what I mean. How are we going to handle this?" quizzed Jeremy.

"You just let 'Tante' (Auntie) Loretta do all the talking for you."

"Do you really think anyone is going to believe that a twenty-six-year-old, young-looking captain is going to be a Brigadier General?" Grant asked anxiously.

Jeremy finally calmed down and began to appreciate the idea. He realized that it could have some serious consequences, but it could also have some interesting possibilities. He looked at the beautiful Loretta and blurted out, "You are the most amazing woman, I have ever met. Let's have some fun and scare the shit out of these Navy squids," Jeremy stated, as they slowly drove over the Bay Bridge.

"Mon Dieu, (My God), thank God, you are finally getting with it. I called and made a reservation for a Brigadier General by the name of Stuart McBarron Fraser III. Can you think of a more obnoxious name than that?"

"Ha, ha!" She laughed. I told them that you were a highly decorated Medal of Honor winner, recovering from wounds suffered in Vietnam. However, as you were a Special Forces intelligence type, your visit had to remain secret to everyone," Loretta explained with glee.

"Wow, I am impressed, madame, but how did you explain your presence? Jeremy asked, his boyish innocence demanding an answer.

"No problema, cheri, I am your personal physician and temporary Aide-de-Camp, oui? I have reserved a room next to you, and I will come and visit you often, n'est ce pas?" (Isn't that so?) She laughed.

"Of course, mon docteur, you can come and check my pulse

anytime you want," he stammered, in his best Maurice Chevalier imitation.

The little red Mustang slowly wound its way down the curvy road to the main gate at Treasure Island. A young Seaman Third Class (PO3) stood in his guard shack and lazily waved them through. Loretta made a right turn, and immediately turned left in the front entrance of the BOQ. She purposely and knowingly parked her car in a slot marked, "Admirals only," Loretta walked into the main lobby and walked over to the duty Yeoman.

"Good evening, ma'am," he stammered, his eyes focused on her twin large caliber guns.

"Good evening," she answered, more formally than she intended to.

"What can I do for you?" he queried, still trying not to stare too hard at her.

"Is the suite ready for the general? I sincerely hope so, as I made those reservations three days ago, and I was assured there would be no problem," Loretta said, her voice projecting impatience.

"Oh, I am sure there won't be any problem, ma'am. Let me get the Chief, he'll, he'll be able to help you." The young Yeoman Third Class (YN3) had never seen an admiral, let alone an Army general. He turned around and grabbed the switchboard cord.

"Chief Mendoza, Chief Mendoza, get up here pronto; I got some general here and no reservation, help me; please," he yelled into the receiver.

Chief Mendoza, a twenty-seven-year veteran of the U.S. Navy, calmly answered the anxious sailor,

"Hold on, don't get all panicky, I'll be there in a second."

Chief Mendoza got up and waddled over to the counter. The chief was an old salt; he had enlisted in the U.S. Navy shortly after the attack on Pearl Harbor and the Philippines. Like many of his fellow countrymen, Chief Mendoza was proud of his Filipino ancestry, but was even prouder of serving in the U.S. Armed Forces. The years had not been kind to him. His once slim and trim body had turned into a quivering mass of flab and sagging skin. He had a particular fondness for beer and ice cream, neither of which was particularly good for his physique. Hercules Mendoza was near the end of his career and there was very little that could ruffle him. He was a short-timer, two hundred fifty-two days and counting. Hercules had actually purchased a small island near the Mindanao group and intended to retire to a life of leisure and debauchery. His short-timer's attitude was obvious to all who worked with him, and it made life particularly unpleasant for his staff. The Chief had the reputation for being fierce and grumpy. He approached the counter ready to rip off the head of the "asshole" who dared to disturb him during his "siesta" time. However, Loretta DeFaut's striking beauty and voluptuous assets quickly changed his mind.

"Good morning, ma'am, can I help?" he casually asked.

"I am Chief Petty Officer Hercules Pacito Mendoza, Non-Commissioned Officer in Charge (NCOIC) of the BOQ billets. What seems to be the problem?" he stated heroically.

"Well, I am obviously talking to the right man," smiled Loretta.

"I called three days ago and made a reservation for the general. It appears that someone didn't inform you. I am sincerely disappointed, but I am sure that you will be able to take care of the problem."

"There is no problem, ma'am. I took the phone call, and in the interest of security, I booked the general under the name of John Smith," he slowly grinned.

"I have been around a long time, and I know how these things are handled," he replied, winking at the same time.

"Yeoman, look under John Smith and Aide-de-Camp, now," he whispered under his breath.

"Right away, Chief. Yeah, here it is, Brigadier John Smith. Sure, sure no problem," said the anxious Yeoman, sensing a pair of dark piercing eyes burning through his skull into his brain.

"Well, I could tell that you were the right man for the job, Chief. If there is anything I can ever do for you, just let me know, hear?" Loretta answered, looking straight into his eyes.

"Okay, I promise, ma'am, if I ever need to have my liver taken out, I'll be sure to have you take care of me," Chief Mendoza slowly grinned at her. He knew when a woman was pulling his chain, but he couldn't remember when he enjoyed it more.

"Yes ma'am, thank you very much," he said once again.

"Your suite is on the third floor, facing the bay and it has been fully provisioned for comfort and entertainment, and your room, ma'am, is right next door," Hercules proclaimed with a large grin.

"Thank you, Chief," Loretta said.

Loretta slowly exited the office and walked through the lobby toward the main exit. She knowingly sashayed her way past two high-ranking naval officers. Their mouths were so wide open that an entire squadron of F-4 Phantoms could have landed inside their drooping jaws. Loretta knew the effect she was having on these poor hapless sailors. She purposely exaggerated her prancing, as she walked out the door.

Jeremy sat in the car, nervously waiting for her to come out, his mind racing with visions of swarms of SP's (Shore Patrolmen) and MP's (Military Policemen) hauling them off to the brig. Loretta slowly walked over to the car and said, "Get out, sweetcheeks, the suite is ready for his lordship," she giggled.

"How did everything go? Any problems?" Jeremy asked.

"Don't be such a little petain (fart/pain) in the derriere (ass); Tante Loretta will take care good care of "Le General."

"Make yourself useful, and carry the luggage upstairs, cheri," she said.

"Excuse me, "Ma Capitaine," don't forget I am a general, and generals don't carry their own luggage, captain." He chuckled.

"Now lookee here, CPT Grant, don't let this general thing go to your head. Allez-vite (Hurry up), pick-up the bags and move," she said in a semiconscious-scolding manner.

Jeremy exited the Mustang and grabbed the luggage, his mind racing with visions of passion, naked embraces and sexual misconduct. However, the closer they came to the building the quieter they grew, Their silence seeming to be the only bond between them with each step imitating the honor guards at the Tomb of the Unknown Soldier. Like mechanical puppets going through the motions, their actions were so forced that it was almost comical. Jeremy felt alone and very insecure. He was amazed at his actions, but only hoped that time would quell his fears.

The suite was located on the third floor, and the climb seemed to take forever. Suite 323 had a living room, a bath and a spacious bedroom furnished in the newest thrift-store fashion. The rooms were recently painted, and were remarkably clean. A large color television sat atop one of the chest of drawers. The large rectangular coffee table was garishly decorated with a flowered table cloth. A large fruit basket, adorned with various tropical fruits, sat in the middle of the table. Two bottles of chilled champagne sat in an ice bucket, waiting to be consumed. A small and lazy Navy gray fan slowly rotated back and forth, its' motion reminiscent of a tired beast slowly shaking his head to and fro. A small white refrigerator purred in the far-right corner. Jeremy walked over and looked inside. An ample supply of Red Horse Filipino beer was lined up on the top shelf. Loretta sneaked up behind him and kissed him on the neck. Jeremy suddenly snapped back into reality, and turned around.

"Wuh, that was nice, let's do it again," Jeremy said, feeling more confident and rambunctious.

He slowly looked down into her beautiful eyes and realized that she was crying, her tears, like drops of crystal, gradually streaking her face. Loretta's head was bowed and her body was rigid.

"What's wrong, darling?" Jeremy whispered.

"Can I help you, sweetness? What has brought the sudden change?" Jeremy inquired, his self-confidence slowly leaving him.

"I am afraid that I am a fraud, cheri. I have deceived you into believing I am some sort of sex fiend. I am only putting on a show to give myself strength, and get through this night. Please forgive me, darling," she slowly whispered.

"Now, lookee here, little Miss Cajun Queen, you don't really think that I bought all of that heavy-handed romancing, did you?" Jeremy shot back.

"Of course not, I just went along with the program in the hope of perhaps finding the real you. Your sweet Southern-Belle charm did not fool me at all," he said.

"Well, I guess I was only fooling myself into believing that perhaps I could find love again, or at least a little romance," she said, her chest heaving sobbing uncontrollably.

"Come here, darling, if there is one thing that I can't stand, is a woman in tears." Jeremy walked over, took her in his arms, and slowly looked down her tear-streaked face. She carefully raised her still quivering lips to his face; they slowly and sensually kissed each other, their kisses merging passionately, becoming stronger and stronger, until his desires were so strong that he could no longer control himself. His right hand sneakily crawled along her shoulder like a snake awaiting its prey. His fingers finally found the small metal zipper of her low-cut dress and struggled to unzip it. Her dress almost exploded off her still trembling shoulders. Jeremy had never seen a more sensuous or desirable woman in his life. The dress had drifted to the floor, and lay crumpled at her feet. Standing before him was a goddess of beauty and desire. Her slinky, sexy, black low-cut brassiere was barely able to restrain her large and quaking bosom.

Jeremy was awestruck by such feminine perfection and beauty. He felt as if his entire body was being set afire and he could no longer wait to quench his flame. Yet, Loretta stood transfixed and apparently petrified with fear.

"Darling, I sense fear and indecision on your part. What can I do to help? Come over here and hug me, please?" he said to her.

Loretta, her eyes still downcast, walked over to Jeremy and said, "Cheri, darling, sweetheart, please give me time. I, I, I have to get over my feelings of betrayal and cheating that I still feel. I once loved a man very much, and the damn war took him away from me. I just don't think I could go through that again," she whimpered.

"Hey, I understand, honey, I want you to know that I am here for you, however you want me. I, too, need to rekindle my heart. I thought I would never find love again. That damn jungle took every ounce of strength, stamina and courage just to keep alive. I haven't thought about love or sex until I met you." I don't want you to worry about anything, anymore. We can do this anyway you want it. I am willing to devote as much time and effort as you need, sweetheart."

Loretta reached over and slowly began caressing his chest in sensuous semicircles.

"All I want now, cheri, is love, love, amour. Please love me now, and we will sort out the details later," she said grinning at him. With her free hand she unbuttoned her bra.

Jeremy whispered, "Ooh la-la," as a pair of perfectly matched, extremely large breasts quickly found relief from the unjust confines of her brassiere. The 42/DDs seemed to gently sag downward, as if looking for a new home; then suddenly finding renewed strength and springing upward with newfound resiliency, her nipples erect and proud like large canons on a battleship. Jeremy plunged his head into her chest and began caressing her cannons with his mouth, lips, face. He could not get enough of her. His massages and caresses began to elicit a response from her. Her body began to gyrate and rotate in an ever larger and larger circle, her moans and quivers increasing in intensity.

Jeremy realized that this wonderful Cajun woman needed as much tenderness and passion as he could muster. Every inch of his body was already prepared for the climactic attack and penetration; yet his mind and heart begged him to wait for her. Grant pensively reflected on the amount of concentration he needed to survive Vietnam; he then applied the same amount of determination to his lovemaking. To his great surprise, he was able to conquer and tame his desires. It was very important for him to satisfy her first.

Jeremy had never known such intense passion and pleasure. Their lovemaking had reached new plateaus of pleasure and gratification for him. Her intense physical demands had, in fact, utterly exhausted him. He could not remember being more tired, or satisfied in his life. Her long, and almost scandalous screams, had convinced him that she had finally broken the chain that bound her to Beau. Later in the night, their lovemaking had taken on a new art form. Both Jeremy and Loretta were willing sexual slaves and victims, their intensity levels reduced by sheer exhaustion to a more romantic and caring relationship. Finally, as the fog horns wailed their final mournful wails, complete exhaustion overcame both of them and they collapsed into a deep and peaceful sleep.

Sometime around eleven-thirty in the morning, a chambermaid gently rapped on the door.

"Excuse me, general, room service, can I come in?" Said the young Filipino maid.

Jeremy dreamily opened his eyes, and looked around the room. At first, he did not know where he was; it took him a few seconds to focus his gaze. A slow panoramic survey of his quarters revealed that he was completely naked and lying on top of the covers.

"No, miss, come back later, please," he yelled out at her, still trying to gather his thoughts.

He slowly began to focus on the vision of loveliness walking toward him. He marveled at Loretta, her sexy, naked hips gently swaying back and forth. Her incredible breasts slowly rocked up and down; a small shy smile on her face, as she approached him.

"Bonjour, mon cheri. How are you, this fine and wonderful morning?" she asked.

"Did you sleep well last night? I hope so, because I slept like the living dead."

"Well, I can't honestly remember being more exhausted in my life. You wore me out, my sweet. Hey, you got to take it easy on me, doctor, I haven't had any sex in over a year," he teasingly chided her.

"Okay, okay, what are we going to do for the rest of the day? What do you have planned for me? I was kind of hoping for a small amount of nutrition, food, K-rations, anything please. I'm starving," he whined.

"Get ready and I'll take you out to lunch," she glowered back at him, in mock disappointment.

Jeremy quickly rose, his head spinning around like a top. He staggered over to the shower and turned the spigot on hot. He stood there, allowing the scalding water to revitalize his tired body. After fifteen minutes, he felt better and got dressed. Loretta was sitting on the couch waiting for him when he exited the bathroom.

"You are so slow, mon cher. I have been waiting for fifteen minutes; let's go now," she said.

"All right, already. Boy, no pleasing you, is there?" Jeremy replied with a smile.

The drive across the bridge took less than five minutes. Loretta took the Embarcadero exit and proceeded to a side street, off of Van Ness. Mama's Place was a small family-owned restaurant, two blocks away from the usual tourist traps on the wharf. They had no problem getting a table. Mama recognized Loretta and said,

"Cara mia, buono giorno, (My darling, good morning), Loretta, how are you, darling? Come in, come in."

"Who is this most hamsomee gentlemen? Your cavalieri (cavalier) grandioso (fabulous) gentleman, you are very big. I bet your mama feed you good. I take care of you, like your mama. Guiseppe, Guiseppe, la doctora is here, give her the best table, in the corner," screamed Mama at an unknown individual standing near the bar.

Loretta and Jeremy walked over to the table, and sat down in a comfortable circular booth, the bright red vinyl gleaming despite age. The red-checked table cloth smelled of fresh laundry soap. A young man, barely out of his teens, walked over and said, "Hi, I am Guiseppe, but please, call me Joe."

"I hate this silly name. My mama gave me this name and I despise it," he said emphatically.

"Okay, Joe, I won't add insult to injury," Jeremy said.

"How about a bottle of your best Chianti, breadsticks and some Antipasto, Prosciutto ham and melon," Jeremy asked?

"Okay, boss, but Mama has given me orders, she will prepare a feast for you, and you know Mama. She always gets what she wants," Joe said.

"Hey, CPT Loretta, are you still going to Vietnam next month?" Joe said, with a frown on his young face.

"I am going to join next month, too," Joe exclaimed, with a proud gesture.

"Airborne, Special Forces for me," Joe exclaimed with a boast.

"Maybe we see each other. Oh, oh, better not, that would mean I would be wounded or dead, and I haven't even told Mama yet," Joe stated, with a look of fear and horror on his face.

Joe realized that no one was listening to him. Jeremy and Loretta were intensely staring at each other. Finally, Jeremy broke the ice and stammered,

"Why, why didn't you tell me? How could you not tell me," Grant demanded.

"Don't you think I understand? "How long have you known?" he demanded.

"I am so sorry, cheri, I wish I could have told you in a different way, but I just didn't have the courage," Loretta blurted out, her voice trembling with emotion.

"I probably would have told you this weekend, it's so difficult," she cried out.

They both stared at each other, not knowing what to do or say. Joe finally broke the ice by once again apologizing for his faux-pas.

"Oh, man, I really stepped in it. I haven't even joined the Army yet, and I already put my foot in my mouth," Joe whined.

Jeremy slowly looked over at Loretta and asked for an explanation.

"I don't know where to start, I am sorry, so sorry," Loretta replied, her eyes welling up with tears.

"I still have about thirty days left, and I hope that you will be able to spend some time with me," Loretta answered.

She looked down and was unable to speak. Her sobs slowly increasing in intensity until everyone in the restaurant stared at her. Jeremy knew he could not resist any woman who cried so passionately.

"Okay honey, enough said; let's forget it ever happened. Let's have some dinner and spend the next thirty days loving each other."

"I am sure I can make them the happiest days of your life; besides if you give me a clean bill of health, I might just go back to Vietnam as a civilian and visit you, or something," he snickered in a less than convincing fashion.

The next twenty-nine days were spent in a wildly passionate and loving fashion, the nights filled with ardent desires needing to be fulfilled. The days were spent taking long and romantic walks along the most beautiful seashore in the world. His love for Loretta increased in intensity and desire. Jeremy had never felt so happy in his entire life. He dreaded the thought of being away from her for an entire year. Yet he knew that she was as dedicated and committed to her job, as he had been, prior to his going over there. October 13 began like so many other days in the bay area, cold, dreary and overcast. Loretta had begged him not to drive her to Travis AFB. Her emotions were confused and chaotic. She strongly wished to see him one last time, and at the same time feared the obvious tearful adieu.

Jeremy solved her indecision by forcing her into the car and driving her to the base.

The drive to Travis normally took sixty minutes. However, today's traffic was unusually heavy, and they seemed to inch along the freeway at ten miles an hour. Neither Jeremy nor Loretta was able to speak. Finally, after nearly one hour of total silence, Jeremy blurted out, "Damn, wouldn't it be horrible if you missed your plane."

"Don't be silly, we have plenty of time, my flight is not scheduled to leave until 21:30 hours and it's only one o'clock in the afternoon."

"Are you really sure you want to do this?" she asked.

"I wouldn't have it any other way my dear," Jeremy answered.

The traffic eventually thinned out, and they made good time the rest of the trip. Grant took the Travis AFB exit off I-80 and drove down the Travis Parkway until they reached the main gate. A young Air Force security policeman checked their I.D.'s and saluted smartly, as they drove past. Travis AFB was and is one of the largest Air Force installations in the world. It played a pivotal role in the Vietnam War. Daily flights of C-130s, C-141s and giant C-5s could be seen landing and taking off twenty-four hours a day. Jeremy slowly drove past the main gate looking for the Operations Terminal building. They were eventually directed to the location by a passing airman. Jeremy stopped the car in front of the building and reflected on the fact that nothing had changed since his first flight to Vietnam.

Loretta got out of the car and pretended to be in a cheerful mood.

"Hey, Jeremy, they even have coffee, candy and soda machines. It's a great way to spend the next eight hours," Loretta whimpered.

Although Loretta attempted to appear cheerful, her facial expressions betrayed her true emotions.

"Damn, I wish we could spend some time alone, and away from this environment," Loretta blurted out.

"Okay, honey, let's go inside and sign in. Maybe we can find some privacy somewhere around in this area," Jeremy said.

"Yes, ma'am, can I help you?" said the young sergeant.

"I am scheduled for flight 2203, Than Son Nhut Airport, Republic of Vietnam, leaving at 21:30 hours," Loretta stated.

"Yes ma'am, I need a copy of your orders, I.D. Card, Dog Tags, and Vaccination Certificate, and I'll take care of you," the sergeant said.

"Window seat?" asked the young sergeant.

"Yes please, and what movie are you showing?" Loretta asked with a grin on her face.

"No ma'am, you got the wrong airline; you should take a good book and a pack of cards. Some of those poker games are a real kick, and you won't have too many other comforts on this flight. One more thing, ma'am, we have box lunches available. Which one would you like? A, B, C or D?" stated the young buck sergeant.

"Wow, what a choice, salami, ham, baloney or chicken. I think I'll take the chicken under glass, with caviar, roasted potatoes and a Caesar salad. Do you have any Beaujolais wine, 1966?" Loretta shot back with a smirk.

"One greasy fried chicken, apple, milk and Snickers candy bar coming up," SGT Fuller countered with a smile.

"What time do I have to be here?" Loretta asked.

"Exactly ninety minutes prior to departure, and don't be late. We wouldn't want you to miss your excursion on our first-class airline. You can check in your luggage now, or bring them back later," SGT Fuller quipped.

"I think I'll check them in now," Loretta said, with a sigh of relief, keeping only her small carry on bag, with the necessary female accouterments.

Jeremy stood there watching the whole scene with a strange and quiet demeanor. He had a sense of déjà vu and felt hopeless and lonely. He watched in silence as Loretta handed her luggage to the young sergeant.

"Here you go, ma'am, your receipt and I'll see you promptly at 20:00 hours, okay?" The sergeant asked with a grin on his boyish face.

"You got it, I'll be here with bells on my toes," Loretta answered.

"What do you want to do now, boss?" Jeremy asked.

"Let's go somewhere nearby and spend some time together, please!" Loretta blurted out, her voice quaking with emotion.

They silently left the flight operations building and got into the car. Jeremy drove out the main gate and headed for the freeway.

"Where are you going?" Loretta asked.

"I am going to take you to the Super 8 Motel across the freeway and we are going to spend some wonderful moments together," Jeremy answered.

Jeremy pulled up to the motel guest parking area and told Loretta to wait in the car until he checked in.

"Hi, can I help you?" the elderly man asked.

"Yes, you can, I would like a room," Jeremy answered.

"How many days will you be staying, and are you alone?"

"One night only, and I am with my, uh, uh, wife," Jeremy answered, unconvincingly.

The old man glanced up and said, "Going to Vietnam, are we now? Don't worry, I understand, you young fellows come in here and pretend you're married. Don't think you are the only one who ever went to war, son." The old man glanced at Jeremy and winked. "Room 202, upstairs and to the back, nice and quiet, if you know what I mean."

Jeremy stood there, not knowing what to say or do. He sheepishly reached across the counter and took the key.

"Thank you very much." Jeremy took the key and shoved it down into his pocket and rushed out of the office. Loretta sat in the car patiently waiting for him to return.

"It's about time, mon cheri, this little girl is tired of sitting all alone in this-here car, my love," Loretta quipped, her eyes gleaming with childlike glee.

"Hey, you should have been the one to get the room, the old man knew we weren't married and he thinks I am going to Nam," Jeremy answered with mock indignation.

"Let's cut all of the bull and get down to some serious loving," Jeremy said.

The room was no better or worse than many other rooms he had seen. The decor was still showing signs of late-fifties styling mixed in with late-sixties ghastly color combinations. The king-size bed stood facing the bathroom and was covered with a hot-pink bedspread. Although the decor was not to his liking, the room was immaculately clean.

Loretta walked in and slowly glanced around the room. Her thoughts were swirling around in her head so fast that she almost passed out. She had to catch herself on the door in order to avoid hitting the carpet, face first.

"Come here, mon cheri, I need you. Please, hold me and love me. Your love will have to last me a whole year," Loretta whimpered to Jeremy.

Large tears slowly ran down her cheeks, staining her shirt. Jeremy walked over and put his arm around her. He gently squeezed her shoulders and softly kissed her lips. His lips felt her moist and somewhat salty lips part and accept his demanding tongue. Their passion grew in intensity and demand. Both of their bodies seemed to require intense passion. All of the tenderness was gone; passion and desire overcame their needs. At times their lovemaking was so fierce that the whole room shook like a 6.7 California earthquake.

Their passion finally abated after two hours of intensive lovemaking, leaving both of them exhausted and drowsy. Loretta put her head on his shoulder and dozed off. Jeremy called the front counter and left word for a wake-up call at 18:30 hours. Jeremy laid in bed thinking about his future and what life would be like without Loretta. Her soft purring sounds made him realize how much he had come to love and need her. She had been his inspiration and moral support throughout his long ordeal, and now she was leaving and he was unable to help her. Without realizing that he had done so, Jeremy had fallen asleep and was awakened by the ringing phone.

"Hello, okay, yeah, thanks, I appreciate it very much," Jeremy said, not fully knowing where he was, or what was going on.

Loretta didn't even budge, *the sleep of 'the living dead',* thought Jeremy. She lay there in a fetal position, her whole body gently shaking, her feet and hands nervously twitching, as if some demon was chasing her and she was desperately trying to get away. It reminded him of a little puppy he once had, Sarge was his name, a wonderful and cuddly chocolate Labrador who had a habit of twitching nervously while sleeping in front of the fireplace. Jeremy decided it was time for her to get up and get ready. He softly began caressing her forehead and gently called out her name.

"Loretta, wake up, darling, it's time."

Loretta suddenly jumped up, and screamed a piercing and mournful sound. It had an almost animal-like quality to it. Her eyes were focused on some distant and painful object. She began to sob, the sobs slowly increasing in intensity until her entire body was shaking violently. It took all of Jeremy's strength to hold her down. Jeremy sensed her distress and continued caressing her forehead, shoulders and whispered to her.

"It's okay, darling, everything will be all right, I love you."

His soothing manner and gentle words seem to calm her. Just as suddenly as they had started, her sobs subsided and she began to regain her composure.

"I'm okay, sweetie, I just had a bad dream, a horrible dream. I, I," she stuttered, her eyes welling up with tears again. Loretta was unable to finish the sentence.

"Don't worry, babe, I'm here and I love you very much," Jeremy answered.

His tenderness and compassion really moved her and she wanted to thank him for his sensitivity, but was unable to do so. She was surprised by his gentleness and affection. Loretta was discovering a new and gentle side of Jeremy.

"Are you ready, Jeremy? I'll be ready to go in fifteen minutes," Loretta announced.

"Hey, what's the rush? It's only 18:30, and you don't have to be there until eight o'clock! Slow down, you'll get plenty of time to see Vietnam, believe me," Jeremy said with a half-assed laugh.

Loretta got ready in silence. Her actions were stiff and automated. Her eyes had a glazed and far away look to them. Jeremy sensed her unhappiness and decided that silence was the appropriate at this time. Exactly twelve minutes later, Loretta proclaimed her readiness.

Jeremy opened the door to the room and Loretta rushed past him to the waiting car. They drove in silence back to the base, arriving exactly at 19:00 hours back at Base Operations Terminal building, one hour earlier than expected. They both sat in silence, until Loretta blurted, "Please, mon cheri, leave, leave now! I can't stand this waiting. I feel like I am waiting for an execution," her eyes still glazed and somewhat hysterical.

"Are you sure this is what you want?" Jeremy demanded, somewhat aghast and taken back by this radical turn of events.

"I really would like to stay with you, and see you off," Jeremy begged, his eyes filling up tears.

Unable to control his emotions, he simply turned around and walked out of the building, his feelings in total disarray. He knew then that he had a lot to learn about women. His feelings were torn between storming back in there and confronting her, or meekly agreeing to her demands and leaving the area. His ego stood to take a beating, but he decided to go back to the motel room and get plastered. He got back into his car and drove out the main gate toward the motel.

Chapter 5

Farewell

Back in Afghanistan, on a high desert plateau, Khalil listened intently for several hours without saying a word. He finally grabbed Jeremy's hand and shook it.

"You have had an interesting life, Jeremy. It's too bad you are not a Muslim, I would let you marry my sister," stated Khalil with emphasis.

"Please tell me more. You are a very good storyteller, please continue," asked Khalil.

Jeremy looked at his friend, and nodded.

"However, you must tell me about your experiences in America someday, too. I am sure you also had many interesting adventures in Sacramento," said Jeremy.

"You are right, my friend, but we must save those stories for another day. Right now we are all interested in what happened to your love, Loretta," replied Khalil, in a somewhat rude manner.

Jeremy continued telling his story to Khalil, however Jeremy noticed that now there were several other men in his tent listening to his tale. Unknowingly the crowd had grown to more than a dozen listeners. Khalil was trying his best to translate as fast as Jeremy was speaking. Jeremy went on with renewed gusto.

"Well Khalil, I spotted a liquor store, directly across the street from the west gate. I got out of my car and walked into the store. A young, friendly clerk greeted me," continued Jeremy, now feeling somewhat self-conscious of his large crowd.

"What can I do for you, sir?" asked the young man.

"Where is your booze?" Jeremy growled back at the youth.

"Well, that depends on what you want. Hard stuff is on the left aisle, wine in the middle aisle and beer on the right," answered the young clerk, his voice less friendly now.

"You got any Chivas?" Jeremy asked, slowly regaining his composure.

"Sure do, and as a matter of fact it's on sale today, $5.95 plus tax. I am also running a special on Miller beer, $2.79 a twelve-pack, plus tax," answered the clerk, his voice once again friendly and cooperative.

"You got yourself a sale, young man, a bottle of Chivas and a twelve-pack of beer. That should do the trick," Jeremy answered, murmuring to himself.

Jeremy grabbed the bag, left a twenty dollar-bill and hurriedly left the store. The young clerk yelled at him, "Hey, buddy, you forgot your change, hey, hey."

Jeremy was so preoccupied with himself, he didn't even notice the clerk chasing after him. The short drive to the motel was a kaleidoscope of color and sensations. He felt that the whole world was in slow motion and he was the comic book hero, the "Flash," whizzing by at the speed of light. His only thought was of getting back to the comfort of his room and drinking from that bottle. He pulled up to the spot in front of his room and got out of the car. He hurriedly ran up the stairs and went inside his room. He then realized that he had forgotten the most important ingredient, ice. *Shit*, he thought. *I'll go downstairs and ask the manager for some ice.*

As he approached the sliding glass door to the motel office, he noticed the manager sitting in his living room watching television.

"Excuse me, sir, I hate to disturb you, but would you have some ice for me?" Jeremy asked, his voice betraying his agitated state of mind.

"Sure, sonny, but you are the last person I expected to see tonight. I thought you were going to Vietnam tonight. Miss your plane? Not A.W.O.L. (Absent Without Official Leave), I hope. I sure would hate to see a nice young fellow like you get in trouble," said the old man with a questioning look in his eye.

"You got it all wrong, sir. My wife, uh, uh, girlfriend is just about ready to take off for Vietnam and I am confused as hell. She doesn't want me to be there when she leaves, and I don't know if she'll be coming back. Believe me when I say, I know what it's like. I spent nearly two years there; three months as a P.O.W. I could not possibly think of a worse place to send your girlfriend," Jeremy answered, his voice still shaking with emotion.

"Well, son, it sure sounds like you have a problem. Maybe an old man like me can point you in the right direction. Why don't you come in and sit down; we'll talk about it."

"What do you have in that bag?" asked the old man.

"A bottle of Chivas, and some Miller beer. I fully intend to get drunk tonight and dream away my sorrows," Jeremy answered.

"I'll tell you what, I'll put the "NO VACANCY" sign up and I'll join you in a drink or two," the manager answered.

"That is, if you don't mind? I know I am being a little presumptuous, but I know from personal experience that company can sometimes help fight the blues. I am also going through a personal tragedy at this time, and I sure could use the companionship. You see, my wife of thirty years, Regina, just passed away last week, and I miss her so much." The old man looked up at Jeremy, tears running down his face.

"Well, it will be a pleasure. I couldn't think of a nicer person to spend the night with, sharing my bottle and my sorrows. I am truly sorry about your wife; I am sure she was a wonderful lady. I must excuse myself, I am Jeremy, Jeremy Grant, Captain, United States Army, on extended convalescence leave prior to discharge."

"Well, it's a pleasure, Jeremy. Braxton, Gilbert, Colonel, retired USAF at your service. I flew twenty-eight missions in WWII and seventy-eight more in Korea, having the honor to be the first aviator in Korea to fly fifty missions!" he said with emphasis.

"B-26s and A-20s, A-26s, B-47s, and even some B-52s. You know the drill," Gilbert answered proudly, as he pointed to the wall full of aviator photos, old planes and lost memories.

"Well, hot damn, Colonel, I kind of knew you had to be a military man; you have that bearing and look of a soldier," Jeremy shot back as he walked into the tidy living room. You have any glasses and ice?" Jeremy asked.

"Sure do, I'll be right back. Sit down and make yourself comfortable," Gilbert yelled as he walked into the kitchen.

Jeremy picked a large and well-used stuffed chair to sit down in. His whole body sank into the comfortable chair.

"Hey, I bet this thing has seen a lot of use," Jeremy quipped, as Gilbert walked back in the living room carrying a large bucket of ice, two whiskey glasses and a can opener for the beer.

"Sure has, it was my Regina's favorite easy chair. She used to sit there, hour after hour, watching her soap operas," Gilbert answered, his voice quivering with emotion.

"Well, let's get down to some serious drinking, old buddy, and let's drink to our favorite ladies," Jeremy answered, pouring both of them a healthy triple shot of Chivas on the rocks, and popping open a couple of beers.

The conversation lasted all night. Both men reminisced about their lost loves and later drifted into war stories. Jeremy finally crawled to his room around sunrise; leaving Gilbert sound asleep on his sofa, a picture of his dead wife in one hand and the empty Chivas bottle in the other. At ten-thirty the next morning, Jeremy opened his left eye first. His head was pounding and his right eye refused to work. He finally forced it open and realized he couldn't focus very well. Last night had been a total blank. Jeremy's mind couldn't concentrate on anything. He finally realized that he had consumed almost the entire bottle of Chivas himself and drank a majority of the beer as well.

Gilbert was nowhere to be seen. He found a note on the chair saying, "Morning Jeremy, I've gone to the store for some groceries and I'll be right back."

Jeremy, feeling relieved that Gilbert had survived the night, rushed out of the living room and walked unsteadily back to his own room. A hot shower, change of clothes, and a cup of hot coffee would do him good. Thirty minutes later, Jeremy was ready to check out of the motel. He walked downstairs and turned in his key.

"Hey, young fellow, what's the hurry? I've prepared breakfast for us, come and join me." Jeremy, realizing it would be impolite to refuse, reluctantly accepted Gilbert's invitation.

"I am terribly sorry, Colonel, I guess I really needed to do that, but now I feel like shit! "Jeremy answered, slowly stroking his pounding head.

Jeremy ate his breakfast in silence, purposely and politely evading Gilbert's questions.

"I think it's time for me to go now, and I sincerely want to thank you for your hospitality and friendship," Jeremy said, as he got up to leave.

"Well, you are welcome, young man, and I hope that someday you'll come back and spend another night here with your wife, uh, girlfriend, when she returns from Vietnam," Gilbert stated as he was extending his hand across the counter. Jeremy shook it firmly and walked out into the bright California sunlight.

Jeremy's drive back to the Presidio seemed to take forever. Traffic wasn't that bad, but his mind seemed to be in a coma and refused to work. It seemed like an eternity before he drove back through the main gate off Lombard Street. Nothing had changed, except that his Loretta was now en route to Vietnam and he was stuck here. He filled his time with endless trips to the "O" Club at night, and long walks along the seashore during the day. His feelings were in turmoil and he was happy for the solitude that the Presidio afforded him. On one such long stroll he bumped into an old friend whom he could barely recognized, CPT Justin Neal Brown, soon to be retired.

"Excuse me, sir," asked the ex-Air Force helicopter pilot.

"Don't I know you from somewhere? You are an awfully large individual to forget, and that streak of white hair. Bingo! I pulled your skinny ass out of the jungle! Right?" stammered Justin excitedly.

"Well, I'll be, it's my savior, the greatest helicopter pilot in the world. Yeah, you sure did. What are you doing on this Army installation?" blurted out Jeremy, too excited to speak clearly.

"Well, a few days after I rescued you, I was shot down and crashed near Da Nang. My left arm was severely injured, and some great Army specialist is supposed to make it better. The Air Force said there was this Army surgeon who could repair the damage. Anyway, I hope so! I am left handed, and it's very difficult to wipe your ass with your right hand," CPT Brown answered.

"I expect it is, but I still owe you that drink, and I am sure going to show my gratitude. What are you doing tonight?" asked Jeremy.

"Well hell, nothing but get drunk with you, buddy. It's not very often I get to meet someone whose life I've saved. Okay, let's meet at the "O" club at seventeen hundred. By the way, my name is Justin, but all my friends call me Neal, "answered CPT Brown with a grin on his face."

"Roger that, Neal. See you there," answered Jeremy.

Jeremy was surprised how eager he was to meet up with Neal again. It somehow brought back memories of Vietnam, and reconnected him to Loretta. He wondered how she was doing, and when he would receive the first letter from her.

At seventeen hundred hours sharp, Jeremy walked in to the officers club, and saw that Neal was already there, and had a head start on him. His old friend Lt./Col Anthony "Glorious" Barnum was also there, and as usual he was showing his photo with John Wayne.

"Oh, come on, "Glorious," if John Wayne knew that you were freeloading off these disabled veterans, he would kick your ass. Besides, that good old boy there is the pilot who rescued my scrawny ass out of the jungle, and if anyone is going to buy drinks tonight it's going to be me," Jeremy stated with authority, so much so, that the whole bar turned and shouted a loud," 'Yes, sir."

Jeremy spent the next five hours with old friends. They told one lie bigger and more incredible than next. Jeremy and Neal spent a lot of time together over the next couple of weeks and it helped him get over his loss. Neal's operation was successful, and he was transferred to the David S. Grant Hospital at Travis AFB. The last Jeremy heard of Neal, he had retired from the Air Force, and now worked for the United States Customs Service in San Francisco.

A few weeks later, Jeremy received his long-awaited honorable discharge and medical separation, and he headed back East to see his parents. He was determined to start a new life, and leave all of this behind him for now.

Back in Afghanistan, Jeremy stood up and told his friends that the story was over for now, and they should now leave his tent, as he wanted some private time. Khalil approached him and said, "Jeremy, it was a very honorable thing for you to do. We mujahidins would never have revealed so much personal information about ourselves. But you Americans are different, so open and free," stated Khalil as he walked out of the tent.

"Yes we are, and perhaps that's what makes us such a great country," answered Jeremy.

Jeremy sat back down and wondered if it was a mistake to reveal to the mujahidin so much about himself. However, he knew his time was limited there, and he hoped that his transfer would come through in the next few months. He also hoped that this "confession" of sorts would allow him to sleep better at night. Although these dreams had awakened long buried and forgotten memories, Jeremy continued to think about his past, and decided he would not reveal anymore information to anyone else. His memories and thoughts were for him alone from now on.

Flashbacks of a little red Mustang and a long trip home crowded his thoughts for the rest of the evening. His mind continued to focus on those long-lost events of twenty years earlier.

Chapter 6

New Life After Loretta

He was hopeful that his decision to drive cross-country along the famous Route 66, now Interstate 80 in some parts, would probably free his spirit. Jeremy hoped he would once again become an almost civilized human being. Jeremy would take his time, and for the first time in his life, really appreciate the beauty of this land. He realized that he never could forget Loretta, but was bound and determined to resume his life again. Jeremy kept writing her every day, and was also resolved to send her outrageously funny postcards from the weirdest places he could find on his route home. Jeremy hoped that these diversions would help him forget the pain he was now feeling. Little in his current life would prepare him for the horrors he would encounter twenty years later in the highlands of Afghanistan.

Loretta had lent him her beautiful little Mustang, and he was bound and determined to keep it in mint condition until her safe return. Early one morning, he got up and packed his duffel bag and checked out of the Presidio's B.O.Q. Jeremy lazily walked down to the Mustang and threw his bags on the back seat. He carefully pulled out of the parking stall reserved for "General Officers Only," and slowly drove down the street to the Lombard Street entrance. There he stopped, and turned around for the last time, and gazed at the Presidio with fond memories. He weaved his way through the early morning Lombard Street crowd until he reached Van Ness. He then took a right on Van Ness and continued up the street until he reached the northbound highway 101, which then led him to once again cross the Bay Bridge. Halfway across the bridge, he stopped at the Treasure Island exit and admired the view from atop the Coast Guard's building. The view from this location is absolutely spectacular. A surrealistic panorama unfolded beneath his gaze. The view from this location brought back many fond memories, and made him feel pains of anguish as well as joy. He decided that it would be best if he left now, while he still could. Jeremy drove back onto the Bay Bridge and headed east toward Sacramento.

Jeremy drove at a leisurely pace, knowing full well it would be a long day. Two hours later he arrived in Sacramento, and drove southward on Highway 5. The drive on I-5 was a rather dull and uneventful trip until he reached Los Angeles. Los Angeles was one of his least favorite cities. He hated the smog, traffic and hectic lifestyle. Every nerve in his body was on edge as he slowly worked his way through the traffic. His survival instinct cried out; he wanted to lash out at these reckless and discourteous drivers. He paled at the thought of someone's smashing Loretta's car. After what seemed like an eternity, he managed to catch the eastbound Highway 10 toward Las Vegas.

Jeremy wanted to spend a few days in Vegas visiting his cousins, Douglas C. Lawyer, a very wealthy and successful criminal defense attorney, and Daniel "Danny" Lawyer, an equally successful banker. Jeremy couldn't help but smile at his cousin's unusual last name. Why would anyone named Lawyer choose that profession?

However, "Dougie or Degoulass" was his most common nickname, but that did not stop him from being one of the most prolific Casanovas in Nevada. Douglas had great success with the ladies, but he also was one of the most brilliant lawyers in the West. His success with the ladies was only surpassed by his immense skill in the courtroom. Jeremy was positive that Dougie would someday be someone of great importance, a federal district judge, or perhaps even a U.S. Supreme Court Justice. His other cousin Danny was a quieter individual. He preferred the finer things in life, and usually partied with a different group of friends then his older brother. As a successful banker his clientele expected a more demure attitude.

Jeremy accelerated the pace of his Mustang in anticipation of a reunion with his cousins. As the Mustang slowly climbed the last mountain pass, just west of the Nevada state line, Jeremy could already see the incredible glow of the neon lights that surrounded Las Vegas. Jeremy was always fascinated by the glamour and glitz that permeated Vegas. The lights, glamour, casinos, and of course the showgirls were of great interest to him. Jeremy could easily understand why a young successful lawyer would pick this desert oasis as a watering hole for life. The Mustang slowly cruised down the "strip," as it was known, an infamous boulevard almost six miles long, cluttered on both sides by immense gambling casinos, motels, gas stations, tourist traps and restaurants.

Jeremy pulled into the Matador Hotel, his favorite place in Vegas. His old war buddy Guido Fontana worked here, and he was anxious to see him as well. Jeremy's Mustang pulled up to the young valet attendant and asked him to please take good care of his car. Jeremy got out of the car, walked up to the front desk and asked if they had a room.

"I'm terribly sorry, Sir, but we are completely sold out, the convention, you know," the front desk clerk answered, without even looking up.

"Gee, that's too bad, does Guido Fontana still work here?" answered Jeremy with an inquiring look.

"Uh, you know Mr. Fontana?" asked the young clerk, his voice rising in excitement.

"As a matter fact, I do, we served together in Vietnam, and he always bragged how he worked in this hotel. Does he still work here?" Jeremy asked.

"Oh, you mean, Junior Fontana. Yes, you might say that. His father owns this hotel, and two others along the strip, and also one in Lake Tahoe. I'll be glad to tell him that you are here, Mr., Mr.?" The young man asked, his weasel-like face gleaming with a sudden, but insincere smite.

"Just tell him Jeremy, from Nam, and he will understand," stated Jeremy, glancing down on the young man.

The young clerk, a rather pathetic-looking kid, barely out of his teens; his face still pocked marked with adolescent zits and horrible acne, rushed to a red phone hanging on the wall, and quickly dialed three numbers.

"Frankie, this is Jim at the front desk. Tell Junior that a guy named Jeremy from Vietnam is here and wants to talk to him," the young kid stammered in the phone.

"Who in the hell is Jeremy Vietnam?" Frankie screamed in the phone.

"No, no, not Jeremy Vietnam, you dummy! Jeremy from Vietnam, Junior's old war buddy," the kid answered, his chest swelling in mock indignation.

"Okay, I'll tell him, but you had better watch your mouth. You ever call me names again, and you'll be sharing a cement bed with the fish at Hoover Dam! Do you understand me, zit face?" Frankie answered, his voice barely rising above a whisper.

Jeremy noticed the young boy first turn beet red, then his scarred face slowly lost all of its color, as he listened to Frankie on the other end.

"Excuse me, Mr. Jeremy, Junior will be right down," murmured the young clerk.

Jeremy turned his back and gazed toward the large gambling area. He hadn't really noticed it right a way, but the din of thousands of slot machines was deafening. He was enthralled by the masses of silver-haired ladies yanking on the one-armed bandits. His attention was suddenly diverted by a large hand gently tapping him on the right shoulder.

"Hi, CPT Grant, you haven't changed much, except for the hair, and you are a lot skinnier than I remember," Guido said, as he embraced Jeremy from behind.

Jeremy turned around and looked down at Junior. Junior was about five-feet-nine, with a stocky build and seemingly no neck. His jet-black wavy hair was beginning to thin on top, but his boyish grin had not changed much. Jeremy reached over and gave him a bear hug. Guido Salvatore Fontana, the ex-Special Forces Staff Sergeant had tears in his eyes. Both men stood there for a second and pumped hands like farmers churning milk.

Guido had been Jeremy's weapons specialist and armorer. He was by far the most skillful and deadliest soldier Jeremy had ever met. He had a natural aptitude with weapons, explosives and knives. Jeremy knew that Guido could always be depended on to carry out his mission. One of his other great attributes was his physique. He regularly pumped iron, and exercised. Four years of heavy weight lifting had molded him into a beautiful specimen of muscle and incredible strength. Guido was one of the strongest men, Jeremy had ever seen. He had developed a typical bodybuilders shape. He had huge arms, a bulging chest and no neck. Jeremy was amazed how little Guido had changed.

Jeremy stared at Junior and had flashbacks of an incident which occurred in Vietnam. His thoughts drifted to the incident, and suddenly he was there again, the flashbacks seeming more real than the actual event. They were on the way to a base camp in the Mekong Delta, just south of Saigon, when their jeep hit a land mine. The explosion was so great that it flung the jeep, and its passengers, ten feet in the air. The jeep crashed and landed on top of one of the men, pinning him underneath. Jeremy was unable to budge the vehicle until SSG Guido S. Fontana brushed himself off, grunted like a weightlifter and picked up the vehicle with a superhuman effort. Jeremy was then able to pull the injured soldier to safety, and carry him to the hospital. On another occasion, their base camp was under heavy attack and their only heavy weapon, a "Ma" Deuce (M-2) .50 caliber, air-cooled heavy machine gun had been blown up by a mortar round. SSG Fortuna ran over to the bunker physically manhandled the heavy weapon and began firing it again. The M-2 had the heavy metal base blown to bits, but Guido was able to brace the machine gun on some sandbags and with his incredible strength continued firing until the attacking forces retreated. SSG Guido S. Fontana earned his first Silver Star during this engagement. Jeremy knew of no other man that could successfully fire and control such a weapon without a gun mount.

A powerful slap on the right shoulder allowed Jeremy's eyes to refocus. He glanced down at Guido. Junior was staring intently at Jeremy. Guido had that deep menacing look that men in combat or cold-blooded killers develop. However, he still had a smile on his face and Jeremy was unable to tell whether or not, he was angry or just brooding. It slowly dawned on Jeremy that perhaps Junior had more than a casual acquaintance with organized crime. That thought suddenly brought him back to reality, and he decided not to pursue the matter right now. He was happy to see Guido and right now that was all that mattered.

"Damn, CPT Grant, you are looking great!" Guido yelled.

"Man, am I glad you are okay! We heard all those horrible stories about you being KIA (Killed in Action), or MIA (Missing in Action), etc. Shortly after you disappeared, I was zapped in the head and ended up in the hospital at Fort Sam Houston, Texas. I have a huge silver plate in my head now. I am okay now, except for the occasional headaches. They were not able to get all of the shrapnel out, but the doctors tell me I should be all right," Guido blurted out in one long sentence, his right hand slowly and unconsciously rubbing a large scar near his right eyebrow and right ear.

"Well, everything you heard was true. I was taken P.O.W., and eventually escaped three months later. I was picked up by chance by a Jolly Green Giant, and here I am today safe and almost sound!" Grant said, his voice trailing off in thought once again.

"Hey Jeremy, what has happened since you came home, what are you going to do? Do you have any plans? Want to work for me?" Guido said, switching to the more familiar Jeremy.

Jeremy explained the rest of the events of the past six months, and told him of Loretta, the Presidio and Travis AFB. Junior listened intently, then dragged Jeremy over to one of the many bars and bought him a double Chivas.

"Guido, you lied to me. You always said you worked here, but you never told me you owned the place! I really appreciate the offer, but right now I am on my way home, and I am not planning on doing anything for at least six more months. Besides, I've been able to save nearly all my pay for the past three years, and I have nearly forty grand stashed away," answered Jeremy.

"Well, would you have believed me if I told you we owned four casinos? You know how G.I.'s are! They lie, steal and get drunk! Not only that, but for obvious reasons, I didn't want everyone to know who I am. You know what I mean?" Guido said, a smile slowly spreading across his face. It was menacing smile, filled with veiled threats, yet genuine and sincere, a somber wake-up call to perhaps a hidden agenda.

"Anyway, that's old news, what brings you here? I know you didn't come all the way to Vegas just to see me. What's cooking?"

"You are right Guido. I am on my way back home, and I decided to stop by Vegas and visit my cousins Douglas and Danny Lawyer, and at the same time say hello to you," Grant exclaimed.

"No shit, that 'shyster' is your cousin? Well, I'll be damned, what a coincidence. He is my attorney, and one of the best guys in Vegas. I knew there was something I liked about him. Why don't you call him and we'll have a party tonight. All three of us, and some friends," Junior blurted out.

"Well, it sounds like a great idea. Let's call him now and get started.

Law offices, can I help you? A young, sexy voice answered, her breath blowing air on the receiver, as if she had been running, or for that matter, being chased by someone.

"Is Dougie there? Grant inquired.

"Who did you want? Doggie? I am sorry, we don't have anyone here by that name," answered the secretary, somewhat irritated by the caller.

"No, not Doggie, Dougie C. Lawyer, my cousin."

"I am terribly sorry, I misunderstood you, I'll connect you to Mr. Lawyer," the young secretary answered.

"Douglas Lawyer, can I help you?" he answered.

"Hey Dougie, it's me, Jeremy; I'm here in town. We want you to join us at the Matador, and Guido is throwing a party tonight. By the way, call Danny and ask him if he wants to join us."

"Hey, that sounds good to me, cousin. I don't think Danny is going to make it, he is visiting my parents up in Redding. I didn't know you guys knew each other. Where did you meet?" Dougie inquired.

"I am surprised he never told you, I was his CO in Vietnam, and we were very close," answered Jeremy.

"Well, he probably never knew I had a crazy cousin named Jeremy Grant. Okay, let me finish up here in my office, and I'll be right over. Where should I meet you guys?" asked Douglas, his voice trailing off.

"Hey Guido, where should Dougie meet us?" asked Jeremy.

"Tell him to come to the front desk and ask for me, they will show him the way up to my penthouse. Tell him be sure to ask for Junior," replied Fontana.

"Doug, come to the front desk and ask for Junior, they will show you the way. See you soon," answered Jeremy.

Junior grabbed Jeremy's arm and escorted him toward a bank of private elevators, guarded by a couple of beefy goons, their bulging suits revealing strange shapes near their left armpits. Jeremy felt a little uncomfortable knowing that Guido could very well be some type of underworld gangster. However, the strong bond they had developed convinced him he should not say or do anything right now.

The elevator quickly rose to the top of the building. It silently opened to a large corridor, also guarded by more beefy goons. There was a series of large doors facing the northern and southern exposures. Junior nodded to a couple of the guards and they opened a large glass door. It led into a huge, magnificent penthouse which overlooked the fabulous Vegas Strip. Jeremy walked over to the immense windows and slowly gazed across the incredible Vegas skyline.

"Wow!" He exclaimed. "This is a magnificent view, no wonder you like to live way up here. Is it always this gorgeous?" Jeremy asked.

"Yep, you got it. We have more lights on the strip than most major American cities have in their entire infrastructure. We are really blessed to have the Hoover Dam, and its unlimited power source. Sit down and get comfortable. What will you have to drink?" Guido asked.

"Well, how about Chivas on the rocks, and perhaps some cold Miller beer for chasers?"

"Sounds good to me. Hey Frankie, take care of it. Also call the restaurant and send up Tony Pascuali. I want to order something really special for my friends. Oh, by the way, ask Rosemary to come up as well," Guido ordered.

Frankie smiled at the mention of Rosemary. She was a grand lady, but of indeterminate age and full of vigor, probably in her early fifties, possibly in her sixties. She was tall, buxom and a splendid redhead. In many ways, she resembled the legendary forties movie star Maureen O'Hara, but was slightly plumper and taller. Frankie sometimes fantasized about what she was like in her prime. Rosemary was the hotel's personal Madame. She watched, controlled, monitored and inspected all the showgirls who also worked the field. The hotel did not allow any overt prostitution, but instead had a covey of willing girls who were available for services for special guests. It was all very well controlled and managed by Rosemary. She could spot a street whore a mile away, and would immediately dash over like an angry mother hen and protect her chicks.

Someone knocked on the door, and Dougie was escorted in by one of the goons. Jeremy got up and walked over to Dougie.

"Hey cousin, how in the hell have you been?"

Dougie was a little shaken by Jeremy's appearance. He had not seen his cousin in almost three years and was shocked by his rather gaunt appearance, and especially his streak of snow-white hair. Dougie walked over and embraced his cousin. Both men stood there silently for a while and slowly parted.

"Hey you, what in the hell have you been doing to yourself? Trying to emulate Twiggy? I really think you should tell your hairdresser to put less peroxide in your hair gel next time." Dougie said, in an attempt to break the awkward silence.

"These things just happen when you are under great stress. The doctors say there isn't much I can do about it. Anyway, I've been told that it makes me look distinguished, and the women seem to like it," answered Jeremy.

Jeremy was happy to see his cousin, but he noticed that Dougie had also changed. He was slightly paunchier, thinning on top and wore a full set of facial hair. Jeremy admitted that the overall impression was favorable. Dougie had that distinguished and fashionable academic look. Jeremy was convinced that the years had been good to his older cousin.

Just then, someone knocked at the door. Mr. Pascuali walked in. He was a rather small, balding Maitre Di, a Don Knotts-looking individual, but with an Italian flair.

"Mr. Fontana, what can I do for you?" he asked with an exaggerated Italian accent.

"I have some very special friends, and I want you to tell the chefs to prepare a very special meal for us. We are celebrating tonight.

What can you recommend?" Guido asked.

"Well, I received a large shipment of Maine lobsters, and the Filet Mignon is very good. Perhaps a Caesar salad to start with, followed by a zuppa a la pomodore? Does that sound good?" The little man inquired, his right eyebrow raising in an anticipatory gesture.

"What do you think, guys?" Junior inquired.

Both Jeremy and Dougie replied simultaneously.

"Great!"

"Can I offer you a drink, Dougie?" Junior inquired.

"Sure, Guido, I'll drink whatever you guys are having, and plenty of it. I told my secretary to clear my calendar for tomorrow; I'm taking the day off!" Dougie exclaimed, with great panache.

Just then, the gorgeous Rosemary entered the room with six of the most beautiful women Jeremy had ever seen. They all were very tall, radiant and leggy. They ranged in color from a chocolate-colored Jamaican beauty, to a spectacular six-foot-tall Nordic goddess, a veritable Smorgasbord of delicious female specimens, a rainbow of feminine creations.

"Sit down, and be quiet," Rosemary ordered, her voice sounding more intimidating than the meanest First Sergeant Jeremy had ever encountered.

All of the women sat down near the window and waited to be introduced. Jeremy, Dougie and even Guido were speechless at the sight of this incredible display of female magnificence. Rosemary walked over to Guido and whispered in his ear.

"I hope you are pleased, Mr. Fontana?" Her head turning slightly to the right in expectation of a positive answer.

"Wow, you once again have overwhelmed me, Rosemary! Where have you been keeping these beauties? I haven't seen them around the casino," Guido answered, his eyes slowly admiring the multitude of beautiful women.

"Well, you might say they are virgins. I mean as far as the casino is concerned," she quickly corrected herself. "I've been saving them for a special occasion, and have not allowed them to be used by anyone else," Rosemary proudly answered, her already large bosom swelling to magnificent proportions.

"You done good, hasn't she, boys?" Guido answered.

A chorus of, "Amen, Hallelujah," greeted him. Jeremy felt the most uncomfortable of the lot. Being recently separated from his lover, he was not yet prepared for this compromising situation.

"Guido, I, I, uh, can you please come over here, I need to talk to you. I don't think I can do anything just yet. Loretta has only been gone for a month or so, and I don't know if I will ever see her again," Jeremy whispered in his ear.

"Hey, don't worry about it. These girls work for me, and they will or won't do anything you want, or don't want. Just think of them as your personal assistants, and they will take good care of you," Guido smiled.

Dougie was out of his seat, and was now standing next to the girls, every one of them towering at least five inches over him.

"Hey you, you have been holding out on me. Had I known that you had so many beautiful women up here, I would have given you a discount on my services. Which one can I have, or better yet, how many can I have?" Dougie asked, his eyes bright with excitement.

"You can have as many as you can handle, but don't let your eyes overload your pecker! As you are obviously the most sexually frustrated individual in our esteemed group, we will allow you the privilege of first pick," Guido stated with a snicker.

Dougie quickly went over to the group and slowly eyed everyone of them. His gaze had the professional glance of a southern tobacco auctioneer reviewing the crop prior to the sale. He had an almost comical way about him. He strutted like a rooster in the barnyard, and everyone was quite aware of his exaggerated mannerisms. Dougie finally stopped in front of a gorgeous six-foot-tall redhead, and promptly said, "You are the lucky one, princess. You will have the honor of romancing me this evening, along with another beauty of course."

"Anything you want, cutie," she answered, her voice barely rising above a whisper. Sandra was her name and erotic passion was her claim to fame.

Dougie continued his search for his second willing partner. His eyes suddenly glanced over to the dark-haired Jamaican beauty.

"What is your name, my ebony Venus?"

"My name is Chastity Williams de Mornay, and I am part French, English and Jamaican. What else would you like to know, my good man? Oh, perhaps my specialties? I can do anything and everything better than all of these women put together," she answered, her eyes simmering with genuine anger and jealousy.

"Hoa, there, Chastity, no reason to get your feather in an uproar. You will all get a crack at the "Incredible Hulk," Dougie replied with a boastful outburst.

"Let's quit all of this bullshit, and let's get down to some serious partying, now!" Guido ordered, his voice rising in excitement.

One of the goons turned on the music, and all of the women began to undress slowly and sensually. It was a mystical and almost magical moment. Jeremy had never imagined a more erotic spectacle in his life. His drive demanded satisfaction, but his still strong emotional attachment for Loretta prevented him from participating in the orgy. During the course of the night, several of these exotic beauties attempted to induce Jeremy into participating, but he graciously declined and left the suite.

Jeremy wandered throughout the casino and ultimately ended up at the Blackjack tables. Blackjack had always held his interest, and he decided to see if 'Lady Luck' would be less of a temptress than those naked beauties upstairs. He played steadily for almost five hours, neither winning or losing, but enjoying it thoroughly and couldn't pass up all the free drinks. At about 04:45 a.m., a gentle yet firm hand tapped him on the shoulder, and said, "I am really surprised to see you here; I thought you would be upstairs with the rest of the gang enjoying all of that carnal pleasure?" It was Rosemary.

"Well, uh, you see, it's a long story. I don't really want to bore you with all the details. I just couldn't participate, as I have someone who is very special to me, and I can't give her up. Can you understand that?" he asked, his eyes rising in anticipation.

Rosemary, eyeing him carefully like a prizefighter staring down the opposition prior to the actual bout said, "Damn, I am really surprised, a man with morals and principles."

"Well Jeremy, I am a good listener, and if you will buy me a drink,

I'll be your mother confessor for the rest of the morning."

"You got yourself a deal, Rosemary. Besides that, my luck is not that hot, and if I stay here I'll probably lose everything I have," Jeremy smiled at her.

"Oh, I wouldn't count on it. You would be surprised to find out how quickly 'Lady Luck' can smile upon you. Guido instructed me to give you the run of the casino, and I think that your luck has just smiled upon you." Turning her attention to the young female dealer, Rosemary whispered, "Jill, this gentleman is a very good friend of Mr. Fontana, and he would be very happy if Mr. Grant could win a few hands in a row. Could you see to it that his luck changes?"

The young blackjack nervously looked over to one of the pit-bosses, and he immediately came over.

The pit boss produced a new deck, and the young dealer began shuffling the new deck. Jeremy cut the cards, and placed a fifty-dollar bet.

"My, how conservative. Why don't you place a real bet and play two hands," Rosemary exclaimed.

"Okay, I'll do it. Five hundred dollars on two boxes, how's that?" Jeremy said shoving his stack of chips across the table toward his two playing fields.

"That's better, now let's hope that I have brought luck to you?" answered Rosemary.

The dealer slowly dealt Jeremy the first card. It was the ace of spades. The first card on the next hand was a six of hearts. The second card on the first box was the queen of hearts. "Blackjack!" he exclaimed. The dealer counted out seven hundred and fifty dollars, and gave him the second card, a black five, giving him eleven, a good doubling hand as the dealer had a four showing, and it was a new deck.

"I'll double down, give one card down and dirty; I don't want to see it," replied Jeremy, as he shoved another five hundred dollars on his box.

The dealer had a ten in the hole, giving her fourteen. She took one more card and got another ten, breaking her hand.

"You win, Sir," she said, as she shoved another thousand dollars toward him.

"Great, this is incredible. I can't believe my luck. Here is a tip for you, honey. "Jeremy gave her a hundred-dollar chip, which she quickly put in her tip box and smiled brightly.

Rosemary insisted that he play one more hand, and really push his luck.

"Come on, Jeremy, give it one more try. Who knows? You might get lucky again," stated Rosemary, a big smile on her face.

"Okay, you have been my good luck piece, and I should give it one more shot. Let's go for broke! A thousand on each hand, and let's hope for the best."

The dealer gave him an ace again on the first box, and a nine on the second hand. The next card was another ace, forcing him to split his aces and doubling his bet to two thousand dollars. He got a ten on the second hand and didn't look at his hole cards. The dealer had a seven showing, drew a ten and had to stay at seventeen. Jeremy gingerly lifted up the first card and saw a ten, giving him twenty-one on the first split. The second card was also a ten, giving him two twenty-ones and one nineteen. He had three winners, and was five thousand dollars richer. His total winnings for the two hands was an outstanding six thousand seven hundred and fifty dollars. He could not believe his good fortune, and promptly tipped the young card dealer another two hundred dollars.

"Well, Rosemary, you brought me incredible luck. Let's go and have those drinks now," Jeremy said, as he grabbed her right elbow and led her to the nearest bar.

The rest of the morning was spent telling her of his recent romantic interlude with Loretta. Rosemary was, in fact, a good listener. She seldom interrupted his conversation, and appeared to be genuinely interested in him and what he had to say. Jeremy noticed that two small teardrops were slowly sliding her cheeks, smearing her perfect makeup.

"I'm sorry. Please, forgive me. I, I feel very touched by your story, and it reminds me of something that happened to me, long, long ago, when I was a very young girl. Rosemary went on to tell Jeremy about a tragic love affair she had with a young B-17 pilot in W.W. II.

Apparently, he had been sent over to Basingbourn, England in 1943 and never came home. His plane and the entire crew had been lost on their very first raid over the submarine pens at St. Nazaire, France. Rosemary did not find about the tragedy until several months later. In fact, the news arrived on the same day that she found out that she was pregnant. She gave birth to a healthy baby boy seven months later. Unfortunately, her son had also followed in his father's footsteps and joined the Air Force. In June of 1968, he had been shot down somewhere near the North Vietnamese DMZ and reported MIA. Jeremy was really moved by her story, and tried to console her by telling her of his incredible escape and good fortune in being rescued three months after his initial capture.

Rosemary then changed the subject and asked him if he had a room. "No," he replied. She then quickly arranged for him to have one of the best suites in the hotel. Jeremy felt very comfortable with this woman and hoped that their friendship would last beyond this surreal setting. The suite was not quite as luxurious as Guido's personal quarters, but it had nearly all the same comforts and the same incredible view of the city. Although daylight had diminished some of the glamour, it still was a spectacular sight.

Jeremy carefully unpacked his bags and was amazed that he wasn't very sleepy. The incredible events of the past twenty-four hours had energized him. The visions of unclad females, and the incredible high he experienced after winning all that money had his heart pumping faster than a speed freak. He realized that he desperately needed sleep, so reached for the phone and called room service.

"Room service, Maria, can I help, sir?" A Latin-sounding female voice answered.

Jeremy asked if they had a bottle of Metaxa seven stars, one of the best cognacs in the world, and a famous Greek export.

"Yes sir, would you like some seltzer water, ice, senior?" She proudly answered. Her strong Spanish accent quickening in tempo to an almost intelligible answer.

"Sure, why not?" he answered.

Although he would never normally mix seltzer with Metaxa, the idea of a cool glass of ice and seltzer water made his mouth pucker.

He could always use the water as a chaser. Jeremy had learned to appreciate this fine beverage while vacationing in Greece prior to going to the military academy. He walked over to the bathroom, undressed and decided to take a shower. The warm water felt somewhat tepid and sticky against his sweating skin. He heard a knock at the front door, and quickly grabbed a towel. He rushed to the door, still dripping with water and opened it. An elderly black man, elegantly dressed in a tuxedo promptly said, "Good evening, Sir, room service. Where would you like it?" He politely asked.

"Well, how about over there, by the bed." Jeremy signed for the bottle and generously tipped the waiter.

Jeremy walked over to the night stand and poured himself a triple shot of Metaxa; he then sat down in front the air conditioner. He took a large swallow of his drink and let the Metaxa slowly trickle past his mouth into his throat. The strong, yet sophisticated taste of the Metaxa slowly relaxed him. He took the towel off, and turned on the air conditioner. He sat there listening to the whirring sound, and twenty minutes later, drifted off into a restless sleep. His thoughts were punctuated by dreams of naked women, B-17 bombers, Rosemary, Vietnam and Loretta. His fitful sleep was a nightmarish kaleidoscope of hellish visions. His thoughts were disjointed and confused.

Jeremy finally reached his deep REM sleep and eventually calmed down. His sleep took on an almost death-like quality. His labored breathing slowed down to an almost imperceptible whisper. His heart rate slowly decreased and he began sleeping almost normally. He was suddenly awakened by a loud knock on the door. The shock of the knock made him sit up in his chair. He was totally confused, and had no idea of where he was or what was going on. Time had completely lost all meaning and it took him several seconds to realize where he was.

"Who is it?" he asked sleepily, his voice barely audible.

"It's me, Guido, and Dougie. Open up!" they shouted in unison.

"Okay, okay! I'll be right there," Jeremy said, as he staggered toward the door, his head pounding like a tom-tom.

"Hey, sleeping beauty. It's about time you got up. Do you know what time it is? It's eleven o'clock in the morning! A day later! You slept almost twenty-seven straight hours, and we were worrying about you, Guido said, a smile slowly appearing on his face.

"I understand you were very lucky last night. A big winner at the tables and scored with Rosemary? You lucky guy, I've been trying for years and she won't have anything to do with me! How did you manage it?" Guido inquired with a lecherous grin on his face.

"Now, let's get one thing perfectly straight. I was lucky at the tables, but Rosemary and I, we only had a very long and interesting conversation. Nothing else! Do you understand me?" blurted Jeremy, his voice rising in anger.

"Hoa, there, cowboy! We were only teasing. How about some breakfast, and I can discuss some business with you," Guido offered.

Jeremy apologized for his overreaction and agreed to meet them downstairs in thirty minutes. Jeremy quickly showered and dressed in a pair of tan cotton slacks, button-down pink Oxford shirt and slipped into a pair of burgundy penny-loafers. Feeling refreshed and revitalized after his marathon twenty-seven-hour, coma-like sleep, Jeremy took the elevator to the lobby and joined Guido and Dougie in the restaurant.

The waitress came over immediately and poured him a cup of fresh hot coffee.

"Well, I must say, you look a hell of a lot better than you did thirty minutes ago," Dougie mockingly said.

"Okay, okay, you made your point. Let's try to eat breakfast in peace. You of all people should talk, Douglas C. Lawyer. I am surprised you are still alive after last night, oops, I mean, two nights ago," Jeremy smiled.

"What do you mean? I only did what you should have done! At least I held up our family's honor, and performed admirably under very strenuous and trying circumstances. Speaking of performance, I understand you made a sizable dent in the profit and loss statement of the hotel last night! How much did you really win?" Dougie answered, his chest swelling like a gamecock in mock indignation.

"Well, if you really must know, it was about six thousand seven hundred and fifty dollars, to be exact. However, I feel that Guido or

Rosemary had something to do with my winning streak. Is that so, my friend?" Jeremy asked, his right brow rising in anticipation.

"Do you remember our R&R in Bangkok, Thailand? We must have spent over two thousand dollars that week, and you paid for everything. This is my way of repaying you the favor. Anyway, the cards fall where they fall and you were just lucky. Accept it and enjoy it," Guido answered with a great big smile on his face.

"How come I never get to win? Every time I come here I lose thousands of dollars. It's a good thing that I am such an excellent attorney and I can stick you with those horrendous legal fees," Dougie sneered.

"Well, if you can keep the feds off our asses, I'll make sure that you win next time," answered Guido, his voice trailing off in deep thought.

The rest of the meal was completed in silence. It seemed as if that subject had touched a raw nerve, and no one wanted to bring it up again. Shortly after breakfast, Dougie excused himself and returned to his office for some pressing business. This gave Guido the opportunity to talk to Jeremy alone.

"Hey buddy, let's relax a little. I've been meaning to talk to you about a job offer, and I don't know how to go about it. I owe you! You saved my life twice, and I am only here today because of you and what you did in Vietnam. My father feels the same way and he has authorized me to offer you the job as the chief of security and operations. You know, kind of a G-2/G-3 kind of a guy. At least $150,000 per year, plus all the benefits you can imagine. What do you say, Jeremy? Interested? Please say yes; it would be great to have you on board again, at least this way I would feel safe again."

Jeremy carefully chose his words. He had no wish to offend his friend, nor did he want to create in him a powerful enemy.

"I am very honored by your offer, but I can't accept it. I really haven't decided what I am going to do. I will definitely go home and see my folks and take a vacation. Maybe after a few months I might be able to choose my course of action. If I change my mind I will let you know. Please tell your father that I am deeply honored by his most generous offer." Jeremy's answer seemed to satisfy Guido's inquiring look.

"Okay, my friend, I can't force you to work for me, but remember one thing, a debt of honor exists between us. I owe my life to you and until it's repaid, I am still in your debt." As an afterthought Guido said, "I don't like being in debt to anyone, but if I had to be in debt to anyone it might as well be you. Is there anything else I can do for you?" Guido asked.

"Thanks, Guido. You have done more than enough. I just need to get started, and things will work themselves out," Jeremy answered, as he got up and walked toward the main lobby entrance.

The same skinny parking attendant was on duty that day, and he immediately ran over.

"Hi, Mr. Grant, I'll get your car right away," the young attendant blurted out as he ran past Jeremy.

A few seconds later, he drove up and with exaggerated flair jumped out of the convertible. Jeremy threw his bags in the back seat, and jumped in. The engine sounded throaty and powerful as he pulled out of the hotel parking lot. He carefully blended in with the heavy traffic and drove northward out of the city. He eventually reached Highway 95 northbound, which led through Nevada, toward Reno.

The drive was a long and boring trip for Jeremy. His only interruption was an occasional tumbleweed or a stray herd of cattle. After what seemed like an eternity, he finally arrived in Reno, "The biggest, little town in the world." His exhausting drive through the desert had given him plenty of time to reflect on his current status, and his lost love, Loretta. Jeremy decided to spend the night in one of the local casinos; his favorite place in Reno, the Sands Regency, and continue his trip the next morning. He was so exhausted that he went straight to bed without even checking out the local scenery. The next morning he awoke early and immediately headed east, toward home. The drive eastward allowed him many lonely hours of reflection. It also gave him the opportunity to think.

Why on earth would anyone in their right mind live in Kansas or Missouri? It was so boring and nondescript, mile after mile of nothing. Despite more than twenty hours of driving through those states, he was unable to come up with a satisfactory answer.

Chapter 7

The "American Imam"

Jeremy had been a product of the U.S. military academy system. The West Point Brotherhood Association had ensured that Grant was properly taken care of, after his release from active duty. His previous connections with the CIA in Vietnam had, in fact, helped him in getting hired by the "Company." In reality, Jeremy was a second-generation "Company" man. His father, Winston Howell Grant III, had been recruited during W.W. II by General "Wild" Bill Donovan and served with the OSS (Office of Strategic Services) in France. Jeremy knew that his father had been an intelligence officer, but had no real knowledge of his father's spectacular successes against the Nazis in France. His father had always been rather modest about his exploits in Paris during the occupation. Jeremy found out after his father's death that Winston Grant had been a highly successful agent and was personally decorated by the French government and the King of England.

Although Jeremy didn't want to admit the fact, his father's influence had also been instrumental in his recruitment, and fast promotion within the CIA hierarchy. After the war, Jeremy's father, a wealthy New England Republican, had successfully run for the Senate and had been reelected three times prior to his mysterious death in an airplane crash in 1984. Jeremy's father had always been a strong supporter of the agency and used his influence to support them publicly and privately. His sudden demise greatly chagrined everyone at Langely. It is surmised that Winston Howell Grant III was the guiding force behind the effort to arm the mujahidin in Afghanistan. His untimely death caused many CIA hawks a great deal of concern. He had been the secret guiding light and lightning-rod behind the Carter Administration's initial decision to support the mujahidin forces in Afghanistan.

Senator Grant had approached his Soviet-hating buddy Bilenczinski, and proposed a plan to arm the mujahidin as soon as possible with the best ordnance we could buy. Bilenczinski was one of the few hawks during the Carter Administration, and was thrilled to receive this support from the powerful Senator Grant. Bilenczinski was convinced that this was the opportunity to bleed the Soviets dry, and he wanted to take every opportunity to make them pay for years of political humiliation, and also become their worst nightmare; Count Dracula Bilenczinski, he laughingly sometimes called himself.

Winston H. Grant III was influential in convincing several of our so-called allies to support the mujahidin. Eventually, the Egyptians, Saudis, Pakistanis and Chinese contributed large sums of money and arms to the cause. American intelligence sources were thrilled at the opportunity to collect first-hand HUMINT (Human Intelligence) and evaluate Soviet hardware. As far as the CIA was concerned this was a WIN/WIN situation and they were extremely eager to support the mujahidin.

The advent of the newly arrived Stinger missiles (Light Ground to Air Missile) had caused a great deal of excitement and confidence among the mujahidin. It was with the arrival of these deadly missiles that Jeremy Grant rejoined Khalil and his followers. Grant had spent nearly three days teaching the mujahidin how to operate the Stinger missiles. He was convinced they could successfully shoot down any low flying Soviet aircraft in this area. Over the past three years, Grant had the opportunity to fight along with Khalil's group on several occasions, and he found them to be well organized, well led and deadly.

Early one morning, after Grant's departure, Khalil was awakened by a loud *whoosh* and a chorus of Allahu Ak bar (God is great). Fearing a possible Soviet attack, Khalil exited his tent with his AK-47 (Kalashnikov 7.62mm automatic sub-machine gun) fully ready for action. Instead he was just in time to see a burning, low-flying Soviet MI-24 helicopter crash on the slope, approximately 2000 meters north of their camp. It was the first victim of the newly arrived Stinger missiles. Khalil and his men were so excited that they wished to share their victory with Jeremy. He sent for one of his most trusted men,

Khadef.

"Khadef, you must go immediately and bring back the CIA man Grant. I wish to have him share in our glorious victory over the Soviet helicopter," Khalil stated emphatically.

"Yes, Khalil, I will leave immediately. Is he still on his way up the mountain to see your brother Youssef?" Khadef asked.

"That's correct, take the mule and bring him back as soon as possible. Also direct that all men be particularly alert tonight. I do not wish to give away our position. We don't know if that Soviet pilot was able to transmit a distress signal prior to his crash. Make sure that all men stay under cover for the next two days. Also send out a small patrol to reconnoiter the crash site, and set up an ambush nearby, in case we receive any unwelcome guests," Khalil directed.

Khadef set off immediately in pursuit of Jeremy. Knowing that Grant was on foot and he had a mule, he expected to catch up with Grant in less than two days. Prior to leaving he instructed all of the mujahidin to move the camp at least five clicks to the west of their current location, and set up a dummy camp near the one they had just evacuated. Khadef knew from previous experience that the Soviets might attack their camp, and it would be a wise precaution to move. Soviet military tactics were still bogged down in W.W. II theory, and a massive artillery and aircraft retaliation was imminent. They only knew how to do things in a grand scale, but it also gave away their intentions, and caused them to get bogged down in Afghanistan.

Khalil had known that many other mujahidin groups had received these new missiles, but was certainly surprised by the immediate success of his Stingers. Previous encounters with this type of aircraft had not been as successful. Khalil pensively looked at the burning aircraft and recalled a previous encounter in which he had nearly lost his life. He unconsciously began to caress his left shoulder, and slowly rubbed the dollar-size raised scar on his chest. The burning aircraft brought back horrible memories of this previous disastrous encounter. He and a group of twenty mujahidin had been on patrol near a Soviet outpost, when an MI-24 helicopter surprised them in the open. A furious and relentless attack ensued. Every member of his group was killed or seriously wounded in the surprise engagement. It was only sheer determination and stubbornness that forced him to crawl back to camp; more dead than alive. Khalil was determined never to let this happen to his men again. He studied Soviet tactics and learned that the Soviet generals had a far different view than the West when it came to the use of helicopters. The Soviet military felt that helicopters were tanks in the skies and could control territory just as their T-55s (older Soviet tanks, still widely used throughout third-world countries) did.

This is one of the reasons why their tactics were not successful against the Afghans. The mujahidin simply moved from location to location and avoided any major land engagements. They knew from centuries of guerrilla warfare, that it would be more advantageous to hit the enemy in the rear areas and avoid open confrontations. Avoid all battles unless you had no choice, or simply overwhelm your adversary when the odds were greatly in your favor. Never try to match strength with the Soviet army, unless everything was in your favor. The arrival of the Stingers would definitely make a difference in any future engagements.

Two days later, almost to the hour of his departure, Khadef returned. He entered Khalil's tent; his face was gleaming with excitement.

"Khalil, I have good news, the American was not that far away. He saw the burning aircraft and decided to hide out until things cooled down a bit. I was able to catch up with him, and he is now waiting outside for you, "Khadef stated with emphasis.

"You have done well, Khadef, Allah be with you. Get some rest and eat some lamb stew; it will do you good. Bring the American inside," Khalil answered.

"Come in, Jeremy, you are most welcome. We have been anxiously awaiting your return. We wish to share our great victory with you," Khalil stated, extending his hand to Jeremy in Western fashion.

Jeremy was rather amazed at the warm display of friendship. Their previous encounters had not been unfriendly, yet they lacked the cordiality and familiarity now shown by Khalil. Although, Jeremy had saved his life on one occasion, he was never really able to penetrate

Khalil's armor, until now.

"Thank you, Khalil. However, I didn't expect you to send a man all the way to get me. After all, we expected great successes from your group, and you have proven that our trust was justified. I am also pleased, but I fear that too much jubilation may attract some most unfriendly company," Jeremy replied, a frown developing on his forehead.

"Allah is great, and he will protect us from the evil, godless Soviet pigs. Do not be too concerned, I have already given orders to move our camp, and set up an ambush.

"You are very wise, Khalil, I apologize for having doubted you," answered Jeremy.

"But now, sit down and enjoy our meal with us. It is time to discuss future ventures. As you know, the Soviets are showing signs of weakness and we must encourage their departure. My spies in Kabul tell me that Mikhail Gorbachev is ready to pull out the Soviet troops and cut their losses. I have called a council meeting with the neighboring clans. We shall discuss our next attack against their garrison at Qonduz," Khalil said, pounding his right hand into his left fist.

Jeremy looked at him in total disbelief. Here was Khalil, about to do what he so vehemently opposed and had preached against doing. Grant almost said something, but many years of training urged him to hold his tongue. He knew that Khalil had something up his sleeve, and he didn't want to spoil it, just now. Jeremy was not about to get himself involved in a major attack against a well-defended Soviet garrison, just when it appeared that the war might be winding down. Grant looked at Khalil, and thought to himself, *I wonder what the old Falcon is up to.*

Khalil noticed Jeremy staring at him, and in turn wished he could look into Jeremy's mind. He often wondered why such a young man had a streak of snow-white hair, and invariably acted wiser than his age. *Maybe he has led a sinful life, or maybe he had some horrible experience as a young man in Vietnam. Someday*, he thought, *I must sit down with Jeremy and solve this puzzle*. With that thought in mind, both men sat down to a feast of lamb, cheese, figs, dates and olives.

Chapter 8

Respect

Grant's hair was a common topic of discussion among the mujahidin. Most of them suspected that the streak had turned snow white as a result of some intensive and particularly vicious torture at the hands of the Vietnamese, or perhaps some other traumatic experience. Jeremy did not like to talk about it, and yet was amazed how much they already knew about him. The mujahidin fighters admired his streak of snow-white hair and full-length beard, as they were unable to grow such marvelous whiskers. Most of their attempts at beard growing were somewhat anemic in appearance. The mujahidin claimed it gave Grant an almost holy and wise appearance.

They called him "***American Imam***" (the leader of a group prayer, spiritual leader). It was an uncommon honor for devout Moslems to honor a stranger with such a name. However, Grant had spent nearly three years fighting alongside the mujahidin and they respected his strength, wisdom and compassion. Grant would often quote the Koran, and his mujahidin compatriots were amazed at his knowledge and respect for their religion. Grant's favorite reply to their inquisitive religious questioning was a quotation from Mohammed Neguib: "Religion is a candle inside a multicolored lantern. Everyone looks through a particular color, but the candle is always there."

He could spend hours discussing their holy book, and would often bring up passages or trivia that they had never learned. Jeremy was blessed with the uncanny ability to retain ninety-nine percent of what he read. Grant enjoyed these relaxing moments with the mujahidin. It was, after all, the only real form of entertainment that these battle-weary men enjoyed. These mujahidin storytellers would often sit around the camp-fires recalling many of the tales that made them famous. Of course, as with all tales, they were somewhat embellished, but generally held true to the events.

Grant's exploits were legendary among the Afghan freedom fighters. One of their favorite stories involved the rescue of Khalil and another man. Grant managed to carry both wounded mujahidin guerrillas on his back for over twelve straight hours; the whole time eluding an elite SPETSNAZ counter terrorism squad hot on his trail. The other mujahidin was, in fact, Khadef's younger brother, Yousef. At fourteen years of age, he had earned a reputation as a fierce fighter, and had also become Jeremy's sidekick. Jeremy could not help but smile when these tales were recounted over and over; always embellished by the enthusiastic storytellers.

Jeremy was concerned about Khalil's decision to attack Qonduz. Qonduz was a regional military headquarters, close to the Soviet border and with plenty of air cover just minutes away. CIA intelligence had given him a pretty good breakdown of the opposing forces. An Afghan Army motor-rifle regiment, the best unit in the entire Afghan army, guarded the valley floor. It was based exactly on the Soviet prototype.

"Khalil!" Jeremy blurted out.

"You know that I respect you very much, and I admire your great military tactics; however, I think you are making a great mistake by attacking this large force," Jeremy stated in desperation.

"Well, American, you may be right, but the Falcon is about to spring the trap, and the Russians are my pigeons. No one can save these Russians or their lackeys." His eyes glowed with anger and disdain.

"Yes, Khalil, I know you are right, but their heavy armor will make mincemeat of you. What about their air power? Do you really know what their composite strength is?" questioned Jeremy.

"I'll tell you. I have received many intelligence reports and they have quite an outfit up there," stated Jeremy. It consists of the following:

"A. A command headquarters element."

"B. A reinforced reconnaissance company."

"C. A complete signals company with all of its equipment."

"D. A tank battalion (three companies)."

"E. Three motor-rifle battalions (each of three companies and one automatic mortar battery)."

"Do you realize how many men we are talking about, so far?" inquired Jeremy.

"Sometimes, Jeremy, you act like an old woman," Khalil answered, mocking his concerns.

"Oh, yeah? I am not done yet, listen to the rest of their strength," answered Jeremy, his voice rising in anger. Jeremy continued listing the strength of their opponents.

"F. A battalion of self-propelled howitzers (three fire batteries and one control battery."

"G. A battery of Grade-P multiple rocket launchers."

"H. A complete SAM battery with replacement rockets."

"I. An engineer company with equipment."

"J. A chemical defense company."

"K. And not least of all, a maintenance company."

"L. And of course a motor transport company with all vehicles. Plus a whole bunch of support troops. Don't forget those SPETSNAZ, who gave us such a hard time last year," stated Jeremy with authority.

Khalil looked at him, but didn't say anything. It seemed as if Khalil was sorting all of this information out in his brain, and would answer Jeremy when he was good and ready.

Jeremy stared back at Khalil and pensively reflected on what he had just said to the still silent Khalil. Granted, Jeremy thought, a regiment of the Afghan army was not as well trained or disciplined as its Russian counterpart; however, it still could inflict major damage on any unsuspecting or overzealous mujahidin. Khalil answered, his voice barely above a whisper.

"My spies have given me an exact breakdown of how many Afghan soldiers are ready for action. Counting deserters, sick and injured, they can only muster less than half of their troops, and almost none of their sophisticated equipment. Spare parts are missing, lack of training, etc. I am convinced that with proper planning, coordination, and Allahs will a major attack can be successfully launched against this stronghold.

"I shall wait for inclement weather, thereby neutralizing their air power. They will be at our mercy," Khalil laughed.

"My only concern is what to do with that company of SPETSNAZ! As you know, Jeremy, this Afghan army headquarters also has a company of Soviet diversionary troops, AKA SPETSNAZ. These elite troops consist of approximately 115 men, of which 9 are officers. All of these troops have received specialized training and would normally operate most effectively in an AO (Area of Operation) ranging between 50 and 300 miles behind our lines. However, due to the continuous pressure put upon them by my troops, they have been sticking close to camp and refuse to go farther than ten kilometers from the area," answered Khalil in a forceful tone.

"Khalil, I am quite familiar with this organization. Due to our current fluid battlefield condition, we have forced them to operate out of their AO," replied Jeremy, pausing just a second before he continued speaking.

"This type of unit, as you know, normally maintains a headquarters platoon, three diversionary platoons and a communications platoon. Once their mission is completed, they normally will reform and regroup into one or more complete units," continued Jeremy, expecting an answer from Khalil.

Khalil continued staring at Jeremy, but slowly began developing a small grin across his normally expressionless face. Jeremy, not knowing how to interpret this newest development, decided to continue with his lecture on military tactics and doctrine.

"Very good, American, you know your enemy well. You have received a lot of good training at West Point and at the CIA. However, I am not a young recruit or cadet, and I do not wish to be instructed like one!" Answered Khalil, his voice showing a slight bit of irritation.

"But how good are you at deception?" inquired Khalil, a grin now spread across his entire face.

"Deception?" asked Jeremy, his voice rising to the occasion.

"What do you mean, Khalil?" asked Jeremy.

"Please, don't continue with your lecture, and then I will tell you how we will defeat our enemies! Your lecture sounds like something you learned in a boring textbook at West Point, and this is not West Point!" Khalil answered in haste.

"As you know," Jeremy continued, "this particular unit has been specially trained in counter-guerrilla and terrorist operations and assassinations. It has received the dubious nickname of 'the Black Cat', because it was never seen; they did their best work at night and brought an evil omen to those who gazed upon them," Jeremy finished. This last statement drew an angry look from Khalil.

Grant knew from previous intelligence reports that many SPETSNAZ soldiers were world-class athletes who openly participated in sporting events, to include the Olympics and World Class Games. These types of venues gave them access to most major European and American cities, and it helped them gain access, knowledge, and intelligence about all major world metropolitan centers. They often participated in parachuting and sky-diving exhibitions with the sole purpose of becoming familiar with that particular airfield or location. They were, beyond a doubt, some of the most dangerous adversaries in the world.

Grant was aware that these Soviet soldiers were particularly tough and vicious soldiers. Several previous encounters with them had shown them to be cold-blooded killers. He had less confidence in the Afghan army units; although they had the best Soviet equipment and training, desertions were commonplace, and conditions were such that some Afghan army soldiers were forced at gun-point to fight. Grant hoped, if Khalil really planned on fighting for Qonduz, that these diversionary soldiers would not be around to participate in the battle.

Grant reflected on his many narrow escapes over the past twenty years of service with the agency, and hoped that his string of good luck would continue awhile longer. He had no intention of dying in these forsaken mountain tops. However, he did not want to show Khalil that he was concerned over their chances of winning the next conflict.

"Well, American, now that you are done whining like an old woman, let me tell you of my plan! Do you really think that I would attack that base, if I didn't have a trap set?" answered Khalil, his smile even wider now.

"Come and listen to my story, and you will perhaps learn something about deception and treachery," quipped Khalil.

"I have been fighting the Soviet army for over eight years now, and I know how they think. My plan is twofold, I am going to set a trap to draw the SPETSNAZ out in the open and away from camp, and secondly I am going to blow up the entire ammunition dump!" Khalil slapped his knees with his open palms, and started to laugh hysterically.

"Jeremy, don't be so serious. I have a secret weapon. His name is Haziz Mohammed, Major Mohammed that is. He is a renegade Afghan army soldier who has had enough of this war, and approached me with an offer I couldn't refuse. He has volunteered to blow up the combined Russian/Afghan ammo dump on my command. In return, he asks only that he be allowed to go back to Germany where he has a wife and child," Khalil stated with an air of authority. He was so pleased with himself that he continued grinning.

"Okay, Khalil, let's say that you can handle the ammo dump, and then demoralize the Afghan troops into surrendering, once you blow the ammo dump. How are you going to get those damn SPETSNAZ, and particularly their brilliant commander, CPT Oleg I. Kolkov, to come out in the open?" asked Grant.

"That is actually the easiest part of my whole plan. What do we know about Kolkov and his troops? Tough, resilient, cold-blooded, etc. Right?" Khalil stated with a snicker.

"Okay, Khalil, get to the point," Jeremy answered.

"There is something else that these Russians have developed a fondness for in Afghanistan. HEROIN, that's right, "white death," many Soviet soldiers have become hooked on the stuff, and they must periodically come out of their little forts and either buy or steal some. Believe me, even the 'Black Cats' have developed a taste for this drug." Gloated Khalil with an air of finality.

"So, you think because a few troops are hooked on heroin that the whole company is going to come out and fall into our trap?" Jeremy replied.

"Once again, American, you underestimate me, and I am disappointed in you. Listen, and listen well. What is the most important target for the Russians in this area?" Khalil asked.

Jeremy looked up, and slowly began to see how Khalil was going to trap them.

"Do you think that is wise? After all, if they capture you, they will have won!" replied Jeremy.

"No, not at all, I do not intend to be captured. They are the ones who will die, and pay the price for invading our land. Kolkov and his group will all die! Khalil screamed, his voice rising to a hysterical pitch.

"Tell me, Khalil, why is it that you hate this CPT Kolkov so much? It's not just because he is a Russian, is it?" Jeremy questioned.

"You are very wise, Jeremy. You know I once had a younger brother named Hamir. He was just fourteen years old when the Russians invaded our land. When the Russians found out that I was one of the main leaders, they took him hostage in an effort to force me to surrender. Well, as you know, I could not surrender, and my brother made a valiant sacrifice. He did not reveal any information, even after they cut off all of his fingers, one by one. He still maintained his silence until he died. CPT Kolkov slaughtered a pig in front of him, and as a final act of torture, slit the pig's stomach and forced my dying brother's head into its belly! Can you imagine the torture my brother must have endured, knowing that his soul was doomed forever, and he would not be going to heaven? For Moslems, this is hell! I swore revenge nearly eight years ago, and Allah will be good to me," Khalil said, his eyes filling up with tears.

Jeremy looked at this brave warrior, and silently sympathized with him. This was the first time that he had ever seen him even remotely emotional. Jeremy was at a loss for words, and just silently bowed his head, as if to acknowledge his grief.

"Enough of this sentimental nonsense, let's prepare our plan now. I will call a council meeting of all the commanders in our region, and we will prepare for the attack. Jeremy, I need you to be the coordinator and help me implement our plans," Khalil ordered.

"Well, if you expect me to help you, I should know the plan, shouldn't I?" Jeremy replied, his brows rising in anticipation.

"Okay, Jeremy, I will now reveal the second part of my plan to you. How do you think we have been financing our war? Is it the measly twelve million dollars the CIA gives us? Or the money from the Saudis? Or Pakistan, our enemy? No, we are blessed that our territory has been one of the historical supply routes for the opium and heroin trade in this part of the world. For centuries, caravans loaded down with drugs have passed just north of here, and for years we have been collecting our tribute. CPT Kolkov also knows this, and he and his men have shown more interest in trying to intercept the heroin shipments than attacking us," Khalil stated, in a matter-of-fact voice.

"I will let it be known that a huge shipment of one thousand kilos of pure heroin will be passing near his camp. I will also let it be known that a certain well-known guerrilla leader will be escorting the shipment directly to Pakistan for distribution and payment. We will then coordinate our attack to coincide with his departure from camp. What do you think?" Khalil inquired, expecting instant approval from Jeremy.

"How can you convince this wily veteran soldier that, in fact, you have this heroin, and that you will lead the convoy?" Jeremy asked, not really wanting to know if Khalil had the heroin.

"It's very easy, one of my men will get himself captured, shortly prior to the attack, and he will talk under torture. It's really quite simple. In our religion such personal sacrifices are a direct link to heaven. This brave soul will be guaranteed immediate access to Allah, and he will be viewed for centuries as a martyr, or in your country, as a saint," Khalil answered, without even batting an eye.

"I am amazed that someone would volunteer, knowing that he would be tortured and possibly killed," Jeremy replied.

"Is that so? I am surprised that you don't know your history, Jeremy. Did you ever hear of the Alamo? Did not those 186 brave Texans, volunteer to stay and fight over 4000 Mexicans, knowing that they would be slaughtered? You forget Jeremy, I studied in your country, and I can remember dozens of examples where American patriots died," Khalil replied.

"Okay, you are right. But I still think it is a pretty incredible thing to do," Jeremy answered.

"Do you, in fact, have this heroin? And what are you going to do with it after the battle?" Jeremy asked anxiously.

"Yes, I do, and that is no concern of yours, Jeremy! You must not judge us, or attempt to stop me, because if you do, you will pay the same price as Kolkov! I will not allow anyone or anything to interfere with our destiny. And please, do not quote me the Koran, Jeremy, I know that our religion prohibits us from using or supplying this 'white death.' This is strictly a matter of survival. We do not have the luxury that the West or the Soviets do! We are fighting for our very existence, and we will do everything in our power to win, and defeat the infidels. I beg of you, Jeremy, don't get in my way!" Khalil finished with a flurry, and walked away from Jeremy. He stopped a few yards away, and turned around slowly. He looked Jeremy in the eyes and said," You, of all people, should question my using drugs to finance a war? Wasn't it your own agency that used cocaine money to partially fund the Contras in Nicaragua? Of course it was, and if your Congress hadn't found out about it, the CIA never would have told anyone about these illegal funds, now would they?" With that statement, Khalil walked away, leaving Jeremy uneasy and speechless.

This new development caused Jeremy to do some deep soul searching. He was at a loss of words; nor did he know how to proceed. His options were severely limited, but he knew that somehow he must stop this shipment from ever leaving the battlefield, or he needed some guidance from his superiors. He started to formulate various options, but in the end he decided to play it by ear, and hope for the best. One thing he knew for sure, he had to maintain Khalil's friendship and trust, but also pass on the information to his immediate supervisor.

Jeremy followed Khalil in an attempt to restart a friendly dialog and break this icy tension which had developed between them. When Jeremy found Khalil, he was sitting by a small fire eating some left-over lamb and goat cheese, and cheerfully talking to his men.

"Hey, Khalil! One thing I always wanted to ask you, why did you return from California after the Russians invaded your country?" Jeremy asked, as he sat down on a small rock near Khalil.

Looking up from his meal, Khalil slowly reflected and asked Jeremy this question.

"Jeremy, what would you do if the Cubans, Nicaraguans, or Mexicans attacked your country? Wouldn't you come back and help defend it? Of course you would!" answered Khalil, his voice increasing in tempo.

"I am also a very religious man, and it is my calling to expel these foreign invaders from our holy country. This is a *"**jihad**"* (holy war) for us, and Allah will see us to victory," continued Khalil.

"When I went to Sacramento, California, on a funding drive, I once saw a movie that greatly inspired me; gave me some of my motivation for carrying on our struggle against the Russians. It was called *Red Dawn*, I believe. It showed how a bunch of young American teenagers rose up against the evil Russians, Cubans and Nicaraguans and fought them to a standstill. We also know that it is our destiny to win. Our real problem will be after the Russians leave," Khalil answered pensively.

"Oh yes, I enjoyed the good life in Sacramento, and the fine things it offered, but deep in my soul, I yearned to return to my mountains. You Americans are very fortunate, you haven't had a foreign invader in your country since the war of 1812, when the British attacked you. We, on the other hand, have been invaded or colonized by dozens of tyrants for thousands of years, and none of them have ever successfully survived our resistance, and I am sure that the evil godless Russians will also perish. Allah is great!" Stated Khalil with intense fervor and patriotism.

Chapter 9

Khalil

The mujahidin were, in fact, fortunate to have the best and most well-liked resistance leader in the entire country. Abdul Ak Khalil was a Moslem holy man, a doctor of Political Science, honors graduate from Sacramento State University 1979, an engineer, and a fierce and determined leader. He was a stubborn and clever spiritual guide who would rather kill Soviet soldiers than visit the holy city of Mecca. Khalil was one of the few mujahidin leaders who was universally respected and admired by all. He had demonstrated his uncanny military skills in over two dozen major engagements with the Soviets and their Kabul-led communist soldiers.

Unlike many of the mujahidin leaders, Khalil came from the privileged class and had the advantage of a formal education. He had received an engineering degree from the University of Kabul, as well as studying four years in Sacramento, California. Jeremy Grant often wondered how an engineering graduate from Kabul, ended up studying political science in Sacramento, California. Jeremy was determined one day to ask Khalil about his American adventure.

Even the once feared Soviet elite special forces, SPETSNAZ, avoided this region like the plague. They had given Khalil his nickname, "The Falcon." Like his namesake, he was a bird of prey who swooped down from above and showed no mercy to those unfortunate enough to be caught up in his claws. From his lofty perch, Khalil could soar near his beloved mountains, usually dusted with a powdery coating of newly fallen snow, and glide over the peaks like a bird of prey in search of a victim.

Khalil had always thought of himself as a gentle and caring man who followed the Koran, the holy book of God's revelations. The Moslem religion does not preach violence for the sake of violence. On the contrary, it demands violence only when the faith is threatened. It even promises easier access to paradise for those faithful disciples who die in defense of Islam. The mujahidin were giving the maximum effort or struggle in support of Islam. Khalil truly believed that he was already dead and therefore had no reason to fear death or the Soviet soldiers. He always attempted to follow the Koran's rules of tolerance, justice, charity, mercy and self-denial. Khalil considered all of his men ***shaheedan*** (war martyrs). He had coached them to believe that martyrdom was Allah's will. His fighters were as resolute, fanatic and determined as Japanese ***kamikaze*** (divine wind) pilots in W.W. II.

Khalil strongly believed in his cause. He was willing to sacrifice his life, the lives of his men and their families if necessary. However, he was unwilling to needlessly sacrifice them. Khalil often quoted a famous saying he had learned while in college in the U.S.A.: "Battles are won by slaughter and maneuver. The greater the general, the more he contributes in maneuver, the less he demands in slaughter. Winston L.S. Churchill," British Prime Minister during W.W. II.

Khalil was convinced that he was ordained by Allah to follow this doctrine. He could be as fierce as the wildest beast, but could also be gentle and caring. His men and his many adversaries respected his wisdom, tactics and concerns. There were many on the Soviet side who totally disregarded any concern for humanity and fought a dirty little war without regard for life on either side. There was one enemy that did terrify Khalil and his men; it wasn't the Soviet army, but Soviet mines. They were so cold and impersonal, destroying mostly young children and farmers. Varying western sources estimated that the Soviet military sowed between twelve and thirty-six million mines. That would average about eighty mines per square mile of Afghan countryside.

Khalil knew that war was an inhuman and cruel beast, but he tried to minimize his casualties, especially the innocent women and children. Khalil was horrified at the sight of small children walking around on crutches, missing limbs, hideously twisted in agony and pain. The Soviet war machine was purposely targeting children and innocent noncombatants in an obvious attempt to overwhelm the already over-burdened medical care system. Many of their mines were disguised to look like toys, and more often than not they targeted innocent children. Khalil always knew that even if they won the war, they could never win the battle against the mines. Khalil hoped that the western powers would come to their aid after the shooting stopped. However, history would prove him wrong.

Khalil's youth had been one of privilege and wealth. He was fortunate to have a wealthy family and grew up having all of the western benefits and advantages that most of his countrymen did not possess. His father had always taught him self respect, charity and godliness. Khalil was heartbroken when he saw the horrors of war and their results on children. This was an enemy that could possibly defeat his fellow countrymen long into the future, even after the conflict ended with the Russians, as innocent victims would continue to perish.

Despite all of his advantages and good intentions, perhaps Khalil was biting off more than he could chew. The attack on this stronghold might swing the balance of power in favor of the Russians. It might even convince them to hang on a little longer.

Chapter 10

Preparation

The garrison at Qonduz was oblivious to the upcoming cataclysmic force which would shortly befall them. The Afghan commander, Major General Abdul Khalif Miszrayen, was continually drunk, and when he was sober he attempted to endear himself to his Russian masters. One of the greatest problems currently facing General Miszrayen was desertion. His actual combat strength was somewhere around 42%. Of those, only about 25% would probably fight. The weather had turned very cold and the continual overcast and torrential rains made reinforcements and re-supply impossible. There was a feeling of impending doom in the camp, and the drunk general was totally out of control. The political upheavals in Russia were making news, and he knew that someday soon his Soviet "buddies" would be leaving his country for good.

"CPT Fahzri, I want you to organize a staff meeting, right now!" shouted the drunken general, as he fell off his chair.

"Yes sir, general. Ah, should I include CPT Kolkov and his men?" asked the nervous captain.

"You stupid pig, don't you know anything. They are leaving us soon, and we are going to be all alone! No! Leave them out for now. I will deal with them later on," shouted the general.

Thirty minutes later a ragtag bunch of unit commanders showed up at the headquarters building, most of them cursing and swearing at the general for bringing them out of their warm bunkers into the miserable cold rain. As the group slowly assembled around the large oval table it was evident that less than half of the commanders had reported for duty.

"So, the rats are leaving the sinking ship," screamed General Miszrayen.

"CPT Fazhri, issue a general order now. All missing commanders will be treated as deserters, and they are to be shot on sight. Additionally, I will personally promote every man who carries out my orders by two ranks!" screamed the general.

An immediate, but noticeable hush settled over the room. The remaining commanders were shocked by this order. However, their strong instincts for survival kept their mouths shut. At this point in time they all knew the stupidity of uttering a single word. After what seemed like an eternity, General Miszrayen began to speak, his voice slurred by too much vodka.

"Listen to me, and listen to me well. I know that most of you don't think much of me, and quite honestly, I don't care anymore. I have but one concern, survival! As you may have noticed, our brethren in arms have already fled, and should the mujahidin decide to attack now, we will be decimated! I do not think that my family would appreciate that fact right now," finished the general with a flair.

The gathered commanders looked at one another; waiting for someone to speak. For several minutes no one spoke. Finally, a brave soul at the back of the room, stood up and said, "Excuse me, general what are your orders, and what would you like us to do? Major Mohammed's voice cracked at the end of his question.

The entire room turned around and stared at the brave soul who dared to utter any words under the current circumstances. General Miszrayen did not react at first. He kept his head down as if he was staring at his feet, but suddenly he jumped up and shouted, "Well, I am glad to see that at least one of my officers has balls enough to ask a sensible question. Is that you, Major Mohammed?" asked the general.

"Yes, yes it is," he answered.

"Guess what? You are now Colonel Mohammed, and you are my new chief of staff! None of these other officers had the courage to ask me a question, so I am promoting you to Chief of Staff!" shouted the general.

"Thank you, general. Thank you, sir. What are your orders?" asked Colonel Mohammed, slightly overwhelmed by the suddenness of the events.

"You are now my Chief of Staff, and I expect you to come up with a proposal for the defense of our garrison," ordered General

Miszrayen.

"I will have a proposal for you within three hours, general," Colonel Mohammed answered.

The general left the room and retreated to his quarters and his vodka. The rest of the commanders stood around perplexed by the sudden turn of events.

"Well gentlemen, here we are, stuck on this forsaken garrison; and nobody wants to be here! Nevertheless, we have to prepare for the worst contingency and I expect all of you to cooperate. Is that clear?" bellowed the newly promoted colonel.

"Yes, sir, yes sir," answered the obviously disheartened commanders as they gathered together to discuss their situation.

"Okay gentlemen, I'll return in an hour and I expect a preliminary proposal, is that understood?" shouted Colonel Mohammed as he left the room.

What luck, what incredible luck. I will make it out of here yet, thought Colonel Mohammed as he entered his jeep. He knew that he had to get word to Khalil as soon as possible. Mohammed drove toward the main gate of the outpost, only to be stopped by a frightened sentry.

"What are you doing, Major Mohammed? You can't leave the post now; it's too dangerous, sir!" exclaimed the young sentry.

"Since when does a private tell a colonel what to do!" Mohammed answered, with an emphasis on colonel.

"I am, I, I am sorry, colonel, I didn't know, but it's very dangerous out there," the private said as he pointed toward the hills.

"Well private, I appreciate your concern, but I am now in charge of the defense of this garrison, and I must inspect the perimeter." With that last comment the colonel drove away into the darkness. The poor private was left there alone and scared.

Mohammed drove quickly to a prearranged meeting spot with the mujahidin. After a winding twenty-minute drive up and down a narrow, and tortuous road, he stopped near a giant boulder. He blinked his headlights on and off three times and waited. Approximately two minutes later, a small hand-held flashlight responded with four short blinks and one long one. Colonel

Mohammed stepped out of his warm vehicle into the cold. The wind was howling and the rain felt like stinging bees against his exposed skin.

Colonel Mohammed raised his arms in the air so as not to be mistaken by his mujahidin contact. He walked slowly toward the point where he had last seen the light. As he approached a small rock outcropping, a voice from the shadows yelled, "Stop right there or I'll send your soul to hell."

"Okay, okay, don't be so jittery; it's me, Major, ah Colonel Mohammed."

"What do you mean colonel?" answered the voice still in the shadows.

"I refuse to speak to anyone who does not show themselves," blurted the now impatient Colonel Mohammed.

"All right, but keep your hands where I can see them," answered the voice, an obvious nervous stammer in his speech.

After what seemed an eternity, a small dark figure emerged from the gloom, his AK-47 held chest high and pointed directly at Colonel Mohammed's chest.

"There is no need for that, brother, I am on your side remember," whispered Colonel Mohammed at the approaching figure.

"Don't call me brother! You and I are not alike. I am one of Allah's chosen warriors, and you are a traitor! I am only here because Khalil has ordered me to wait for your signal. What is it that you want?" answered the yet indistinguishable man.

"Have it your way; I have come with some very important information. Listen and listen well." Colonel Mohammed proceeded to explain the events of the past few hours.

The darkly clad small young man sat and listened to all of the interesting information and made mental notes. After what seemed like forever, he stood up and repeated the important points back to Colonel Mohammed.

"Okay, I understand. You will blow up the ammo dump at 02:30 two days from now, and that will be the signal to attack. You will meet Khalil here, and he will arrange safe transport for you. Is that correct?" asked the young mujahidin, his eyes rising in expectation.

"Yes, that is correct, and please tell Khalil not to be late," replied Colonel Mohammed as he walked away from the young mujahidin.

The young soldier looked at the back of Colonel Mohammed and had a sudden urge to blow his head off. A sudden feeling of revulsion swept over him. His finger tightened on the trigger of his assault weapon, but at the last moment he lowered his weapon and spat on the ground instead. The shadowy figure of the colonel got back into his jeep and drove away, his lights quickly dimming in the darkness.

Colonel Mohammed was proud of himself. Everything was working out well, and he was convinced that he would shortly be back in Frankfurt, Germany. His German-born wife and three children had not seen their father in over four years. Mohammed drove back to the camp in less than twenty minutes, and was in time to review the commanders' plan of defense.

"Well gentlemen, I am glad to see that you have spent your time well. Let's see if we can coordinate this into a workable idea and I will present it to the general," Colonel Mohammed said as he leaned over the large table.

"Good, good. I am glad to see that you have thought of all possible eventualities, even the destruction of our ammunition dump. Congratulations, CPT Biruz, I will make you personally responsible to ensure that all charges are in place by tomorrow evening, and that a fail-safe back-up system exists. I want the primary destruction mechanism placed in my personal bunker. I also want an electronic detonation device capable of setting off the charges from at least three hundred meters away. Is that understood?" Smiled the colonel, unable to hide his glee.

"Yes, yes sir. I will personally make sure that everything is tested and double-checked," answered the eager captain.

It seemed that everything was falling into place. What a stroke of luck. He could not have planned it any better himself. However, he now had to deal with the unpleasant side of this adventure, CPT Kolkov. Colonel Mohammed walked out of the warm bunker and headed towards the Russian compound. After what seemed an eternity, he reached the barbed-wire enclosure surrounding their area. A firm and menacing voice challenged him.

"Stop, and identify yourself," shouted a Russian soldier in a heavily accented Armenian speech.

"Comrade, it's me, Colonel Mohammed. I am coming to see your commander, CPT Kolkov," yelled the colonel, above the howl of the wind.

"Step forward into the light, and I will call the commander," answered the edgy Russian soldier.

As the young soldier spoke into the field phone, he never lost sight of Colonel Mohammed. There was an inherent distrust between all SPETSNAZ troops and Afghan soldiers, even a colonel. The colonel stood in the rain awaiting permission from a foreigner to enter his own garrison compound. *How ironic* thought Mohammed, *I can't wait until they all die or leave my country.* Just then, the Russian motioned him forward and pointed him toward the main Russian bunker.

It was an impressive structure, thought Mohammed, as he approached it, at least fifty meters wide, bristling with heavy machine guns, rocket launchers and mortar positions. Every angle of the bunker was covered by at least two separate fighting positions. A well-built fort, he thought to himself, as he entered the structure. He was once again challenged, and had to experience again the humiliation of being held at gun point in his own base. One day, one day soon. He smiled inwardly, as he was finally given permission to enter the inner sanctuary of this fortress.

"Welcome, welcome, major, ah, I understand now colonel. Have a seat, please." CPT Kolkov extended his hand in an unconvincing gesture of friendship.

"What can we do for you, colonel? Is there something special you need done or is this a simple courtesy call?" asked Kolkov, with a smile on his face.

"No, CPT Kolkov. I am now the Chief of Staff, and as such I have been given the task to organize and coordinate the defenses of our garrison. As you are part of our garrison, I would like to include you in our discussions. I hope you don't mind," stated Colonel Mohammed, his voice sounding more excited than he wanted to.

"No, not all. I am honored that I am the second person you have visited tonight," answered Kolkov, his eyes peering deep into the colonel's eyes.

This sudden statement caught him off guard. He needed time to figure out if Kolkov knew. What did he mean? Was he talking about the staff meaning or did someone follow him to his rendezvous with the mujahidin? Unsure of himself for the first time this evening, he decided to take the offensive.

"Yes, CPT Kolkov, your participation is very important in our plans, and we hope that we will have you complete cooperation," he said as he vainly attempted to stare Kolkov down.

"Colonel, you and your men can always count and expect the cooperation of the Russian forces until the day we leave your country. Let me show you how much we intend to cooperate with you, colonel," he announced as he pointed to a dimly lit back room.

There, in the farthest corn of the room, sat a man, or at least what appeared to be a human shape. An animalistic moan escaped from his lips. His whole body quivered in an almost rhythmic fashion. He was securely fastened to the arms of a sturdy wooden chair. Perched above him was a brute of a man. He was at least six-foot-five and weighed at least 280 pounds. He was bare-chested and completely covered with a thick mat of hair. Had Colonel Mohammed not known he was human, he would have guessed that a huge ape of some kind had penetrated their compound. The ape held a field telephone in his hands and was enjoying winding the handle as fast as he could. Every time he did so, the poor helpless victim would begin to moan and quiver all over again.

At first Mohammed could not see that the field phone wires were attached to two metal clips, and they in turn were attached to the poor man's testicles. Every turn of the phone sent an agonizing jolt of electricity through his genitals. Colonel Mohammed also observed that the man had several of his fingers missing, and hideous looking burn marks throughout his body. Colonel Mohammed stopped and stared at the helpless human being and inwardly prayed to God that he never would be in such a position.

"Colonel Mohammed, meet Warrant Officer Ivan. He is our interrogator, and he has never failed to extract information from his victims." CPT Kolkov pointed to the ape and smiled.

The huge beast temporarily stopped his torture, and slowly turned around to see who had come in the room. He looked at everyone present; right through them, and then resumed his hideous work. Upon gazing at this human monstrosity, Colonel Mohammed had no doubts that humans and apes were closely related.

"Well CPT Kolkov, have you gotten any information from this poor soul yet? I am sure that he has told you his entire life story by now," blurted Colonel Mohammed, as he turned away from this disgusting scene.

"Yes indeed, colonel. I know everything I need to know. I am only allowing Ivan a little playtime before we kill him," answered CPT Kolkov with a disgusting smile.

Before Colonel Mohammed could answer, CPT Kolkov leaped toward the helpless man and shot him between the eyes with his standard issue Makarov pistol. The poor man's head exploded like a ripe watermelon, sending pieces of skull, brains and blood everywhere. The suddenness of the action caught Mohammed by surprise; the gunshot erupted from the barrel with such fierceness that the noise bounced off the thick walls for minutes afterward. Ivan, the interrogator, turned around and stared at Kolkov, his eyes glowing with hate and frustration. Kolkov had interrupted his sadistic playtime and he was obviously angry.

"I am sorry, Ivan. He had served his purpose, and it was time for him to meet Allah. The mujahidin would be proud of this man. He was truly a shaheedan or war martyr," stated Kolkov.

Warrant Officer Ivan slowly packed his hideous instruments of torture into a large black leather case. He walked out of the room without so much as a grunt.

"Would you be so kind as to share some of the intelligence you have so skillfully gathered, CPT Kolkov? Or is this another secret Russian operation?" questioned Colonel Mohammed, as he walked toward the corpse.

"Not at all, colonel, we will share as much information with you as you normally share with us," answered CPT Kolkov with a grin.

"This man swore that a large-scale offensive might take place in the next few weeks, and that it might even be led by our longtime nemesis, Khalil! I am convinced he is telling the truth. Aren't you, colonel?" answered CPT Kolkov, nodding to the colonel.

"Well, I could have told you that, without torturing this poor soul. We know that the mujahidin are planning something, but we feel that it might take place after you leave. As far as Khalil is concerned, how often have we heard these stories. The man is a ghost, a shadow warrior. I don't believe it! In any case, we Afghans have to settle our own mess, when you Russians leave our country," answered Colonel Mohammed, as he left the room.

Mohammed was now more convinced than ever that the wily Kolkov knew more than he was letting on. He only hoped that he didn't know about his plan with Khalil. Mohammed decided to continue with his plan as outlined. He had no other choice. Kolkov or not, in two days this place was going to disappear and he did not plan to be around.

CPT Kolkov called his staff together and discussed the information they had learned from the wretched Afghani prisoner. Everything except the information about the heroin, that is. Kolkov wanted to keep that information from as many persons as possible. Kolkov was now thinking about a new plan. It did not involve the Afghans, the Russian army or most of his colleagues. It was a plan of survival and escape. Kolkov had no intention of ending up like many of his dead colleagues, or even worse, missing an arm or a leg. The Russian system as he knew it was collapsing around him and he was going to make the best of it.

Chapter 11

The Betrayal

As soon as Colonel Mohammed drove away from the meeting location outside the camp, the young mujahidin sentry waited another twenty minutes in the shadows. He knew that the SPETSNAZ had night-vision devices, and he had to be extremely careful. The American Imam, Grant, had also given them several American-built night scopes, and he was now scanning the landscape for any signs of the enemy with his new toy. *How wonderful,* he thought, *I can see in the dark!* Just then, about a hundred meters away, a movement. Was it a gazelle, a donkey? No it had to be a man. He was now convinced that the Russians were observing Colonel Mohammed.

The shadowy figure made no hostile advances toward him. He seemed to back down the hill as fast as he could. For a moment there was no action, and then suddenly a loud noise pierced the night. Despite the ferocity of the wind, the distinct sound of a motorcycle could be heard. A few seconds later, a single low-beam headlight left the area back toward the camp. What could this mean? Did the Russians suspect Mohammed? Who was this person? Youssef decided he could no longer linger in the neighborhood. He scampered down the hill, and eventually found his donkey. He managed the whip and pushed his ancient beast back to his camp in less than three hours.

"Khalil, Khalil," shouted the young man as he entered the tent. "I met with him, I met with him and, and," stuttered Youssef, his words mingling so fast that no one could understand them.

"Slow down, and take a deep breath. Tell me exactly what happened. Don't leave anything out," replied Khalil, looking up at the still panting and excited Youssef.

Youssef sat down, gulped down a large breath of air and started recounting the entire episode, word for word. After what seemed like an eternity, he stopped talking and looked up at Khalil. His brown eyes resembled a young Cocker Spaniel awaiting a treat from his master, after a good trick. Khalil paused for a few seconds, looked around the room and said quietly, "You have done well, Youssef. Very well indeed. Why don't you go back to your tent, have some food, and rest a little. I will call you if I need you again. Make sure that your replacement is well on his way. We must ensure that someone is always there, do you understand?" replied Khalil to the youth.

"Yes, of course, Khalil. I have already arranged for Salim to replace me. As a matter of fact, he should already be halfway there," answered Youssef, his small chest puffing out like a rooster's.

Youssef backed out of the tent and disappeared into the night, his thoughts racing back and forth between the excitement of his scouting mission, and his homecoming. *I have done well, yes indeed, I have done well,* he thought to himself. *Maybe Khalil will make me a commander now,* he thought.

"Well, my brothers, the plan seems to be working. However, I don't like the fact that the Russians are following Mohammed around. Do you think they suspect something?" questioned Khalil to the gathered men.

Grant was the first to speak. He stood up, and looked around the tent. He knew he had to carefully choose his words. He had to express his pessimism, but at the same time not offend anyone.

"You know what my feelings are. I think that this is a foolhardy thing to do at this time. However, I will support any action on your part, and I will give you 110% of my effort. Just be wary of Colonel Mohammed," replied Jeremy, as he sat back down.

One by one, each mujahidin commander stood up and voiced his opinions. The vast majority expressed overwhelming support; some expressed similar concerns about Mohammed. Overall, the consensus was to proceed, but with caution.

"Well then, it's settled. We will attack the main base at 02:30 in two days. However, we will have to draw out the SPETSNAZ earlier that evening, at least their commander, CPT Kolkov. I am sure we can handle them once we have killed their top officers and noncommissioned officers. Our brother Kahmir sacrificed his life, earlier today. I am sure the Russians have fallen for our trap, and we will annihilate them with the lure of our 'White Treasure'." A chorus of "Allah be Praised" was heard around the tent.

"I know that the American Imam does not agree with our plan, or the use of heroin, but I am sure he can live with it, isn't that so, Jeremy?" stated Khalil as he looked at Jeremy.

"You are right, Khalil, what you call 'White Treasure,' I call 'RED SNOW.' The ground will be covered in blood, the Reds will be white as snow after we kill them, and the snow will also be red with their blood. Don't worry, Khalil, I will support you to my death if necessary," Jeremy answered. A renewed chorus of "Allah be Praised" could be heard throughout the large tent.

Although he used the words *to my death*, Jeremy was seriously concerned about his survival. Jeremy knew that his position was now tentative, and that he had to somehow alert his superiors of the current situation. Unfortunately, his satellite uplink telephone system had been damaged, and he was unable to get across the border to Pakistan. Jeremy had only his wits and survival instincts to carry him through these dangerous times.

Jeremy was asked by Khakil to assist them in coordinating the combined efforts of the four regional mujahidin groups. For the next thirty-six hours Jeremy's military and logistical knowledge was heavily taxed. He was unable to get any sleep at all. After what seemed forever, he was able to convince the four group commanders to follow his recommendation. Dealing with these diverse opinions was worse than arguing with his mom, he thought.

Jeremy walked over to Khalil, and told him that he was exhausted and wanted to go to his tent for a few hours rest before the attack. Jeremy left the enthusiastic group of mujahidin leaders and strolled over to his tent. He could not believe that in less than twenty-four hours the entire countryside could be engulfed in some of the fiercest fighting since the beginning of the war. He was in a difficult predicament, but he could not readily see an easy way out. Perhaps the easiest thing to do was to relax, and hope for the best. Jeremy soon fell into a deep sleep.

Chapter 12

The Attack

Meanwhile thirty-six hours earlier, back at the secret rendezvous, Vladimir watched Colonel Mohammed meet with the shadowy figure. They appeared to talk for a few minutes, and then Mohammed got back in his jeep and headed back toward the garrison. CPT *Kolkov was right*, he thought. "That sneaking, treacherous, piece of pig shit!" screamed Vladimir into the wind. "Wait until Ivan is done with him," he will regret ever messing with us. After quietly observing his nemesis through his night scope, he decided to rush back to camp. He slid down the hill and climbed on his motorcycle, and drove away at a high rate of speed.

Vladimir was so excited to see his commander and explain what he had seen that he missed seeing the large boulder in the middle of the road. His motorcycle hit the boulder with such force and impact that he was catapulted head first over his cycle. Unfortunately, the edge of the road was only fifteen feet away, and his unconscious body slid over the precipice and plummeted one thousand feet or more to the valley floor. The motorcycle came to rest on the right edge of the dirt road.

Back at the base camp CPT Kolkov called Senior Sergeant Andropov and expressed his concern over Private Vladimir's absence.

"What do you think, Andropov? Should we send out a patrol out looking for him, or should we wait?" Asked Kolkov.

"Well sir, if you want my opinion, I think we should send a patrol out immediately. Vladimir is one of my most reliable soldiers. In two years of combat, I could always count on him. He was always punctual and reliable. Let me organize a patrol, and we will know what happened to him in a few hours, "requested Senior Sergeant Andropov.

"Okay Yuri, you know best. Please, let me know as soon as

possible. I have some urgent matters to attend to, and I need to know the whereabouts of all my men," replied Kolkov, as he walked out of the room.

"Damn, damn, and damn," shouted Kolkov as he exited the room. I hope nothing has happened to Vladimir. He is one of my best men and he knows about the heroin! I hope that the Afghans have not captured him and made him talk. What shitty luck, now that things are falling into place. All of these thoughts raced through his mind as he tried to reorganize his thoughts. Vladimir's cousin LT Antoniv was going to be the MI-8 helicopter pilot who was prepared to fly them all out, heroin and all, if the shit hit the fan.

Calm down, calm down, he thought to himself. *You have been in worst situations than this. Maybe Vladimir's motorcycle just broke down, and he is on his way here right now.* One thing he knew for sure, the Afghani that Ivan tortured had been very sure about the shipment of heroin and Khalil. He would make sure that Khalil died and he collected the one ton of pure heroin. Kolkov didn't know much about drugs, but he knew that a ton of heroin had to be worth a lot of money. Getting rid of the heroin afterward might prove to be more of an obstacle than acquiring it. However, he felt sure that things would work out. His cousin Yuri in Moscow had always been on the fringes of the underworld, and he would be a good contact point to help him sell the drugs.

Although he loved "Mother Russia", he now felt betrayed, and the heroin would somehow repay them for their pain and sacrifices. He thought about his many comrades and he swore revenge against Khalil and all mujahidin. One thing he knew for sure, he had less than thirty-six hours to organize and plan the ambush on Khalil and his men. All of the intelligence indicators, and the recently tortured mujahidin informant had told him as much. Kolkov had, in fact, discovered the true ambush plan, and would double-cross Khalil. Kolkov got satisfaction from the knowledge that, for once, he would be able to snag the "prey" before Khalil. He wasn't quite sure how to handle the rest of the plan, but was confident that something would come to him in the next few hours.

Senior Sergeant Andropov and his men carefully drove up the

winding road. Years of combat training had taught them to be extremely careful. These mujahidin, were a cunning, resourceful lot. They were well trained and had the best Soviet or American equipment. It was no time now to be careless. Each member of his patrol scanned every nook and cranny of the road and mountain. There was very little said, but every one of them knew his job.

After about four hours of careful searching they came upon the scene of the accident. Sgt. Andropov was the first one to approach the motorcycle. He skillfully inspected the scene and could not find any evidence of foul play. The lack of skid marks, and the large boulder in the middle of the road were evidence that an accident had occurred.

Private Vladimir was nowhere to be found. Sgt. Andropov told his men to take cover and wait for sunrise. The next two hours were extremely tense and nerve-racking. The SPETSNAZ were trained to operate in both darkness and daylight, but felt extremely vulnerable in the daylight in enemy territory.

After what seemed like the longest two hours in history, Andropov crawled out of his hiding position and sneaked a peak over the edge. His powerful binoculars were able to show him the mangled corpse of Private Vladimir at the bottom of valley. Lacking any evidence of foul play, he correctly assumed that Vladimir had simply driven too fast and went over the edge.

Sgt. Andropov then began to wonder what had made Vladimir drive so fast. Was it the enemy? Surely not, there would have been some physical evidence such as spent cartridges, etc. CPT Kolkov had sent Vladimir on a special mission. That mission was to observe and follow Colonel Mohammed and report back as soon as possible if he saw anything of importance. Andropov was now more convinced then ever that Colonel Mohammed was somehow involved in an act of betrayal. CPT Kolkov must be notified as soon as possible; however, they would not make the same mistake that Private Vladimir had made.

"All right, men, we have spent enough time exposed to the elements. Let's get of the truck, and get the hell away from here. I have no intention in ending up like Private Vladimir," screamed Senior Sergeant Andropov to his patrol.

Sgt. Andropov was anxious to communicate with his commander, but was unsure whether or not to trust his radio or personnel. He knew that the way down would take far less time than the way uphill in the darkness. I will wait until we return, and report in person to CPT Kolkov, he decided.

Sgt. Andropov had correctly guessed the willingness of his truck driver to find his way safely home. It took four hours to go up the mountain, but only twenty-five minutes to come down the hill. The young truck driver displayed amazing driving skills. Just as the sun cleared the tallest mountain, Andropov and his patrol screeched to a stop in front of the Russian compound. Andropov dismissed his men, and he went directly to CPT Kolkov's quarters. He knocked loudly on the door three times, and entered without waiting for a reply.

"Excuse me, sir! We are back! I found Vladimir's body at the bottom of a ravine. It appears that he simply had an accident and went over the edge. I found absolutely no evidence that mujahidin interfered with him. Unfortunately, the body is in an unreachable location. It would take a mountain goat with wings to reach the corpse. I did not think it prudent to spend too much time exposed to enemy positions.

"Although there was not any direct evidence of mujahidin involvement, I strongly believe that Vladimir had seen Colonel Mohammed with the mujahidin, and he was hurrying back to warn you," stated Senior Sergeant Andropov with emphasis.

Sgt. Andropov had caught CPT Kolkov napping. Kolkov slowly rose and looked Andropov in the eyes, up and down, and repeat what you said in such a manner that I can understand," answered CPT Kolkov.

"I am sorry, sir. I was so anxious to bring you the news. Yes, we found his body, but it appears to be an accident. There was absolutely no evidence of Afghani involvement. I think he simply drove too fast and didn't make the curve. However, the reason he drove so fast was that he had news of Colonel Mohammed," replied Sgt. Andropov.

"Well, so be it. I am sorry for Vladimir. Two years of combat and not a scratch, and now this unfortunate accident. Yes, I agree with you. The main sentry gate log indicated that Colonel Mohammed returned about the same time that Vladimir disappeared. I don't believe in coincidences. We must keep our eyes on Mohammed; he is not to be trusted," answered CPT Kolkov.

"Please put Private Vladimir in for some appropriate decoration. No, make it the Order of Lenin, or some other high-ranking decoration. Notify graves registration, I hope some day we will be able to recover his remains. Make sure that you and your men take a much needed rest, and see if you can track down his cousin LT Antoniv. I want him to report to me as soon as possible, is that understood?" barked Kolkov.

"Yes sir. Do you want me to stick around after I have located him?" asked Andropov.

"I guess so, now that Vladimir is gone, I have to trust someone else," replied Kolkov with a smile.

LT Antoniv was easy to find. He was drinking vodka, way too much vodka, with his squadron mates. Sgt. Andropov walked in on the party and was greeted with choruses of boos, and whistles.

"Excuse me, sir. CPT Kolkov would like to see you right away," said Sgt. Andropov to LT Antoniv.

The drunken lieutenant turned his head toward the voice and said, "***Zsopa!***" (Asshole). A silence descended upon the crowd. No one spoke, whistled or drank anymore. For ten long seconds there was a long silence. Then, Senior Sergeant Andropov repeated his statement.

"You tell that asshole CPT of yours, that I'll get there when I am good and ready, do yoooooouuu-" slurred the drunken lieutenant.

Before he could quite finish his words, CPT Kolkov walked in the room and growled at LT Antoniv.

"Is there something you wanted to say to me, LT?" asked Kolkov, his voice low and filled with anger and passion.

"UUh, aahh, I am sorry, sir. I was speaking to the sergeant and not about you. I didn't mean tooooo!" Lied the drunken pilot.

"Well, that's even worse then. How dare you talk about anyone in my command that way. I order you to report to my quarters in ten minutes, and you will apologize to Sgt. Andropov now! You worthless piece of pig shit!" Screamed Kolkov, his veins nearly bursting from his throat and forehead.

"I, I, ah, uh. I am sorry for what I said, Sergeant Andropov," stammered LT Antoniv.

Senior Sergeant Andropov was visibly upset, and had to maintain his composure. He looked disgustedly at the LT and the other drunken officers and walked out. He was so upset that he didn't see CPT Kolkov behind him.

"I am terribly sorry, Yuri. You deserve a lot more than this. Don't worry. If we didn't need that piece of shit, I would have put a bullet in his head right now. His time will come, and when it does, I will make sure that you are around to see it," said CPT Kolkov, as he put his arm around his sergeant.

Less than ten minutes later, the still drunken lieutenant knocked on his office door.

"Come in," shouted the still angry Kolkov.

"LT Andrei Andreinovich Antoniv reporting as ordered, sir," yelled the weaving pilot.

"I have good news, and I have bad news. I am sorry to inform you that your cousin Vladimir, a valiant member of my unit, was killed in the line of duty. The good news is, I am not going to kill you now," whispered Kolkov as he kicked him in the shin as hard as he could.

The drunken pilot let out a yelp and collapsed to the floor. He grabbed his damaged leg and began to cry. The tears seemed to infuriate Kolkov even more, and he began to rain blows all over the prone pilot. The more he whimpered, the more Kolkov struck him. The cringing and cowering pilot, in a feeble attempt to protect himself, rolled up in a ball. CPT Kolkov was so enraged by now that he grabbed his service automatic and stuck it in the pilot's ear. All of a sudden Antoniv seem to stop quivering, and slowly begged for his life. Kolkov stood there for several seconds, undecided as to what to do. Then Sgt. Andropov walked in and screamed, "No! Don't do it. He's not worth it. Please, I will take care of it myself. Please, sir!"

The sudden appearance of Andropov brought Kolkov back to his senses, and he put his weapon away. He straightened up and looked down at the quivering mass of flesh beneath his feet. The once-drunk pilot suddenly sobered up, and now lay in a pool of his own urine and feces.

"You disgust me, Antoniv! You are not a man; you are not a soldier! How did such a brave soldier like Vladimir have such a coward for a relative? Hissed Kolkov at the still prone Antoniv.

"Sir, sir, sir I, I beg you, don't hit me anymore. I am truly sorry for what I said," whined the quivering coward Antoniv.

In an obvious attempt to change the conversation, and perhaps save his life, Antoniv asked Kolkov, "How did my cousin die?" his voice breaking at the last moment.

"I dare not mention his name in the presence of such a coward. You know all you need to know. Did your cousin brief you well, Antoniv?" asked Kolkov, his eyes piercing Antoniv's skull like an arrow.

"Oh, yes sir. I promise I won't fail you. I know exactly what to do, and you can count on me. The MI-8 helicopter will be properly fueled and ready for a sixty-second takeoff. However, no one has informed me of our destination yet," whined Antoniv.

"Get out of here for now, and be ready for my signal. You will be notified in the air as to our target. It is no concern of yours!" answered Kolkov, still fuming at the cowardly lieutenant.

Kolkov still had misgivings about trusting Antoniv, but he was the only pilot weak enough to participate in this scheme, and to keep his mouth shut. Kolkov knew that Sgt. Andropov could also be trusted, as he was eager to leave Afghanistan alive. Andropov was tasked to select a few good men to join him in this venture. Kolkov only revealed as much as he thought would be necessary; the final details would be revealed at a later date. Kolkov wanted to make sure Andropov cooperated, as there was simply too much at stake.

Kolkov reviewed the ambush plan with Andropov, and trusted him to inform the rest of the crew. After what seemed hours, both men put the finishing touches on the plan and called it a day. Kolkov told Andropov to take the initiative and select a few good men who would follow orders without question. Kolkov then gave orders not to be disturbed, unless they were attacked.

Senior Sergeant Andropov spent the next twenty-four hours trying to identify and select a few good, trustworthy men to participate in the plan. After an exhaustive quest, he selected the Paparov twins, Igor and Mischa, as well as Abdullah Salim Puriz, a native of Tajikistan and fluent in the Afghan language. One additional advantage that Abdullah had was that his older brother Kaziz was a former helicopter pilot. As luck would have it, he was living near the Russian military helicopter base at Dushanbe, Tajikistan, near the border of Afghanistan. Should that cowardly Antoniv not work out, they could always exchange him for Kaziz. It was always good planning to formulate a back-up plan, thought Andropov to himself. "I think I have everything covered," he murmured to himself.

Andropov's only minor concern were the twins. They were excellent soldiers, but somewhat undisciplined at times. However, their hulking figures and superb close-in fighting ability made up for any shortcomings in discipline. The twins had other values. The Paparovs always bragged about their connection to Russian organized crime. Apparently they had an uncle, on their mother's side, who had the reputation of being a highly placed in the Moscow underworld. Andropov deduced that someone of this caliber would be a helpful connection. Although CPT Kolkov had not directly informed him of the final mission, he was wise enough to plan ahead, and hoped Kolkov would be pleased with his choice of men.

Senior Sergeant Andropov was confident that this five-man team could handle anything the mujahidin threw at them. Andropov decided to inform Kolkov of his success, but did not want to disturb the captain until the next morning, as both men desperately needed sleep. Andropov returned to his quarters.

Prior to going to bed, Sgt. Andropov, thoroughly briefed his men, as far as he could. He also gave specific instructions to everyone to get as much sleep as possible. He knew from many years of combat experience that lack of sleep, could sometimes be as deadly as the mujahidins bullet. Sgt. Andropov was so physically and mentally exhausted that he fell into a deep bear-like sleep.

Meanwhile back at Khalil's camp, everything was proceeding at a feverish pace. All of the advance forces were thoroughly briefed by Jeremy. Most of the participating combat units had already moved out into their respective areas of operations, and were merely waiting for the signal to attack. Coordinating all of these mujahidin freedom fighters had been more of a challenge than expected. It seemed that every commander had a different agenda. A great deal of diplomacy, courage and plain old "ass kissing" finesse had to be used by Jeremy to get everyone on the line and ready to go. The chess pieces were falling into places, and maybe Khalil could, in fact, pull it off.

"Jeremy, Jeremy, it's time to get ready," stated Khalil as he pushed the tent flap open.

"No problem, Khalil. I am ready. I was only going over a few last details in my mind. How is the weather holding out?" asked Jeremy, rising from his makeshift ammo box chair.

"Allah is on our side. Allah's mine sweepers are hard at work on many fronts," answered Khalil.

"Allah's mine sweepers?" asked Jeremy.

"Yes, didn't you know Jeremy? This freakish weather has caused large hailstones in some areas, making our eventual attack a lot easier," replied Khalil with a grin.

"Additionally, we intercepted a weather report from CNN and it is still favorable. The weather is overcast, cold, rainy, and in some areas large hailstones will fall, for the next forty-eight hours. There is a slight chance of clearing, but none of their aircraft can fly in this weather; not at this altitude, at least none of their combat aircraft," answered Khalil, his voice rising in anticipation.

"Good, good. You might get lucky yet, and pull this thing off. Let's get down to the jump-off point and wait. Did you want me to go with you, Khalil?" asked Jeremy as they started to walk out of the tent.

"Of course I do. However, you must make a promise. You must swear by Allah not to interfere with my operation, even if it involves 'Red Snow', as you call it. Do I have your word of honor, Jeremy?" asked Khalil, his voice rising in expectation.

"I will swear not to hinder your military operation in any way. However, once the action is over I must make every effort to stop you. Do you understand, Khalil?" asked Jeremy, his eyes staring down on Khalil.

"You are my brother, and I respect you. Once this conflict is over I strongly urge you to leave the area. I will no longer offer you my hand in friendship. However, I will grant you sanctuary until you leave our country. I am sorry it has to come to this, Jeremy. But this money will keep our people going for several years, and I cannot afford the luxury of not dealing in 'Red Snow.' Allah be with you, my brother," stated Khalil with emphasis.

"And with you, my brother," replied Jeremy, as he walked out of the tent. He was troubled with the situation, but his hands were tied now. He would go along with the plan for now.

Over the next few hours, hundreds of mujahidin fighters made their last preparations. Heavy weapons were brought up close to Quondoz. Extra ammunition, food and supplies were brought in by mule, trucks, and by heavily overburdened individuals. At 01:30 hours everything was ready for the forward push. Khalil, Jeremy and his followers were already within sight of the large base at Quondoz. Khalil gave final instructions to his men, and waited for the ammo dump to explode on time.

Across the small distance separating the colonel from Khalil, Colonel Mohammed sat patiently in his room. Everything was going as planned. Even the general was pleased with the defense plans. Colonel Mohammed made sure that everyone knew that he was going on a perimeter check at 02:00 hours. It was a great way to establish an alibi, should he need it.

Unbeknown to Mohammed, CPT Kolkov and his men were also preparing to leave the camp. They had been observing Mohammed and were convinced he was going to meet up with Khalil somewhere near the large boulder on the road which led to the border of Tajikistan. CPT Kolkov had already sent Senior Sgt. Andropov and the twins up ahead in a truck to set up the ambush. He would follow later in the helicopter, weather permitting.

Andropov and the twins drove up the lonely road and parked the truck four hundred meters from the boulder. Using their skill and training they were able to approach the meeting location unobserved.

"I am glad we took precautions. This area is crawling with mujahidin. Did you guys see the two sentries to the left and right of the boulder?" whispered Andropov to the twins.

"Yes we did, Sgt. Mischa and I will circle around them and eliminate them," answered Igor, his eyes glowing in the dark.

"Go ahead, but be very careful. These dogs are treacherous."

Without a further word the twins removed all of the excess ammo, gear and equipment. They would be a lot quieter this way. Igor was going to take the sentry on the left, and his brother the one on the right. The weather was definitely on their side. The gusty wind and rain made their approaches almost invisible. Igor climbed up and over the fallen rocks as if he was a panther. His movements were so fluid and graceful that he appeared to be a large cat on the prowl for his prey. The mujahidin sentry did not even hear a sound before his throat was slit from ear to ear. The sentry fell to the ground and bled to death within a few seconds. Mischa caught the other guard equally unprepared. The man had been trying to light a cigarette in this wind storm and had his back to Mischa. Mischa killed him instantly with a savage thrust of his commando knife to the back of the skull. His spinal cord was severed and he died without making a single noise or grunt. His body just dropped to the ground like a sack of potatoes.

Sgt. Andropov then advised both men to plant the explosives and then take the mujahidin sentry posts, and keep their eyes open. They could always communicate through their throat microphones. Andropov would wait down below for Kolkov and the rest of the team. The ambush was already set and Khalil would likely fall into a deadly trap.

Back at the base camp, Colonel Mohammed looked around his room and smiled. *This will be the last time I ever have to spend a night in these stinky quarters*, he thought to himself. It took only a few minutes to pack a few of his personal possessions into a black leather attaché case. He left the room without looking back. He made sure that the electronic detonating devices were safely stored in his bag. As he approached the front gate in his jeep, he couldn't help but feel a moment of unease. He couldn't explain it, but he felt that someone was monitoring all of his moves. He looked around, but no one was in sight. *I guess it's just nerves,* he thought to himself, and continued driving to a knoll approximately three hundred meters from the main gate. He stopped and got out of his vehicle. He looked upon the base with a sense of sorrow, and yet he knew he had to press the trigger or he would never get back to Germany and his family. It was still a few minutes before 02:30 hours. He sat on the hood of his jeep and waited for the time to finally arrive.

CPT Kolkov and Abdullah were, indeed shadowing his every move. Both men could sense the feeling of impending doom and disaster. They followed him as far as they could. When they saw him stop on the knoll, they returned to the heliport where LT Antoniv was waiting for them. After what seemed an eternity, they arrived in front of the MI-8 helicopter and did not see Antoniv!

"That drunken S.O.B. Wait until I get my hands on him. I'lllll killlll him. I'lll," screamed Kolkov at the top of his lungs.

Before Kolkov could finish his sentence, a small squeaky voice was heard to say, "Good evening sir, I have been waiting for you. Is tonight the night?" asked Antoniv, his voice breaking at the last moment.

"Well, well, you did listen to me after all. Good for you, Antoniv. I was about ready to go look for you," answered Kolkov, his voice rising in anger.

"Well, you see sir, I thought it would be best if I slept in my helicopter. That way I could always be ready for you. However, I don't really think anyone or anything could fly tonight," answered Antoniv with a sheepish smile.

"I am glad you are here and ready to go. Start your copter now, and let's get the hell away from here, "screamed Kolkov to Antoniv.

"But, but sir, the weather is horrible. I don't know if she will make it. I don't think it's a good idea," answered Antoniv in a plaintive way.

"Listen LT, we don't have time to discuss the situation. You either take your chances with me now, or die on the spot. What will it be?" replied Kolkov.

Both Kolkov and Abdullah, loaded their gear aboard the chopper. Antoniv resigned himself to the situation, and started the copter. The blades began to rotate slowly. After a few seconds, the chopper slowly lifted off the ground. Antoniv turned around to ask Kolkov what heading he should take.

In the same instant, four hundred meters away, Colonel Mohammed glanced at his Rolex, a gift from his German wife Heidi, as the second hand smoothly advanced to 02:30 hours. He firmly pressed the remote detonator. For a split second, nothing happened. Then the whole world erupted before his very eyes. The entire horizon seemed to flash in one continuous wave of explosions. The road he was driving on shook and quivered from side to side. Massive fireballs lit the sky for miles around. One by one, the different ammunition bunkers were destroyed. They, in turn, ignited the camp's fuel supply, which added a huge black cloud to an already black sky. Mohammed was unable to believe the amount of destruction he had created. For a few precious seconds he sat there, unable to move, but then reality set in when a human torso came crashing down from the sky. The impact was so terrific that it nearly frightened him to death. The torso crashed right on the axis of the hood of the car and windshield. The force was so enormous that it completely shattered the windshield and bent the hood at such an angle that he was unable to see. He stopped the jeep, and using the tire iron, banged the hood back down so that he could see again. A red, oozing mess of flesh, bones and gore covered the front of the car.

He was petrified to be outside his jeep. Human debris, unexploded shells, vehicle remnants, etc. were whizzing through the air with such force that contact with any one of them would mean instant death. Not wanting to waste any more time, he put the jeep in gear and sped away from the scene, still hearing muffled multiple explosions as he sped over the hill to safety. He never looked back.

Back at the helicopter, Kolkov and his men were preparing to follow the small beam of light which led away from the camp.

"I suspect that…" Kolkov started to say.

Kolkov was unable to finish his sentence. The helicopter was rocked by what seemed like a giant fly swatter. Antoniv struggled with all his might to keep the chopper in the air. Not only did he have to contend with the bad weather, but the air was filled with one explosion after the other. The only thing that saved the chopper from immediate destruction was the fact that it was already airborne and flying at a thousand feet or more. All three men were stunned by the sight that was unfolding below them. It appeared to be Dante's Inferno coming to life. Every few seconds finger-like explosions rocked the aircraft. LT Antoniv used every bit of skill in his possession to keep the machine flying.

"What, what, what is that?" stuttered Antoniv on the intercom.

"Just shut up, and keep this crate flying! You should be happy you are not down there with those poor souls right now," replied Kolkov, his voice rising in anger.

Kolkov was an experienced combat soldier. He thought he had seen all there was to see about war, but this was a nightmare. He felt pains of anguish for his fellow comrades. After what seemed like hours, but in reality was only seconds, Kolkov regained his composure and screamed at Antoniv through the intercom: "I want you to follow the main road out of the camp northward for approximately ten minutes. That is the highway that goes to Tajikistan. There should be a pair of moving headlights on the same road; follow in that direction until I tell you what to do. Do you understand?" asked Kolkov.

"Yes, yes, yeesss sir. What on earth happened down there?" asked Antoniv, his voice still showing traces of instability and panic.

"Don't worry about it. You are safe for now, and you should be happy that you are with us, and not them," replied Kolkov, his voice now under control.

Of the three men, Abdullah seemed the most quiet and reserved. He showed little emotion or feelings. However, one could sense that underneath that calm exterior, a deep, brooding and foreboding exterior existed. He finally looked at Kolkov. "How did you know? How did you know? What made you pick this time to leave?" asked Abdullah, his voice not showing any emotion or sentiments.

"Well, I guess you can call it luck, intuition, good intelligence and a dead mujahidin, a combination of all four. The question now is how do we best use it. We still have to get Khalil, and our reward. This journey is far from over," answered Kolkov, in an unusually casual and flippant manner.

"Sir, sir. I see some headlights heading up the road toward the pass and Tajikistan. Someone besides us managed to get out on time. I would guess from the speed he is going that he is in a hurry to get there," stated Antoniv, now slowly regaining composure.

"Well, I'll be damned. I bet that would be our friend, Colonel

Mohammed, en route to collect his reward from Khalil. I guess we will have to burst his bubble now, won't we!" replied Kolkov into the aircraft's microphone.

"LT Antoniv. There is a junction in the road about twenty kilometers from here. It is within walking distance of the rendezvous. There is a small meadow there. Do you know the place?" asked Kolkov.

"Oh, yes sir. I have been there many times on maneuvers," answered Antoniv, his voice high with excitement.

"All right then, show us what a hot-shot pilot you are, and drop us in there without the benefit of lights or illumination. Not only must you drop us in, but you must wait for us to return with our booty. Can you handle it?" asked Kolkov, his eyes fixed on the back of Antoniv's helmet.

"Well sir, I don't have much of a choice now, do I?" replied Antoniv, in a plaintive voice.

"You are finally catching on, LT. Keep your head together for a little while longer and you might be a very wealthy man someday," replied Kolkov, with a smirk.

"Abdullah, you and I must make contact with Sgt. Andropov and the twins. We then must finish our plans for the ambush," stated Kolkov to Abdullah.

"Absolutely, sir. I am anxious to move on. We must make sure that we are as far away as possible by noon tomorrow. Because weather or no weather, every Russian element in this part of Afghanistan will be moving in our general direction," replied Abdullah, his voice once again showing little or no emotion.

Kolkov began to put the finishing plans on his ambush, and realized that at some time Senior Sgt. Andropov should be made aware of the final plans involving the heroin. He was purposely being kept in the dark, and had no idea of what was really going on. He was following orders, and suspected that they could possibly make a lot of money someday. Kolkov switched the channels on his hand-held radio and spoke:

"Tiger two, Tiger two. This is Tiger one. How do you copy? Over!"

Almost instantly, a highly agitated Sgt. Andropov answered back, "It's about time. What in the hell is going on! What was that fireball? And whaa…" stammered Sgt. Andropov like a machine gun.

"Hoa there, slow down! All in good time. Not over an open net, remember Sgt.? All in good time. Our first customer is probably on his way up to your area. Do not, I repeat, do not reveal your position until I get there in ten minutes or so," ordered Kolkov, in an authoritative voice.

"Understood, sir. We will stand by," replied Andropov, angry at himself for violating one of the cardinal rules of radio communication.

The helicopter slowly hovered over the landing area. LT Antoniv seemed to hesitate. His depth perception was not particularly good at short distances from the ground. The night-vision devices did not compensate too well when one was a few meters from the ground. Besides, the visual conditions were so bad that his landing was less than perfect. The chopper hit the ground with such force and so unexpectedly, that both Kolkov and Abdullah thought that it had crashed. After realizing that everything and everyone seemed to be relatively intact, they packed their gear and gave final instructions to Antoniv.

"Okay, you have done better than expected. I expect you to continue in this manner. But to ensure that you do not suddenly abandon us, give me your night-vision device, your microphone and your weapon, now," ordered Kolkov, with authority in his voice.

"Sir, I object. You do not think that I would do such a thing? Really, it's quite unnecessary. I, I…!" stuttered Antoniv, in a less than convincing fashion.

"Stow it! Just be ready when we come around the corner, and be prepared for all contingencies. By the way, what is the maximum weight capacity of this chopper?" asked Kolkov in parting.

"Well sir, it depends on the weather conditions and type of load, and, and…" replied Antoniv.

"Oh, never mind. We will plan accordingly upon my return," answered Kolkov, as he and Abdullah walked away from the aircraft.

It didn't take them more than eight minutes to reach Sgt. Andropov's position. Kolkov was extremely pleased with the ambush plan. Sgt. Andropov had his men so well hidden that even Kolkov was unable to spot them. Abdullah practically tripped over the twins before they were seen.

"You have done a good job, Yuri. We can expect both of our fishes in the next few minutes. I know you have a lot of questions about the camp, but save them for later. I think I see our treacherous Colonel Mohammed coming up the road now. Remember, don't do anything until Khalil and the shipment get here," stated Kolkov with emphasis.

Colonel Mohammed was so pleased with himself, and the success of his mission, that he drove by the hidden helicopter without even noticing the strange shape in the darkness. LT Antoniv, on the other hand, nearly shit in his pants when he saw the headlights coming around the bend. He had momentary thoughts about leaving, but his inherent fear of Kolkov changed his mind. It took him several minutes to calm himself down.

Mohammed drove up to the rendezvous point expecting a handful of jubilant mujahidin. Instead, he found no one, or so he thought. He got out of his car and nervously paced the immediate area in front of the vehicle. He wanted a cigarette so badly, but did not know whether or not he should allow himself the pleasure. After a few minutes of deliberate hesitation, he lit one and took a long, slow drag. The twins, Abdullah, Andropov and Kolkov all looked down the barrel of their respective weapons and wished they could pull the trigger. Kolkov reminded everyone on the throat mike walkie-talkie to sit tight and hold their fire.

Chapter 13

The Aftermath

Back at the base camp after what seemed forever, Khalil and his men waited and watched for the signal. When it came, it was more than anyone had envisioned. The explosions were so loud that Khalil wondered if his Pakistani neighbors could see or hear the explosions two hundred kilometers away. Khalil gave orders to his sub-commanders and ordered them to proceed with the attack. He wasn't quite sure as to the whereabouts of the SPETSNAZ unit or its commander, but he was convinced that Colonel Mohammed or his sacrificial lamb would draw them out of their fort into the open. He thought to himself, *maybe the devastation is so complete, we won't have to worry about them after all.*

The results of the explosions were far more spectacular than anyone had imagined. Khalil was convinced that no one or anything could survive such a barrage of explosive power and still have the will to fight. He did not think his fighters would have much to contend with. However, explosions were still detonating in the main ammo dump and it would be several hours before anyone could safely approach the area. The detonations had also destroyed the underground fueling storage area, communication and transportation centers, and he was sure that no help could arrive for at least twenty-four hours. He dared the Russians to attempt an overland approach, as his men had every avenue of approach sealed off. Khalil was also confident that his newly arrived Stinger missiles could destroy anything the Russians had to in the air.

One of his advanced units had reported the possible takeoff of a Russian helicopter shortly before the explosions but the weather conditions were so bad, and the visibility was so poor, they could not be certain. Besides, a few seconds later their entire peripheral field of view was so filled with explosions, fires and devastation that they lost sight of the ghost ship. The incident was duly noted and passed on to Khalil. All in all, Khalil felt confident in leaving the immediate battle front to his sub-commanders. He gave instructions to his men. The overwhelming success had charged him up so much that he screamed out, "Let's get it on with the SPETSNAZ." The momentary success of the explosions had clouded his judgment. His men were somewhat taken back by this sudden burst of enthusiasm. They all knew Khalil as a modest and reserved leader.

Khalil was anxious to meet with Colonel Mohammed. He was now convinced more than ever that Mohammed would give him news directly about Kolkov and the SPETSNAZ. Khalil still had some reservation about the SPETSNAZ. However he thought, *Mohammed will give me intelligence that will allow me to decide, if they were a force to reckon with or not.* The temporary euphoria slowly disappeared and a more realistic scenario took its place.

Khalil was now going through a rather complex and difficult time. His emotions would swing from ebullient to dark and somber. Although he wanted to believe that everything would be okay, he would then reverse himself and think, *As long as I have not seen their corpses, I will consider Kolkov and his men a possible threat to my rear elements. Although* he felt confident that his trap would work, he still felt somewhat unsure about the remaining Russian officers and men. Had they survived the carnage? Were they out looking for him? He had an uneasy feeling. These were thoughts that left him feeling quit very insecure for now. Was it a premonition?

Khalil put his doubts behind him, and hastily arranged with his transportation element for a nearly new Mercedes five-ton truck (a gift from their generous Saudi benefactors) to be loaded with his men and the bait. Khalil knew that the lure of the heroin would surely draw out Kolkov and his thugs. Of course he had no way of knowing that most of the SPETSNAZ company had perished in the initial explosion, and only Kolkov and his five remaining soldiers remained.

Jeremy, Khalil and a dozen of his best mujahidin fighters boarded the truck for the twenty-minute ride to the meeting site. The truck was heavily laden with the mujahidin, the heroin and the explosives they intended to use on the Russians. Jeremy could not believe that he was sitting on fifty kilo bales of heroin, and was powerless to do anything about it. On his way to the rendezvous, Khalil suddenly became serious, and told Jeremy that they would shortly have to part company.

"Jeremy, my brother, you have served us well; however, it is now time for you to leave us in peace. I will arrange for you to take Colonel Mohammed's jeep, and I will give you a guide. You should be able to make the Pakistani border in less than four hours. However, I ask that you witness my greatest triumph, the annihilation of Kolkov and his men. If there are any left, of course," stated Khalil with emphasis.

Jeremy knew better than to argue with Khalil. He was sure that Colonel Mohammed would be joining his ancestors in Allah's kingdom, as soon as he provided Khalil with all the pertinent intelligence about the camp and or the SPETSNAZ. Although the plan had originally been to draw out Kolkov and his men, now it seemed a mute point as they probably did not survive the ammo dump inferno, thought Jeremy.

This was no time to further contemplate the realities of war, but better to ponder the chances of surviving this fiasco. Jeremy decided to follow the path of least resistance and make it across the border alive. *There* he thought, *I have many more resources, and perhaps we can put a stop to this shipment of heroin.* Jeremy had several friends in the D.E.A. who would love to be involved in this type of case. Jeremy's main goal for the next few hours was to live long enough to report back in one piece.

The drive to the rendezvous was uneventful enough; that is, if you consider racing along mountain roads in the middle of the night at breakneck speeds uneventful. The driver of the truck was obviously better suited at driving a donkey than a Mercedes truck. His near misses with disaster had everyone on board nearly frightened to death. After a terrifying yet stimulating ride, the truck and its passengers arrived near the prearranged meeting place. Khalil barked orders to his men. He was still leery enough to attempt a stealthy approach.

Better cautious than stupid, Khalil thought to himself. He had half his men get out of the truck and instructed them to reconnoiter the area, and the remaining half stayed on board the truck with him.

Kolkov and his men watched silently through their night-vision devices as the Mercedes truck stopped three hundred meters from their ambush sight. They were able to clearly observe the splitting of the forces. Half of the mujahidin began approaching the meeting place in a typical patrol formation, while the other half, Khalil and Jeremy continued on the truck. Kolkov thought to himself, *sly old fox, he is trying to outfox the fox.*

Khalil had no way of knowing that Kolkov and his troops had already mined the whole area with claymore mines, and any attempt by the mujahidin to advance would end in disaster. Under orders from Kolkov, the twins had crept up on Colonel Mohammed, and taken him captive. Mohammed was so shocked at the appearance of these two ghostly figures that he passed out. *So much the better* thought Kolkov, *we won't have to deal with him until later.* Mohammed was tied to the front seat of his jeep, bound and gagged. Anyone approaching the scene would think that he had fallen asleep.

Khalil ordered the truck to stop fifty meters from the large rock; they all dismounted and approached cautiously. His advance patrol had failed to make contact with the mujahidin sentries, but he was not overly concerned. Apparently these two mujahidin fighters had a reputation for falling asleep on the job, and they were convinced that they would find them asleep somewhere.

"Well, you see, Jeremy, Colonel Mohammed is already here and waiting. I am sure he has good news for me," stated Khalil as he approached the jeep.

Before Khalil could get close enough to look inside the jeep, Kolkov and his men detonated the claymore mines. The claymores had been placed in a semicircular fashion in front and around the jeep, facing outward in a typical killing-zone format. The initial explosion had been so violent and effective that nearly all of the mujahidin had been seriously wounded or killed. Khalil had been the closest to the explosion. He had no time to react to the explosions and was literally torn to shreds by the thousands of steel pellets and explosives. Before the steel pellets imbedded themselves in his body, Khalil had time to curse himself for not being even more cautious, and *how ironic* he thought, *I am about to die in the fashion I fear most, minefields.*

Men were moaning and groaning everywhere. The other half of the patrol faired no better. The SPETSNAZ had also placed claymores and other mines all over the area and they were also brought under fire by the well-hidden Russians. Looking through their night scopes, they were able to easily pick off the fleeing or wounded mujahidin with accurate rifle fire and machine-gun fire. Most mujahidins were unable to fire off a single round before they died.

Jeremy was once again blessed, to be alive. Khalil and the men around him took the initial blast. Jeremy, who was fifteen meters behind them, was bowled over by the explosion. He felt several sharp blows in his legs, arm and head. He looked down at his feet and saw that his right foot was nearly severed, and his left one did not fare much better. In addition to the severe wounds to his feet and legs, he had received numerous other shrapnel wounds to the right side of his head, and left arm. The initial shock of the explosion caused him to pass out and fall down a small ravine. He lay there unconscious for a matter of minutes. When he came to, the battlefield was once again quiet, too quiet he thought. *Why aren't the mujahidin returning fire?* he wondered. Of course he had no way of knowing that everyone was dead.

Jeremy had been hidden in the depression. The three-meter deep ravine, and his unconsciousness prevented anyone from seeing him. His disappearance and silence did not draw any particular attention from the SPETSNAZ. After lying there for a few minutes he finally regained his senses. Not wanting to give away his position, Jeremy lay perfectly still for another few minutes. He then slowly raised his head; there, not ten meters away, was a Russian giving orders to his men. Jeremy looked at the man carefully and recognized him as Kolkov, a face he would never forget.

After the successful ambush, Kolkov and his men had individually shot all the remaining wounded mujahidin. After assuring themselves that everyone was dead, they hastily returned to the waiting helicopter. The Mercedes truck and its precious cargo were driven back to the clearing and off-loaded aboard the chopper.

Once Jeremy heard Kolkov and his men depart the area, he raised his head again and looked around. There were no signs of the

Russians. He carefully and painfully made his way up the ravine, and what he saw made him gag in horror. Every mujahidin had been horribly mutilated, and both Khalil and Mohammed had been decapitated. The still warm headless body of Colonel Mohammed sat upright in the seat of his jeep, and Khalil's body was barely recognizable. The initial explosion had severed several limbs and the Russians had severed the head, so that all that was left was a disfigured stump.

This grisly sight brought him back to his senses, and he knew if he did not get medical attention shortly, he would probably bleed to death. His tightly-laced boots were keeping the wounds on his feet somewhat under control, but he felt his strength ebbing away, and began to panic. *Calm down, calm down*, he thought to himself. He tore the shirt off his back and wrapped his wounds well enough so that the blood flow slowed to a trickle.

After a few indecisive minutes, Jeremy attempted to pull Colonel Mohammed's headless body away from the front seat. The headless corpse was still secured to the seat of the jeep. Jeremy had to use his boot knife to release him from the seat. The front seat was covered in blood, guts and shit. Jeremy needed an extra couple of minutes to wipe up the mess. *A coward to the end*, thought Jeremy as he wiped the shit from the seat.

Every movement sent sharp pains throughout his feet and legs. Jeremy knew that this was his only salvation. He sat on the blood soaked front seat and started the engine. Miraculously it started on the first try. Jeremy knew that the mujahidin had a first-rate combat-trained medic back at their camp.

Although both of his feet were severely wounded, and he could barely see out of the right eye because of the blood flow from his head wound, he managed to push the little jeep at a high rate of speed. The closer he got to camp, the weaker he got. As the rays of sun cleared the farthest mountains, Jeremy's borrowed jeep came to a slithering stop in front of the first aid tent. That was the last thing Jeremy remembered.

Chapter 14

The Recovery

"Jeremy, Jeremy, Imam! Wake up, Jeremy, wake up! How are you doing? Are you feeling better? You are okay," screamed the medic at the still drowsy Jeremy.

"Where am I? How did I get here? I, I…" stammered Jeremy, as he slowly opened his eyes.

"Well, you drove here this morning, and you have been unconscious ever since. How are you doing? Are you feeling better? You are blessed by Allah, Jeremy Imam. Lie still and meet your savior, Doctor Jean-Pierre Perrin. He is a member of a group called 'Doctors for Humanity.' They had been in a nearby village, when we asked them to come and treat you," said the young medic Moustafah, with a grin. They did not want to get involved at first, especially with a CIA man, but we managed to convince them," he said with a wink.

"Tell us, Imam, what happened to you and the rest of the group?" asked Moustafah and the rest of the assembled mujahidin leaders.

"I, I, I don't know for sure, but I am sure that Colonel Mohammed led us into a trap. I am surprised they were able to ambush us. It appears that Mohammed could have been working both sides. The Russians had the perfect ambush set up, and we never had a chance. Most of us never had a chance to fire our weapons!" answered Jeremy, his voice breaking slightly at the end.

"Those damn Russians will pay! We found Khalil and the rest of the men. Did you see what they had done to Khalil?" asked Moustafah, anguish in his voice.

"Yes, yes I did. I, I promise you that Kolkov and his men will have to answer someday for what they did today," answered Jeremy, raising himself on his elbows. Sharp pains in his feet and leg forced him back down.

"Moustafah, tell me how did the rest of the battle go?" asked

Jeremy, his voice barely a whisper now.

"Imam, Allah is great! We defeated the Russians and wiped out the infidels. However, the damage to the Qonduz garrison was greater than we had ever imagined. Approximately, 90% of the defenders were either immediately killed or severely wounded. The remaining 10% were so disheartened that the resistance was negligible. Our losses were insignificant, Allah is great. Our biggest problem is what to do with the one hundred and fifty prisoners we have. Many of our fighters want revenge, but for now we have them under control. We have relocated them in the mountains; we will wait and see what happens to them," answered Moustafah, his voice trailing off.

"The most amazing part is that the Russians still haven't responded. It is as if they are paralyzed by the enormity of our victory. We have interrogated a few of the surviving SPETSNAZ, and they all stated that Kolkov, and a few other men, escaped prior to the attack. Of course we know what they were really doing, but there is no need to inform the Russians," answered Khadef, his voice gaining in strength as he spoke.

"Yes indeed, Moustafah. Khalil was right after all. It is only too bad that he was unable to see his glory," replied Jeremy, attempting once again to get up.

"Monsieur, monsieur. You must not move; you will bleed to death if continue to wriggle like a worm. You are incredibly lucky to be alive. When you drove up here this morning, you were within a minute of dying. You had lost nearly half of your blood! I must insist that you remain perfectly still, or you will die. Not even the barrel of your friend's AK-47 will save your life," stated the French doctor with authority, pointing toward Moustafah and smiling.

"Our three-month tour is now over, and I must return to France. I have made arrangements for you and some of the other severely wounded to be taken across the border into Pakistan. Proper medical care can be given to you and the other men. You are in need of several critical surgeries, but I am unable to perform them under these conditions," stated the tall French doctor to an already unconscious Jeremy.

The ride across the frontier in an old French Citroen station wagon was a living nightmare. Eight severely wounded men, along with Dr. Perrin, were crammed in this old heap. The shocks were so worn that every new pothole started a series of roller-coaster-like motions which lasted for several minutes. Jeremy, by now, was so doped up that most of the ride seemed like a series of Van Gogh paintings, a few flashes of brown, beige and black across a nightmarish landscape in hell. Somehow, this contrasting Hades reminded him of a previous, and even more frightening nightmare. The countryside now appeared in deep shades of green, and the wounded mujahidin suddenly took on the appearance of Vietnamese villagers, and Dr. Perrin resembled Major Dong, that evil little Vietcong. Jeremy was by now hallucinating, and had completely lost touch with reality. Jeremy's mind reeled between unconsciousness and madness. Flashes of Vietnam kept forcing him to scream out in terror. Suddenly, he remembered that little green millipede he had eaten in his cell. It had by now grown to gigantic proportions and was eating his brain. He screamed in terror, and awoke to find Dr. Perrin giving him another injection of morphine, and trying to calm him down.

"Monsieur Jeremy, it is okay, calm down, please calm down. We are approaching the border to Pakistan, and you must be quiet," said the tall Frenchman.

Jeremy awoke just long enough to notice that the Citroen had suddenly gotten less crowded. Three of the severely wounded mujahidin had died en route and, due to circumstances were unceremoniously dumped from the vehicle. Jeremy lapsed back into insensibility shortly after seeing a road sign written both in Arabic and English which said, "Karachi" 275 Km. Jeremy's next conscious thoughts were of sweet-smelling perfumes, and clean sheets. He slowly opened his eyes, and observed the second biggest set of tits he had ever seen. Somehow these magnificent mammary glands reminded him of a long-lost love, Loretta. He refocused his eyes and looked up to see a very young, heavyset nurse. She said, with a strong British accent, "I say love, you must be all right. You can't stop staring at my bloody knockers, can you?" stated Stella, with a smirk on her face.

"I am terribly sorry, miss. I was unconscious, and when I, I regained consciousness, well I saw you, ahw, dahw," stuttered Jeremy, too embarrassed to speak any further.

"Well, don't you fret, none. Dr. Perrin told me to take good care of you, and I intend to do just that!" answered Stella with authority in her voice.

"Okay, I'll go along with that, but please tell me where I am. I haven't a clue how I got here. Has the American embassy been notified? Can you get me a phone? I, I need toooo…" stammered Jeremy in one long sentence.

"Now, you just hold your britches, Mr. embassy man. I know who you are, and what you do. This is the British Embassy hospital, and we are the only ones around here with medical facilities. Your Mr. Tom Symons asked us to take good care of you and he would return later, when you take your nap. I said nap. Do you understand English, Mr. Grant?" ordered Nurse Stella with a stern look on her face.

"Okay, okay, I'm sorry. Don't bite my head off. I, I just…" replied Jeremy, lying back down on his pillow.

"All right, love. Take your nap, and when you get well Nursie Stella might let you put your head on her bosom. And yes, Mr. Grant they are real, British boobs, born and bred in jolly old England," she replied with a smirk on her lips. Jeremy's only comment was a soft, "Great…"

Jeremy drifted off in to a drug-induced sleep. Despite the heavy doses of medication, his mind kept racing between the green hell of Vietnam, and this new "Brown Out". At times he was unable to tell which was worse, or where he was. The shock of the last forty hours had scrambled his brain. After what seemed forever, his mind finally quieted down, and he was able to turn off all of his nightmares and slip into a great black void. Nine hours later, a gentle, sweet voice brought him back to reality.

"Mr. Grant, Mr. Grant, wake up, wake up! You have a visitor. Awh, come on love, you've slept enough for today. Wake up now," said Stella, as she gently shook his shoulder and his chest.

"Uhw, ahw, okay, okay I, I am awake. Don't rip my arm off, Nurse Ratchet! I felt your gentle touch, and what was that you said about caressing your giant 'boobs'?" Replied Jeremy laughingly as he opened his eyes, and stared at his tormentor. Jeremy wasn't sure, but Miss Stella Crockett turned three shades of red and hurriedly left the room.

There before him, at the foot of the bed, stood a middle-aged man. His hair was cut short, but could not hide the large bald spot on the back of his head. He wore a conservative three-piece blue business suit, a heavily starched white oxford shirt, and a striped red, white and blue tie. Jeremy could not see his shoes, but he could guess that they were either black oxfords, or penny loafers. Jeremy wondered silently, *why do these CIA bureau chief have to look the part*? The man extended his hand and said, "Hi, I am Tom Symons; call me Tom, the economic attaché at the embassy in Karachi. Welcome back. From what I can see, you had a rough time of it, didn't you?" asked the friendly man.

"Well, you might say that, Mr. Symons. Oh, excuse me, Tom," replied Jeremy.

"Please forgive me, but everyone seems to know who I am, and what I do, why the cloak and dagger stuff?" Asked Jeremy, propping himself on one elbow, and staring at Tom.

"Can't help myself, old habits die hard. You just take care of yourself, and we will debrief you tomorrow. By the way, we have arranged for an Air Force C-141 and medical crew to pick you up in a couple of weeks. Your end destination will be Rhein Main Air Force Base, in Germany. They have the best medical staff in Europe, and they will take good care of you and your particular medical needs. Any questions?" asked Tom, as he walked out the door.

"Yeah, send nurse Stella in for a second, will you?" asked Jeremy plaintively.

"Okay, Jeremy, see you tomorrow," answered Tom, as he walked out the door.

"Well, well, well, I understand you need me?" asked nurse Stella as she walked back in the room, and stood in front of the bed.

"Does that offer still stand? You know—the pillow, huh?" asked Jeremy shyly.

"I have been sleeping in the mountains for the past few years; spending a few minutes resting my head on those magnificent breasts of yours, would surely do more for my recuperation than any more drugs. How about it?" asked Jeremy, his voice rising to the occasion.

Before he could answer, she turned around and started walking toward the door. Jeremy suddenly felt extremely embarrassed, but she had made the offer after all. Stella walked slowly toward the door, as if to leave, locked it and turned around. She stared at him, her arms reaching behind her bra.

"By God, I knew you were a tit man when I saw you staring at my knockers," answered Stella as she approached the bed.

By the time she had reached the foot of the bed, her size forty-four DD bra was lying on the floor. Her incredible breasts were squeezed together between her opened shirt, and her incredibly long nipples were pointing at him like a double-barrel, twelve-gauge shotgun. Jeremy just stared for a second, and said, "Wow". Stella leaned over the bed and her nipples brushed against his mouth. Jeremy's reaction was involuntary. The white sheet suddenly rose and resembled nearby Mount Everest.

"My, my, at least we know that's still working. However, your physical condition does not allow you to get out of the bed, so there will be none of that for now, although, I must say, I get very excited every time I gave you a sponge bath. You must content yourself with fondling and kissing my knockers. Okay love?" asked Stella, as she bent over and kissed him passionately.

Jeremy had not been this close to a woman in years, and the smell of her perfume drove him crazy. It was a musky, sensuous smell. Jeremy's lips latched on to one of her nipples and he began to fondle the other one with his good hand. Stella seemed to rise to the occasion, and began grinding her hips against the bed. Jeremy increased the intensity of his fondling and she grew even wilder. After a few minutes of intense petting she began to moan, and before he knew it, she let out a cat-like growl and pulled back from him. At first, Jeremy was puzzled, but he soon realized that she had experienced an orgasm.

"Yeah, that's right, honey. I am one of those few women who have their clits and tits in the same spot. I can have an orgasm after a few minutes of intense petting. Thanks much, love." stated Stella, at the still incredulous Jeremy.

"Well, I am glad I was able to satisfy your needs so quickly. You are an amazing woman, and a great nurse to boot," replied Jeremy with a smile.

"Don't you worry, honey. I will make sure you sleep well tonight." Smiled Stella, as her hand reached under the sheet and found his still erect canon.

Jeremy laid back and wondered if all patients of nurse Stella received this wonderful welcome on her ward. Jeremy's excitement was so great that he had lasted about as long as a sixteen-year-old boy on his first lovemaking attempt. Stella took the opportunity to give him another sponge bath, and wished him a safe return home. Her parting words were, "I am sure that you will never receive better treatment in any hospital, will you love? It's time to go to bed now, if there is nothing else I can do for you now," said Stella as she walked toward the door.

"No, not now. But tomorrow, I would like to meet that great French doctor again. It's not often that a Frenchman says or does anything good for an American," answered Jeremy as he blew her a kiss with his hand.

For the first time in a long time, Jeremy slept like a baby. The incredible events of that evening, and the peace and quiet of the sterile hospital allowed him a feeling of security. His dreams were not convoluted or dramatic. Strangely enough, Stella's intense sexual passion brought memories of another love. He drifted off into a comfortable and relaxing rest thinking of Loretta.

Jeremy's restful sleep was interrupted by a knocking at the door. At first, Jeremy was unable to focus his eyes or determine his whereabouts. As the figure got closer to the bed, he was able to recognize it as Dr. Perrin.

"Well good morning, Jeremy, how are you feeling this morning? You look well rested and content. I understand you wanted to see me before I left. Here I am, what can I do for you," stated the French doctor as he smiled at Jeremy.

"Well, you see doctor, I owe my life to you, and I would like to thank you before I leave. You are a great humanitarian and you deserve a lot of praise for what you do," remarked Jeremy to the doctor.

"I will take that as a compliment, Jeremy. I am not in favor of what you do, but I guess someone has to do it. My own father is a colonel in the Deuxieme Bureau, and has been involved in this type of business since World War II. As a matter of fact, I am going to visit him in Paris before I return to my home in Reims. I would like you to have my card, and you ever need anything in France, please call upon Papa or myself, his name is Colonel Auguste Gaston Perrin," said Dr. Perrin, as he handed the card to Jeremy.

"What a coincidence, Dr. Perrin. My father was with the OSS during the war and spent a great deal of time in Paris during the occupation. I would not be at all surprised if they knew each other," answered Jeremy with a smile.

Before Jeremy could make any additional comments. The tall French doctor was out the door. Jeremy lay there for a while and reflected upon his adventurous life. He looked down at his legs and knew that, as an active agent, his career would probably be over.

The next few days were a continuous series of debriefings, medical checkups and reflection. Unfortunately, nurse Stella had a few days off, and was not around to comfort Jeremy. Apparently, she had a visit from an old boyfriend and was out amusing herself.

Jeremy's life became a daily routine of injections, dressing changes and endless hours staring at the ceiling. Approximately three or four weeks later, Tom Symons visited Jeremy, and informed him that all arrangements had been made for the flight back to Germany. At thirteen-thirty in the afternoon, an unmarked ambulance arrived at the British embassy for Jeremy. Two burly medics and two armed security guards arrived at the back of the hospital to pick up Jeremy.

The four men arrived in front of his room and knocked on the door.

"Come in," answered Jeremy.

"Hey, how are you doing?" asked the youngest one to Jeremy.

"Well, considering the circumstances, I guess I am doing reasonably well. Where are we going?" asked Jeremy, directing his question to the young man who had greeted him earlier.

"We have received orders from Mr. Symons to transport you and your nurse to the airport and send you off to Germany," replied the polite young man. He seemed to be the only one in the mood for friendly conversation.

"Oh, my nurse Stella is coming along to the airport?" asked Jeremy with a smile.

"No, I don't think so. Her name is Gretchen Schwarzkoff, and once you meet her you'll never forget her," answered the same polite paramedic with a snicker.

Jeremy was carefully strapped to the gurney and wheeled out the front door. Jeremy never realized how large the British Embassy hospital was. Now that he was conscious, he was able to see that it was at least one hundred yards long and three stories high. *Quite a sizable hospital for such a remote location*, he thought to himself. He could tell by the construction and the paint color that it was probably built by the British during W.W. II.

The medics and security officers stopped in front of a large double-sized gleaming metal elevator door. The door opened and inside stood the biggest and nastiest looking female species Jeremy had ever seen. She was several inches over six feet tall. Her weight was hard to judge, but if he had to guess probably, two hundred seventy-plus pounds. Her two massive arms were anchored on her huge hips like tree trunks. Her white uniform fitted her incredibly large frame like a rubber glove. Perched on top of this massive specimen was a repulsive head. Some would call it a monstrosity, but to most it was a gargoyle-like head. Many a man would envy her twelve-o'clock shadow. Jeremy stared at her, unable to speak at first.

All four of the other men were visibly moved by her presence. They all seemed to cringe and twitch in unison. Even the armed security guards cowered and stepped to the rear of the elevator. Normally this size elevator could comfortably hold twelve persons and a gurney, but Gretchen's presence and size had them all jammed in a corner. No one spoke a word for a full thirty seconds. It seemed as if all the air had been sucked out of the elevator. No one moved or dared to speak. Finally, Jeremy dared to speak. He extended his undamaged hand and said, "Hi, I am Jeremy, and you must be…"

The beast stood there not moving, her oversized nostrils flaring like a bull ready to charge, her deep brown eyes glaring at everyone. After an additional thirty seconds or so, she replied, "Ja, und? (Yes, and?) I am Fraulein Schwarzkoff, and I will be your escort to Germany, Ja!" (Yes), she replied with finality in her voice.

Jeremy was beyond speechless. *This can't be true. Why is this happening to me? Maybe someone found out about Stella and me, and this is my punishment?* All kinds of strange and devious ideas crossed his mind as they drove him to the airport. Every once in a while, he dared a glance toward Ms. Gretchen and shuddered at the thought of, *What if Germany had won the war*? The remaining ride to the airport was made in complete and utter silence. Jeremy fervently hoped that the Air Force nurses would be better looking than this one.

After what seemed like the longest ride in the world, Jeremy saw the large C-141 in the distance. The green Air Force camouflage paint job contrasted greatly with the tarmac. The ambulance pulled up to the rear hatch door, and off-loaded him. A couple of burly Air Force crew members picked up his stretcher and carried him on board. The hold was full of cargo and a few other injured or ill military personnel en route to home. To his great chagrin, Ms. Gretchen waddled up the ramp and boarded the aircraft too. Even though he knew better, he thought that the aircraft listed to one side when she sat down next to him.

"Nah, Schatz, wie geht es Dir?" (Hey honey, how are you doing?) asked the burly nurse.

"Ah, I am sorry. You don't speak German, do you, Herr Grant?" asked Gretchen.

"Aber selbsverstaendlich, Fraulein. Ich kann einiger massen gut Deutsch sprechen, nicht war Fraulein Schwarzkoff?" (Yes, naturally fraulein. I can speak German pretty well, isn't that so, Miss Schwarzkoff), replied Jeremy in his best Rheinisch dialect.

Nurse Gretchen's mouth dropped so far down that the entire C-141 could have parked in it. She seemed to stutter for a second, and then slowly a smile spread across her face. She stared at him for a while longer and got up and walked away. Jeremy was shocked to see that Gretchen was able to smile, and what a ghastly smile. It reminded him of a slit in a large watermelon.

A good-looking blond second lieutenant nurse walked up to Jeremy and said, “Hey buddy, what did you do to get stuck with the ‘beast’?”

“Well miss, your guess is as good as mine. One moment I am being spoiled by a sweet British nurse, and the next thing I know it’s, Frankenstein!” replied Jeremy to the young second lieutenant.

“Can I ask you a question, lieutenant? Why is it that military nurses are not allowed to care for me? Why do I have to be treated like this?” asked Jeremy.

“I am not sure of the answer, but I think it has to do with your status, and politics. The Pakistanis must maintain this charade of neutrality so as not to anger the Soviet Union. However, that seems like a farce now, doesn’t it? As far as we know, you are a civilian, and we are not allowed to care for civilians unless ordered by headquarters. Miss Frankenstein, however, is a civilian employee of the British Embassy, and as soon as you get to an American installation you might get military care. We will take off shortly, and our flight time is less than six hours, including a quick layover in Ryad, Saudi Arabia. If there is anything you need let me know. Our physician is very good and he will take good care of you, unofficially of course,” replied the young second lieutenant as she walked away toward the front of the aircraft.

Jeremy laid back down in his bunk; he noticed that Gretchen was nowhere to be seen. Good, he thought, maybe she’s found another victim for now. Jeremy was so exhausted that he fell into a deep sleep. The whirring of the jets, and the hum of the engines seemed to have a lulling effect on most of the crew and passengers. Jeremy did not notice how long he slept, until a blast of warm air entered the aircraft and woke him. He looked out the window and immediately noticed that they were not in Germany yet. The landscape was too sandy and it was hot, real hot. They had landed in Saudi Arabia and were picking up additional injured personnel for transport to Rhein Main AFB.

Jeremy was staring out the window so intently he did not notice Nurse Frankenstein putting her extremely large hand on his leg. Her action startled him, and he involuntarily cringed from her touch.

"You should not be jumpy, Herr Grant, after all it's only me, Nurse Frankenstein," she said as she looked at him.

At first, Jeremy was too shocked to reply. Had she heard the conversation with the pretty blond lieutenant, or was he imagining things? Her stare was less aggressive than earlier; as a matter of fact, he detected a bit of compassion and sorrow in her voice.

"Fraulein Schwarzkoff, what do you mean? I think you misunderstood what I said, I, I, I" he said, looking directly into her big brown cow eyes, and not knowing how to finish the sentence.

"It's okay, Herr Grant. I have been called a lot worse things in my life. You don't have to apologize," she said waving her hand in front of his face.

Jeremy was extremely embarrassed and unsure what to say at this time. He decided to say nothing and wait for the next opportunity to apologize to her.

"It's time to change your bandages and clean your wounds, Herr Grant. Turn over and be still!" She said with authority, her voice going back to the old Gretchen.

Gretchen professionally removed, cleaned and replaced all of his dressings. She did not utter a single word during the entire procedure. Jeremy noticed how gentle and caring the big woman could be. All of her moves were done with great care and professionalism. When she was done she patted him on the behind and turned him back right side up. Jeremy was undecided whether he should broach the subject or not. *After all* he told himself, *I have faced death in many wars; been held as a POW, how bad could this really be?*

"Fraulein Gretchen, would you please forgive my earlier indiscretion? It was very cruel and odious of me to say those things about you. I really feel sorry for what I did, and I hope you will forgive me, Bitte?" (please?) asked Jeremy.

Fraulein Gretchen was standing at the foot of his bunk. Her head was lowered as if she was inspecting her handiwork. After an extremely long and uncomfortable pause, she raised her head and looked at him. Very large teardrops were slowly gliding down her face. She did not speak, but her tears mirrored her true feelings. For a moment Jeremy was unsure of his next move. He felt compelled to reach out and comfort her, but did know how she would take it. Finally he overcame his initial fear and reached out and touched her hand.

"Verzeihen Sie mir, Fraulein." (Please forgive me, miss) whispered Jeremy to the shocked nurse Gretchen.

"You don't have to do that, Herr Grant," she said as she pulled her hand away.

"You see, I am used to it. God punished my parents for what they did, and I was their burden. I am accustomed to this by now. I have lived with many worse insults throughout my life. Don't trouble yourself any longer. By the way, Herr Grant, your special treatment from nurse Stella was not so special. She is a nymphomaniac and does that to most of the new patients," replied Gretchen as she looked away. Jeremy was shocked, but thought it best to keep his mouth shut for now.

A few moments later, Jeremy sat up and asked Fraulein Gretchen to sit down next to him. For the next three and a half hours, they had the most frank and interesting conversation. Fraulein Gretchen's parents, in fact, had been evil people, and she always believed her looks and size were God's punishment. Her father had been a member of the Waffen SS, and her mother had been a female camp attendant in the Buchenwald concentration camp. Both parents had been tried at the Nuremberg war criminal trials, and been sentenced to long prison terms. Gretchen had been a little girl and did not see her parents again until she was seventeen years old. Jeremy listened to her long and tragic story. He promised himself that he would never again judge a person solely on their physical characteristics. The remainder of the flight whizzed by. By the end of the flight both Gretchen and Jeremy were good buddies and promised to keep in touch.

Chapter 15

Escape to Nowhere

Meanwhile, a few days earlier back at the ambush scene, Kolkov and his men were finishing off the mujahidin one by one. The twins seemed to take particular pleasure in exterminating everyone. They made sure that all the mujahidin were dead by putting several extra shots in their brains. They also volunteered for the grisly detail of decapitating Colonel Mohammed and Khalil. Then the twins approached Kolkov.

"Hey, what do you want us to do with these heads? Why do you need them?" asked Misha.

"I would normally have no use for them, but my friends, do you forget the reward for Khalil? And how are we going to explain to our superiors in Dushanbe about our survival? We have to come up with a good story, or we are all dead, do you understand? The head of Colonel Mohammed will verify our story. We will tell everyone that we were out on patrol looking for Khalil when this double-crossing piece of shit led us into an ambush. We were able to fight our way out, and in the process killed Khalil. We then returned to Qonduz, only to find out that the enemy had overrun it. We have to make sure that all of us know the story by heart. Let's grab the Mercedes and load the helicopter as soon as possible," answered Kolkov angrily.

As the men set about clearing up the battlefield and loading the truck, Kolkov looked around once more just to make sure that no evidence was left behind that would later incriminate him. Despite assuring himself that everything had gone better than expected, he still had the premonition that something was not right. He walked back to the area where the chopper was hidden, just in time to help the men load their equipment and the drugs. He approached LT Antoniv, who was still shaking in his boots, and asked him, "Antoniv! How far can this crate fly before needing fuel?"

"Well, sir, as heavily loaded as she is, maybe 300 kilometers," answered Antoniv, his voice quaking in fear.

"Where is there a fuel depot?" asked Kolkov again.

"There used to be an emergency fuel depot at Herat. However, I don't know whether we still control that area or not, and it is nearly at our maximum flying range," answered LT Antoniv.

"How much weight will we have to lose to be able to reach it?" asked Kolkov impatiently.

"I would estimate, at least 500 kilograms," answered Antoniv.

Kolkov evaluated his chances. He had 1000 kilograms of pure #4 heroin. An article he had recently read in Pravda described the worth of various drugs, and he remembered that heroin sold in America for about $200,000 a kilo. The estimated wholesale value was maybe $200,000,000. Retail, who knows, maybe one billion, he thought or even more, the amount was mind-boggling. Could his cousin Yuri handle anything of this size? He began to have some doubts, and hoped everything worked out well.

The helicopter would be carrying five men, weapons and ammunition. All I have to do is get rid of approximately 500 kilograms. It was an easy decision. He called a meeting in front of the aircraft; made sure that all the men, except Antoniv, were present. After they all sat down and were waiting his instructions, he unslung his AK-47 and mowed them all down on the spot. He emptied an entire magazine; reloaded and emptied the second magazine. They didn't stand a chance. They were all gunned down in seconds. LT Antoniv came running out of the aircraft and viewed the scene in horror. Kolkov stood there holding the still smoking AK-47 and smiling. He had solved his problem and eliminated all the witnesses, but one.

"Kolkov, Kolkov, what has happened? I, I, I don't understand," cried Antoniv as he witnessed the horrific scene.

"I just can't understand it, Antoniv! They all decided to commit mass suicide, and I couldn't stop them. It really is an awful shame, isn't it? You don't have any such feelings, do you?" asked Kolkov as he swung his AK-47 toward the timid pilot.

"Oh, oh, no sir. I, I will make sure you get to Erat and Dushanbe, don't you worry," replied LT Antoniv as he was backing toward the aircraft entrance.

"Okay then. Get in and get us the hell away from here," growled Kolkov at the still shaking Antoniv.

LT Antoniv sat in his pilot's chair. He was so scared, his entire body began to shake uncontrollably. He sat and stared at the instruments for a full two or three minutes. His fear was promptly eliminated when the cold barrel of the AK-47 pressed against his ear, and Kolkov whispered, "The only reason you are still alive is because I need you. Do you understand that?" asked the still angry Kolkov.

"Don't you worry, we will make it to Erat and beyond. I have no intention of letting you down," answered Antoniv, his voice quaking with fear.

Antoniv pushed the stick forward and the helicopter lifted slowly in the air. The weather was still not cooperating, but it was flyable as long as one kept flying northward away from the storm and the winds. Antoniv kept glancing back every once in a while, expecting Kolkov to be there behind him. He did not have to worry, as Kolkov had no intention of harming him now. However, he knew that Antoniv was the sole living witness and eventually he would have to die.

Kolkov was still a little unsure of how to best handle the situation. He knew he couldn't just fly to the airbase at Dushanbe with 1000 kilograms of heroin. They would shoot him on the spot. He had to find a way to stash the dope and then pretend that they were the only survivors of Qonduz. He could damage the aircraft's radio in such a way that no one would notice, and then at the appropriate moment eliminate Antoniv. Kolkov began to formulate a plan in his mind that would involve Abdullah's older brother, the former helicopter pilot who had been stationed in Dushanbe, and was still living nearby. Apparently, he still worked at the base as a aircraft maintenance engineer. The plan slowly began to unfold. He picked the intercom microphone and pressed the key.

"Antoniv, how are we doing for fuel? Are we going to make Erat?" asked Kolkov.

"No problems, sir. We will make it with fuel to spare. We should be there in approximately one hour and twenty minutes," replied

Antoniv.

"Good. I want you to wake me up when we are twenty minutes away, okay? I am really tired and I need a nap," stated Kolkov with emphasis.

"Yes, sir!" answered Antoniv, too scared to say anything else.

CPT Kolkov found a spot between two bales of heroin and quickly fell asleep. LT Antoniv kept turning around nervously. He didn't trust Kolkov, and he knew his chances of survival were diminishing the closer he got to Dushanbe. He was evaluating his options when the red warning fuel light indicating low fuel went on with a loud buzz. He quickly looked down at the gauge and could not understand why it showed nearly empty. He tapped the gauge with his finger hoping it would budge from its position, but it did not waver.

The loud fuel alarm woke Kolkov with a start. He jumped and promptly hit his head on the overhead cross beam. He looked down at Antoniv and screamed.

"What the hell is all that racket? Shut that fucking noise off," ordered Kolkov.

"Yes sir. It's only the fuel warning alarm system. It's telling me we only have about 100 liters of fuel left, sir," replied LT Antoniv in a low moaning voice.

"What does that mean, in plain language? Are we going to crash?" asked Kolkov, with vengeance in his voice.

"Yes sir. The winds probably shifted, and we were using more fuel than previously estimated. However, I still think we should land somewhere near the Erat Reserve Fuel Depot. It's not much farther, I am positive of it," replied Antoniv with more confidence in his voice than he felt.

"I hope you are right. Because if the crash doesn't kill you, I will," answered Kolkov, patting his AK-47.

Just as things seemed to got from bad to worsen, Antoniv spotted a light on the horizon. As the craft grew closer, he spotted a few more lights. All he could see now was a grass runway, strewn with old and obsolete aircraft, a few hangars and a wonderful fuel tank farm. He turned around and asked Kolkov, "Where should we land?"

"What is protocol?" replied Kolkov, unsure what to do now.

"Usually, we report to the tower personnel, and request permission to refuel. However, I don't see any lights in the tower. We could just land near the fuel bunker and help ourselves," answered Antoniv.

"Okay, let's do that and whatever you do, don't speak to anyone. I will do all the talking, is that understood?" asked Kolkov, as he pressed the barrel of a silenced automatic against the pilot's head.

The barrel of the automatic was pressed so firmly against his temple that when Kolkov pulled it away, a deep, round red welt stood in its place. LT Antoniv reflected once again on his chances for survival. If he was going to do something it had to be soon. His chances were vanishing by the second. Kolkov ordered him to set the aircraft down near the largest of the buildings. The aircraft hovered over the area for a few seconds and gently touched down. Kolkov waited for a few minutes expecting ground personnel to come out and service their aircraft. Seconds became minutes. After five minutes elapsed and no one came out, CPT Kolkov decided to take action.

"Antoniv, remove the primary fuses out of the fuse box and come with me," ordered Kolkov.

"I am telling you, if you don't act normal, you will be dead a man. Is that understood, Antoniv?" asked Kolkov as he jammed the barrel of the automatic in his spine.

"Yes sir, sir there is no need for that. I have the fuses here in my hand and the aircraft cannot fly without them. I will follow your orders; don't worry, sir!" replied Antoniv with a feminine squeal in his voice.

Both men stepped out of the aircraft, Antoniv first, and Kolkov close behind him. Kolkov held the automatic close to his side and watched Antoniv like a hawk. Both men walked slowly forward; they could see a hangar near the nearest fuel station. The light was on inside, and the door was open. Kolkov ordered LT Antoniv to head toward the open door. As they approached the door, a young private stepped out of the door and cupped his hands together as if to light a cigarette. He had his back to them and did not see then until they were right next him.

"Private, come to attention when a superior officer is near you," screamed Kolkov at the inattentive private.

The suddenness of their presence made the private whirl around and drop his cigarette. He attempted a half-assed salute and was once again reprimanded by Kolkov. *Great* thought Antoniv, *the only help I have is this poor excuse for a soldier.* Both men noticed that he was unarmed and disheveled. He looked like he had just gotten up out of bed.

"Yes sir. I, I, I did not see you come. I am sorry, sir, it won't happen again. Private Gregor Markarian reporting, sir!" shouted the now fully awake private.

"Where is your commanding officer?" shouted Kolkov, still keeping his eyes on Antoniv.

"You see, sir, this is a small post, seldom used by anyone. We have only a sergeant and five soldiers on duty here, now. Rumor control has it that the war will be over soon, and no one feels that we are a threat to anyone this close to the border of Mother Russia. However, two of the privates are now on leave," answered the now fully alert young soldier.

"We are an inspection team from Dushanbe, and we need to talk to your sergeant immediately, where is he?" asked the now irate Kolkov. Kolkov had emptied his canvas mussette bags and now held the pistol inside of it.

"Sgt. Volonchekof and Private Brezchenko are inside the building. Sleeping, sir. *Great* thought Kolkov, *this will be easier than I thought.*

"Where is the other private?" asked Kolkov with authority.

"He, he should be at his post near the fuel cells," replied the nervous guard.

"Let's move inside and talk with your lazy sergeant. I really want to know why this important fueling center is only manned by so few troops!" ordered the still agitated and increasingly nervous Kolkov.

The young private did a snappy about face and marched inside the building. Kolkov could immediately see that this building, for that matter, the entire installation was a British W.W. II leftover and forgotten post. It smelled of stale food, gasoline and body odor. The private marched in and flicked on the lights. The brightness at first startled both Antoniv and Kolkov. Two sleeping forms in the corner cursed and yelled out obscenities.

"Gregor, you fool, what are you doing?" shouted the now angry sergeant.

"Attention," screamed Private Markarian at the top of his lungs.

Both sleeping forms sat straight up in their cots and attempted to stand up at once. Both men landed in a pile on the ground. Kolkov couldn't help, but wonder, *what has become of mighty Russia*? Fools like this will someday lead to the destruction of all he loved, he thought. He ordered LT Antoniv to sit down in a chair in front of him, and waited for the other two buffoons to settle down.

"Now, which one of you two idiots is the sergeant?" asked Kolkov accusingly. For a second both men failed to respond. Finally Sgt. Volonchekof timidly raised his hand and attempted to salute at the same time.

"I am, sir. What can I do for you, CPT?" answered the still confused sergeant.

"What you can do for me, is answer me one question! Don't you know there is a war on in this country? I will make sure this gets in my report, sergeant," threatened Kolkov as he shook his fist in mock indignation.

"I, I, I don't understand CPT No one told us of an inspection. We were not expecting anyone," complained Sgt. Volonchekof.

"Notified! Advised! This is a surprise inspection, you fool. Show me your records for the past three months! Be quick about it!" ordered Kolkov with anger in his voice.

As the sergeant came within ten feet, Kolkov drew out his silenced automatic and fired twice at the sergeant and twice at the private by the bed. Both hit the ground without so much as a whimper. Antoniv stared down at both men and marveled at the almost identical entry wounds. Both men had a hole between the eyes and another in the heart. They never knew what hit them. Private Markarian just stood there, transfixed by the events. In his small, limited mind, he thought perhaps this was some sort of punishment for being caught sleeping on duty. Before he could further evaluate the situation, Kolkov pointed the automatic at him and asked him if they had a functioning telephone. "Of course," he answered," pointing at the small office in the corner.

"Do you use any codes when contacting headquarters?" asked Kolkov.

"No sir. We just report in every eight hours or so. The phone system is one of the few things that actually works around here," answered the still shocked Private Markarian.

"Okay, when was the last time you made a commo check?" asked Kolkov.

"I think it was at least six or seven hours, maybe it's been eight or so. I am not exactly sure," replied the worried private.

"I want you to make a commo check now," ordered Kolkov.

"Yes sir," replied the scared private.

Kolkov, Antoniv and Private Markarian walked over to the tiny office in the corner. Markarian picked up the phone and made his call to headquarters. Kolkov kept near him the whole time and listened to every word that was said. He was unable to detect any codes, ruses or whispered calls for help. LT Antoniv stood there and was mesmerized; still unsure what to do or how to react to the ever-worsening situation. Antoniv knew that Kolkov needed him to fly the chopper, but they were getting closer and closer to Russia, and closer to his death.

"You have done well, Private Markarian. You have done so well that I am appointing you acting sergeant," stated Kolkov with authority.

The young private stared at Kolkov like a reindeer in the middle of a road, not knowing what to say or do. He mumbled something sounding like, "esss sirrrrr."

"I want you now to call the other private at the fuel cell depot, and ask him to come over. Tell him there is an inspection going on, and he must report here as soon as possible," asked Kolkov, in a more gentle and friendly matter.

"Yes sir!" answered Private Markarian, acting Sergeant Markarian, that is.

Markarian called the other private on the phone, a fellow Armenian by the name of Garneyonian, and ordered him to report right away. At first, the fuel cell private seemed to hesitate, but when Markarian told him a SPETSNAZ captain was here conducting an unannounced inspection, he decided he had better come over. He grabbed his AK-47 and started the quarter-mile walk back to the hangar. He had seen the helicopter land, and was surprised. En route he began to think how unusual it was that Markarian ordered him and not Sgt. Volonchekof. *Was there something wrong*? He wondered?

Garneyonian decided to use the back entrance just to be on the safe side. Private Garneyonian slowly approached the hangar from the east side, hidden from view in the shadows of the buildings. He entered the building and passed through a darkened corridor toward the light at the other end. When he arrived at the glass partition he carefully peeked above the wooden rail and looked in. There, not more than thirty feet away, stood a SPETSNAZ captain holding a silenced pistol in his hand. In front of him sat another officer, but he was unarmed. Next to the unarmed officer was Markarian, who was near the telephone. They were all looking away from him toward the front door. Because of the office walls, he was unable to see in the sleeping quarters, where the dead bodies of Sergeant Volonchekof and the private were obscured from view. Garneyonian had no clue as to what was really going on. However, he decided to be cautious and unslung his weapon. He checked the magazine and took the safety off. He walked in carrying the AK-47 in a fashion that would indicate his seriousness and concern.

Suddenly he was there behind all of them. Kolkov was the first one to feel his presence and turned around. What he saw made him nervous. For the first time in a long time, an adversary had been able to sneak up behind him. He smiled at the private and said, "You must be Private Garneyonian? I must commend you for your tactical entrance. I am CPT Kolkov of the SPETSNAZ Group and we are here to conduct an unannounced security inspection," stated Kolkov, his voice icy calm and controlled.

"Good afternoon, Sir. I am Private Garneyonian," replied the suspicious private.

"Where are Sgt. Volonchekof and Yuri? And why do you find it necessary to hold a gun to my colleague and that other officer?" asked the now cocky Garneyonian.

Kolkov was a little surprised at the tone of voice and the challenge from this young soldier. He also noticed that the soldier held the AK in a comfortable, but professional manner and the safety was off, and that he also had his finger on the trigger. *Bad odds,* thought Kolkov. *I must distract him somehow.* Kolkov took a very bold and deadly risk. He put his pistol down on the desk near him; then he turned and faced the spunky private.

"You have done well, Private Garneyonian. Very well indeed, your exemplary reactions and security awareness will be noted favorably in my report. I wouldn't be surprised if you got promoted. Good job!" stated Kolkov.

Kolkov extended his hand as if to shake Garneyonian's hand. Garneyonian now felt at ease and comfortable. Years of harsh indoctrination had made Soviet soldiers into robots. It was not very often that an officer extended him a hand and congratulated him for an action well done. He mistakenly removed his finger from the trigger area and started to extend it toward Kolkov. Before both men could shake hands, LT Antoniv decided it was now or never. He dove for the automatic on the desk, and simultaneously screamed as loudly as he could, "No, no. Stop, shoot him, shoot him he is a traitor and murderer!"

The whole scene had taken only a fraction of a second, but Kolkov's world-class martial arts training was more than the young private could defend against. His right hand grabbed Garneyonian's extended hand and twisted it in a reverse wrist lock, simultaneously pulling on the gun barrel with his left hand. The AK came flying out of his grasp and into Kolkov's hands. Kolkov spun him around and used him as a shield. Antoniv's managed to get his hands on the pistol and began firing wildly in all directions. The first two rounds caught Garneyonian in the throat and chest. The third round nicked Kolkov's left shoulder. Kolkov fired one long burst near Antoniv arm and shattered his left hand. The intense pain caused him to scream out in agony.

Kolkov raised the AK again and told Antoniv to drop the gun. Antoniv did not have to be asked twice; the automatic slipped to the ground and then Antoniv began moaning, and crying. The other private did the only smart thing he could, and that was hit the ground. Kolkov ordered him not to move. "I am surprised LT Antoniv; I didn't think you had it in you. This is probably the bravest thing you have ever done in your entire life, is it not?" shouted Kolkov as he scooped up the automatic.

Private Garneyonian made one final gurgling sound and stopped breathing. His uninjured comrade was still lying face down and hoped that this was only a bad nightmare. Kolkov looked down at him and screamed.

"Do you know how to fuel an aircraft?" asked Kolkov while nudging the back of his ear with the barrel of his automatic.

"Oh yes, sir. We do it quite often. I will show you," replied the anxious private.

Kolkov turned to the still whining Antoniv and told him to prepare to fuel the aircraft. Antoniv looked up at Kolkov, his eyes showing both fear and anger.

"What do you mean, fueling? Can't you see I am seriously injured? I need some time to recover. My left hand is useless, I, I, I..." answered the quivering Antoniv. Kolkov looked at him in disgust and said, "I don't have to tell you what will happen to you if you can't fly anymore, do I? You will be a total liability and must die. I have no further use for you. Besides, how many arms do you need to fly this helicopter? If need be, I will be your left arm," replied Kolkov as he leveled the automatic in his direction.

"I, I, understand. I will cooperate. Can we find something to bandage up my wound," asked Antoniv with an expression of pain on his face.

"Sure, there is a first-aid kit over there. Bring something back for me, too. I want to stop the bleeding in my shoulder," replied Kolkov, remembering that he was also wounded.

While Antoniv walked over to take care of his hand, Kolkov was planning ahead. He sat in the office, which was more like a glass cubicle. It was surrounded on three sides by glass, and Kolkov could observe both the private and the cowardly Antoniv. He picked up the phone and asked the operator to connect him with Dushanbe airbase. After a few minutes a young cordial voice answered, "Dushanbe operator, can I help you?"

"Yes, can you please connect me to the helicopter maintenance shop, a MR. Kaziz Salim Puriz. Thank you," said Kolkov, in his most polite voice. After what seemed forever, a husky voice came on the phone.

"Kaziz here, can I help you? Hello," replied the voice.

Kolkov knew that Antoniv was too occupied with his wound to pay attention to this phone call. Kolkov would make his final plans and it didn't involve Antoniv.

"Yes, hello are you the brother of Abdullah Puriz?" asked Kolkov.

"Yes, of course I am, has anything happened to him, is he okay?" asked the worried Kaziz.

"I am terribly sorry to report that he died in combat. He died a hero of the Soviet Union, and you should be proud of him," replied Kolkov in his most dramatic voice.

There was a pause on the phone and Kaziz explained to Kolkov how he always knew something terrible would happen to his brother. He finished the sentence with, "It was Allah's will." Kolkov was surprised at the lack of grieving on Kaziz's part; maybe they were not very close. Kolkov then asked him if his brother had discussed the possibility of doing some off-duty flying. Kaziz replied in the affirmative. Kolkov then proposed that they should meet at grid coordinate VT-0236 and GH-9084 in approximately two hours.

Kolkov also asked if he could bring a large truck. Kaziz said, "No problem, I am the maintenance engineer and I have access to all the trucks on post. You realize that this grid coordinate is about forty kilometers from the post?" asked Kaziz.

"Don't worry about it. Your brother informed you that there was money to be made, and I promise you will become a very rich man. Just be there on time and bring the truck," finished Kolkov with a flair.

"Don't worry, CPT Kolkov, I will be there in two hours or less," replied Kaziz, as he hung up the phone.

Antoniv walked back toward the office; his left hand was wrapped in white gauze and he was carrying a field dressing for Kolkov. Kolkov ordered both men to sit down and be quiet until he was done bandaging the wound. From this vantage point he was able to watch both men and still take of his field dressing. He unwrapped the sterile pad and tied the two long ends around his left shoulder. Because the injury was only a minor grazing wound, it should last him for now.

"Get up, both of you, we are going to fuel the aircraft," ordered Kolkov.

Both men stood up, and looked at Kolkov for further instructions. Kolkov nodded his head in the direction of the helicopter and waved his gun at them. That was enough to get them motivated. They hurriedly scrambled outside.

"You, private, bring that fueling truck over here, and remember that this AK-47 can blow up your tanker in an instant if you try to flee," Kolkov reminded the young private.

"Yes sir, no problem from me, sir," he replied.

"Antoniv, why don't you get aboard your aircraft and prepare for refueling? Same thing applies to you," Kolkov reminded the still shaking Antoniv.

"Yes sir," he answered as he boarded the aircraft. It was difficult to climb aboard with only one hand, but on the third try, he managed.

Kolkov stood there and observed the private refueling the aircraft. He reflected on what to do next. *How could he destroy all the evidence, and make it look like a band of rogue mujahidins had also ambushed the garrison at Erat*? The young private looked at him through the window, expecting his next order. Kolkov boarded the aircraft and ordered LT Antoniv to take off immediately. Antoniv whined and complained, but managed to take off. CPT Kolkov ordered him to fly approximately one hundred yards from the fuel tanker and hover.

Antoniv did as he was told, and immediately knew what Kolkov was going to do. Kolkov rested the barrel of the AK against the nearest bale of heroin and fired one long burst at the truck. It took a millisecond for the tracer rounds to penetrate the oblong tanker. There was a tremendous explosion and the truck disintegrated into a million pieces. Kolkov now ordered Antoniv to fly over the fuel cell farm. Kolkov noticed that each 50,000-liter container was close enough to the other that if one went, they would all blow.

"Antoniv, I want you fly about two hundred meters above the tank farm and hold steady for a second," ordered Kolkov with a grin.

Antoniv realized by now, that complaining wouldn't do any good.

He flew his aircraft over the lower left bladder and waited for the explosion. Kolkov decided to use grenades and tracer fire this time. The results were equally devastating. The entire base was engulfed in one massive eruption of fire and explosions. One bladder after the other exploded, until all four had spewed their contents into the atmosphere. The helicopter was rocked by the explosions, and Antoniv moved away from the area. He turned around and asked Kolkov to join him in the co-pilot seat. He explained to him that his hand was hurting and he needed some help. In actuality, he wanted to keep him in close proximity. Antoniv felt ill at ease when Kolkov was behind him.

"So captain, what do we do now? Do you still want to go to Deshanbe?" asked Antoniv in an inquisitive manner.

"As a matter of fact, I do. However, starting in fifteen minutes or so you will fly below radar coverage and maintain this minimum altitude until we arrive at the position indicated on the map. Do you understand, no deviations will be allowed!" barked Kolkov, handing Antoniv the map.

"CPT Kolkov, would you mind turning on that light above the console, so that I may better see those grid coordinates, and if you expect me to maintain this low altitude, I will need you to help me at the controls," replied Antoniv with a little more confidence in his voice now.

Antoniv knew that Kolkov had not forgotten the retaliatory incident in the hangar, and first chance he got he would kill him. This might be the last opportunity to get away alive. Antoniv's mind kept racing ahead in search of some escape plan. He knew that every chop of the blade could be the next chop on his head. He had no intention of ending up like those other two heads he had seen. His mind kept thinking of new and possible solutions to his problem, but just as quickly he would discard them as impossible. While he was still in this daydreaming phase, Kolkov startled him with an abrupt command.

"You fool, I told you to keep below the radar detection height, and you are now slowly creeping up to a dangerous level! Down, now! Down!" ordered Kolkov with the tip of his AK-47 pressing into the pilot's rib cage.

"Okay, okay. I am not doing it on purpose. I am having a difficult time controlling the aircraft with only one hand," replied Antoniv, his voice returning to the blubbering mode.

"I told you, if you needed any help let me know! I am sure with your instructions I am quite capable of holding this aircraft steady. Don't you ever go up without my permission, do you understand?" asked Kolkov, with venom in his eyes.

"Yes, yes sir," replied Antoniv, timidly.

"You see that junction on the map? On the main highway, near that clump of woods behind those low hills? I want you to come in as low as you can and set it down between the hills and the treeline. That way, our approach will be hidden from any traffic on the road. Do you understand?" repeated Kolkov with emphasis, the barrel of his weapon poking Antoniv in the ribs.

"I, I understand, Sir. We should be there in twenty minutes, or so," replied Antoniv, knowing his minutes on earth were disappearing fast. He was slowly gaining some form of inner strength. He had been a coward his whole life, but he was unwilling to end it here and now. He slowly formulated a plan in his head. The choices left to him were minimal, and the best plan would seem to include a controlled crash landing and hope that Kolkov would somehow be injured.

Antoniv was positive that Kolkov didn't know the emergency auto-rotation feature on most helicopters. This was a system to enable the blades to continue rotating slowly, and one hoped to allow for a somewhat soft and controlled crash landing. Antoniv knew that these landings could more often than not, end up with total destruction of the aircraft. However, he figured his twenty percent chances of living here was better than his one hundred percent certainty of dying at Kolkov's hands. Antoniv's plan grew more in scope and dimension. He even fantasized a plan to tilt the aircraft at the last moment; hoping the chopper would crush Kolkov. Suddenly, Antoniv felt a little more confident and ebullient, so much so that Kolkov saw the smile on his lips, and asked him, "What are you smiling about, Antoniv? Do you think someone or something is going to save you at the last minute?" asked Kolkov with a devious grin on his lips. Antoniv just turned around and smiled back. For the first time since this adventure began,

Antoniv felt a certain degree of confidence and fearlessness.

"There, there it is!" exclaimed Kolkov, pointing to a location about three kilometers ahead.

Antoniv began to gain altitude, pretending to struggle with the stick and the strong wind currents. He told Kolkov that he had to gain some altitude to clear those hills, near the forest. Kolkov was so intensely looking for Kaziz that he did not notice what Antoniv was trying to do. When the aircraft reached the designated height he cut the power and turned on the auto-rotate mode. The chopper dropped like a stone at first; then it slowed down as the blades began to slowly rotate and catch the air. Kolkov looked at Antoniv in horror, and screamed out, "You rotten son of a bitch, I am going to kill you! He pointed the automatic at him and fired two rapid shots.

Due to the turbulence and gyrations Kolkov's first shot missed him completely and put a gaping hole through the window. The second shot, however, caught him square in the jaw. The impact of the bullet at such close range was devastating. It literally blew off his jaw and continued through his throat, and into his brain. Death was instantaneous. Antoniv's last thought was, *at least the bastard is going to die with me!*

Kaziz watched in horror as the chopper fell from the sky not more than one kilometer from his location. He had gotten there early and hidden the truck near a stand of trees. When he heard the chopper approach, he pulled out to see if it was they or not. As an experienced helicopter pilot he could tell that it was on auto-rotate, and someone might survive the fall. The chopper came down faster than Antoniv expected, but as luck would have it, struck a large oak tree prior to hitting the ground. The tree's immense branches acted like a giant basket, and seemed to reach up and catch the aircraft in midair. The chopper hit heavily, but reached the ground in one piece. Had Antoniv not been shot through the jaw, he probably would have survived the crash.

Kolkov was thrown about the aircraft, and landed upside down beneath bales of heroin. The initial contact with the tree had knocked him out, but upon contacting the ground, he regained consciousness. His first and immediate concern was fire! He tried to push the bales of heroin off of himself, but made no headway. He was stuck in the upside down position with a dozen or more bales of heroin piled on top of him. A few minutes later he heard a voice, an unfamiliar voice calling his name.

"CPT Kolkov, is that you? Are you okay?" asked a concerned Kaziz.

Upon seeing the helicopter crash, Kaziz had put the truck in gear and driven the short distance to the crash site.

"Yes, yes, yes! Get me out of here; I am trapped, help me, please!" replied the now panicking Kolkov.

"Don't worry, I'll get you out," answered Kaziz as he frantically removed bales of heroin from the aircraft.

"I see you, I see you. Don't move; I'll get you out!" replied Kaziz with renewed enthusiasm.

A few seconds later, Kolkov was a free man. He had a few bumps and bruises and the crash had reopened his shoulder wound, but all in all, he was doing pretty well. He stood up and looked at Kaziz: a man of about forty, or so; one hundred fifty pounds and deep black eyes.

"Are you okay? Are you injured? You are bleeding from the shoulder CPT, is there anyone else alive in there?" asked the seemingly concerned Kaziz.

"I am okay; I am fine, but my pilot didn't make it. He died just before we crashed. There is no hope for him. Thank you for saving me; I will always be grateful," replied the now confident Kolkov.

Kolkov explained the situation to Kaziz in a matter of minutes. Kaziz understood and nodded in agreement. Kaziz had brought a large Russian military truck, and both men quickly loaded the heroin aboard. Kolkov's plan was a simple one. He would destroy the aircraft; fire has a way of destroying evidence, and continued on to the airbase with two hundred kilograms of heroin. He would tell his superiors that he had ambushed a mujahidin patrol led by Khalil and had recovered the heroin. Being concerned that such a valuable cargo arrive safely at its destination, he had decided to personally escort it. Shortly after his departure from Qonduz, he had heard and seen the explosions coming from the base, and assumed that all was lost. He would further tell them that he and Antoniv, being the only survivors, had crashed landed forty kilometers short of the base and Antoniv had been killed in the crash. Kaziz's presence would be explained as a mere coincidence. He happened to be en route to a supply depot to pick up some parts when he observed the crash and rescued Kolkov from the flames.

Kolkov would further explain that both he and Antoniv had previously been wounded by the mujahidins, near Erat, thus explaining the destruction of the fuel center. Kolkov would again explain that he had some rudimentary flying knowledge, and that Antoniv had also given him some basic flying instructions prior to his crash. Additionally, to make matters more complicated, their radio had been damaged and he was unable to radio ahead.

Kolkov hoped that his story would not sound too complicated or unbelievable. The two hundred kilos of heroin should, help convince his superiors that he was telling the truth. It was a small price to pay in order to cover his tracks. He figured he could afford to be generous with $200,000,000 at stake.

After destroying the aircraft and all its evidence, Kolkov and Kaziz headed toward Dushanbe. Kolkov asked Kaziz if he knew of a good hiding location for the rest of the stash. Kaziz thought about it for a while; then a giant smile crossed his face.

"Yes, yes, of course. I know exactly the spot. Perfect, just perfect," said Kaziz, as he slapped himself on the forehead with his hand.

"Well, where? Where is this perfect place? Don't keep me guessing!" asked Kolkov with impatience.

"The nuclear missile silos. They were closed after the last disarmament treaty. All of the missiles were removed and destroyed, last year. To make things even better, they are only ten kilometers from Dushanbe. No one ever goes there now. The local farmers think it is haunted and everyone else think it's unsafe to go in there, radioactive stuff you know. That's just a bunch of garbage, it's been swept, and it's as clean as your ass. I am sure I can get the key through the maintenance shop. We can then store your heroin, and recover it at a later date. How does that sound, comrade?" asked Kaziz with a big grin.

"You are a genius, Kaziz. That sounds perfect. Why don't we go to your shop first and get the key, drop off the stuff, and turn me over to the hospital?" replied Kolkov with a smile. It seemed that his plan was working out after all.

Kaziz was able to obtain the master key to one of the silos. All went well and the drugs were successfully smuggled in and hidden in the safe that normally kept the small arms used by the underground personnel. He looked around for a place to hide the key in case he was found out. He looked down on the ground and found a steel support beams running the length of the hallway. At one time it must been used for some kind of track. The closest end was slightly raised and there was enough room to jam a key down in the crack. *Double safe* thought Kolkov. *Nothing can happen to it now.*

Kaziz drove up to the operations headquarters building and ran inside looking for the Chief of Staff. After locating the acting Chief, Senior Major Bolotin, he explained his long and sordid tale. Bolotin immediately called a base ambulance and Commanding General Turkov at home.

"General, this is Bolotin. You must come over right away. I have some news of great importance. Hurry, hurry, yelled Bolotin at the still groggy general.

"Okay, okay. I will be right over. This better be good, Bolotin. Or I will arrange a transfer to a very cold place. Do you understand me?" replied Turkov angrily.

Turkov's, Chief of Staff Bolotin and a few other staff members listened to the incredible flight and heroic actions by CPT Kolkov. After Kolkov had finished recounting his exploits, he sat down and winced in mock pain as he grabbed his shoulder.

"Get this hero a doctor right away, you must be exhausted," exclaimed the admiring general. General Turkov was an ambitious officer and he knew that two hundred kilos of heroin could buy him a lot of favors. He knew that the war in Afghanistan would soon be over, and he had better look after his own interests. Turkov thought, *maybe I should keep this quiet for now, until I find out all of the details*. He decided that he would send out reconnaissance patrols and aircraft as soon as possible.

Kolkov was taken to the base hospital and well treated for the next twenty-four hours and released, pending home leave. On the second day he met with Kaziz outside the post.

"How are things going?" asked Kaziz with genuine interest.

"I am feeling much better, and I owe it all to you. Let's go and have a few drinks, my friend. Oh, oh, I am so sorry. I had forgotten that you are a Muslim and don't drink," replied Kolkov with a grin.

"Don't you worry. I am a Muslim, but I don't practice my religion. Why don't we go to my house?" asked Kaziz

"You have yourself a deal, comrade?" answered Kolkov.

The ride to Kaziz's house took only ten minutes. Kaziz, like so many other Russians, lived in one of those cheap concrete monstrosities that the Russians were so fond of building. Kaziz lived on the fourth floor of a twelve-story building. Unlike many Russians, he did not have to share his two-room apartment with anyone. After all, Kaziz was a highly decorated Russian pilot, and an engineer at the base. The apartment showed signs of bachelor-hood: clothes everywhere, dishes still in the sink etc. Kaziz invited Kolkov in the living room/bedroom and sat down on his couch. Both men drank from the bottle, and told war stories recapping the glory of "old Russia". Kolkov, unlike Kaziz, kept going to the toilet and spitting out his vodka. Kolkov had no intention of getting drunk tonight. He had a plan. Kaziz was the only remaining witness and he had to die, just as the other ones had. It had to look like an accident, however. Kolkov kept offering toasts to old war comrades, including Kaziz's brother and anyone else he could think of. As the night wore on, Kaziz kept getting drunker and drunker.

At around midnight, Kaziz finally passed out on the couch. By now even Kolkov was a little unsteady. He reached down and pressed on the arterial vein in Kaziz's neck. He knew from experience that this would cause unconsciousness or even death. Kolkov poured an entire bottle of vodka on Kaziz and the couch; lit a cigarette and threw it on Kaziz's body. He stood there for a second and contemplated his handiwork. Apparently Kaziz had already died from the alcohol and the neck pressure. He looked around and made sure he had not left any incriminating evidence; then he quickly left the apartment and ran down the stairs. When he got to the ground floor he could already hear the screams of the other tenants in the building. He went across the street to make sure that the apartment was fully engulfed before he called to report a fire.

Kolkov walked around for a while trying to work off the effects of the alcohol. He did not particularly like to drink a lot and this was more than he was used to. Around two-thirty in the morning he took a taxi back to the air base. He had the taxi driver drop him off in front of the main gate. He walked up to the sentry and showed him his identification. The sentry nodded his head, and started to salute when he suddenly yelled, "Stop or I will fire."

Kolkov was already ten yards past the main gate; at first he thought it was a joke or not meant for him. The sentry raised his weapon and fired a warning burst in the ground in front of him. The sound of the bullets hitting the ground and bouncing off made him stop and turn around. Kolkov was ready to chew this young man a new asshole, but when he saw the intensity and determined look in his eyes he stopped, and asked him, "What are you doing private? Are you crazy? How dare you fire upon an officer! I will have you court-martialed," screamed Kolkov at the young private.

"CPT Kolkov, by order of the Commanding General, I am to place you under immediate arrest. If you resist, I have been authorized to use deadly force! Do not make me shoot you. Put your hands on top of your head and freeze!" shouted the private with authority in his voice.

Kolkov was totally surprised. What could have possibly gone wrong? There was no one around to break his cover. There were no survivors, no one could possibly know anything. He stood there, mentally going over every single detail of the past few days. It was impossible; nothing had escaped his attention. He decided the best thing to do was wait for an officer to explain to him what was going on. He didn't have long to wait. Within five minutes a jeep drove up to the main gate. Sr. Major Bolotin and two heavily armed privates jumped out and came running over to him. Bolotin approached him carrying a set of heavy manacles in his hands.

"CPT Kolkov, by the powers invested in me, I hereby place you under arrest for the crimes of treason, murder, and desertion. General Turkov has personally signed the arrest warrant. Do you have anything to say?" asked the overbearing major.

"Of course I do, but this is neither the place nor time to do it. Please, take me to General Turkov and we can resolve this misunderstanding right away," explained Kolkov with a flair.

"You will be detained in the military prison, and if and when General Turkov has time, he will call for you. As of this moment, CPT Kolkov, you are a prisoner and will act accordingly. Now shut up, and go with these two soldiers!" yelled Bolotin at the still shocked and devastated Kolkov.

The two soldiers walked over; one of them was carrying the shackles that Bolotin had been previously carrying. They thoroughly searched him and placed the shackles on both his hands and legs. For the first time in his life Kolkov felt really alone and desperate. All of his scheming and plotting had gone for naught. He was being jailed without knowing the reason or cause. Kolkov was transported by jeep to the post's military prison. Russians, were not known for their belief in rehabilitation. Prisons were meant for punishment and this one was no exception. It was a dark-gray structure about four stories high, surrounded by barbed wire, gun towers and a moat. It had to be early seventeenth century, judged Kolkov as he was driven through the courtyard.

Kolkov was offered no special treatment or privileges befitting his rank and status. He was stripped naked, deloused and given rough prison work clothes. After enduring this humiliating ordeal, he was taken to a small cell on the second floor and left alone in the dark. Kolkov's whole world was suddenly upside down. Here he was in prison for an unknown crime, when perhaps others should be.

His life became a daily and boring routine, lights on at five-thirty a.m. A breakfast consisting of gruel, bread and tea was brought to him around six. Lunch was served at noon and it consisted of some type of boring soup made from cabbage, potatoes and the like. Dinner was not much better. He was allowed one hour of exercise in the courtyard between four and five p.m. and was then returned to his cell. Kolkov found out through the jail grapevine that he was considered a special prisoner; not allowed any contact at all with anyone. Kolkov endured this regimen for nearly a month, when he suddenly received a visitor. A young baby-faced lieutenant by the name of Orloff came to visit him one afternoon.

"CPT Kolkov, I am your state appointed advocate. You will be tried this afternoon, and found guilty! Your sentence will be death by firing squad. Do you have anything to say before we go to the tribunal?" asked the obviously bored and uninterested young lieutenant.

"Yes, hell yes! I have been stuck in the miserable abyss for nearly a month, and no one has told me what the charges are!" replied Kolkov with rage.

"Listen to me and listen to me well. You are a traitor, a coward, a murderer and a deserter, what kind of treatment and sentence do you think you should get? We even have a witness to your crimes. A Private Markarian survived your attempted assassination of him and has told us everything. Do you remember him from Erat? The explosion threw him away from the fire. He was severely burned, and we had to wait until he could testify in court. We also did a ballistic examination of your personal sidearm and it matched the bullets found at Erat and the helicopter pilot's head. Do you now understand? You are being blessed with a personal visit from the tribunal president, General Turkov, and I suggest that you listen to him," stated Orloff with venom in his voice.

Kolkov was in a trance. How could this happen? He was worth over $200,000,000 dollars, yet he would soon be executed. How ironic, he thought. And now the visit from the tribunal president, General Turkov, how convenient. Slowly a plan began to develop in his head. What if Turkov took the two hundred kilos and never reported it to Moscow? Maybe he could work out a deal. The door to his cell slammed opened and General Turkov walked in.

"Out, out all of you, except Kolkov! I need to speak with him alone," demanded the general, as he physically manhandled Lieutenant Orloff, and the jailer out of the cell.

"CPT Kolkov, I want you to sit down, and not say a word until I am finished, do you understand?" demanded Turkov with a growl in his voice.

"Yes sir, yes sir. I, I, I will not say anything," replied Kolkov as he sat on the bed.

Turkov paced up and down the small cell for a few seconds and finally stopped at the foot of the bed and looked down at the helpless Kolkov.

"Do you know the predicament you are in, Kolkov? You have been found guilty. Oh excuse me, will be found guilty of all the charges and executed today. I hope you understand that clearly?" stated Turkov with confidence and certainty.

Kolkov nodded his head, but remained speechless as instructed to. Turkov went on to explain that the only way Kolkov could survive the firing squad would be not to mention the heroin in the official court transcripts; these transcripts were taken by a civilian civil servant and members of the press might be present, much too difficult to cover up. Turkov went on to explain that poor Private Markarian had suddenly taken a turn for the worse today and died, thereby being unable to charge Kolkov with the most serious crimes. If Kolkov agreed not to mention heroin, he would see to it that he receive a lesser sentence, and once the interest subsided he would pull some strings and have him exonerated. All in all, it didn't sound too bad. At least there was some hope, and as long as he was alive he could make deals for the future.

"General, how much time do I have to think about this?" asked Kolkov with a great deal of sarcasm in his voice.

"Of course I'll do it. However, are you willing to put your offer in writing?" asked Kolkov with a smile.

"You really want to die, don't you?" Was Turkov's reply as he started to walk out of the cell.

Kolkov suddenly stood up and grabbed Turkov's arm, and spun him around. He looked deep into his eyes and said, "If you do not keep your promise, I will find you and I will kill you!" stated Kolkov, icily staring Turkov down.

"You are pretty brave, for a man facing the firing squad. But, unlike you, Kolkov, I am a man of honor and I will keep my promise. I will sentence you to, let's say, six years, plus your time already served.

Is that agreeable?" asked Turkov grinning as he walked out the door.

Kolkov could not believe his bad/good luck. Here he was back among the living, but would probably have to serve some time in prison. It was better than being dead, he rationalized. At one time Kolkov had actually thought about telling Turkov about the rest of the heroin, but what was to prevent Turkov from keeping all of it and then having him executed? *No*, he thought. *Stick it out and some day you will be rich, richer than you could ever imagine. Maybe I can make some friends in prison and get out sooner anyway.*

Turkov kept his promise and reduced the sentence to six years. It was to be served at Gulag fourteen, near the Crimea. Well, thought Kolkov to himself, at least it won't be as cold as some places I have been to. When the jailers came to take him away that day, he actually had a smile on his face.

Chapter 16

Almost Home

The giant C-141 circled the Rhein Main airport, near Frankfurt, in a holding pattern. The pilot was following a series of civilian jets ahead of him, and was forced to wait for them to land first. Frankfurt/Rhein-Main was one of the busiest airports in Europe. Since the close of W.W. II this giant airport has served as both a military and civilian airfield.

Jeremy was anxiously peering out of the window next to him. It had been a long time since Jeremy had been here; he hardly recognized the landscape. Jeremy was amazed at how much the countryside had changed. The city had really expanded in all directions, and the downtown area had several new skyscrapers. *It's been nearly twenty years* reflected Jeremy pensively. Although he hoped his stay in Germany would be more productive than his stay in Pakistan, the nearly four weeks there accustomed him to the hospitalization routine. He was far from well, and he knew that his feet and legs required delicate surgery which could only be done in Germany or in the U.S.

Jeremy was so captivated by the green landscape and new skyline that he didn't even notice Nurse Gretchen walking up to him. She was making sure that all of his dressings were changed and cleaned. After all, she didn't want these young American nurses thinking she wasn't doing her job properly.

"Herr Grant, you are almost home and I wish you many happy and wonderful years ahead. May I make a suggestion, Herr Grant? Get out of this type of business. Find yourself a good German girl and settle down, and make many babies," stated Gretchen, the corners of her big dark eyes glistening with tears.

"Is that a proposition, Fraulein?" asked Jeremy in return.

"I, I, I wished it was, Herr Grant, but I am destined to remain single." replied Gretchen with a deep and sorrowful sigh.

Gretchen once again turned away from him, and walked toward the rear platform. Jeremy could not help but feel sorry for this giant of a woman. Maybe someday she could marry someone compatible, thought Jeremy. *I wish her luck.*

The sound of tires skidding on the runway brought him back to consciousness. He realized that although Germany was not America, he was near home, and would be around Americans for a while. The large aircraft taxied for a very long time and finally came to rest at the western end of the airport. The large rear door was dropped and he, along with the other injured personnel, were carefully transported to the nearby hospital. Wiesbaden had the reputation of being the best American hospital outside the continental United States. Jeremy was given a short ambulance ride to the nearby hospital, and discretely taken to the north wing. The north wing had a reputation as a special wing. VIP's and the likes were often secluded here, away from prying eyes.

Jeremy's room was quite spacious, and offered a wonderful view of the hospital gardens, and the distant city skyline. He had a large color television in the corner, and even a small refrigerator with cold soft drinks and mineral water in it. *Hey, first class* thought Jeremy. However, he also noticed that he was all alone in this wing, and the nearest human company was the nurse's station, thirty or so yards away. *Well you can't have everything*, he thought to himself as he dozed off in his comfortable bed.

Jeremy did not know how he had been sleeping, but a soft and gentle voice awakened him.

"Mr. Grant, Mr. Grant, there is someone here to see you. Please wake up," asked a middle-aged nurse wearing captain's insignias on her lapels.

Jeremy opened his eyes, not knowing exactly where he was. He tried to sit up in his bed, but the nurse pushed him back down and asked him to lie still for moment. He squinted one eye toward her and noticed that she was adjusting some type of intravenous device to the back of his hand.

"Okay, Mr. Grant, you can move now," she said with a gentle

smile on her face.

Jeremy noticed that she was around his age, had brown hair and a large wedding ring on her left hand. Jeremy couldn't help but smile. *At least this time I won't have to worry about anything "special" from her*. She noticed his smile and was curious.

"Mr. Grant, is there something you want to tell me? Have we met before?" she asked.

"No, not really. It's just a personal joke; you would not understand. Excuse me, captain, was it your name?" asked Jeremy.

"Nolan, Patricia Nolan, captain, United States Air Force. My friends call me Pattie, and as we are going to be seeing a lot of each other, you can call me Pattie, too," replied Pattie, extending her hand to him.

She had a firm grip, and a great smile. Jeremy knew he would get along with her. He sat up in his bed and looked around the room. It was then that he noticed the tall thin man sitting in the corner lounge chair. He had been extremely quiet, too quiet, thought Jeremy.

"And you are?" asked Jeremy inquiringly.

"Hi, I am James Brown from the embassy. I am to notify the military attaché and press attaché when you wake up," answered the young man, without so much of a smile.

"Okay, James Brown. I am awake. So go tell your boss to come over," replied Jeremy.

Jeremy laid back down in his bed and reflected on the last twenty-five years of his life. He had more scars on his body than a professional boxer, lumberjack and bullfighter combined. He had done just about everything there was to do. There was nothing left to prove. Maybe it was time now to buy a piece of property somewhere, and become a country gentlemen. *Yeah, that's what I'll do,* he thought to himself. His inheritance and wise investments over the past twenty years had made him a millionaire. He didn't have to work anymore if he didn't want to. Just as he drifted off into a deep sleep, a booming voice was heard to say, "Excuse me, huh, Jeremy? I am Frank N. Pimmelkopf, the resident in charge," stated the voice in the background.

Jeremy was not quite awake yet, but he thought he heard the guy say, "Pimmelkopf" That can't be the guy's real name. That means "Dickhead" in German, Jeremy slowly opened his eyes and stared in the direction of the voice. There stood William Foster Scardale, Major, U.S. Army (retired), ex-Special Forces, ex-Vietnam buddy, ex-everything. Jeremy suddenly sat up in his bed and saw "Bill". Some called him "Billy Bob", and many called him a lot worse things. The years had not been kind to Bill. He had put on weight, gone bald and now sported unflattering horned-rimmed glasses. He looked like a Harvard English teacher.

"You old so and so, what on God's green earth are you doing here? I haven't seen you in twenty years or more! What a coincidence. How in the hell are you? You, you Pimmelkopf! What a perfect name for you," shouted Jeremy with jubilation in his voice.

"I guess I am just lucky, old buddy. Got myself this cushy assignment in Frankfurt, and I will retire here someday. I am not going to ask you how you have been, old buddy. You look like shit," replied Bill with a smile and a handshake.

"Ain't it the truth, but at least I got my hair left," stated Jeremy, still smiling and pumping his arm for all it was worth.

What to do you mean retire here someday? You can't possibly mean here, as in here, can you? Germany? Why?" asked Jeremy unbelievably.

"Well, you see, old chap. We have this German attorney who occasionally handles our legal affairs, Baroness Heidi Von Schuldschein. They even own a castle and a vineyard around here somewhere. She has a set of tits my friend, out of this world! Well you know the drill, I can't marry her as long as I am still in the 'company.' She obviously doesn't know that I am who I am, but that's okay too. I know her deceased father was a former high-ranking Nazi with a devious past, and I don't hold that against her," bubbled out of Bill, before Jeremy could get in a word in edgewise.

Bill sat down and both men recalled their lost pasts. It seemed as if both men had experienced similar career paths, expect Billy Bob had elected a more sedate diplomatic career path, and Jeremy was more of a field man. Bill interrupted their pleasant reminiscing by informing Jeremy that his field days were over, and rather than being downcast,

Jeremy was jubilant.

"Are you kidding? No way Jose, I am not going back to Virginia for a cushy desk job! I am officially turning in my resignation the moment I am healed up, and out of here," answered Jeremy with a strong affirmation in his voice.

Billy Bob was pleased that his friend had taken it so well, but was somewhat perplexed by Jeremy's intense vocalization and apparent joy. Bill wondered if this was the effect of all those years in Afghanistan or did Jeremy have an ulterior motive?

"You realize that you are not out of the woods yet, don't you? I have been informed that a couple more operations are needed to repair those horrible leg wounds you received. Don't be concerned, I have been told that the staff in this hospital trained under the famous Dr. Frankenstein, and they are now out digging up the countryside for spare parts," Bill said laughingly.

"Okay, wise guy. Cut the crap and tell me the straight story," Jeremy asked in a serious tone of voice.

Bill carefully informed him of the all options that were available to him. One was getting the necessary surgeries performed in Germany or to wait a couple of weeks and have them done at Bethesda Naval Hospital, when he returned home. Jeremy was determined to get moving with his new life and he elected to have the military doctors at Wiesbaden perform them as soon as possible.

Jeremy's life was slowly returning to normal. He had successfully undergone three serious operations in the past two months and was well on his way to getting out of his wheelchair. His legs and feet were slowly getting back to normal, but he would always have a "Gentleman's" limp, and would have to walk with a cane. He would also have a hard time going through airport metal detectors. In order to reattach his right foot, several pieces of stainless steel had to be used to reconstruct the ankle and part of the foot. He also still had several steel pellets lodged in his body from the detonating Claymore mines. Billy Bob had been a true friend. His constant visits and horrible jokes had kept him in from falling in to a deep depression.

On several occasion, Bill had brought Fraulein Baroness Heidi Von Schuldschein to visit. Jeremy had found her to be a very pleasant and charming woman, somewhat plain looking, but a gracious lady none the less. She had, in fact, invited Jeremy to visit her castle and recuperate there. Jeremy was giving it serious consideration. He would have to wait until his physical therapy was completed, but he hoped someday to visit Heidi and Bill at her castle.

The doctors were anxious to get Jeremy started on an individualized physical therapy program, but were waiting on the availability of a specialized therapist. This specialist had worked on several similar cases and had achieved amazing results. Unfortunately, he was so good that his services were in high demand throughout the European theater of operation.

Jeremy passed the time by attempting to do leg strengthening exercises on his own and practicing his German with the janitorial staff. Jeremy was extremely anxious to resume his physical conditioning program; all those years in Afghanistan had seriously affected his physical appearance.

His current situation often forced his thoughts back to a different time and a different war. *How ironic,* he thought, *I find myself back in the same boat I did twenty years ago, but I don't have Loretta around to comfort me.* He was amazed how often he'd been thinking about her in the past few months, and promised himself he would try to locate her upon his return to America.

One late afternoon, when he was feeling particularly down, he had an unexpected visitor. Fraulein Gretchen had inquired as to his whereabouts and came to visit him.

"Herr Grant! How are you doing? You are looking well, and how are the nurses treating you here? You tell me if they're not being kind to you, and I will scare them in to reality," snickered Nurse Gretchen at Jeremy.

Jeremy went on to explain the delay in his rehabilitation program and how much he would like to get started. Gretchen stood up, all six-feet-two of her, and said, "I am disappointed, Herr Grant. You should have called on me before now. I am the best nurse in the world, and my first cousin Otto is, in fact, the best physical therapist in Germany. I am positive that we can somehow manage to get you back on your feet. Now you tell me how I can get a hold of Herr Pimmelkopf, I mean," she jokingly knew him by that name, too, "and we will take care of everything."

"That would be great, Nurse Gretchen."

Billy Bob was a great organizer. While in the Army he was the only man to practically memorize every single Army regulation and use them to his advantage. Bill's organizational skills were put to a real test. Jeremy's dead father's influence had to be used on several occasions to convince agency "pinheads" to release Jeremy from the hospital. The fact that Nurse Gretchen was an on-call nurse for the American Embassy made Jeremy's transfer to her care a great deal easier. He still had to report in once a week and be examined by a physician, but he was well on his way to an almost complete recovery. Heidi had offered her castle as an ideal location for therapy, and Jeremy had promptly accepted. Bill had told her that Jeremy was a victim of a terrorist attack while working in the Middle East somewhere. Jeremy had, by this time, turned in his official retirement package and was now only waiting for the bureaucrats to do their jobs, and process his retirement.

Once the preliminary battles had been fought with the "pinheads", the transition to the care of Nurse Gretchen and Otto was well planned and organized. Bill had arranged for an ambulance and all five of them had taken a leisurely ride up the north-south Frankfurt Autobahn toward Koeln. From there, they took small and scenic highways until at nightfall they reached the wonderful river town of Cochem, on the Moselle river. It was a picturesque German post-card town with small alleyways, ancient buildings and, of course, a majestic castle looming nearby.

This part of Germany was dotted with beautiful historic castles. Sometimes the ravages of time and war had reduced them to ruins. Most of them were perched on hilltops, or on small islands near or in the middle of the river. It was one of the prettiest spots on earth, thought Jeremy, as they drove down the small two-lane road which ran parallel to the river.

This part of Germany was historically referred to as part of the "Rheinland ***Gebiet***'." (area). This area was still occupied by French troops in 1936 when Hitler reoccupied it. It was nearly the "early beginning" to WWII. Hitler once referred to the inhabitants of this area as the "***Scheiss*** Rheinlaender" (shitty Rheinlanders). Anyone who lived west of the Rhein River was once looked down upon as impure Germans. This area at one time in history had belonged to France, under Napoleon, and further back in history, Charlemagne had been crowned "Emperor of the World" in the city of Aachen. Hitler's derisive terms had only made them prouder of their heritage and tradition. The people in this part of Germany were friendlier than in other parts. One of their traditions was only celebrated in the Rheinland, "***Fasching-Karneval***" (similar to the Mardi Gras in New Orleans, but with a German flair to it). It was, and is, an ancient joyous celebration that lasted six riotous days. Because of their friendly and folksy way they have always truly enjoyed a glass of good wine, and have made some terrific beers throughout the centuries. The Moselle area produces some of the best white wines in the world.

"Don't worry, our castle is ten kilometers south of here, and we are off the tourist attraction list. We do not allow uninvited guests on our property. My father was a very private man. The road leading up to our castle is a private one and we control the access. Our vineyard is directly behind the castle and will offer you many miles of pleasant walking paths, of course once you are on your feet, Herr Grant."

The ambulance pulled up and stopped near a large metal gate. It was obviously old and antique in design. The Schuldschein family crest was carefully centered between the two gates. From what he could see of the gate, the crest appeared to be of an eagle or bird of some kind. Although the gate was old, Jeremy noticed the well-worn, but well-maintained metal grooves that ran parallel to the gate. A six-foot-high, rough stone wall ran on each side of the gate as far as the eye could see, and two well-placed video cameras guarded the entrance. *Why all the security*, thought Jeremy to himself. *At least,* he thought, *no one is going to disturb me.*

The gate slowly opened and the ambulance wound its way up a long cobblestone driveway toward the castle. The castle stood perched on a small hill directly on the river. Jeremy was sure that at some time in history a direct connection to the river was possible from the castle.

Several ancient stone remnants were strewn between the main castle exterior and the river's edge, indicating that at one time a connecting wall and fortification must have existed. Jeremy could not help but also notice many WWII era bomb craters and heavy machine-gun damage to many of the parapets and buildings. It would seem that the last inhabitants put up quite a struggle not too long ago.

The ambulance pulled up to what was the main entrance to the castle. A large set of stone stairways led to an impressive massive oak door. The two ambulance attendants carefully lifted Jeremy and carried him inside. Heidi saw to it that he got a lower-level room with easy access and egress to the garden area behind the library. Jeremy was amazed to see that the castle was conveniently equipped with a twenty-five meter lap pool, Jacuzzi and a complete gym. In addition to these marvels, it was also equipped with an elevator giving him access all the way to the third story. Heidi explained that her father, Baron Kurt Von Schuldschein, had been wheelchair bound and these conveniences had been installed for him shortly after the war ended.

Jeremy room was a rather large high-ceilinged affair. Large French windows opened to the rear of the garden, and gave him a magnificent view of the hills behind the castle. Well-groomed and century-old cultured vines grew abundantly on the terraced hills. Both Gretchen and Otto had rooms on the second floor overlooking the courtyard and main entrance.

Gretchen and her cousin kept their promises to Jeremy. They developed a grueling set of exercises that would task a fit young man. Slowly over the next three months, Jeremy's condition improved dramatically. At the end of this period, he was able to walk up and down the terraced hills with the aid of a gnarly grapevine root cane. Jeremy felt quite healthy and was almost back to his old self. He had gotten accustomed to the cane and occasionally could walk without it, with a strong limp, however. He had kept his weekly doctor's appointment and was given a clean bill of health. One of the surgeons had recommended that sometime in the future, he seek out a specialized orthopedic surgeon and review his progress. Modern medicine had made miraculous strides and it was possible that something could be done for his limp someday. However, for now he was about as good as anyone could be.

Billy Bob had used his organizational skills to expedite Jeremy's retirement paperwork and after much delay and headaches, Jeremy was finally officially retired. He did not want to overstay his welcome with Bill and Heidi, and decided to do a little traveling in Europe prior to returning to America.

Chapter 17

Short Vacation?

Jeremy was trying to put his Afghanistan experience behind him, but he still had lingering memories of Khalil and the other men who died that day. On one hand he wanted to forget the horrors of war, but the realities of modern life made that impossible. News coverage of the final Soviet departure from Afghanistan and the continuing ongoing domestic turmoil made forgetting very difficult. The upheaval in both the Former Soviet Union (FSU) and in Afghanistan did not allow him to forget. The daily CNN news bulletin kept him apprised of the situation in those countries. As hard as he tried to forget them, he was continually reminded of those events.

More surprising than anything else were the events happening throughout the former Soviet Empire. Nation after nation was trying to rid itself of the crushing Soviet yoke. As the months rolled into years, it became more apparent that the house that Stalin built, was crumbling down and no one could fix it.

Jeremy tried for twenty-one months to see all the wonderful European sights, but he just did not have his heart in it. He wandered around for almost two years without an itinerary, and eventually gave up. He no longer had any interest in drifting like a cork on the sea. He needed some structure in his life, and he decided to return to California, and either become a writer or get back in the intelligence field. Maybe, if he were lucky, he could do both.

After trekking around like a gypsy, Jeremy felt a strong sense of urgency to go back to Frankfurt, Germany and see his friend Bill. He was sure Bill could help guide him, or at least offer some probable solutions. One thing he was certain of, he did not want to work for the "Agency". They were too restrictive, pigheaded, and lacked flexibility; perhaps Bill could give him some ideas or at least point him in the right direction.

Jeremy found himself in Paris, when he impulsively packed his bags and bought a train ticket from Paris to Frankfurt. If he was going to do it, now was the time. He walked to the Gare de Lyon station, and transferred to the Gare du Nord for the connecting express train. The train stations in Paris were all of interesting designs and architecture. The Gare du Nord was a prime example of a 19th-century French train station. Jeremy admired its massive granite Corinthian columns and facade which took up at least two blocks of the Avenue Magenta. The interior is contained in an immense hall with at least sixteen rail sidings. The ceiling is covered with a glass roof which allows a certain amount of filtered light. Jeremy would swear that the interior had not changed since the days of the great empire.

Although a few modern ***accouterments*** adorn its halls, it has remained basically unchanged for the past three or four decades. As he walked through its immense hall, he expected to see Humphrey Bogart waiting in vain for Ingrid Bergman, or some black shirted **SS** trooper yelling for his arrest. Jeremy was sorry that he did not have more time to spend in this neighborhood. He was across the street from one of the most popular ***brasseries*** (Pub/restaurant) in this part of Paris, Brasserie de la Gare. It specialized in seafood and also in fried mussels. It was also less than a block from his father's old stomping ground during WWII in the OSS. His father had worked out of the Hotel de Londres et D'Anvers, on the Avenue Magenta, and operated his entire OSS infrastructure hidden in this ***quartier*** (neighborhood). Jeremy spent many a day as a child listening to his father's adventures in the OSS and his beloved Paris.

Jeremy was somewhat confused by the complex and puzzling route to Frankfurt. It was a weird and convoluted way of getting there, but he had time and eventually he would arrive there. Jeremy boarded the Trans-European Express (TEE) with great excitement and anticipation.

The high-speed TEE left Paris at exactly thirteen hundred hours, and headed northward through the flat French countryside. It passed historic WWI battlefields of the Marne and Ypres, as it sped toward Germany. It made only two stops before it arrived in Germany, Brussels and Liege Belgium. In less than six hours he was in Aachen

(AKA Aix-la-Chappelle) Germany, the wonderful historic frontier city. From there, he caught a connecting train to Koeln and then to Frankfurt.

One of the few pleasures Jeremy had truly enjoyed in the past two years was the European train system. It was consistently good from the tip of Norway to the southernmost corner of Portugal. One could travel in first-class luxury and be anywhere in Europe in less than eighteen hours. He thoroughly enjoyed the efficiency and punctuality of their magnificent rail system.

His long and relaxing train ride allowed Jeremy many opportunities to ponder his future. He was particularly excited about returning to Virginia, and especially California. One of the problems with his job at the agency was his necessary separation from most of his family and friends for the past twenty years. He looked forward to seeing his family again.

However, one thing always nagged at the back of his mind, and it would not go away. He had come to accept the fact that Khalil and the men had been killed, but what had happened to the heroin? One of his first priorities would be to check into the missing heroin. Quantities in this amount are not always easily processed, let alone captured by the authorities. As far as he knew, no one had ever reported any such quantity in the past three years and he was determined to locate it. A seizure or disposition of such a large quantity could easily affect prices worldwide.

Perhaps, if he were lucky, he could even locate the source country, or its original manufacturer. Jeremy was equally sure that the original purchaser or promised end user would also be interested in trying to locate it. These underworld figures had also made bargains and agreements with their customers, and there would be hell to pay all along the line. Jeremy also wanted a small dose of revenge, and retribution; after all, it was partly responsible for his injuries and the death of so many men.

Billy Bob and Heidi were there to pick him up at the station on Bahnhofstrasse, in Frankfurt. Jeremy still needed help with his luggage, and it always embarrassed him. He could manage one suitcase, but anymore than that was impossible. Bill was a gracious host and escorted him to his waiting car.

"Welcome home, stranger, it has been a long time. How have you been? We received your postcards, but you were never anywhere long enough to contact you," said Bill in a gracious manner.

"Greetings to both of you. Well, considering everything, I would say pretty damn good. I have seen everything there is to see in Europe and it's time to go home. However, I need to talk to you in private about something important," replied Jeremy just as graciously.

"Sure, old buddy. Can it wait until we get home, or do I have to throw Heidi out the car so we can speak freely?" Bill shot back with a smile.

"Now darling, if you men have business to talk about, just drop me off at the shopping mall, and I will be out of your hair for a couple of hours," answered Heidi in a simulated huff.

"No, of course not. It can wait until later on. I am just anxious to get going on this project, and I need Bill's help, that's all," answered Jeremy.

A few minutes later, Bill's gray Mercedes pulled up to a large white house in an affluent neighborhood on the outskirts of Frankfurt. It was a rather large house, three stories and an attic, and of course, as in all houses in Germany, a cellar. It had an electric metal gate, and Jeremy noticed the omnipresent video camera. It was surrounded by a six-foot-tall cinder block wall, topped with spiny thorn bushes. As the car drove through the driveway, two very large German shepherd dogs jogged alongside.

Jeremy was impressed, as Bill's status as a resident chief had some perks after all. He also had a butler and housemaid, courtesy of Heidi, she didn't want her "sweetie" to suffer when he was away from her. It was also her way of keeping tabs on her wandering-eyed Wild Bill. Bill did have a reputation with the ladies after all. *Wow*, Jeremy thought, *maybe I should have become a pencil pusher instead of a field operative.* No, he never regretted his decision; pinheads were pinheads and he could never have endured all the ass-kissing necessary to become a bureau chief, European desk in Frankfurt or not.

As a trained agent, Jeremy was immediately conscious of the many watchful eyes in the tree lined street. Before Bill could say anything else, Jeremy advised Bill that there was possible surveillance on his house.

"Yes, of course, Jeremy. I am glad of it. You see that car over there, pointing to a black Opel sedan, parked near the corner. Those are our friends from M.A.D., (Militaerischer Abschirm Dienst), our German intelligence boys. They always watch my house in the hope of catching the other guys watching me. I also have two heavily armed members of the German Bundes Grenzeschutz watching my ass, twenty-four hours a day, terrorists you know. I am probably the best protected prick in the country," laughed Billy Bob.

"You said it 'old boy,' the biggest prick in the country," replied Jeremy in the affirmative.

Jeremy retraced his last few weeks in Afghanistan and explained how they had been ambushed by some SPETSNAZ, and that a ton of heroin had disappeared in the process. As far as he knew, it had never reappeared anywhere. A shipment of this size would have certainly made news headlines anywhere in the world. Nothing had been seen or heard of it. Jeremy expressed his suspicions, but had absolutely no proof of anything. Bill sat there not saying a word for the longest time. He finally lifted his large eyebrows and said, "Oh, boy. You are bringing up a very controversial subject. After your return, we had access to the reports you filed, and believe me when I say, "HOT", I mean hot in the hottest sense of the word," replied Bill with gusto and emphasis, his bushy eyebrows curling upward in the process.

Jeremy stared at him, not knowing what to say or do for now. *Let him talk, he will eventually get to the point.* Bill had a propensity for the gab, and to say that sometimes he was longwinded was an understatement.

"Man, oh man, did you ever open a can of worms with that report. Some enterprising French reporter interviewed a returning French doctor who had been there, and that's how the story got out to the world. However, the story came out much different than the facts you presented. For weeks European and American papers ran headlines screaming, "CIA involved in one-ton drug deal!" You of course were oblivious to the whole thing, and because of health considerations you were not questioned. You know the rep we have. Some politicians were trying to tie us in again, and claim that this was just another case of the 'agency' trading something for something. Let me tell you Jeremy, this was so hot that no one in the 'agency' cared or wanted to know what had happened to that ton," finished Bill finally.

"You are kidding? You mean to tell me that no one has attempted to find out what happened? That's incredulous; that's criminal!" replied Jeremy with anger in his voice.

"What I am telling you, old buddy, is let it be. Don't push it or someone will bite your hand. You are not going to get anyone in the 'agency' to help you. I mean no one!" stated Bill with emphasis.

Jeremy stared at his old friend, and wondered how deeply Bill had been involved in the cover-up of this information. Jeremy understood Bill's reluctance, but had honestly been hoping for a little bit more information from his old friend. Well, so be it. I'll dig up what I can from here, and hope I can do something once I am back home. I still have some contacts in Europe, and maybe they can help, thought Jeremy.

"Bill, I have a special favor to ask. Can you take me to the airport? I need to take a flight to Paris as soon as possible, I have forgotten something there and I need to retrieve it prior to returning home. Will you do that for me?" asked Jeremy of his longtime friend.

Bill stared at Jeremy for at least thirty seconds before replying. He knew what Jeremy had in mind, but also knew it would be impossible to talk him how of it.

"Okay my friend, I can't stop you from committing suicide, but I don't have to pull the trigger either. I'll dig around, and let you know what I have found out. No promises, you understand. This matter has been officially buried, and I don't want to be the gravedigger!" replied Billy Bob, with concern in his voice.

Jeremy was amazed at Bill's reluctance to help. Jeremy had always known Bill to be an ass-kicking kind of guy, but the loss of the heroin had him scared and running. Well, if Bill turns up anything, fine, if not, so be it. Jeremy knew what he had to do. Paris was the key for now, and he needed to get back there as soon as possible. Bill drove him to the airport in silence. For the first time in his life, an uncomfortable schism existed between them, and Jeremy did not like it. Just as the car pulled up to the valet parking near the Lufthansa terminal, Jeremy said, "Look Bill, I know this is difficult for you, and I don't want our friendship to be strained because of this. Do what you can, and I will call you on a regular basis and let you know where I am. How is that?" asked Jeremy, extending his hand in a gesture of friendship.

"Sounds like a deal, old buddy. I hope you don't think I am chicken, but I am this close to my pension, and my marriage to Heidi. I really don't want anything to interfere with those plans. You will hear from me, if I have anything of value, and it's safe to reveal, okay?" replied Bill, shaking his friend's hand like a pump.

Bill helped Jeremy with his luggage again, and drove away in silence. Jeremy had an hour's wait before his flight. He walked over to the first-class lounge and tried to organize his plan of attack. He knew that Paris, the reporter and Dr. Perrin were immediate clues that needed to be followed. The flight to Paris was only forty minutes or so. There really wasn't much time to get comfortable before the plane started its descent into Charles de Gaulle airport at Roissy, outside of Paris.

The Parisian sky was gray and overcast. The airport itself was fairly modern, yet out of place. Its buildings seemed disconnected and disjointed. Jeremy was not an architectural expert, but someone had screwed up royally. The whole complex had conflicting architectural styles, and it was not aesthetically appealing. Jeremy did not feel comfortable here, and wanted to get out as soon as possible. He picked up his luggage and hailed a taxi.

It was then he realized, I don't know where to stay. *Where do I start?* he thought to himself. The young taxi driver asked again, "Where to, monsieur? Do you know where you want to go? If you don't I can recommend several nice hotels, said the young man, eagerness in his voice.

"No, I do know a place, it's on the Avenue Magenta, near the Gare du Nord, Hotel de Londres et D' Anvers. Do you know the place?" inquired Jeremy of the taxi driver.

"Of course, I do. Are you sure you want to stay there? After all, it's only a two-star hotel, and I can recommend much nicer quarters for the same price," replied Yousif, the taxi driver.

The ride from the airport to the hotel took nearly forty-five minutes, longer than the flight from Frankfurt to Paris. Yousif was a young Moroccan, from Spanish Morocco. He was married and had two children. Jeremy learned nearly his entire life history by the time they arrived at the hotel. Yousif even offered to chauffeur Jeremy around twenty-four hours a day for a "special price", Yousif gave Jeremy his cell phone number and home number and told him to call him anytime he needed anything.

The hotel was exactly as his father had described it, a little worse for wear, but still presentable. It was a typical turn-of-the-century, five-storied French hotel. It was now mainly used by the budget-conscience tourist. Its main attraction was the proximity to the Gare du Nord and Gare de L'Est.

Jeremy stared at the hotel and gave it a "tactical" intelligence rating of five stars. He could easily understand why his father's group had selected this location. This hotel had one secret advantage that most German Gestapo agents, or current tourists never saw. It was connected through the basement with four adjacent buildings, and was also connected to the building directly behind it on another street. Two of these underground entrances were connected to parking areas, making for perfect rendezvous points. It allowed for surreptitious entries and exits, and often befuddled the watching Gestapo officers. The cellar also had a direct sewer connection, which on occasions offered a readily accessible, if somewhat smelly, emergency escape.

Jeremy walked up to the front desk, and rang the brass bell. A tall and strikingly handsome elderly gentleman came to the counter. He was well dressed in a dark three-piece suit. He sported a gold watch chain in his left front vest pocket, a carnation in one buttonhole and a small colored ribbon in the other, indicating he was a ***Chevalier*** (high French decoration).

"May I help you, please?" asked the distinguished-looking gentleman, in impeccable English.

"Yes, I would like a room. I don't know for how long yet, but it should not be for more than three or four days," replied Jeremy.

"Well, I am sure we can help you. Would you please show me your passport, and fill out this card for the police. Thank you, monsieur," replied the clerk.

Jeremy handed the elderly clerk his passport, and began filling out the form as required by French law. At first the clerk glanced at the passport, checking the number, and then suddenly looked up at Jeremy, his eyes scanning the picture and face, over and over.

"You are Jeremy Grant? Did you have a father by the name of Winston?" asked the now excited clerk.

"Well yes! He was my father, Senator Winston Grant, from Virginia. Did you know him?" asked the astonished Jeremy.

"But, of course, ***mon petit*** (my little one). Your father and I worked together during the war, right here in this hotel. I am sorry, let me introduce myself. I am Colonel Auguste Gaston Perrin, retired of course."

Jeremy stood there like a deer paralyzed by headlights. Unable to move for a second, he looked at the distinguished gentlemen, and it dawned on him that Dr. Perrin, Jeremy's savior, was probably his son. *Too incredible to be true*, he thought to himself. Colonel Perrin dragged Jeremy to the small bar in the lobby, and for the next two hours grilled him for information about his family, work, etc. When the colonel found out that it was his son who had saved him, he broke down in tears. His sobs were so loud that Jeremy was embarrassed for him.

"I am sorry, Jeremy. You could not possibly understand. The 'debt' is now repaid. It is repaid," sobbed Colonel Perrin.

Jeremy was still unsure of what the colonel was referring to, but he was sure the colonel would tell him. The colonel went behind the bar and pulled out a bottle of his best Courvoisier and poured each a healthy three-finger drink.

"You see, Jeremy, I was captured by the Gestapo, and tortured for days. I refused to talk, so they decided to shoot me like everyone else in that group. Your father and some of my fellow countrymen decided to free me. They knew that all condemned prisoners were taken to the soccer stadium for execution. So they set up an ambush, and on the day of my expected execution, I was freed by your father. I swore on that day, that I would repay this 'debt.' My wonderful son has kept that promise, and I will be eternally grateful. Just a second, Jeremy, I must show you something," stated Colonel Perrin, bubbling with enthusiasm and fervor.

Colonel Perrin came back with a worn and tattered photo album. He sat down at the bar and flipped through several pages before suddenly shouting, "Come Jeremy, you must see your father in his glory. He was a brave and valorous soldier," continued Perrin, emotion in his voice.

Jeremy looked at the old album, and there before him was a photo of his father. A young and dashing-looking Winston Grant was in civilian clothes, but carried a Thompson .45 caliber submachine gun, a bandoleer with extra clips and several grenades. He was wearing a rakish beret, and also had a French "Croix de Lorraine" patch on his sleeve. This was the symbol of the "free French". Jeremy had to admit that the old man looked pretty good. Jeremy also noticed that standing next to his father was an equally young Colonel Perrin, and a very beautiful young woman.

"Excuse me, colonel. Who is that beautiful women? She has such striking looks," said the still puzzled Jeremy.

"That woman was almost your mother! Had the OSS not recalled your father, he would have married my Yvette," replied the still grinning Colonel Perrin.

"What do you mean mother?" asked the surprised Jeremy.

"Your father and Yvette were very much in love, and had the war not come between them, you probably would have been half French! I, on the other hand, am very glad that the OSS called your father back. I was able to respond to her needs and in time she became my wife. Unfortunately, she died last year, but I always carry a locket of her hair in my wallet, near my heart," said Colonel Perrin with great pride, excitement and some chagrin in his voice.

Colonel Perrin reached in his left coat pocket and pulled out a beautiful tiny cut crystal vial containing a small locket of golden blond hair. Colonel Perrin then stood up and gave Jeremy the obligatory French hugs, three of them as required by custom and tradition. It was then that Jeremy noticed that the colonel had a small tear running down his cheek. Not wanting to embarrass him, Jeremy turned away and pretended not to see it. The colonel quickly wiped it away, and quietly said, "I, unlike many Frenchmen, like Americans. I will always be grateful for what you did for my country and for me. All of these whining liberal Socialists who don't like Americans should take a ride to the cemeteries at Bellou Woods, St. Michelle, Normandy and many others just like them to see thousands upon thousands of American crosses lined up in neat little rows. Those dead Americans paid the price for French democracy. Those graves are the voting ballot receipts that gave the Socialists the current right to vote! Here, and only here, they can see the price paid for France and Europe by America. Should you ever need a favor, do not hesitate to ask me. I will do everything I can," stated the colonel with elegance and grandeur.

Things have a way of working themselves out, thought Jeremy. Dr. Perrin had casually mentioned that his father was in the same business as Jeremy. What an understatement, thought Jeremy. Here was a Frenchman who not only liked Americans, he was crazy about them, and he also had the advantage of having been a high-ranking French army colonel with connections. To top it off, he was a friend of his father, and also a retired member of the French Deuxieme Bureau. Jeremy was elated. He felt as if he finally had a partner on his side.

"Colonel Perrin, I wonder if I could impose upon you for a favor? I am trying to right a wrong and I don't know where to start. Maybe you could be of help?" inquired Jeremy hesitatingly.

"Of course, anything you want. Anything at all. I would be glad to assist you," replied the colonel with enthusiasm.

Colonel Perrin did not say a word. He merely listened to Jeremy's story, occasionally scratching his well-groomed beard or grunting approval. After about twenty minutes of dialog, Jeremy stopped to take a sip of his delicious cognac. Colonel Perrin took this opportunity to ask a few pertinent questions.

"As you know, Jeremy, I too am retired. However, I still have well placed colleagues who owe me a favor or two. As you know, we French have developed a special relationship with the Russians, and I even have some contacts over there. The 'New Russia' is still difficult to deal with, but maybe we can get some information for you. I will also try to track down this newspaperman for you, and you can take it from there. How does that sound, Jeremy?" replied Perrin in the affirmative.

"That would be fantastic, Colonel Perrin. I need a lead, and this could be it. I sincerely appreciate your offer of help," replied Jeremy.

"After all, it is the least I can do for the son of the man who risked his life to save mine. I will show you to your room now. Number 105, the one your father used to always stay in," answered Perrin.

Jeremy and the colonel took the elevator to the second floor. It was exactly as his father had described it to him. The elevator was about the size of a refrigerator. It was made of an ornate cast-iron grille pattern. However, over the years it had been painted so often that it was almost one solid sheet of paint, and hardly allowed any light in at all.

His father's favorite room in the hotel, was also an antique, small in size, not more than fourteen by twenty feet. A large window faced Avenue Magenta; there was a very small bathroom and a mixture of fifties and modern furniture. One of the interesting features this room had, was the connecting door to suite number 106. This was the corner suite and it had a complete view of the entire ***quartier*** for several blocks. The access had now been covered by a cheap 1950s armoire, and he could no longer gain direct access from his room. Colonel Perrin gave him the key to both rooms. Jeremy took the opportunity to personally inspect his father's home away from home during WWII.

Jeremy felt strangely at ease in this room. His father's presence and memories seemed to linger in the walls, and it somehow comforted Jeremy. These rooms were party to many important events in history, and he felt a deep sense of sorrow, and at the same time exultation. This was a moving event in his life and he was glad his father's memories could trigger such emotions in him. He inspected every nook and cranny expecting to uncover some hidden secret or mystery. He was hoping that somehow he could find a trace, maybe a remembrance of his father, but alas the rooms were clean and had been painted over several times. Nothing there, just memories of a father he had almost forgotten.

Jeremy spent his time in Paris, for the next several weeks, doing what most men wanting information do. He hit the pavement and tried to uncover some usable information. He spent many hours everyday at the home office of the *International Herald Tribune*, a very old and respected American newspaper with its home offices in Paris.

Jeremy became an expert at reading microfilm of the papers old editions. After several weeks of fruitless search, he found what he was looking for, a clue or at least he thought it was a clue. There buried on the fourth page, was a small story that rang a bell: "**MUJAHIDIN ATTACK RUSSIAN FORCES AT ERAT.**" Jeremy continued reading and was shocked to read that mujahidin forces had allegedly attacked Erat less than twenty-four hours after Qonduz! The story said, "A large force of mujahidin attacked and completely destroyed the reserve fuel center at Qonduz, etc., etc. He read and reread the scant storyline, and still could not believe that he didn't know about this alleged attack. After all, he had been appointed the operations officer, and he would have known of any such plans. There was something wrong, and he was going to find out what it was.

Jeremy rushed back to the hotel and found Colonel Perrin reading his Paris '*Match*' magazine at the bar.

"Well colonel, do you have anything for me yet? I was hoping that by now, you would have had something for me. Well, that's okay for now. I found something and I want you to follow it up. Do you think you could do that?" asked Jeremy inquiringly.

"Of course, I can. I am only sorry that my sources have not tracked this newspaper man down yet! I have been told that he may be on vacation or covering a story outside of France. What is it that you need, Jeremy?" responded the colonel anxiously.

Jeremy carefully explained what he had found. The colonel agreed with Jeremy; it would have been a tactical error for the mujahidin to expose their forces to the Russians, particularly so close to their frontier. Colonel Perrin promised to approach his Russian source and ask him to dig around and see what happened. Jeremy was not having very good luck. All of his known sources were drying up, or were unwilling to talk to an "ex-company man." Jeremy began to realize that he needed to get back in "intelligence," if he was going to do anything constructive.

Just when his luck seemed to have run out, Billy Bob called and asked to meet with him in Geneva, Switzerland. Bill was quiet secretive, and would not talk on the phone about it. Jeremy agreed, and told Bill he would meet him there tomorrow at the Groesse Gerau Inn, near the airport, around sixteen hundred. Jeremy was full of hope and expectations, and asked Colonel Perrin to keep his rooms until he returned. Perrin informed him that he would, and hoped to have some information for him upon his return. Jeremy left Paris, feeling better than he had felt in a long time.

The flight to Geneva was a short one, only-thirty five minutes or so. The flight was on time, and the service impeccable. *Just like a Swiss watch*, thought Jeremy. He took a cab to the inn, and checked with the desk clerk for messages.

"Ja, can I help you, please?" asked the young clerk, with his typical sing-song Swiss accent.

"Yes. I am Jeremy Grant, do you have any messages for me?"

"Just a second please, I will check," replied Hans, the clerk.

"Yes sir. A Herr Scarsdale called and said he would be delayed for about an hour, and you should meet him in the bar. ***Ja, danke bitte***." (Yes, thank you, please).

"Okay, thanks. If he should call, I will be waiting for him there," replied Jeremy, as he sauntered over to the bar.

"Ja, bitte," stated the bartender.

"A double cognac, anything good," ordered Jeremy.

"Will a Metaxa do?" asked the bartender, now switching to perfect English.

"Of course, Seven Star if you have it, but Five Star will also be good," replied Jeremy with anticipation.

It had been a long time since the word *Metaxa* had been brought up in his memory banks. He searched for a few seconds, and suddenly remembered Las Vegas. He began to smile, and just as suddenly heard, "Hey Bud, is this bar stool taken?" It was the unmistakable voice of Billy Bob that brought him back into focus.

"I can't believe an hour has gone by so fast already," answered

Jeremy staring at his old friend.

"Let's go over to a quiet corner, and talk. First of all, greetings from Heidi and Nurse Gretchen. Now that is out of the way; let's get on with the business at hand," stated Bill with authority.

"It's your dime, and your time," answered Jeremy, a little less formally.

Billy Bob went on to explain that he was here strictly off duty, and he would deny it, etc., etc. Jeremy got the drift, and asked Bill to quit playing the Bozo game and get on with it. Bill began unfolding an incredible tale of espionage and counter-espionage that would rival any James Bond movie. Bill had recently found out through unnamed sources that a certain Russian general has been trying to peddle a very large quantity of heroin for several years, but had not had much luck. The heroin market is apparently a pretty lucrative market, and the existing "Merchants of Death" have a monopoly on the market in that part of the world, and are not willing to share it with just anyone. Additionally, the original owners of that heroin may also want a piece of the action. The source is willing, for a certain price of course, to negotiate with the general, and or act as a "gopher".

"That's a great story, but what proof do we have that this guy is telling the truth? He could be spinning a yarn, and only wants to collect a reward! I need details, lots more detail!" replied Jeremy, his face showing no excitement at all, although his insides were doing a rumba.

"I figured you would say something to that effect, and I am here on his behalf to offer a proposal. He will tell you all he knows, if in exchange, you will give him $100,000. The money is to be paid by you in cash after you are satisfied with the information," countered Bill with a smile.

"Do you trust him? Can he be reliable? How much experience do you have with this guy?" Jeremy asked in rapid fashion.

"Remember, old buddy. This is off the record. He was one of our small-time moles. He occasionally came across with some interesting bits of information, but never major enough to warrant us getting him out. As you know the tide has changed, and he finds himself on the outside looking in. We no longer have any use for him, and the new

Russians don't want him, either. You might say, he is screwed. He can't live on his measly pension, and he keeps contacting me in the hopes of making some money. Officially, I kissed it off as a crank call. Unofficially, well you know the rest," continued Bill, in his usual ponderous monologue.

"$100,000 you say? How do I meet this character? You don't think I am going to go there, do you? Fuck no! Cold war or no cold war, they are still looking for me, and I am never going over there!" replied Jeremy, indignation and outrage in his voice.

Before Jeremy could finish his sentence, Bill raised his hand and said, "I knew this sounded pretty good, so on my own authority and expense, I took the liberty of flying him over here. He is upstairs, waiting for us. Can you get that kind of money on such short notice? I will make the introduction, and then I am out of here," stated Bill.

"Yes to both questions. I knew you had it in you. Geneva is the home of many of my bank accounts. I can call the Credit Suisse, and have the money here in an hour," answered Jeremy, slapping Bill's back in the process.

"Right, go ahead and make the arrangements and I will tell him to hang on for an hour or so. I hope this works out for you, Jeremy. I also forgot to inform you, as of next month, I will commence my official debriefing, retire and finally marry Heidi. I hope to have you at the wedding. Will you come?" asked Bill.

"You know I will. I hope both of you are very happy," replied Jeremy, giving Bill a bear hug.

Chapter 18

Moleman

Bill led Jeremy up the stairs to room 412, on the fourth floor. Room 412 was at the end of the corridor, near the emergency exit. *Well thought out, at least this guy is no beginner*, thought Jeremy as he approached the door. Bill knocked twice, paused and then knocked four more times. After a slight pause, the door was cracked open, and Jeremy got a glance at his mole.

Senior Major Andrei V. Bolotin, late of the FSU armed forces, former acting Chief of Staff at Dushanbe, and currently unemployed, opened the door. The room looked a mess. There were seven or eight empty mini liquor bottles strewn all over the bedroom. Candy wrappers and towels were equally distributed throughout the room. Bolotin stood there in his stocking feet; he held a can of German beer in one hand and his crotch in the other. First impression was not very good, thought Jeremy as his eyes swept the room.

Bolotin was no more than five-foot-eight and weighed a hefty two hundred and ten pounds. His hairline was down around his ears, and he had the ugliest kisser Jeremy had ever seen, even worse than poor Nurse Gretchen's. Major Bolotin had the face of a fighter who had lost more than he had won in the ring. Jeremy paused and then looked at Bill.

"Is this guy for real? I, I don't think we can do business together, I, I," stuttered Jeremy, as he looked down upon this poor excuse of a human being.

"Don't, don't jump to conclusions, Jeremy. I know he looks a little rough, right now, but his information has usually been reliable, and he's your only clue, after all. Listen to what he has to say, and if you don't like it, don't pay him," replied Bill, holding up his hand.

"Okay, let's sit down and talk, but the moment I think you are not telling the truth, I am out of here, and you have to find your own way home, Andrei," replied Jeremy, as he sat down on the only clean chair in the room.

Bolotin began his exciting tale of espionage and treason. As a CIA mole he had planted a hidden microphone in General Turkov's office. Over the years he had heard many secrets, but what he had heard on that particular day, made his few hairs stand up and cry for joy. He had overheard the general making plans to sell heroin to the highest bidder, and on another occasion, jail a soldier to a six-year prison term sentence for various and assorted charges. Before Bolotin could use this information to his best advantage, the general had not been very discreet politically, and had been thrown in jail after a coup attempt against the new regime. Faced with a possible death sentence for treason, he bargained away most of his drugs for a lesser sentence. General Turkov was now a prisoner somewhere in central Russia.

"Well, that's a great and wonderful story, Bolotin, but how does that affect me? What can you tell me? I don't really care about this Russian general," replied Jeremy, in a ruse trying to goad more information out of Bolotin.

"Hold your britches, Jeremy! Just listen to what the man has to say. Go on, Bolotin, tell him the rest. By the way Jeremy do you want me to leave, or stay?" countered Bill, trying to intervene.

"Okay, okay Bill stay a little longer," replied Jeremy.

"Well, if you look at the dates of the phone calls, you will note that they began shortly after the disappearance of the shipment in question. I have not told you how he came to acquire these drugs yet. A captain of our SPETSNAZ forces arrived at our base about the same time as these calls started. I was not supposed to know about the deal he made with Turkov, but the microphone, you know," continued Bolotin, now sounding more confident.

Suddenly, Jeremy became very alert and still. Bolotin may have something after all, he thought to himself. It would be prudent to let him continue, and see what he has to say.

"This captain made up some weird and incredible story about Qonduz, Erat, mujahidin, a shot-down helicopter and a large shipment of heroin. Unfortunately, he was found to be a liar and a traitor and sentenced to a long prison sentence. His death sentence was commuted by the general himself, at the last moment," finished Bolotin with a flair.

"Do you happen to know the name of this officer?" asked Jeremy, every nerve in his body tingling with excitement and anticipation.

"Of course, I do. However, first I must know if this is something that interest's you or not. Excuse me, I forgot the most interesting part of the story. This officer brought evidence with him. Not only did he bring the heroin, but he also brought back two severed heads. One was a mujahidin leader, and the other, uh, uh, I don't remember. You surely must know who they were," replied Bolotin, an evil smile developing on his face.

Jeremy was now convinced that Bolotin knew Kolkov, and might even know his current whereabouts. However, he had to let Bolotin say the name without any acknowledgment on his part. Jeremy stood up and paced the room, always keeping Bolotin in front of him.

"Go on!" whispered Jeremy, now turning his back on Bolotin and Bill.

"Kolkov, CPT Oleg Kolkov, of the SPETSNAZ, and you also know him, don't you?" inquired Bolotin.

Jeremy stopped his pacing. He turned around and faced Bolotin.

"If what you are saying is true, where is this Kolkov now? Is he still alive? Can you answer these questions?" asked Jeremy, hoping for an affirmative answer.

"Do we have a deal? I gave you most of what I know, and you have not shown any good faith money yet. I want my money now!" screamed Bolotin, his face turning a deep crimson color.

"Yes! We have a deal. However, I must know where Kolkov is now! Can you get this information for me?" Asked Jeremy, as he walked to the phone, and arranged for the money to be sent from his bank.

"I possibly could, but that was not part of the deal. I am not going back to that world ever again. I have burned all my bridges, and it's time for me to go to California. I have a cousin living in Sacramento, and he has told me wonderful things about California. I want to take the money, open a small shop, and live a quiet life for the rest of my years," replied Bolotin, as he walked over to the bed and sat down.

"Jeremy, it sounds like you have what you want. At least, it is a lead. I believe Bolotin kept his part of the bargain, and as previously arranged, I have to get back to Frankfurt before I am missed," stated Billy Bob, extending his hand to Jeremy in friendship.

"Bill, for once in your life you are right to the point, and correct. Thanks for your help, and I will definitely try to make your wedding. Give me a few weeks' notice, okay?" Replied Jeremy as he shook Bill's hand in return.

Bill left the room without any further comment or action. Jeremy looked at Bolotin and thought, *what would make a man do what Bolotin was doing? Was it the money, the excitement, the adventure? After all, betraying ones country for so many years was probably the lowest form of life Jeremy could imagine.*

Jeremy called for room service and ordered a luxurious meal for both men. The remaining hour and a half dragged on and on. The tension was almost as bad as a hooker waiting for her trick to leave after the sex part was done. Both men ate their meal in silence, and barely cast a glance at each other. Just when the silence seemed the most strained, a knock on the door made both men jump up in unison. Jeremy got to the door first. The Suisse armed guard stood there with a large canvas bag chained to his wrist. Jeremy asked him to come in. The guard handed over the bag, asked for a receipt and left.

"Is it all there? Is it all there?" asked Bolotin, jumping up and down like a child at his birthday party.

"If you will wait a minute and let me count it!" barked Jeremy at the over anxious Bolotin.

Jeremy went through the procedure and was satisfied with the amount. He turned around to hand the money to Bolotin, and to his amazement Bolotin was standing there with a gun in his hand. It was a SIG Sauer Model 226, 9mm. Miraculously, Bolotin had sobered up, and was now pointing the automatic at Jeremy's midsection. Jeremy could tell that this man knew how to handle firearms. His hands were steady, arms extended and slightly bent at the elbow, his feet spread eighteen inches apart and his arms extended shoulder high.

"Well, Mr. CIA man. What do you think about my plan now? Maybe, I think that $100,000 is not enough! You paid this amount without flinching. Maybe, you can come up with a lot more money? I want $500,000 more dollars brought to my room, or you will die!" screamed the now crazy Bolotin.

"I worked for fifteen years for the CIA, and they always gave me empty promises and very little money. Even my wife Karina has left me. I have nothing but memories. They made vacuous offers, and now I will collect on those promises. Now I am in control, and you will give me more money or you die!" screamed the now ranting Bolotin.

"I am not in the CIA. I, I…" Jeremy answered.

The crazed Bolotin would not hear any of it. "Once CIA, always CIA," insisted Bolotin. Jeremy knew that it would be impossible to deal with Bolotin in his current condition. He had to play for time, and stall. One question crossed his mind as he stared at the automatic. How did Bolotin get the gun?

"Bolotin, just calm down and point that thing in another direction. I am sure we can work this out. I don't have that kind of money to give you. What you got was everything I had. Let's talk about this," said Jeremy, hoping to subdue the fanatic Bolotin.

"Talk, talk, that is all you Americans do. I am through talking! You either make that phone call or I will kill you right now! I have nothing to lose. Do you understand?" replied Bolotin, slowly grabbing a pillow and placing it over the barrel of the automatic to act as a silencer.

Jeremy knew that he had to act fast, or he was a dead man.

"Okay, Bolotin you win. Now just put that thing down, will you? I will make your phone call," replied Jeremy as he slowly walked to the phone and turned away from Bolotin. He picked the receiver, and pretended to call his bank. His right index finger was inconspicuously placed over the receiver. Jeremy carried on a conversation with himself for about one minute, and hung up.

"Okay, you got your money. It will take them a little longer for that amount. They estimate it might take as long as four hours. You will just have to be patient. Would you like anything else to drink or eat? I can order it from room service," offered Jeremy patiently.

"Yes, sure thing, Mr. CIA man, you are paying for it. I am still hungry. I want a bottle of vodka, some caviar, a large steak and French fries; that last little sandwich you ordered was not enough. You can have anything you want," replied Bolotin, grinning and slowly lowering the gun.

Jeremy once again walked over to the phone and placed the order with room service. The whole time thinking of a way to catch Bolotin off-guard. Bolotin assumed an advantageous position in the corner of the room facing forward and kept Jeremy in full view the whole time. *This guy was a sly fox*, Jeremy thought to himself, *I will have to wait until the food arrives before making a move*. Time seemed to drag on forever. Bolotin just sat in the corner, unflinching and never letting his guard down.

The knock at the door seemed to spring both men into action. Bolotin tried to get to the door first, but once again Jeremy beat him to it. Jeremy opened the door and there stood the room service waiter with the food. The waiter walked in and set up the dinner on the table near the window. Jeremy tipped him and he left.

Just before Bolotin began to eat his meal, the phone rang. Both men stared at the instrument not knowing what to do. Jeremy responded first by saying that it might be someone from the bank. He picked up the receiver and said, "Hello? May I help you?

"It's me, Billy Bob. Can you talk?"

"Well, no I can't just now," replied Jeremy.

"Okay, just listen. I am the one who gave Bolotin the gun. He felt very insecure, and would not go through with the deal unless I gave it to him. I gave him the gun, but no bullets. It's empty! In case he tries anything, don't worry about it. Good luck, old pal!" Before Jeremy could answer, Bill had already hung up.

Bolotin must have known that his ruse had failed. He gave Jeremy a cold stare and asked.

"Who was that? What did they want?"

Jeremy just looked at him and smiled, thinking to himself all along, which side of his head am I going to hit first? He walked over to the table and stared down at him from above, his six-foot-five frame casting a shadow across the room. Bolotin raised the gun as if to fire, and Jeremy simply reached over and twisted it away from him. *Let's have some fun*, Jeremy thought.

"Well, Major Bolotin, look who is the boss now. I hold the gun and you are going to die!" growled Jeremy.

Before Bolotin could react, Jeremy was on top of him, the gun held tightly against his right temple.

"I will give you exactly three seconds to tell me where Kolkov is or you die! Tell me now!" screamed Jeremy at the now hapless Bolotin.

"Don't, don't, please. I beg of you, show mercy. Please, don't shoot," cried Bolotin, tears streaming down his face.

Jeremy looked down on this wretched human being, and pulled the trigger. The sound of the hammer hitting the firing pin was the loudest sound Bolotin had ever heard. He sat there cringing, waiting for the loud crash that would end his life, but it never came. Instead, Jeremy got up and smiled at him. He looked down on Bolotin and noticed a large wet spot slowly spreading across the carpet.

"You didn't really think that Bill would give you a loaded gun, did you? You poor stupid bastard. You had better tell me what I want to know, or else! I now control the situation, and you have to play by my rules," stated Jeremy with a mischievous grin on his face.

Bolotin started to get up, but Jeremy's right foot caught him square in the jaw. The blow was so powerful that four of Bolotin's teeth fell out of his mouth. He was spitting up blood and moaning.

"Don't even think of getting away. You and I have a lot of talking to do. Now, where is Kolkov?" continued Jeremy.

Bolotin sat there, blood oozing out of both sides of his cheeks. At first glance, thought Jeremy, he looks like a vampire, but this vampire won't be able to bite anyone for a while. Bolotin continued moaning and groaning, but was not yet talkative. Jeremy then decided to use harsher measures. He walked over to the window curtains, ripped the cords from the wall mountings and walked back to Bolotin. Bolotin's eyes were bulging out of their sockets in fear and anticipation.

"Major! Please believe me when I say I don't really enjoy this, but I learned from the best. When I was in Vietnam I was tortured by a little ghoul, and he was very good at it. Unless you want to learn everything he taught me, you had better tell me what I want. Now!"

stated Jeremy with emphasis in voice.

Major Bolotin just sat there, his chest heaving up and down, air escaping through his broken teeth. He suddenly lunged toward Jeremy, a double-edged boot knife held in his right hand like a sword. The knife caught Jeremy by surprise. Jeremy stepped into the blade, swinging his left forearm against Bolotin's right arm, and pushing the blade away from himself. Jeremy's right forearm delivered a crushing blow to the right shoulder joint area with such force that Jeremy felt Bolotin's bone crack and his shoulder muscle tear. The impact was so great that the shoulder was completely shattered.

Bolotin collapsed to the floor, animal-like groans coming out of his broken mouth, his right arm dangling uselessly at his side. He lay there for several minutes, his back heaving up and down. His entire meal and most of the alcohol came churning out of his stomach in one giant belch. Jeremy knew that Bolotin was a broken man, and would now talk. Jeremy also learned today that his broken ankle and leg had healed well enough to save his life, and that was comforting to him. Despite his many previous injuries, he was still able to handle himself. He had not forgotten any of his martial arts skills; however, he was a lot rustier than he remembered ever being.

Bolotin began talking; it was endless rabble about communism, capitalism and his missing wife. After a little prodding from Jeremy, he eventually came to the point, and told Jeremy everything he knew about Kolkov, the heroin and Dushanbe. It wasn't as much as Jeremy had expected, but it gave him a couple of clues. Kolkov was apparently still in prison in the Crimea, or so he thought. His savior, General Turkov, was faring no better; he was either still in prison or dead. After what seemed an hour or so, Bolotin ran out of things to talk about and crawled over to the couch and sat down in it. He begged Jeremy for the bottle of vodka, and when Jeremy handed it to him, Bolotin took two long swigs of it.

"What are you going to do with me, now? Are you going to kill me?" asked a still groggy Bolotin.

"That's up to you, major. I thought we had a deal, and you had to go ahead and spoil it. You are no longer a valuable asset, are you now?" replied Jeremy.

"I beg of you, please don't kill me. I promise not to talk. I..." answered Bolotin tearfully.

"Aw, quit your whining, major. I will not kill you, as long as you behave yourself, and don't try anything else until I leave. Is that understood?" replied Jeremy in a more serious voice.

Jeremy walked over to the chair where Bolotin was seated. He gathered up the window curtain cord, and tied Bolotin up like a steer at a rodeo. Bolotin began trembling, and sobbing again. He kept whispering." Please, please don't kill me." Jeremy went to the bathroom and retrieved a towel and he stuffed it in Bolotin's mouth. The sobbing stopped, but Bolotin still had that crazed look of a man about to die. Jeremy pulled up another chair and began talking to him quietly.

"Listen, and listen to me good. I made a deal with you. You kept your bargain, but you then got greedy. You must now pay the consequences of your actions," stated Jeremy with determination in his voice.

Bolotin's eyes rolled up backward, and Jeremy thought for a second that he had fainted. Jeremy slapped him hard across the face, and Bolotin's eyes focused again.

"I am going to leave you tied up for about five hours. I will leave word with the front desk to come up in exactly five hours to free you. That will give me plenty of time to make my escape. Three years ago, you would not be alive now! However, I guess I have gotten soft in my old age," stated Jeremy.

Bolotin could only grunt and nod his head in approval. Jeremy went about cleaning up any evidence of his presence. All of his prints were meticulously wiped clean, the room was straightened out as much as possible. To fool the local police, should Bolotin call them, Jeremy left a love note indicating a lover's spat between two homosexuals had taken place.

After half an hour of hard work Jeremy was ready to leave the room. He picked up the canvas bag and started to walk out the door. Bolotin's eyes got as big as billiard balls. Jeremy could sense his enemy's desperation and misery. Jeremy reached into the bag and pulled out three stacks of hundred dollar bills, thirty thousand dollars in all, and tossed it to Bolotin. Although Bolotin had been an asshole, he still deserved the reward for helping Jeremy with Kolkov. It might also cover his hospital bill, and make him less likely to talk to the local gendarmes.

Jeremy walked out of the room, closed the door and put the "DO NOT DISTURB" sign on the door. He used the back fire escape and hailed a taxi when he was at least one block away from the hotel. When he got to the airport he called the front desk and told them not to disturb him in room 412 until later that afternoon. Jeremy emphasized to the clerk to allow him at least five hours of rest.

The flight back to Paris was equally trouble free. He touched down at Orly Airport exactly on schedule. From the airport Jeremy took a cab back to the hotel. The afternoon traffic in Paris made the ride long and tedious. French drivers must hold the world's record for discourteous behavior. The driver turned around and asked Jeremy, "Monsieur, do you know of anyone that would be following you? There is a black BMW on our tail since the airport," stated the taxi driver with anxiety in his voice.

Jeremy turned around and carefully watched the traffic patterns behind him. About four cars back, a black BMW tried to maintain a discreet vigil. He was good, very good, but unfortunately for him, Paris afternoon traffic makes it very difficult for anyone to conduct a successful surveillance. Jeremy could not for the life of him figure out who would be watching him, and why.

"Driver!" shouted Jeremy, above the traffic din.

"Yes, monsieur. Can I be of service?" replied the taxi driver.

"What is the biggest tip you ever earned?" asked Jeremy.

"Well, I once drove a sheik around and he gave me 1000 francs, that's about $200 dollars. Why?" replied the driver, now feeling a little more confident. The word *tip* was a word that he understood in nineteen different languages,

"You see, the man in that BMW is the husband of my lover, and I don't want him to see me meeting her tonight. I will give you four hundred dollars, that's about 2000 francs, if you get away from him, and get me to the vicinity of La Gare du Nord," offered the resourceful Jeremy.

Love, and lovers, is one thing that the French understand. The taxi driver would have made Mario Andretti proud. The streets of Paris would never be the same again. He managed to get to the train station in less than thirty-seven minutes. Jeremy was sure he was not followed, and tipped the cabby accordingly. As the cab pulled away from the curb, he examined all avenues of approach and could not detect any surveillance, but just to make sure, Jeremy walked into the station, bought a French beret and some sunglasses from a street vendor. He looked around for the nearest men's room, saw the sign "***Hommes***" and an arrow pointing downstairs. He took his coat and tie off, reversed his sweater inside out, tucked his hair under the beret and looked at himself under the mirror. He had done a relatively good job, but his six-foot-five frame really towered above these Frenchmen. Just when he thought he would chance it, an ***Ancient Combattant*** (old veteran soldier) stumbled down the stairs. Jeremy reached over to help him, and was promptly cursed and spat upon by this old veteran.

"Oh, leave me alone. I can still piss by myself, I don't need any help from young people," cursed the old man, while shoving Jeremy's helping hand away.

Jeremy could tell that the old man had drunk more than he should. He propped his crutches on one wall, and hopped around on his one good leg trying to maintain his balance. It was a valiant effort, but most of the urine was being equally sprayed in all directions. He finally collapsed in the corner, and conceded defeat.

"Okay, young man. Please hold me up while I piss," stated the old man, extending his hand to Jeremy.

Jeremy reached down again, and pulled him up on one foot. Jeremy held him steady while the old veteran pissed like a racehorse. Jeremy had never seen anyone piss as long as the old man. After the old veteran was done, Jeremy bought his old gray coat, and one of his crutches. Jeremy was now properly disguised, and the old man was $500 richer. The use of the crutch made Jeremy five or six inches shorter, as he stooped down to reach the crutch. Jeremy now felt more comfortable leaving the station without being recognized.

When Jeremy emerged from the station, he blended in with the busy afternoon crowd crossing the street, and proceeded to walk to the street behind Avenue Magenta. Because of the simulated limp, the walk took longer than he expected. After fifteen minutes of agonizing walking, he found the back entrance that would lead him to his hotel. When Jeremy walked into the lobby, Colonel Perrin was still sitting at his favorite spot, smoking those foul-smelling Gitanes cigarettes, and reading *Paris Match.*

"Excuse me, monsieur, you cannot hang around my lobby unless," Colonel Perrin started to say to the man with the gray coat, crutch and beret.

"I am pleased with my disguise, Colonel Perrin. It's me, Jeremy!" he said taking off his beret, glasses and coat.

"But why are you doing this, Jeremy? Is there a problem? Did you find out anything in Switzerland?" replied Perrin, extending his hand in friendship.

Both men embraced, and Perrin looked at Jeremy for the longest time. He finally said, "Your father used to look just like that when he was worried. What is troubling you, Jeremy?"

Jeremy and the colonel sat at the bar, and talked for the next two hours. After their conversation, Perrin easily understood why the disguise was necessary for Jeremy. But both men could not figure out who that was in the black BMW. A process of elimination was used, and four possible choices came up: the Russian mob and or KGB, CIA, or local police. After a couple more drinks, the CIA and local police were eliminated from the quest. The other two possibilities brought back old memories and new worries for Jeremy.

"Oh, never mind, I am glad you are back, Jeremy. I may have some information for you after all. I spoke with some of my colleagues, who then spoke with some of their contacts, and we were able to verify some of the information you were seeking. The Russians are now saying that one of their helicopters did make a crash landing on that date and there was a survivor. A CPT Oleg Kolkov was his name, late of the SPETSNATZ, and now a convict in the Crimea. However, there was no mention of any heroin. My source was also very scared, and did not want to go into the subject matter any further," finished Colonel Perrin with a flair.

"Thank you very much, Colonel Perrin, I think things are

beginning to become clear. I think my time in Europe is slowly coming to an end. I will be returning home shortly, but I hope to keep in touch in case we have any new developments," replied Jeremy with a warm handshake and a hug, French style.

"Don't worry, Jeremy, I will keep tracking down that reporter, and I will get the information to you, as soon as possible. Keep in touch," stated Perrin, as Jeremy went back to his room.

Jeremy packed his clothes, and looked around the small hotel. It was not the most luxurious room in the world, but it had brought back many fond memories. Jeremy took out the keys, locked room 105 and opened room 106 for the last time. He looked inside hoping to rekindle one last moment with his father. Just as he was ready to leave, he glanced out the window, and there on the corner was the black BMW. Two men were standing next to it, looking up and down the street trying not to be conspicuous.

Damn, he thought, *how could they possibly have spotted me?* Or maybe they already knew his address. Someone had leaked some information, and he was not willing to wait around. He grabbed the phone and called Perrin.

"Come up quick! It's urgent," he said before Jeremy could put the phone down. A huffing and puffing Colonel Perrin was knocking at the door.

"Come in, and carefully look out the window toward the corner," instructed Jeremy to the colonel.

The colonel got down on one knee, and barely pulled back the curtain. He spotted the two thugs immediately.

"They are not French, that's for sure. By their stature, profile and mannerisms, I would say Russian. KGB or Mafia, just as we guessed. But how on earth did they find you so fast? And why would they be after you? Do you think that they perhaps followed Bolotin to Switzerland and he never picked up their tail? I am surprised your CIA buddy did not spot them, either. Okay, it does not matter now. Let's get you out of here for now and I will track down their registration number later.

"Sounds like a great idea, but how do we get rid of them for now?" asked Jeremy, inquiringly.

"Just watch my friend. Here in France we do not have so many laws restricting temporary arrest for suspicion reasons. I will call some friends at the Anti-terrorist Squad and these guys will disappear for a couple of days. It might also give me time to find out who they are. You just wait in the lobby, and you will see a show," stated Perrin with authority in his voice and demeanor.

Less than five minutes later, three dark-blue Citroen vans full of heavily armed French gendarmes came to a screeching halt in front of the BMW. One of the men tried to flee, but he was shot down on the spot when he pulled out an automatic. The other, more intelligent, slowly raised his hands and was taken away without a struggle. Colonel Perrin made one more phone call, and told Jeremy it was safe to leave now. They used the same back entrance, and their car quickly blended in with the traffic.

The ride to the airport was very quiet. Jeremy hoped for a new life back in America, and Perrin once again had felt the adrenaline rush of a warrior. It had been many years since Perrin had been actively involved in the intelligence community, and quite honestly, he missed it.

"Jeremy, I will keep in touch. As soon as I develop any leads on those two assholes, I will contact you. Do you know where you are going to be staying?" asked the inquisitive Colonel Perrin.

"No, not really, but I have a cousin in Los Angeles who is a deputy-sheriff, or I might stay with an old friend in northern California. I have not decided yet. I am also expecting a possible job in northern California. In either case, I will leave my cousin's phone number, and you can always get a hold of me somehow. I will make sure to call you periodically," replied Jeremy, shaking his hand once more and giving him the hug that all Frenchmen require.

Jeremy got out of the car, and turned around to wave good-bye. Colonel Perrin had already pulled away from the curb and was slowly blending in with traffic. *Strange*, Jeremy thought. *No, not really. Most Frenchmen do have some rather unusual social behavior, and Colonel Perrin was just expressing his.*

Jeremy needed some help with his luggage. An unusually friendly curbside attendant checked in his three bags, and verified his first-class reservation on Air France to Philadelphia. As Jeremy wandered through the halls at Roissy, Charles de Gaulle, he noticed the stringent airport security measures. It comforted him to know that the French were taking airport security and terrorism very seriously. He did not particularly want to end up blown up into a million pieces at the bottom of the North Atlantic. Less than an hour later, he was seated in the first-class section, thirty thousand feet in the air and on his way home.

Chapter 19

Back in the USSR (FSU)

Kolkov sat excitedly in his cell. For some unknown reason he had been segregated from the general prison populace and told to expect good news. Any good news coming from the monster guard Alexander, was dubious at best. The guard had made it a habit of picking on Kolkov and had made his life miserable.

The past three years had been hard on Kolkov. Prison conditions had been atrocious, yet he managed to survive. He had lost nearly twenty pounds, and in the process developed all kinds of intestinal ailments. His deal with General Turkov had gone up in smoke, and he was still stuck here. The only way he managed to stay alive was to strike a bargain with the local convict Mafia chieftain, Vladimir Kazmicha. Vladimir was considered a ***Pakhan*** (a leader, boss) in the Mafia hierarchy. The Pakhan normally controlled at least four other intermediary criminal cells run by a "Brigadier." The Pakhan would then employ two spies to watch the brigadiers. These spies would ensure that the brigadiers remained loyal and did not try to gain too much power. At the bottom of the pyramid were the enforcers. They carried out the rules, and made sure everyone followed the code. Although these structures were normally used for organizations outside of the prison system; they were also often used in prison. Kolkov was drawn into this spider web out of necessity.

The entire Russian organized crime system ran on a code of conduct, ***Vorovskoy Zakon*** (the thieves code). This code was strictly enforced, and violators were often executed. In prison, the rules were even harsher, and Kolkov often was tempted to tell Vladimir everything. However, Kolkov knew that his salvation depended on telling him only as much as he needed to. For over three years Vladimir and Kolkov played a dangerous game of chess. However, the loser would lose more than just the game. Kolkov had seen

Vladimir's power enforced ruthlessly to both inmates and guards. At the flick of an eye Vladimir could have someone executed. For the first time in his life, Kolkov was afraid of another human being.

Kolkov was apprehensive of Vladimir because he knew that Vladimir could always reach out and touch him, even in his cell. Prison guards were known to have carried out executions for the Mafia; no one was safe, and Kolkov knew it. Kolkov knew that his best course of action was to lie low and hope for a break. Well, it came in the form a presidential amnesty. When President Boris Yeltsin was elected, he proclaimed a general amnesty and decided to release as many political prisoners as possible. A long list of possible candidates was sent to the various penal institutions for review. However, most prisons assumed that this was the final edited list and released everyone on it, including Kolkov. Prison officials were not accustomed to operating under a democracy, and were still fearful of Big Brother.

Kolkov was given some clothes, a new identity card, a few rubles and a one-way train ticket back to Moscow. At the time of his release, Tajikistan was embroiled in a deadly tug of war with various factions within that region. Russian forces were trying to prop up the hard-line government (pro-Soviet) against various democratic forces. Islamic rebels, some based out of Afghanistan, were conducting cross border raids in the hopes of upsetting the power structure. Kolkov knew that his fortune was still relatively safe in Dushanbe, but he had to get there as soon as possible. Now was not the moment, however. He would first have to regain some capital and support. The only person who could possibly help him was his cousin Yuri. His cousin had always been on the fringes of lawlessness since their childhood, and could possibly offer a way to dispose of the heroin.

Kolkov boarded the train near the port city of Sebastopol. The journey home would take nearly five days of continuous monotonous travel. The vast Russian countryside unfolded before him, day after day. Late on the fifth day, the train pulled into the main Moscow station. Kolkov was glad, because he nearly had run out of money. Because of the late hour, it was not as full as it normally would be. Still, there was a certain amount of hustle and bustle. One thing

Kolkov noticed, right away, the dozens of kiosks. Late at night, still brightly lit, they peddled everything under the sun. He noticed right of way, a change in the appearance of most Muscovites. They wore more brightly colored clothes and appeared to have a reason for living. This was his first time home in nearly six years, and the changes were quite evident.

Kolkov had to get to his cousin's house as soon as possible. He was almost out of money, and he was very hungry. Yuri was his first cousin on his mother's side. As children, they had spent many years living together. Yuri's father had died in an industrial accident, and his mother had sent him to live with the Kolkovs. A large man by European standards, he stood nearly six-foot-two and weighed two hundred and twenty pounds. However, he was as solid as Rocky Balboa. Yuri always prided himself in his physique, and at one time had been a famous Russian athlete, specializing in track and field, and boxing. His boxing skills later earned him a job as a bouncer and enforcer for the mob.

As Kolkov walked down the narrow street toward Yuri's house, he pondered his cousin's fate. He had not seen Yuri since the last time he came home, for Kolkov's mother's funeral. Yuri had been there for him, and was very supportive at the time.

As Kolkov approached the street corner, he immediately noticed several large European sedans parked near the entrance to the large apartment complex. He thought to himself, some people have done well for themselves, haven't they? Such expensive European sedans were not common in this neighborhood. Kolkov approached the stairway, only to be stopped by a burly goon openly carrying an SKS assault rifle.

"Who are you, and what do you want?" asked the goon.

"Well, if it's any of your business, my name is Oleg V. Kolkov, cousin of Yuri Valenkov, and what is your name?" asked Oleg, pushing his right index finger up the guy's right nostril until he yelled uncle. The poor slob fell to the ground bleeding like a stuffed pig.

Oleg ran up the stairs before the goon could recover, and stood in front of Yuri's door. Before he could knock, it was opened violently and a pair of rough hands yanked him in.

"You are about to die, so you better tell me why you came here," spat out his cousin Yuri.

"Slow down, cousin, it's me Oleg, Oleg Kolkov," replied Oleg, slowly grabbing Yuri's strong wrists and pulling them off his chest.

"That can't be you, Oleg. You look so different. My God what has happened to you in the past six years?" Replied Yuri inquiringly.

"Well, it's a long story. Do you have any vodka? I'll tell you a story you won't believe," answered Oleg, as he was being ushered in the dining room.

Oleg and his cousin Yuri reminisced about their youth and the good old days. Oleg recounted his life story, and although Yuri was his cousin, Oleg left out the more incriminating details on how he obtained the drugs. Yuri was told the details about the drugs and the imprisonment, and his three years in the Crimea. However, Oleg still kept the exact location of the heroin secret. Cousin or no cousin, anyone would sell his soul for that kind of money. Yuri just sat there, shaking his head in amazement, disbelieving.

"You mean to tell me you have eight hundred kilos of heroin still waiting for you? My God, Oleg, you are a wealthy man! The question is, how are you going to collect it? And most importantly, how are you going to sell it in America!" replied Yuri, his voice rising emotionally.

"Why America? Is there no one else who can handle a shipment this large?"

"Dear Oleg, you have been in prison a long time, and you are not familiar with narcotics trafficking like I am. The United States is the only country capable of consuming that large a quantity, and still maintain the market in a relatively stable condition. Our associates in New York have established very strong ties with the Italian Mafia, and I am sure we can distribute this whole quantity," replied Yuri.

"I was hoping you would help, cousin. I would of course share some of the profits with you, if you could help me. It is obvious to me now that this sort of business is right up your alley. However, the political situation in Tajikistan is very unsettled at the moment, and someone with a lot of influence will have to step in and coordinate the whole affair," continued Volkov.

"Oleg, you casually mentioned that while in prison you formed an association with a ***Pakhan.*** Who is he, and what kind of deal did you make with him?" asked Yuri.

"It wasn't really a deal, it was an arrangement. I told him if he took care of me, I would take care of him later, when I got out," answered Oleg.

"My dearest cousin, how naive you are! Any agreement is cast in blood! Who is this man, and what is his name? Tell me!" demanded a now angry Yuri.

"Calm down, Yuri, I am sure I can get out of this situation. His name is Vladimir Kazmicha, but don't worry, he still is in prison and won't be out for years!" laughed Oleg.

"Vladimir, did you say? Vladimir Kazmicha?" screamed Yuri, the blood draining from his face.

"Yes, that is what I said! What is the problem? His sentence is due to expire in the year 2015! By then we won't have to worry about anything. Calm down, and tell me who he is," insist, a now impatient Oleg.

"Vladimir! Oleg, of all people to make friends with! He is known as Vladimir the Vampire. He is the most ruthless barbarian in the system! 2015! Hell, I had dinner with him last night! He was one of those presidential pardons guys, and unlike you, he flew home three days ago. I was one of his brigadiers while he was in prison. I work for him, you fool!" screamed Yuri, desperation in his voice.

The news hit Oleg like a ton of bricks. This was not good, definitely not good at all! How could he have gotten himself in such deep shit, so soon. *Damn! What I can do?*, he thought. *Maybe I can con him, or maybe Yuri can help?* As Jeremy was pondering his dilemma, his cousin Yuri sat in the corner, his eyes closed, deep in thought.

"Oleg. Maybe I can help. I have a plan, a good plan. I have been running Vladimir's organization for the past seven years while he sat in prison, and I am pretty good at it. If that drunken fool Yeltsin had not let him out of prison, I would still be boss. Being boss is better than being a brigadier. Maybe we can solve this problem after all," grinned Yuri, as he reached for the phone.

"Hello, this is Yuri. Tell the boss that my cousin Oleg will also be here tomorrow night for dinner. Oleg is an old friend of Vladimir's from prison. Tell him I have a special surprise for him, very good news," laughed Yuri as he hung up the telephone.

"Cousin, I have just saved your life, and at the same time I will allow you to perform you first repayment for my kindness," replied Yuri, a gleam shining in his eye,

Yuri went on to explain that Vladimir and his three other brigadiers would come over for dinner tomorrow. While they were having dinner, Oleg would go down and plant a bomb in the car. When the car was at least a mile away it would detonate and Yuri would be the "new boss." Oleg would no longer have anything to fear, and Yuri would only ask for a small 50% commission, of course. Oleg was a little shocked at the 50% commission, but he didn't have much of a choice. It was still a whole lot of money, and he could comfortably retire on some deserted island.

"How do you expect me to make and place a bomb on such short notice?" asked Oleg inquiringly.

"Very easy, my friend. I have all the ingredients right here, and my goon downstairs is quite the explosive expert. You'll pretend to go downstairs and relieve the driver for dinner, plant the bomb, and the rest is history. On second thought, the goon will help you plant the second bomb in the bodyguard vehicle," stated Yuri, with uncontrolled enthusiasm.

"It's not really a very good idea to detonate two bombs right in front of your house, is it now?" replied Oleg, skepticism in his voice.

"No, you fool! Remote control, we only use remote control. We had a meeting in Rome six months ago, and our Italian colleagues sold us a crate of state-of-the-art electronic detonators. We wait until they pull away and are a kilometer or so away, and then *boom, boom,*" answered Yuri, clapping his hands like a kid at a birthday party.

"That part sounds easy enough. However, do you think you have the power to control the rest of your gangsters? After all, aren't these guys loyal to the death? I really didn't come this far to end up in some gang shoot-out in Moscow," replied Oleg, still skeptical.

"Why don't you leave the worrying to me. I promise you

everything will be fine. When you have this kind of money, miracles happen. This is a minor problem compared to trying to get the drugs out of Tajikistan. However, I think I may have a solution for that as well. There is a certain general who commands the Russian forces in that region who might be willing to exchange a favor for a favor. In the past, he sold me large quantities of arms and ammunition. Maybe we can work something out between us. One quick question, Oleg. How are the drugs packed? Are they in satchels, boxes, how?" asked Yuri.

"No, they are packed in two-kilo bundles, and then twenty-five to the larger package, wrapped in bulletproof nylon, and clear coated with three sheets of plastic, and finally wrapped in canvas bags which are stitched together with nylon string. Pretty secure, huh?" replied Oleg, pleased with his answer.

"Good, very good. However, let's take care of one problem at a time, okay cousin?" stated Yuri, a big smile spreading across his scarred face.

"I am sorry, Yuri. I can't help myself. This is all I have been thinking about for the past forty-two months. I can't let anything go wrong now! We have too much to lose. I am glad you think you have solved the problem about recovering the drugs. But what about getting it to America? That sounds more complicated, doesn't it?" answered Oleg, hoping for an equally positive answer.

"Well, maybe yes and maybe no. We now have a lot more resources in America. Our contacts are very good, and don't forget the Italian Mafia. They have agreed in the past to work with us, and they already have an established distribution network. The hardest part is going to be getting such a large quantity in the country, safely of course. Once it's in, no problem! I promise you, we will have success. Our organization has contacts in Anchorage, Alaska; Seattle, Portland, Sacramento, San Francisco, Los Angeles and San Diego. We even have some connections in Tijuana and Juarez, Mexico. Some of these organizations were ex-KGB men who suddenly realized there was more money to be made in criminal enterprises. What better crooks than those who oppressed us all those years!" finished Yuri, finally running out of air.

"I guess all those years in Afghanistan, and in prison really put me behind. I had no clue as to what was really going on. I just found out that the Ukraine is an independent and sovereign country. Things really have changed! I really don't care about anything or anyone anymore. All I want is my money and a chance to spend it. Do what needs to be done, and let me know how I can help. Is there anywhere I can sleep? I am really tired and I need some rest," stated Oleg.

"Of course, my cousin. I am sorry. Just go out into the hallway and pick any of those apartments. They are all empty now. I convinced the tenants to sublease them to me. They are all fully equipped with sheets, pillows, clothes, food and vodka. Help yourself, and sleep well," stated Yuri, waving his hand majestically toward the hallway.

Oleg began to realize that his scheme might work; after all Yuri certainly had come a long way, from a two-bit street thug to a soon-to-be drug lord. Oleg reflected back on his childhood with Yuri, and was astounded at the transformation. Yuri had been a quiet and studious child, often afraid of his shadow. Now Oleg was a gregarious, often charming bully who could, on occasion, be a cold-hearted killer.

"Yuri, thank you for your hospitality. I will be seeing you tomorrow morning," Oleg stated as he walked out the door.

Oleg looked down the deserted hallway, and was unsure which apartment to occupy. He wandered up and down for a few minutes, until he decided on number D12, which was the nearest one to the stairway. Although Oleg felt relatively safe in his cousin's environment, his years of training forced him to take precautions.

Oleg entered apartment D12. He stood in the doorway and looked into the dining room/living room/kitchen area. This apartment had similar dimensions to the one Yuri had, except that it also had a large balcony facing the street. Oleg looked around and found some sheets, a pillow and some blankets in a cupboard, and was soon in a deep sleep.

Oleg's first night in a non-cell environment was a restless and anxious one. He kept having horrible nightmares the entire night. He practically relived his entire Afghanistan campaign, and every single horrible murder he committed. One face after another appeared at the foot of the bed, as if to taunt him, each one horribly mutilated and decomposing. He kept waking up in horror, expecting them to be at the foot of the bed. One episode got so bad, and his screams so loud, that Yuri and the bodyguard came running in the apartment, weapons drawn. Oleg sheepishly explained the situation, and Yuri went back to his room. A few minutes later, Yuri returned with a large bottle of vodka and some hot tea. He told Oleg to mix them in equal amounts, and drink as much as he could. Oleg was amazed how three large cups of sweet tea, mixed with vodka, allowed him to sleep for eight straight hours.

Oleg awoke the next morning rested, but with a major headache. It had been a long time since Oleg had consumed so much alcohol, real alcohol that is. On several occasions, while in prison, he had tried some homemade "pruno" that made him terribly ill. After those experiences, he abstained from alcohol, until yesterday and this morning.

Oleg decided that a hot shower might cure his hangover. He searched and found the small bathroom and took a long shower. Oleg was amazed that it actually had hot water, and everything functioned as it should. *Yuri really must be a big shot*, Oleg thought to himself. After cleaning up for the first time in years, Oleg felt like a new man and wandered over to Yuri's apartment.

The goon, Gregori was his name, was hard at work putting the finishing touches on two almost identical bombs. Each bomb consisted of ten kilos of Soviet issue military explosive ordnance, made in Czechoslovakia. PLASTEX was its commercial name and it was twice as strong as Plastique or C-4. Oleg watched him for over twenty minutes and could not detect any flaws or mistakes. However, he could not help thinking, this much explosive detonating in a confined space, such as the apartment, would probably blow up the entire floor, and Oleg was glad that the goon was apparently very adept. Oleg admired professionalism, and Gregori knew what he was doing. The caps, electronics and transmission device were equally well assembled and installed. The actual electronic detonator appeared to be constructed from a TV channel changer and other components. Oleg asked Gregori a simple question. "Hey, what would happen if someone in a nearby building had a similar channel changer and pressed it?"

"Don't worry, I have set up a series of channel numbers that must be pressed in sequence before it can detonate, a sort of combination. Nothing can go wrong! By the way, your cousin has asked that you just hang around until he returns. He is trying to organize something special and he hopes to have some good news for you later on," replied Gregori, without even cracking a smile.

"That is great news. Have you got anything to eat? I am starving," Oleg said in return.

"Sure do. Look in the 'fridge.' We have just about anything you'll ever want. Remember, Vladimir is coming this evening, and we must make sure that they are well fed before we kill them," replied Gregori, smiling for the first time.

Oleg walked over to the 'fridge' and opened it. Oleg had never in his life seen such delicacies: every imaginable sliced cold cut known to man, several salads, caviar, potatoes, cold chicken, sausages, pickles, beers, wines, vodkas and desserts. Oleg was overwhelmed by it all. He had never seen this much food in his entire life. He grabbed a large plate and heaped it full of everything in the fridge. He also grabbed two European import beers and sat down in front of the large-screen television. Oleg proceeded to gorge himself over the next two hours. He knew that eating this much food prior to a mission was not a good idea, but he just could not help himself. Oleg had never known such luxury, and he was beginning to like it very much. He leaned back and dreamed of what he could do with his share of the millions. His thoughts drifted off to a Pacific island, white sand beaches and beautiful naked island girls. Just when the dream was getting to a climatic moment, a deep voice woke him out of his slumber.

"Oleg, Oleg! Wake up, wake up. I have some people here I want you to meet," said Yuri to the sleeping Oleg.

Oleg awoke with a start. In front of him stood several naval officers. Oleg's eyes were not quite focused yet, but he did recognize the rank of vice admiral of the fleet, one captain and one lieutenant. Oleg jumped up, as if to salute, as years of training had him accustomed to doing so, but he controlled himself. Instead, he acknowledged their presence with a simple nod of the head. He looked over to Yuri and indicated that he would like to talk to him alone.

"What is going on, Yuri? Please don't ever do this again. I don't like surprises. What are these 'squids' doing here? I thought our meeting tonight was with Vladimir and the boys?" stated a somewhat confused Oleg.

"Don't fret, my cousin. While you were having nightmares, I was thinking of a plan to ship our goods to the United States. I came to the conclusion that perhaps the best way to ship our 'goods' is on a ship! I have a very dear friend in the Navy, and I thought Admiral Zurkov might help. I went over to see him this morning, and by God, does he have a plan! I am sure you will like it very much!" replied Yuri, a big smile on his face.

"Do you think it wise to tell everyone about the heroin? I hope you are being very discreet, my cousin. After all, 'Loose lips, sink ships.' And we still have the small problem of recovering my heroin from a war-torn nation!" stated Oleg, with a frown on his face.

"You do mean, our heroin, don't you, Oleg?" answered back, an un-smiling Yuri.

"Yes, of course, it was a slip of the tongue. I am sorry, Yuri, it won't happen again," replied a smiling Oleg.

"I hope so, because cousin or no cousin, no one double-crosses me!" retorted Yuri with emphasis, his index finger poking Oleg in the chest.

Oleg did not like anyone poking his chest, let alone his cousin. However, he realized this was neither the time nor the place for a showdown. Oleg soon began to understand the Mafia mentality, and realized that Yuri must always 'maintain face' in front of his colleagues, especially when Yuri was making such a strong power play. Both men stared at each other for a second, and after a long pause gave each other a big hug. That seemed to end the tension for now.

"Okay, Yuri, tell me about this great idea. I am dying to hear it. Well, not really dying, but you know what I mean. Ha, ha! That's funny!" answered Oleg, slapping himself on the leg.

Yuri asked Admiral Zurkov to come over and join them and explain this "wonderful" plan. It would be a lot easier that way.

"Admiral please, take a seat and let me offer you some vodka. Now please elaborate on this idea you have," asked Yuri, extending a chair to the vice admiral. The other two officers sat down next to him and did not utter a word.

"A few months ago we conducted the first joint naval exercise with the United States Navy since the end of World War II. The exercise was called '***Cooperation From The Sea '94***' and it was held in Vladivostok, Russia. This particular exercise tested the joint disaster relief cooperation between our nations. This exercise was the first of many such exercises that will be held between the Russian Federation Navy and the United States in the years to come. Next year, in less than eight months as a matter of fact, we are holding '***Cooperation From The Sea '95***' in Pearl Harbor, Hawaii." Admiral Zurkov took a pause and looked over at both Yuri and Oleg.

"Any questions, gentlemen? If not, I will proceed," said Zurkov, proud of himself.

"***Cooperation from the Sea '95*** will be the first time Russian warships will have visited Pearl Harbor since 1907. As you can well imagine, there will be many arrival ceremonies, officer receptions, social functions and celebrations. Guess who will be the commanding Russian Federation Navy Admiral? Yes, you guessed it. Me!" finished Zurkov with a flair.

Both Yuri and Oleg saw the tremendous possibilities. They asked Zurkov many pertinent questions and got immediate and promising answers. However, there was one question that Oleg wanted to ask, but was not sure he should ask the admiral or Yuri.

"What happens to the merchandise, once it leaves Vladivostok? Who will guard it until it arrives in Hawaii? What happens after that? I will never allow myself to be separated from it again. I must see to it that it arrives safely," stated Oleg with emphasis.

"I agree, Admiral Zurkov. We must ensure that someone accompanies the shipment to its final destination, the mainland of America. After that, we can negotiate with our colleagues to handle the rest," chimed in Yuri.

"I really don't see a big problem, gentlemen. I am sure CPT Kolkov can speak English well enough. I will make sure that he has the appropriate documents showing him to be a civilian employee of the Naval Department, and he can accompany it to the USA. As far as the mainland is concerned, there will also be a sister city exchange program between representatives of Vladivostok and San Diego, California. Our fleet is scheduled to make several port of call visits to the West Coast of the United States," finished the admiral with gusto.

"Well, it seems to me, gentlemen, that I should go to sleep more often. You have just about everything worked out, except the actual delivery of the drugs to our contacts," replied Oleg.

"I have a possible solution to this problem. This is why I brought these two other officers with me, Captain Chetskiy and Lieutenant Nikolayev. They are both weapons officers aboard my vessels, and they have come up with an excellent idea. How about if I let Captain Chetskiy tell you, gentlemen," stated Zurkov.

"Thank you, Admiral Zurkov. The problem seems to be how to get a large quantity of heroin into the United States without drawing too much attention. Is that correct?" "That's correct Captain." answered Yuri.

"I have, on several occasions, been in the United States, and I know for a fact that U.S. Naval Intelligence, the CIA, FBI, U.S. Customs Service and U.S. Coast Guard all keep our ship and personnel under close surveillance. Why don't we ask them to off-load, let say a new type of 'Top Secret' ship-to-ship/ship-to-shore missile. Why don't we call it H-800 of the SS-N-12 type of missiles, for example. We can also pretend that for a price, we will turn it over to them and at the same time ask for asylum. After all, we still have our 'friend' in the CIA, and I am sure he will arrange the necessary introduction, for a fee of course.

"We could pretend to have been on the wrong side during the coup attempt, and seek political/refugee status. The Americans are so kind-hearted and liberal, especially now that Clinton is in the White House," paused Captain Chetskiy, as he took a large drink of vodka.

"They would agree to just about anything to make a goodwill gesture. As a show of good faith we will sell them the missile for three million dollars. In actuality, we will completely strip one of our SS-N-12 missiles, paint it a different color and fill the interior with the contraband. Lieutenant Nikolayev or I will be responsible for watching over the cargo until it arrives in the U.S.A. Your man, CPT Kolkov or yourself Yuri, could then make the arrangements for the actual off-loading with the CIA. Our friend could ensure that everything is setup ahead of time," finished captain Chetskiy with a grandiose gesture.

"I like your idea, captain. However, it might be difficult to convince the Americans to go for it. After all, our stupid politicians are pushing ***Perostroika***. Maybe their politicians are just as stupid. To show you how far things have gone, former President Gorbachov has an office in San Francisco, and gets paid $100,000 per year as a consultant. Can you believe that?" replied Yuri.

"I think you are wrong, cousin. I have a lot more experience than you in intelligence matters, and this is exactly the type of plot that the CIA would go for. They have been severely burned in the past few years, and they would eagerly go for this deal, if it were properly presented. They could claim a giant coup, and make their arch rival, the FBI, look bad. Let me develop this point with some of our contacts in California and let's see how far it goes. As you know, many of our Russian Mafia friends are, in fact, ex-KGB or current agents with the necessary contacts. We will let it leak through them, and let them tease the CIA. Our friend will ensure the necessary connections. We do have time, after all, and we must recover the drugs, before we can even proceed," stated Oleg with authority in his voice.

"Let's see how far we are in another thirty days. We will then decide what to do. Let's make a firm plan based on those assumptions, and correct them later if we have to. Gentlemen, I thank you for coming, and I will see you in thirty days," finished Yuri, as he was handing each of the naval officers a large envelope stuffed with 100-dollar bills.

Yuri escorted the officers downstairs, and returned a few minutes later. He was very relaxed for a man who was about to make the biggest move of his gangster career. He checked with Gregori, and confirmed that the bombs were completed and properly secreted downstairs for quick access. Both Yuri and Oleg went over the plan, and agreed on the series of events which would lead to the eventual destruction of Vladimir the Vampire and the rest of the goons. Oleg was incredulous at the speed and proficiency that Yuri achieved in resolving difficult and complex operations. Had Yuri been a military officer, he would have surely been a general by now, reflected Oleg. Oleg looked at Yuri and said, "They seem pretty competent. However, do you trust them? How can you be so sure of them?" asked an inquiring Oleg.

"Dear cousin, you have been behind bars for so long that you don't really know the 'New Russia.' Anything and everyone can be bought for cash, cold American dollars, Deutsche Mark, etc. We are now a capitalist country, and these poor slobs can be bought for a few thousand dollars. I promised them a bonus of $300,000 if everything succeeded. I know I can trust Admiral Zurkov. We were the ones who worked out the deal to sell that surplus Typhoon class submarine last year. It was bought by an enterprising Australian businessman and it now sits in Sidney Harbor as a tourist attraction," answered Yuri with a smile.

"A submarine you say? A whole damn submarine?" replied an incredulous Oleg.

"You heard right! A whole submarine for a mere two hundred thousand dollars. To make it even worse, they allowed him to pay on credit, $20,000 a month. If that isn't capitalism I don't know what is!" answered Yuri, feeling very proud of himself.

"You mean that our own government doesn't care?" asked Oleg, still not quite believing the story.

"Not only did they not care, but they participated in it and got a cut through the KGB," stated Yuri.

"In a way, I am glad I was in prison. I don't think I would survived the transition," answered Oleg as he walked away shaking his head in disbelief.

"Enough of this chit-chat. Let's go over once again the details for our dinner," ordered Yuri.

Both men sat down, and for the third time that day, reviewed their plan of attack. After a twenty-minute session, everything was checked and double-checked. All that was needed now was the victims. After agreeing that nothing more could be done, both Oleg and Yuri watched porno movies on the large-screen television and drank vodka. Oleg was still amazed at the freedom and wealth that was exhibited by some Russians under the new capitalist system. Oleg was so engrossed in the movie that he did not even notice Yuri get up and answer the door.

"Welcome, Vladimir, welcome. Please, gentlemen, come in, and have a seat. Vladimir, I am sure there is no need to introduce my cousin Oleg," stated Yuri, extending his arm in an inviting manner.

Vladimir glanced in Oleg's direction and walked over, his right arm extended in the form of a handshake.

"Greetings number 773298, Oleg Kolkov," said Vladimir in a very formal and cold voice.

"How are you? I see you also were on the pardon list. I am glad you are out of prison," replied Oleg, shaking Vladimir's hand in the process. Oleg looked at the other men and nodded his head.

"Your cousin Yuri is a trusted and good brigadier. He tells me you are willing to cut me in on an enormous profit that you already promised me in prison. Is that correct?" asked Vladimir inquiringly.

"Yes, that is correct. If you will allow me I will explain to you in detail exactly what our plan is, and I hope it meets with your approval," finished Oleg.

"Good, let's sit down and eat and drink," said Vladimir.

Vladimir and the rest of his mob sat down at the table. Yuri and Gregori did their best to keep the plates and glasses filled. Oleg observed the whole show from the corner, and quietly went downstairs to relieve the other drivers. He instructed them to go upstairs and help themselves to food and drink. One of the drivers was reluctant to do so, and Oleg had to tell him it was an order from Vladimir before he would leave his vehicle. Oleg quietly and expertly placed both bombs in the trunks, near the fuel tank. He then stood by as the obstinate guard came running out and yelled at him, "Why did you tell me Vladimir ordered me upstairs? You knew that wasn't true!" yelled the highly agitated driver.

"Calm down, calm own. It must be a misunderstanding. I will go speak to Vladimir, just calm down," replied Oleg, not wanting to irritate the driver.

Oleg knew if he showed his face now, it might lead to complications. The best thing he could do was to sneak into another apartment and wait for the whole thing to calm down. Oleg quietly climbed the stairs to the fourth floor, and entered apartment D15, at the end of the hallway. He closed the door, and waited patiently for the dinner to end. Almost two hours later, Oleg heard a commotion in the hallway. He cautiously opened the door and peaked outside. Vladimir and his men were going apartment to apartment looking for him. *Oh boy*, he thought, *this is not very good.* Just when things looked like they were going to get ugly, Yuri yelled down the hallway, "I sent Oleg on an errand and he probably won't be back for several hours."

That bit of information seemed to calm Vladimir down, and he temporarily stopped his search. He returned to Yuri's apartment and asked him why hadn't he been informed of this earlier? He instructed Yuri to have Oleg report to him first thing in the morning, or else. Vladimir and the rest of the thugs bid farewell and departed. Oleg observed them getting into their cars and hurried over to Yuri's apartment.

"Boy, that was close. The second driver almost caught me in the act of placing the bombs, and I had to make up a story. I simply told him that Vladimir had ordered him to come upstairs," stated Oleg excitedly as he entered the apartment.

"Don't worry. Watch this!" answered Yuri, leaning out the front window and pressing the detonator.

Both of Vladimir's cars had just come to an intersection and halted for a red light. They were approximately one thousand meters away from Yuri, when the explosion rocked "The Avenue of the Red Banner". The avenue was a long and wide street, and could normally accommodate at least eight lanes of traffic, but suddenly it disappeared into a storm of fire and hell. The avenue was divided by a broad swath of grass; it was also suddenly turned into a blazing field of holocaust and death. When the bombs detonated, every window within a quarter-mile shattered, and a deep rumbling could be felt and heard all the way up the fourth-floor apartment. Car and human remnants were hurled hundreds of yards from the scene.

Gregori approached the scene, and cautiously videotaped the carnage for posterity. He was very proud of his work, and kept a gruesome video library of his handiwork. Gregori managed to talk to a passing policeman and confirmed that there were no survivors. In addition to the eight occupants, eleven civilians had also been killed, and many more wounded. Both Oleg and Yuri looked out their window in silence and observed the carnage. Oleg was the first to speak.

"It was them or us, and I like the 'them' much better than the us. I hope we can now move on with our lives," stated Oleg, in a somber mood.

"You are right, my cousin. The future is ours and we have but to take it. Part one is accomplished; we have to worry about the other parts now, namely the drugs and the trip to America," replied Yuri, in a less somber mood.

Both men sat down at the table and poured each other a healthy shot of vodka. They drank in silence and toasted each other. The next several weeks were spent in reorganizing, enforcing and establishing territory within the Mafia hierarchy. Yuri's power play was accepted well enough by most other leaders; however, many of them had a hard time dealing with Oleg. They did not like the fact that he had served in the military; nor that he had been sent to prison for treason and mayhem. Even among thieves, they had a code and they did not like Oleg. Yuri's power and influence were able to smooth over most rough spots. Once his empire had been established and consolidated, Yuri and Oleg went about organizing the retrieval of the heroin.

Chapter 20

Back in the USA

Jeremy departed Roissy, Charles de Gaulle airport, at 1700 hours. His Air France flight would land at Philadelphia's international airport in about eight hours. The solitude in the first-class section afforded him the opportunity to reflect and plan his future. Although he had initially thought about retiring from all intelligence activity, the opportunity to work again excited him. He knew that because of his injuries he would have to be a desk jockey, but that didn't seem to bother him anymore. Jeremy had finally found peace within himself and looked forward to returning to San Francisco. The town that had challenged him emotionally so many times in the past was now beckoning to again.

At Jeremy's request, Billy Bob and other CIA associates had arranged for him a great new job within the United States Custom Service, Division of Law Enforcement in San Francisco. He would be given the title of senior intelligence analyst and would be directly responsible to the director of intelligence. Billy Bob had chosen the U.S. Customs Service, at Jeremy's request, and because he knew that Jeremy had expressed a strong dislike for continued service with the CIA, and had always regarded the Customs Service with high esteem.

After a few days visiting his relatives in Virginia, he would once again head out to California. His visit home was a terrible disappointment. Since the death of his father, his mother had turned more and more to the bottle for comfort. He tried on several occasions to have a dialog with her about her problem, but she refused to acknowledge it and told him she was only a social drinker, and that he should mind his own business. The situation seemed to escalate day by day. There wasn't a day that passed by that his mother didn't collapse or fall down in front of him. Jeremy felt totally hopeless and angry that he was unable to do anything about it.

One day she passed out and struck her head on the coffee table. She hit her head so hard that she received a severe concussion and had to be hospitalized for several weeks. Jeremy took the opportunity to extricate himself from the delicate situation and left his mother's home. He was sure that his sisters could cope with his mother and seek professional assistance for her. He was rather disappointed by the whole affair, but somehow could sympathize with her. She had dedicated her entire life to her husband, and now she felt desperately lost and lonely.

His arrival in San Francisco was filled with mixed emotions. On one hand he was overjoyed at the prospect of starting a new job in an exciting city; on the other hand, he was terrified at the prospects of being alone in a city without friends, acquaintances or lovers. Jeremy decided to let fate take its course and he had hope for the best. After all, he was still a handsome man, in the prime of his life. The slight limp and the occasional use of a cane shouldn't prevent him from finding friends.

The immediate challenge was to find a place to live in and around San Francisco. The prices for residential apartments in the city center ran as high as three thousand dollars a month. Jeremy was unwilling to pay these astronomical prices, and he also felt it was not a very good security risk to work and live so close together. Although his career at the agency was now over, he still had certain security concerns and would have to be careful for the rest of his life. The Bay Area had a large ethnic population, and had in recent times become a hotbed of Russian Organized Crime (ROC).

Due to these and other factors, he decided to find a home on the outskirts. He at once thought of his old friend Gilbert, who ran the motel near Travis AFB. He could stay there as a temporary lodging, until he found something more appropriate. On the first day back, he drove to the motel near Travis AFB. He hardly recognized the area. In the past twenty-seven years or so, the entire area had changed drastically. New homes, businesses and construction had dramatically changed the landscape, but the old motel was still there.

Jeremy pulled in to the driveway marked "guest parking". The motel had not changed at all, except it had recently received a new coat of paint. Jeremy walked into the lobby and immediately noticed all of the airplane pictures and photos of Colonel Brigdon were still hanging on the wall. *Great!* He thought, *the old guy is still alive, and maybe we can party again.* At least he felt reassured at the fact that he knew someone.

Jeremy rang the bell, and an attractive sixty-something woman came out of the rear office.

"Can I help you?" she asked in a sultry kind of way.

"Well, I hope so. I once stayed here about twenty-seven years ago, and I got to know the owner pretty well, a Colonel Gilbert Braxton. Is he around?" asked Jeremy.

"I wish he was," answered the woman.

"I am Suzanna, his wife. Gilbert passed away just a few months ago and I do miss him terribly," replied Suzanna, a small tear appearing in the corner of her right eye.

Jeremy felt awkward and did not know what to say or do. He looked at her for a few seconds and reached out and hugged her. Suzanna let out a loud sob, and began crying, her chest heaving as convulsions wracked her body. Jeremy was at a loss. He just held her silently. After a few minutes, she stopped crying and pulled away from him.

"Thanks. I needed that. I am sorry I had to soil your shirt with my mascara, but I haven't really cried since Gil died," answered Suzanna, pulling away from Jeremy and wiping her eyes with a handkerchief.

"Did you know Gil? Was he a friend of yours? You seem pretty young to have been in the same unit. Where did you meet?" rattled on Suzanna, without giving Jeremy a chance to reply.

"Yes, ma'am, I did know him, but only very shortly. We met sometime in 1968 or 1969, and I kept in touch by sending him postcards from all over the world. My name is Jeremy Grant," replied Jeremy.

"Yes, of course you are. He told me all about you, and your girlfriend who went to Vietnam and never came back. Yes, I think you two developed quite a friendship over the years. I married him shortly after you left the area. I am terribly sorry that he died before seeing you again. What are you doing in the area? I hope you will have time to spend a few days here before you move on," stated Suzanna.

"Well, as a matter of fact I was looking for temporary lodging, until I can buy a home or find something nearby. Do you have anything available?" asked Jeremy.

"Of course I do! As a matter of fact, I have just the thing for you. It's a two-room suite, with a small kitchen area, microwave and a large TV, HBO of course. How does that sound, Jeremy?" replied Suzanna.

"Perfect! I can move in today, if you don't mind? I came with only two suitcases, and I'll buy things as I need them," answered Jeremy, extending his hand.

"Of course you can, and as you are such a good friend of Gilbert's, I will let you have it at 1968 prices! $110.00 a week! How does that sound?" answered Suzanna, a warm smile spreading across her face.

"You don't have to do that. I can pay whatever the going rate is. Please, don't lose any money over me," replied Jeremy, imploring her to take his offer.

"Look Jeremy, Colonel Braxton was a stubborn man, and by God so am I. $110.00 or I won't rent it to you. Understood?" replied Suzanna, her voice rising.

"Well, because you are so generous, I wonder if I could ask one more favor?" asked Jeremy, raising his right eyebrow.

"I don't know if your husband knew what kind of work I was involved in or not. Sometimes things can get very dangerous, and for security reasons, I may have to occasionally leave the area or use a different name. Do you understand?" asked Jeremy, emphasizing the **NAME** part.

She nodded her head, then raised her hand and pointed her finger at him.

"Only if you accept my reduced rates. That is my final offer!" replied Suzanna, a big grin spreading across her face. She knew she had won, and wanted him to know it.

Jeremy looked at her, and decided it was quite impossible to change her mind. He thought he might make it up to her by doing something special for her later on. He finally gave in, and extended his hand in defeat. He registered under the name of Beau DeFaut, and did not list any car in the registration form. Jeremy felt it would make it more difficult for anyone to track him down this way.

Jeremy next project was to go and recover his precious red Mustang convertible. Prior to leaving Virginia, he had it shipped via Amtrak to Oakland, California. The little red beauty was waiting for him at the Amtrak office in Oakland. His beautiful little car had been sitting in a secure storage garage for the past twenty some odd years, and was in excellent condition. He arranged with the rental car company to have someone pick up his rental car, and he drove the little red Mustang home.

Jeremy had an eerie sensation driving the same car, along the same route, to the same motel. It brought back a variety of lost feelings and emotions. He once again could almost sense her presence, smell her delicate magnolia-like perfume. He was so enthralled in this thought that he nearly collided with a car in front of him. No matter how hard he tried, he couldn't get Loretta out of his mind. He thought about the possibility of trying to track her down, but the fear of knowing what had become of her, scared him, and he put the thoughts temporarily out of his mind.

The haunting thoughts of Loretta and their wonderful love continued to obsessively disturb him. Not knowing what to do, he impulsively got in his car and drove back to San Francisco. Maybe if I drive around, I will see her, he thought. Hs little red car seemed to instinctively drive him back to the Presidio of San Francisco.

The exterior appearance had not changed much, he thought. However, he did notice the lack of military personnel. He drove to what used to be the 'O' Club, only to notice a large steel chain blocking the entrance. He finally spotted a mounted police officer, and stopped to ask him what was going on. It was only then that Jeremy realized that the Presidio was in the process of being converted to a national park. His treasured memories of this location were now a distant and almost forgotten memory of his past.

Chapter 21

New Job

Jeremy was not expected to report to his new assignment for another week or so, but he was so anxious to get started that he decided to show up a week early, and hope they could accommodate him. Not knowing what the traffic would be like at that time of the morning, Jeremy got up at 04:00 and left his motel at 04:45. Traffic was pretty light at that time of the morning. It was only forty miles to his office, and he arrived there at 05:55 hours. His office was situated at the old Customs House, 555 S. Battery Street, in the heart of the financial district. The building was a grayish stone monolith of some four or five stories, built around the turn of the century. It had the distinction of being one of the few buildings that survived the 1906 earthquake. His office was situated on the second floor, west side.

As his office was the "Regional" Intelligence Center, it was not so indicated on the door. It said only, U.S. Customs, San Francisco, California. Jeremy knocked, and a voice answered, "Come in." Jeremy entered the room, and could not immediately see the person who had said come in. He once again said, "Hello." A head peeked around the corner, and greeted him. Jeremy stared at the bearded man, and for a moment did not recognize him, but he suddenly looked in the man's eyes, and he immediately recognized CPT Justin Neal Brown, his helicopter pilot savior from Vietnam.

"I can't believe it; I just can't believe it!" stated Jeremy, too shocked to say anything else.

"You can't believe it? I was thrown for a loop when I was told that I would be getting an ex-CIA agent to work for me. When I saw your name, I was just incredibly overjoyed. I hope you are as happy as I am. This is a great place to work at, and by a small coincidence, it used to be the main office of the CIA in San Francisco. As a matter of fact, that vault over there used to be their 'clean room'." replied Neal

Brown, pointing to a large metal safe door on the north side of the room.

Jeremy's office was situated in the west side of the building and had a magnificent view of the Immigration and Naturalization Service building right across the street. The view obscured the entire block. His office was situated next to Neal's office and next to the secretary's office, Pearl's. It was still early, and no one else had arrived yet. Neal called him to his office and started to familiarize Jeremy with the staff and the organization. There would be three other analysts, and they would report directly to Jeremy. Additionally, there would be two analysts working in conjunction with, but reporting to another Customs Enforcement, supervisor.

Neal and Jeremy spoke about old times and reminisced about Vietnam, the Presidio and life in general. It was at this time that Neal outlined Jeremy's new duties and explained to him some of the current trends in narcotics smuggling in the general bay area. Neal was particularly interested in tracking and controlling any possible leads leading to the arrest and conviction of ROC criminals. They were currently targeted by the powers to be in Washington as the next criminal organization to watch for on the West Coast. Neal was familiar with Jeremy's background and was convinced that Jeremy's former Russian experience, and fluency in the language would lead to some positive results.

Neal went about organizing his office, and began developing ideas and concepts. He had some ideas, but he wanted to wait for the rest of his staff to arrive, before he could really develop them properly into a cohesive and organized concept. The first to come in was Pearl Johnson; she came in around 07:30. Pearl was a rather large, rotund middle-aged black woman. She wore bright and garish clothes, and also wore some expensive looking Nike Air tennis shoes, an odd contrast, Jeremy thought. One of her remarkable features was an incredible smile, and a set of the most beautiful teeth Jeremy had ever seen.

"Hey, you must be Jeremy," stated Pearl, extending her hand to Jeremy.

"Yes, that's right, and you of course must be the 'beautiful' Pearl, I have heard so much about," replied Jeremy.

"I know I am going to like you, Jeremy. Just keep giving me compliments, and you and I will be friends forever," replied Pearl, with a smile.

Slowly, one by one, the rest of the staff arrived and became acquainted with Jeremy. Everyone seemed very friendly and professional. Jeremy was surprised to learn that one of his analysts was an active duty Army Warrant Officer, on a special counter-drug program. He was apparently brought to active duty from an Army National Guard Intelligence unit, and had specialized in counter-intelligence. He had a very interesting background, extensive law enforcement experience, and had over ten years experience as a cop.

His other staff members were equally interesting. Pattie Wong was a lovely twenty-five-year-old Chinese-American. She was trained as a special agent, but had been assigned to the intelligence unit for the past eighteen months. She specialized in heroin trafficking, Nigerian and Chinese gangs. The third member of the crew was a highly motivated former U.S. Marine, Alexander Madrid Santiago. Alex was a twenty-five year veteran of the Customs Service. He knew everything there was to know about smuggling, and the Customs Service. *What a diverse, yet qualified crew,* Jeremy thought. I am sure I will be able to meet the job goals, and perhaps even exceed them. After briefly reviewing their backgrounds, he called for a meeting.

"Hi, I would like to officially introduce myself. I am sure some of you are curious as to why I was appointed to this position," he said, introducing himself to all.

Jeremy briefly went over his background, leaving out his direct connection to the "company", but hinting at a classified government job. All of them understood his mysterious background, and accepted the fact that he did not officially want to talk about it. Despite his retirement he still had certain oaths and security requirements that had to be met. Each member of his team introduced him/herself and gave him a brief outline. It was at this time that he conveyed Neal's new requirements and asked them to concentrate as many sources as possible on the Russians.

"Well, if it's Russians you want, Russians you'll get," replied Alexander.

"There are several law enforcement agencies in both Northern and Southern California that have banded together for the purpose of exchanging information about criminal gangs. There is a monthly meeting, held in Sacramento. If you want to learn the 'ins and outs' of ROC, that would be the place to go," stated Alexander with a matter-of-fact voice.

"Great that's exactly the kind of stuff I am looking for. If any of you would like to go to this meeting with me, let me know. I intend to attend as many as possible, and I hope you will do the same, answered Jeremy.

"You might also want to contact the Western States Information Network, AKA WSIN, also in Sacramento for information on narcotics. They are a government-financed, state-run agency which specializes in analytical work. They have some of the greatest analysts in the business, and they possess some of the most current analytical computer software in law enforcement. As a matter of fact, they are having their annual conference in a few weeks, and I understand that one of their guest speakers is a Russian General with the new MVD. He apparently is the head of the Organized Crime Task Force for the eastern part of Russia. It might be worthwhile for you to contact the supervising manager and introduce yourself," offered Pattie Wong.

"Wow! This is great stuff. I never realized that local law enforcement had so much information concerning ROC and other gangs. I am really excited, and I hope that we all succeed. Let's get to work," encouraged Jeremy.

Jeremy and his staff established a positive and successful routine for the next few weeks. Jeremy fell into a routine that he liked and he was comfortable with his environment. He had remained at the motel, simply because it was quite convenient, and because of his flexible work schedule he always avoided the peak rush hours. It was during this period that his cousin from Southern California called him.

"Hey Jeremy, it's me, Jason Munger. What's up old buddy? The reason I am calling you is that some French guy called, and was trying to contact you. Not knowing who he was, I didn't give him your phone number. However, I did promise I would call you right away and give you the message. His name is Colonel Perrin, and he asked me to emphasize *'**tres important**,'* if you know what I mean!" stated his cousin Jason.

"Great! I am so glad you called, and thanks for the info. By the way, can you give me some information about ROC?" asked Jeremy in return.

"Well, I'll see what I can do. However, you know that's not my specialty. I'll call some of the guys in the Intelligence Unit and ask them to contact you directly. Take care of yourself, and I'll be seeing you soon," said Jason, before Jeremy could reply.

Jeremy hoped that Colonel Perrin had some positive information for him. Jeremy had been so busy for the past few weeks that he had neglected to contact his old buddy in Paris. He immediately got on the phone, and called the colonel.

"Hello! Hello! It's me, Jeremy. How are you? Thank you for your phone call to my cousin Jason. I understand you have some information for me," Jeremy stated to his friend in Paris.

Over the next twenty minutes Colonel Perrin recounted an interesting story of murder, espionage, terrorism and smuggling. "Jeremy, apparently the two men who were spying on you in Paris were ex-KGB men who have formed close associations with the ROC and had been hired by them to follow you. Unfortunately, the second man was 'shot trying to escape," stated Colonel Perrin.

Jeremy understood the subtle hint from Perrin. The French authorities had a reputation for toughness when interrogating terrorists. These two individuals were enforcers for some of the local gangsters and had a very nasty reputation. Jeremy listened silently and thanked the colonel for his assistance. He asked the Colonel one more favor.

"Would you please ask your contacts in Switzerland if Bolotin ever left their country, and what has happened to him since?" asked Jeremy.

"Of course, my friend. Give me your direct number, and I will call you back in a few days," replied Colonel Perrin as he hung up the phone.

Jeremy reflected on the new information and hoped that perhaps his new focus on ROC might assist him in tracking down Kolkov and the stolen heroin. Despite the many miles and years, there wasn't a day that went by that he didn't remember the horror that had occurred in Afghanistan. Moreover, San Francisco's cold and damp weather continually reminded him of his injured legs, and he could never overlook the pain and suffering of those hideous moments.

Jeremy began planning a strategy that might assist him in fulfilling his quest. He took every opportunity to get his name in the papers. He attended every press conference; offered his testimony as an expert witness and was as visible as a Hollywood starlet. He hoped that perhaps he could somehow entice the Russians rats out of hiding if he offered a large enough piece of cheese: himself. As a matter of fact, he was so visible that his boss chided him for the unwanted publicity. Jeremy sat down with Neal Brown and briefly explained his past history and current scheme for recovering the heroin, and coaxing the rats out of hiding. Neal's only comment was, "Be careful, and keep me informed."

Jeremy took Neal's advice and sought help from agencies that specialized in ROC, and enlisted their cooperation in tracking known ROC members in the greater Sacramento/San Francisco area. Jeremy was carefully developing a trap for the rats. Jeremy visited both the FBI and DOJ's WSIN on several occasions, and participated in some of their monthly intelligence meetings. These monthly meetings proved to be informative and he was able to learn that a Sacramento-based family of the Russian Organized Crime (ROC) family might have connections to other ROC families in Brighton Beach New York; Portland, Oregon, Seattle, Washington, Anchorage, Alaska, and of course, in Europe, including Paris, France. What he found particularly interesting was their connection to the Italian mob in New York and Nevada. Many of his intelligence sources were strictly open sources and a lot of the information had not been verified yet. Jeremy was sure that he could get a handle on all of this current intelligence and somehow put it in a working format.

The Russians had apparently found democracy to be a wide open system filled with opportunities, and freely dealt with just about every known gang. They had already established direct connections to the Black Street gangs, both Crips and Bloods, Hell's Angels, Italians, Colombians, Mexicans and others. Apparently, seventy-five years of communism had hardened them to just about anything, and they were tough enough to take on every known organization. On one of his visits to Sacramento, Jeremy asked the FBI to print out a computer-generated listing of every known Russian criminal or his associates in the greater Northern California area. He was hoping to perhaps scare a rat out of hiding. He also requested the INS to do a similar computer report of all pending and current visa applications for the past twelve months. He hoped to cross-check the applications with the names of the known ROC members and associates in California.

Jeremy and his staff continued to develop new and interesting facts about the ROC. Jeremy met on several occasions with members of the FBI, CIA, Coast Guard and Naval Intelligence. The results of these meetings produced several interesting developments. One of the most fascinating one was the fact that many of these so-called ROC gangsters showed similar characteristics to trained KGB agents. Their 'modus operandi' (MO) was right out of a textbook. It was surmised that many of these gangsters had once been in the employ of Mother Russia, and were now in the employ of the mob, or both. Of course all of these theories had yet to be proven.

Chapter 22

The Trap

Meanwhile in Sacramento, several members of the Varmessy crime family had been called for an important secret emergency meeting. The pressure being put on by the FBI, DOJ and now U.S. Customs was finally having an effect on their operations. Several of their members had been detained, harassed or had observed possible surveillance by the law enforcement community. Varmessy and his three generals had to be sure that all members were aware of the existing crisis, and expected them to act accordingly. No one could be trusted, and they were instructed to watch for hidden microphones and video surveillance.

On a Thursday evening, somewhere in the northeastern part of the city, a half-dozen or more cars pulled in and parked at various locations around a well-known restaurant parlor. The location had been carefully checked for microphones by a trained professional. All of the men, except two who stood guard, entered by the rear exit door.

Everyone entered the large room and stood around until a tall brutish-looking man called the meeting to order. He looked around the large round table, and began to count heads, sounding off names.

"One, two, three, four! This is ridiculous! Is everyone here? Are you sure you were not followed?" growled Viktor Varmessy, the crime family leader, to the assembled mass of ROC members.

"As you know, I called you together for this extraordinary session. We have a grave and dangerous situation developing. There has been a lot of unwanted publicity in the past few weeks, and our names have been mentioned more than once in various newspapers and magazines.

I have warned all of you on numerous occasions to be as discreet and low key as possible. Yet some of you have decided to ignore me and create unwanted attention! Not only that, there is a U.S. Customs official making headlines about the threat of Russian Organized Crime in America. We must always be discreet and take care of our problems internally. I want someone to learn everything there is to learn about this Customs official and report back to me, as soon as possible. I am warning all of you! Do this discreetly, and report back to me. Is that understood? Any questions? Good. Get started and report back to me as soon as possible."

One by one the gathered gangsters nodded their heads and left the restaurant through the same back door. Finally, the next-to-last member hesitated and turned around toward Varmessy and spoke.

"Excuse me, Mr. Varmessy I, I, I…" stuttered the short, bald and stocky individual.

"Get on with it; I don't have all day. What is it?" asked the obviously irritated Varmessy.

"That man, the one in the newspaper article. He looks vaguely familiar. I am not one hundred percent sure, but he looks like a man I once dealt with, a man who owes me a lot of money" finished the bald-headed man with a smirk on his face.

"So you think you know this man? Okay! Go and tail him and find out what he is involved in. Report directly back to me! Is that understood?" replied Varmessy with emphasis, his right forefinger poking the man in the chest.

"I understand, sir. I will start immediately," replied the man, as he walked out the door.

Bolotin could not believe his luck. Right here in Sacramento, a headline on the front page of the *Sacramento Bee.* "**Customs Officer Warns of Renewed Russian Threat!**" Right there was a photo of the man who had humiliated him in Switzerland, and not paid him the agreed-upon sum of money! "I will get my revenge! I will get even!" swore, a still angry and agitated Bolotin! Bolotin did not want to reveal everything he knew about Jeremy. He wanted to keep an ace in the hole, just in case he needed it. He would tell his boss just as much as he needed to know.

Bolotin had somehow managed, under the liberal immigration policies, to get a visa and move to Sacramento with his cousin. His cousin was one of Varmessy's generals and it was easy for his cousin Radnik to vouch for Bolotin. Bolotin's intelligence background had helped him to assist Varmessy in establishing one of the most respected crime families on the West Coast. Unaware of his secret past, everyone working for Varmessy, highly respected Bolotin.

Meanwhile Jeremy and his staff continued their relentless pursuit of information. Jeremy was slowly building quite a dossier on all known ROC members in Northern California, and particularly the greater Sacramento valley. For some unknown reason, Sacramento had become a hub for Russian immigration, especially Russian mobsters. Based on the evidence that he had, Jeremy asked WSIN to officially open a case and provide analytical support. WSIN assigned an analyst who began tracking, collating and analyzing pertinent bits of information concerning the ROC drug activities in Northern California, and in particular, the Varmessy family. One thing became very evident, the ROC was actively involved in drug dealing, smuggling and distribution, as well as a myriad other illegal activities which included: murder, narcotics trafficking, robbery, tax evasion, conspiracy, car theft, welfare fraud, racketeering, etc.

Jeremy continued his daily routine commuting between Fairfield and San Francisco. He felt so comfortable with Suzanna and her wonderful service that he did not even contemplate seeking another form of accommodation. Her warm hospitality and courteous manners lulled him into a false sense of security. Jeremy's many years of combat and intelligence work had been slowly dulled by the routine of a semi-normal and monotonous life. He did not expect anyone to locate him at his home.

Bolotin and his men knew the location of most law-enforcement agency buildings and had routinely staked them out. Based on the information provided by the local papers, he knew that Jeremy and his staff worked on Battery Street, in downtown San Francisco. It was an easy enough task to watch that location and track everyone who went in and out. Although Jeremy had a "Reserved" parking space, he still had to enter and depart through the main door. Bolotin and two of his colleagues watched him depart one afternoon.

Due to heavy traffic that day, Jeremy was forced to use the one readily available freeway ramp to Highway-80 eastbound, the Oakland Bay Bridge. Jeremy merged with the eastbound traffic and was unable to monitor the two cars that were alternately tailing and leading him through traffic.

After a miserable ninety minutes stuck on the bridge near the Oakland exit, traffic lightened up, and Jeremy was able to push his little convertible up to thirty-forty miles an hour. Traffic was still extremely heavy, but at least he was making some progress. Bolotin and his buddies had no trouble following him all the way to Fairfield. Jeremy took the North Texas exit and immediately pulled into the motel. His room was at the south end of the parking lot. Jeremy drove his car around the motel looking for a parking spot. Apparently, everything was occupied that night. When he couldn't find a parking spot near his room, he pulled up to the "Guest Parking" spot in front of the main office. Bolotin and friends were caught by surprise. They had seen Jeremy go in, but he never came out. They waited in their car for over two hours; when nothing happened, Bolotin decided to go and inquire about a room, and at the same time look for Jeremy. He approached the front door and knocked loudly three times. After thirty seconds or so, Suzanna came out of her apartment and pointed to the "No Vacancy" sign on the door.

"Can't you read the damn sign?" she mumbled under her breath.

"Please, it's very urgent. My car broke down, and I need some help!" replied Bolotin, in an excited manner, his partners stealthily hiding behind Jeremy's car.

"Okay, okay! I'll be right there. Hold your horses!" answered Suzanna, her voice showing signs of agitation.

Suzanna saw only Bolotin standing in front of the door. She was unable to see the other two men hiding behind the car. She unlocked the door, and all three came rushing in at her.

"What, what do you want?" she asked, her voice showing a hint of fear.

"Shut up, lady, and you won't get hurt!" blurted Bolotin, as he deftly swung behind her, and put his arm around her throat.

Suzanna immediately felt the strength of the man, as he held his arm tightly around her throat. Suzanna attempted to struggle, but he began to squeeze tighter and tighter. Suzanna felt herself go limp and blacked out. The other men came up to Bolotin and told him to stop.

They had not gotten the information yet and it would be foolish to kill her. Bolotin let go of Suzanna, and she fell to the ground like a wet noodle, her body curling up in a natural fetal position.

"You fool," screamed one of the men.

"Oh, don't worry, she is not dead. Had I wanted to kill her, I would have done so! She is only temporarily unconscious. She will come to any moment now," replied a highly agitated Bolotin.

Right on cue, Suzanna shook her head from side to side, and tried to get up. Her mind was willing, but her legs were still a little wobbly. Bolotin grabbed her by the hair, and dragged her to the large easy chair in the living room. Before Suzanna could react, Bolotin was already strapping her down to the chair with a large roll of duct tape. Bolotin yelled at the two other men to watch the entrances.

"What do you want? I will give you all the cash I have," Suzanna blurted out, her voice now very low and husky.

"Shut up, lady! When I want you to talk, I will let you know!" replied Bolotin as he stuffed a handkerchief in her mouth and bound her mouth with duct tape.

Bolotin and one other man searched the office and living quarters. The third goon watched the exits. Bolotin soon found out why Jeremy had given them the slip. There was another exit to the office area, and it came out on the west side of the motel. From this location anyone could either go to his room or leave the motel unobserved.

"Lady! Where is the man who came in here two hours ago! The tall one. Where is he?" screamed Bolotin at the still tied up Suzanna.

"Mumble, mummbllee," replied Diana, her mouth still taped and gagged.

"Oh, excuse me! You wanted to say something?" replied Bolotin, as he cut the tape around her mouth with his stiletto-sharp boot knife. He removed the handkerchief from her mouth, allowing her to speak.

"Just who in the hell do you think you are!" screamed an irate Suzanna.

"You sons of bitches can't just come into my motel and start bossing me around! What man are you talking about? My motel has been full since noon, and I haven't had a guest check in since then. I have over eighty guests staying here, and I can't remember all of them," answered Suzanna, hoping to fool the men.

"Look grandma, we saw the tall man come in. Jeremy is his name. Just give me his room number and you won't get hurt," shot back a now angry Bolotin.

"There is no Jeremy checked into my motel," replied Suzanna, now realizing that these men were not simple robbers, but were looking for Jeremy. She would never tell them what they wanted; her mind was made up.

"Oh, we don't need you, grandma! We will just check the register." Bolotin grabbed the register and thoroughly checked the entire book. Bolotin screamed at Suzanna, "No Jeremy Grant, anywhere!"

"Of course not! I don't have anyone by that name here," answered a now defiant and pissed-off Suzanna.

"Okay, what was the name of the man? The tall man, who came in here about two hours ago! Tell me, or you won't like the consequences!" screamed a furious Bolotin.

"I don't know who you are talking about. Many of my guests use my back door. I quite often don't know who comes in and out," answered a now desperate Suzanna, hoping that Bolotin would believe her lies.

"Maybe she is telling the truth," replied one of the thugs as he stared at Bolotin.

"Bullshit! She is not telling the truth! I will make her talk!" yelled a now deranged Bolotin in Russian to his colleagues.

"Russians! What would you want with this Mr. Jeremy anyway?" asked Suzanna, finally realizing what language these men were talking.

Bolotin walked over to Suzanna and leaned over her as if to say something to her. Before Bolotin could react, Suzanna used her one free leg to kick him as hard as she possibly could in the groin. Suzanna had done a good job, because Bolotin collapsed to the ground without uttering a single sound. He just lay there writhing in pain. He rolled from side to side for a couple of minutes and finally stood up. He stared at Suzanna for a few seconds, as if trying to make up his mind what he would do to her. Quick as a cat, Bolotin leaped upon Suzanna with a fury and frenzy. He punched her several times in the face with his huge fists. The first blow alone was enough to send her chair spinning backward. He reached up and grabbed her hair and brought her back to a sitting position. Suzanna's ears were still ringing from the punch. Before she could say or do anything, Bolotin lunged at her and stabbed her in the throat with his knife.

"Die, you bitch. I don't need you anymore!" screamed, a mad and insane Bolotin.

The other two men were shocked at his actions, but dared not say anything. Bolotin slowly pulled out the knife and then with one swift motion, cut her throat from ear to ear. Suzanna's blood squirted out from her wounds, and ran down her white blouse. The blood soon covered the entire chair and nearby floor, her bare feet squirming around in her own blood. Within twenty seconds she had bled to death, and now lay there pale, gray, and gaunt, her eyes still wide open in shock and horror. A once cheerful and vivacious woman now lay dead, still guarding the name of "her" Jeremy.

"Why did you do this? She can't talk now! You fool! Varmessy will be very angry. It will draw unnecessary attention to our cause!" stated the taller of the two goons.

"You dare question my actions? You will watch your mouth, or perhaps you might wish to join her?" answered a now angry Bolotin.

"No, not all. I only meant we should be careful, and not raise unnecessary suspicion, that's all," answered the tall goon.

"Okay then. Both of you shut up, and follow orders. Let's make this look like a robbery. Knock things over, open drawers and be sure to wipe your fingerprints from everything you touch. We can then go and park up the road, near the gas station, and observe most of the rooms. I am sure we will be able to spot our target when he comes out of his room during the commotion," ordered Bolotin.

All three men drove up to the nearby Shell station which looked down upon the motel. They climbed out of their car and went across the street behind the theater. About a hundred yards away stood a pyramid-shaped hill with a bunch of microwave dishes and antennas. Bolotin and his thugs broke the lock on the fence and climbed to the top of the hill. From this vantage point, they could clearly observe about seventy-five percent of the motel, and one hundred percent of the road. Bolotin picked up his cell phone and called 911 to report the crime.

Within a few minutes, several city, sheriff's and CHP officers pulled up to the scene. An ambulance was called, but Bolotin knew it would be in vain. Bolotin and his two goons had parked their cars on a small knoll behind the Shell gas station and had a direct view of most of the parking lot. However, what they didn't know was that Jeremy was no longer in the motel. Jeremy had gone up to his room, taken a quick shower and had been picked up by Neal Brown for dinner. Neal's vehicle was a large Chevy GMC Suburban with dark tinted windows. While Bolotin and the boys were watching the front of the motel, Jeremy had unknowingly evaded their observation by going out the back door.

Neal lived right down the road in the small farming community of Dixon. The town of Dixon has been a small sleepy agricultural town for over a hundred years. The skyrocketing home prices in the bay area, had made it an ideal community for first-time home buyers, or for folks who wanted to avoid the overpriced homes in the bay area, and the ever-rising crime rates in city neighborhoods.

Neal's home was a well landscaped lot with a two story, five-bedroom modern house. Jeremy could tell by the pristine condition of the home that Neal's wife was certainly a dedicated homemaker. Jeremy walked in and was greeted by Neal's wife, Sally. She was a statuesque blonde with an attractive figure, and a great smile. Jeremy and the Browns spent a pleasant evening discussing family and school problems, none of which particularly interested Jeremy, but somehow attracted him to this suburban way of life. As he got in his car for the short drive back to his motel, he once again felt strong nostalgic feelings about Loretta. He wondered what his life would be like if he was married and had a family.

The evening being still young, he decided to go see a movie. He drove a few miles westbound on Highway 80 and took the Vacaville exit. Jeremy had not been to a movie in years. He pulled into the Vision 8 Cinema, and watched two movies. By the time the second film finished it was well past midnight. Jeremy drove up to his motel, only to find the whole area cordoned off by the cops. By this time Bolotin and the goons had given up and returned to Sacramento.

Jeremy got out of his car, showed his credentials and asked what happened.

"Well, sir, we don't really know. It appears to be a robbery-homicide. If you want anymore information you'll have to ask the homicide detective over there," answered the police officer, pointing to a rather rotund man.

Jeremy walked over to the man, who was rather busy giving instructions to the coroner, other officers, and at the same time trying to keep the press at bay.

"Excuse me. My name is Jeremy Grant and I live here," Jeremy said, as he produced his credentials.

The heavy-set man stopped what he was doing and looked at Jeremy. He brushed everyone off and started walking toward Jeremy.

"You live here? Isn't that kind of unusual? Do you mean part-time, or do you consider this your permanent abode?" asked the detective.

"Hi, let me introduce myself. I am Sergeant Victorio Lopez-Sanchez, Homicide Unit," stated the detective, extending his right hand toward Jeremy.

Jeremy looked at the detective, and firmly shook his hand. Jeremy stood a good eight inches taller than the sergeant, but the detective's grip was just as strong. Both men stared at each other for a few seconds, and the detective slowly released his grip. Jeremy looked down on the man, and had to smile. What just transpired reminded him of two fighting gamecocks who had just met and were trying to establish their territory.

"Well, Mr. Grant. You live here?" asked the detective, once again.

"Yeah. That's right. I already explained the situation to you. What's the problem? Has anyone been hurt?" asked Jeremy, his voice rising.

"Well, as a matter of fact, yes. The owner, a Mrs. Suzanna Brigdon, was murdered tonight," replied the detective.

Jeremy's heart skipped a beat. He stood very still and took a deep breath. His eyes got very small and he stared at the detective.

"Did you say, Suzanna Brigdon?" asked Jeremy, knowing the answer.

"Yes. I am sorry. Did you know her well?" asked the sergeant.

"As well as anyone can, after living here for the past several months. She was like a mother to me. It was very convenient for me to live here. Eventually, I probably would have gotten a house elsewhere, but I felt comfortable here," answered Jeremy, his voice trailing off.

"Well, I see. Do you know of anyone who might want to harm her?" asked the sergeant.

"Why do you ask? One of your men said it was probably a robbery-homicide. Why anyone would want to harm such a sweet old lady is beyond belief!" replied Jeremy, somewhat surprised by the question.

"Someone tried very hard to make it look like a robbery, but it doesn't fit the mold. She was already dead when the furniture was tipped over. All of her blood is underneath the furniture, none on top or on the furniture. She was first murdered, then they tipped the furniture over," replied Sergeant Lopez-Sanchez with a satisfied look on his face.

"That is a pretty clever deduction, detective. But that would mean that someone took the time to plan the entire murder. What were they after? Money? No, I don't think so. She never kept more than a couple hundred dollars in her cash drawer. Do you mind if I look at the crime scene, Sergeant Lopez-Sanchez?" asked a determined Jeremy.

Both men exchanged glances, and the detective nodded his head in acquiescence. Detective Lopez-Sanchez led the way past the yellow tape into the office. Her body had been removed, but Jeremy could see the large pool of dried blood around the chair. It was almost as if someone had stood on top of the chair and quietly poured all her blood on the carpet below. The scene was too contrived, too artificial. Jeremy shuddered in horror when he thought of poor Suzanna sitting there, bleeding to death.

"You are right, sergeant, she was murdered first and then someone went around tipping over furniture. I have seen a lot of dead people in my life, and this looks to be phony. I just don't understand why anyone would harm this sweet old lady," replied Jeremy as he walked closer to the scene.

"Sergeant! Look at this!" Jeremy exclaimed.

Jeremy squatted down on his haunches and carefully looked at the patterns left by Diana's naked feet. When first examined, they appeared to be the impressions left by someone in the process of struggling and thrashing about. However, upon careful examination, a semblance of letters appeared to come to the forefront.

"Sergeant Lopez-Sanchez, come and take a look at this! What do you make of it? Could it be that she was trying to leave us a message? Have you taken photos?" asked Jeremy, as he carefully examined the dried blood.

"Would you look at this! She was trying to tell us something," screamed Jeremy as he pointed to the blood.

"It looks like the letters R U S…! What does R U S mean?" asked a now inquisitive detective.

Jeremy froze in his tracks. Could it be that Diana was trying to tell him RUSSIANS? Yes, Suzanna was a very intelligent woman. It was her last dying attempt at trying to protect him. She apparently used her big toe to scribble the letters R U S before she bled to death.

"Detective, I know what that means! Russians! Damned Russians!" explained Jeremy to a skeptical detective.

"Russians! Why Russians?" asked Lopez-Sanchez, as Jeremy had now gotten his attention.

Jeremy went on to explain some of his historical background, and his current assignment. The detective was still not one hundred percent convinced, but it was the only clue they had. Both men agreed to follow the lead and keep each other informed.

Jeremy knew if the Russians had taken such a radical step, they would stop at nothing to get at him. He even surmised that they might still be watching the motel. Jeremy explained his concerns to Sergeant Lopez-Sanchez, and a plot was contrived to get Jeremy out of their direct line of sight. A police officer of similar stature was brought into the crime scene. He entered the office wearing his field jacket and duty hat. Once inside, he gave Jeremy the jacket and hat. Jeremy went out the back entrance and entered one of the police units. Even if the Russians were watching the front office, they would never be able to see him get away.

Jeremy had the officer drive him back to San Francisco, where he called Neal Brown and explained the situation to him. Neal was obviously very concerned, and recommended that Jeremy go to one of their "safe houses." These apartments had been especially prepared for such occasions, and he could comfortably stay in one of these units for months. The rat had now bitten the cheese, but the question was how best to trap these guys.

The "safe house" was, in fact, a luxurious apartment right in the middle of the financial district in San Francisco. It was elegantly furnished and had all the comforts of home, plus some extras. All windows were bulletproof; all doors were also bullet- and pick-proof. It had an emergency fire escape, and a sophisticated video-surveillance system which monitored the parking lot, the main entrance and all the hallways. Additionally, the porter, bellman and several other building employees were San Francisco police officers. Jeremy felt as secure as he could under the circumstances. He would ride out the storm here, for the time being, and attempt to collar them at the appropriate moment.

Chapter 23

Recovery

Back in Russia, Oleg and his cousin Yuri had taken the time to plan and organize the recovery of the heroin. Every detail had been carefully worked out, and all the expected bribes had been paid out to government officials, at least they hoped so. "**Cooperation From The Sea '95**" was less than a month away and it was imperative that they recover the heroin as soon as possible.

Getting down there would not be a problem. Getting out and getting the heroin to Sevastopol would be difficult, however. The ongoing conflict in Tajikistan was still a cauldron of rebel activity. The existing government had been removed by force (pro-Soviet), and the rebels were trying to regain control. It made for a difficult situation.

Yuri and Oleg were convinced that their "special forces" would cope with any situation. Yuri had organized a force of about twenty ex-SPETSNAZ and military officers. These men were picked because of their training, ruthlessness and loyalty to Yuri. Oleg was given the task of organizing the training, and maintaining discipline. Each man was paid $1,500.00 dollars a week, plus a bonus of $20,000.00 upon successful completion of the mission. These huge amounts of American dollars ensured loyalty, temporarily anyway. At the current exchange rate of approximately 7,000 rubles per dollar, they were earning more than the president of Russia!

Local intelligence information had shown that the silos were still taboo and off-limits to the local populace. It also indicated that no one had entered the area since the withdrawal of the missiles years earlier. Unfortunately, intelligence also showed that a small Soviet radar unit had set up camp nearby. According to the best estimates, they were within one thousand meters of the silos, and would obviously have to be eliminated. Contingency plans were made for the destruction of this unit.

"Oleg, how many could possibly run this radar station?" asked Yuri, inquisitively.

"Well, that's a difficult question to answer. At the most six to ten men per shift. Probably only four or five. I am sure we won't have any problems. We have sufficient firepower to wipe out an entire company! Just leave everything to me. I promise you, Yuri, everything will be all right," answered Oleg, in a matter-of-fact voice.

"I hope you are right, cousin. We don't need any screw-ups at this point in our plans. You make sure that all details are secured and I will make sure that our transportation is here on time.

Yuri contacted Admiral Zurkov, and demanded that he provide at least three ***MI-24 Hind*** attack helicopters for their mission. These aircraft would be ideally suited for the mission. They could carry at least eight fully armed men, plus three crew members. They were both heavily armed, and armored against small arms fire. Their range was not great, only three hundred miles or so, but arrangements could be made for refueling en route. The admiral informed Yuri that three helicopters could be available in seventy-two hours, however it would cost an extra $100,000.00 in bribe money. Additionally, the crew would have to receive the same salary as the other men. Yuri agreed, and within a few hours sent the money over with a courier.

The final details would have to be worked out in the next few days. Time was getting critical, the fleet was making preparation to depart Sevastopol in less than a few weeks, and the heroin still had to be rescued from the silos. Three days later Admiral Zurkov and CPT Chetskiy arrived at Yuri's temporary headquarters. He was in good spirits and apparently had great news for everyone.

"Well, I am glad to see you, Yuri. I have obtained the three helicopters, and I have organized the necessary refueling points en route to Sevastopol. However, we must depart shortly. I heard from our friends in the weather department that a big storm is due to hit that part of the country. It will have high winds, rain and possibly severe dust storms," stated a confident Admiral Zurkov.

"You have done well, admiral. If the Russian government had more men like you, we would not be in the predicament we are in right now!" replied a satisfied Yuri.

"Oh, I almost forgot. Here you are, Yuri, the 'papers' for Oleg and yourself. These are not forgeries, but original documents appointing Oleg as 'chief translator,' and you as a 'commercial Attaché.'" answered the admiral, with a bit of conceit in his voice.

"All right, admiral, you have done very well. We will meet again in forty-eight hours, and proceed to our meeting point."

Yuri, Oleg, Gregori and the rest of the twenty-man assault unit met one last time at Yuri's house. Every detail was meticulously gone over. It was agreed that the helicopters would not be used until after the heroin was secured and the radar station destroyed. Yuri was afraid that they might have sufficient time to broadcast and send a distress signal. The helicopters would be standing by at Dushanbe Airport, ready for takeoff. Oleg and Yuri remained behind after the men went to sleep.

"I noticed you did not tell them about the heroin, Yuri," said Oleg.

"It doesn't pay to tell everyone. I only told them it was of vital interest and very expensive. Some of them actually believe it's some type of plutonium that was left behind. Well, so much the better. Let them have their own fantasies. Once we have it in our possession, I don't care if Pravda knows!" replied Yuri.

All of the men including Yuri, Oleg, Admiral Zurkov and the rest of the advance unit left by plane for Tajikistan the next day. Admiral Zurkov had once again used his influence to obtain three large military trucks and one sedan. Upon arrival at Dushanbe Airport the entire team was given a specially-coded "Top Secret" clearance which allowed them to have access to a large hangar.

All of the plans, and contingencies were discussed and X-hour was set for the next morning at 04:00 hours. Oleg personally checked each individual and was confident that everything would go according to plan. Oleg and two other men took a drive out to the radar site, and reconnoitered the area. They were able to observe only a single sentry post, and two other technicians. *Great*, thought Oleg, *we should be in out of here in five minutes*. Upon returning to the hangar, he instructed the rest of the troops and Yuri.

"It looks real easy, maybe too easy. Just be careful; we have a lot at stake and I don't want anything to go wrong. Do you understand, Oleg?" replied Yuri, his eyes squinting in a way that Oleg had never seen before.

Oleg looked at Yuri and nodded his head. Oleg held one last meeting with his troops and instructed everyone to get some sleep. At approximately 22:30 hours all the men crawled in the back of the truck and promptly fell asleep. Oleg woke everyone up at 02:30. A quick meal of warm tea and sandwiches was consumed by all. Oleg and Yuri went over the details once more.

At exactly 03:02, all vehicles left the hangar en route to the silos, by way of the radar station. The distance of ten kilometers could normally be covered in less than ten minutes, but because of the enforced no lights driving directive, it would take them about twenty or so minutes.

All three vehicles were driving single file down a deserted goat path toward the radar station. They were blessed with a beautiful full moon, which gave them sufficient light to see everything around them for hundreds of yards, but it also gave the one hidden sentry plenty of time to spot them.

Private Eugeniy Vakayian was a bored conscript from the southeastern part of what used to be the Soviet Union. He was extremely irked, and this assignment was particularly boring. Unlike most conscript, Private Vakayian was a pre-med student, and had a higher than average intelligence. Unfortunately, this above-average IQ had, for some unknown reason, irritated his sergeant; the private found himself on guard duty seventy-five percent of the time.

Vakayian had always fantasized about being a hero. He often daydreamed that he saved his unit from a band of rebels or terrorists. At night, he would often play imaginary war games in which he would single-handedly wipe out all the bad guys. This night, like so many others, was no different. He sat on the ground behind a large dirt wall, near the entrance to the radar site, and dreamt of being decorated by a general. His daydream was shattered by the sound of the three trucks coming down the goat path. He suddenly looked up, and observed that all three vehicles had their lights turned off. His first thought was to run and get the sergeant, but he then thought he might be able to handle the situation by himself. *Let's wait and see what develops*, he thought.

He observed the strange behavior of the vehicles and their occupants. They stopped about three hundred meters from the radar site. Strange groups of men, all dressed in black, got out, and deployed in a tactical manner. He could plainly make out their weapons, and then he began to worry. He then suddenly came to the realization that perhaps he should call the sergeant after all. He depressed the key on his hand-held radio and called the sergeant.

"Hey sergeant! Hey sergeant! I think you better get up now," yelled the young private in the microphone.

"What's going on up there?" answered the still drowsy sergeant.

"I don't know, but I think you better come up and see for yourself," replied the now nervous private.

He pointed his weapon in the general direction of the mysterious group, and hoped that the sergeant would get his lazy ass up there.

"Okay, I'll be right up," answered the now angry sergeant.

Sergeant Bulkimov was a veteran of Afghanistan, and really didn't like the new bunch of soldiers they were sending him. Too many of them thought of democracy, free speech and all of that capitalist bullshit, he thought. They forgot how to obey orders, and always whined and complained, especially that Private Vakayian. *I'll ream his asshole, if he woke me up for nothing*. By the time the sergeant had reached the sentry post, most of the dark-clad figures had vanished from sight. However, you could still see the trucks, and a couple of men standing by them.

"You fool! You stupid fool! You woke me up to tell me that some idiot broke down near here. I'll break your bones, I'll…!"

Sergeant Bulkimov never finished his sentence. Two black-clad individuals shot both men dead on the spot, two perfectly silenced wounds to the head and heart, double-tap. No screams, no noise, just a final silence. The black-clad strangers carried silenced automatic weapons, and the only noise to be heard was the diesel motor which provided power to the radar site.

Oleg's men rushed the radar site, and threw several explosives inside the van. Six seconds later, a large flash destroyed the radar site and the other two occupants. Oleg regrouped the men and headed for the silos. A small scouting party was sent ahead to recon the area, but only a handful of goats were found in the vicinity.

Oleg and Yuri were the first to go in. The one access door had been locked and double padlocked; however, a small charge of explosives had taken care of the first door. As Oleg and Yuri entered the concrete stairway, immediately they detected the strong odor of urine, dampness and just plain filth! They stopped to regain their composure, and started to descend the dark and cavernous interior. After what seemed an eternity, they finally reached the area where the drugs had been hidden. Oleg approached the weapons safe. He made sure that no one had interfered with his bounty. He secured the area and placed a small charge of explosive material on the door.

The explosion blew the hinges off the door, and a loud *boom* reverberated throughout the underground silo. After a few seconds, Oleg swept his flashlight across the interior of the safe, and there, unharmed and still intact, were his eight hundred kilos of heroin. Both men jumped up and down, and danced a little jig of joy. All of their work had apparently paid off.

"Let's go get the men, and get the hell away from here," shouted Oleg to Yuri.

"Don't worry, I'll be right back," answered Yuri as he ran up the stairs.

A few minutes later, ten or so of the men came clattering down the stairway. They were still uncomfortable, and looked suspiciously at the packages. As far as they knew this was some sort of nuclear material and they were scared of it.

"Don't worry, men. The quicker you get this stuff out of here, the quicker you will get your bonus," stated Yuri.

"Oleg, have you called the helicopters? Now that the radar site is destroyed, they shouldn't have any problems getting here unobserved," said Yuri.

"No problem. Everything is taken care of and we should have 'touchdown' any moment now," replied Oleg.

No sooner had Oleg said "touchdown", than the familiar sound of the large helicopters could be heard. It was an odd sound, not much like a helicopter, thought Oleg, but more like a giant windmill. Several of the men popped flares and the three choppers landed near the silos. Oleg organized the men, and in less than eight minutes, the entire cargo was transferred to the waiting choppers. Half of the men were released on the spot and told to go home with the trucks. The other twelve or so boarded the choppers and departed the area at high speed.

Both Oleg and Yuri were ecstatic. The entire operation had gone extremely smoothly, and they were on their way to Sevastopol and their rendezvous with Admiral Zurkov. All they had to do was make two or three fuel stops and they would be home free. Yuri had the pilot radio ahead and contact Admiral Zurkov.

"Admiral, this is Yuri. Yes, everything went well, and we are homeward bound. Have you arranged transportation from the airport? Yes, okay! I don't think we should be any later than 18:00 hours this evening. Don't forget those hotel accommodations, first class, please!" stated Yuri, a big smile spreading across his face.

"Yuri, it sounds like everything is working out according to plan. I only hope our relatives in America are as well organized. Have you had any feedback since your last conversation?" asked Oleg inquiringly.

"Yes, I have had direct contact with the West Coast boss, and he assures me that direct contacts with the CIA have been arranged. They believe they are buying a new 'Top Secret' Soviet missile, as well as a couple of defectors. We still have to work out the details, but we can do that, once we arrive in California. Trust me, Oleg, everything will work out fine," replied Yuri in an officious manner.

The remainder of the journey went without a hitch. All helicopters functioned as smooth as silk, and the fuel was there on time and at the right location. All three copters arrived in Sevastopol and flew over the airfield at precisely 18:00 hours. The admiral had arranged for transportation, and storage. A large commercial heavy-duty tractor-trailer truck was parked on the tarmac. The merchandise was off-loaded by Oleg's men, and they were released to enjoy the pleasures of Sevastopol.

Sevastopol is a large and ancient city on the Black Sea. It is now the home port for the Russian and Ukrainian navies. Strangely enough, the Russian navy was in the Yuzhnaya Harbor (South), near Lazarena Square, and the Ukrainian navy was in the Kamyshovaya, approximately thirty minutes from the center of town, and fifteen minutes from the Streletskaya Harbor, which is the civilian harbor. Both navies now co-exist peacefully, in a post "Cold War" world.

The admiral had made reservations at the Hotel Ukraina. These were first-class accommodations; this luxurious hotel was in the Ushakova district and near everything worth mentioning in Sevastopol. It had its own disco, nightclub and casino. Sevastopol was a cosmopolitan and exciting city. Oleg, Yuri and the rest of the men spent several days enjoying the modern conveniences and pleasures of this historic city.

Admiral Zurkov and his staff made arrangements for the upcoming exercise and the departure of part of the Russian fleet. Oleg and Yuri were not to board the ship until shortly prior to departure.

Among the many Russian ships taking place in the exercise was the ***Kiev***. This aircraft carrier was also to be the ship carrying the heroin, in a hollowed-out missile, as well as transporting Oleg, Yuri and the rest of the smuggling crew.

The ***Kiev*** was a magnificent ship; it was previously designated as a ***KURIL*** class aircraft carrier. Western sources had called her the "First Russian aircraft carrier" but, in fact, it was not a true carrier in the Western sense of the word. Her keel was laid in 1970, and she was eventually launched in 1972. Western intelligence had finally classified her as a "cruiser carrier" designed to trap and engage in long-range anti-submarine operations. Most of her armament was designed for that specific purpose. The ***Kiev*** had the capability to engage in long range land and or naval targets with SS-N-12 missiles, and also attack other aircraft by means of her ***Forger VTOL*** (fighter-bombers). These aircraft were similar to the Harrier jets and could carry out attacks on both ground targets (ground support) and obviously other marine targets. She weighed nearly 37,000 tons (loaded) and was nearly 900 feet in length. Admiral Zurkov had picked a splendid ship to hide and transport the heroin cache to America. One of the SS-N-12 missiles would be repainted and disguised, and used as a "Trojan Horse".

The ***Kiev's*** voyage to America also served another purpose; she was **FOR SALE.** The Russian navy had lost control of most of its ships to the "new KGB and greedy "admirals"; they, in turn, worked very closely with the ROC. It was hoped that some foreign power might see her on this exercise, and purchase her for several million dollars. The ***Kiev*** was to be a victim of the "Cold War".

The Russians (KGB and ROC) had already sold several submarines and other pieces of equipment to India, Australia and other countries. This trip served a dual purpose for Admiral Zurkov; however he was not going to advertise it to everyone, not just yet. Admiral Zurkov's "exercise" preparations went as scheduled, and the entire armada, heroin, Oleg and Yuri departed for America. After a rather nondescript voyage they arrived off the coast of Hawaii for the scheduled exercise.

Chapter 24

Preliminary Bout

Several weeks of hiding in the "safe house" had made Jeremy Grant restless and nervous. He was sure that his pursuers had lost his scent and it was time to resume the offensive. Jeremy had always believed that the best defense is the attack! Jeremy went back on the street prowling for information on the Russians, and on any new sources of heroin.

Over a period of three weeks, his sources and snitches began putting out the word that something "Big" was going to happen soon. His sources were somewhat vague, but heroin and Russians kept popping up in the same conversation. It seemed as if all the usual heroin suppliers along the West Coast were waiting for this "Big" deal to go down. In fact, it made many of them very nervous because anytime a large shipment showed up, the prices tumbled. The Nigerians, Chinese, and Italians were all hoarding now in an attempt to drive the street price up.

Jeremy continued looking day after day, but still no results. Rumors were rampant, but most of them were so unreliable that he had to ignore them. Early one Friday morning, he received a phone call from a longtime friend at the CIA.

"Hey Jeremy, this is Ray from Evergreen Shipping Company. I was wondering if we could meet for lunch today," asked the smooth-talking man.

Jeremy did not know anyone by the name of Ray, but he knew that Evergreen had at one time belonged to them, and perhaps they wanted to talk to him.

"Sounds good to me, but it will have to be on my home turf," replied an insistent Jeremy.

"No problema. You name the place and time, and I'll be there," answered an overly friendly Ray.

"Okay! In an hour at the Green Sandwich Inn in Fairfield. Do you know where that is?" replied Jeremy.

"Sure do, but an hour is cutting it kind of close, don't you think?" replied Ray, anxiety showing in his voice.

"No, not really. The inn or nothing!" answered Jeremy with authority.

Jeremy knew that this would give anyone trying to set up an ambush very little time to do so. Additionally, it was a public place and it had a direct route to the freeway in both directions. Jeremy was pretty sure that Ray, if that was his name, was with the CIA, but he didn't want to take any chances. Just to make sure, he called one of his sources at the "Agency" to verify Ray's identity. His source was only able to tell him that someone with the "Cover" name of Ray did, in fact, work there, but could not verify anything else. Jeremy was now convinced that this was a legitimate meeting, because only the CIA would go to such lengths to hide it.

Not wanting to take any chances, Jeremy arranged for two of the "special agents" to provide cover for him. Jeremy hurried down to his car and sped away. It was eleven forty-five in the morning, and Jeremy had no problem making the forty-two mile drive in less than forty minutes. Jeremy acknowledged the presence of the other agents and conducted his own reconnaissance of the restaurant. After satisfying himself of the "all clear", he went in and took a booth at the back of the restaurant. From this position he could monitor everyone coming in the restaurant and he would also have a speedy exit to the parking lot through the emergency door.

About twenty-two minutes later, two typical government "G" cars, large Ford sedans with cell-phone antennas, pulled up to the front entrance of the restaurant and parked in the "Handicapped Parking" spot. That, in itself, gave Ray and his watchdog away. These two guys did not look like they were handicapped, and because they were driving untraceable cars, they didn't really care where they parked. *Poor technique and no style* thought Jeremy as the guy named "Ray" walked in and looked around for a minute. The other goon stayed in front of the door and tried to look inconspicuous. Ray looked around the restaurant and spotted Jeremy.

"Good afternoon, Jeremy. Do you mind if I sit down?" asked "Ray" as he sat down.

Jeremy looked at him for second, and answered back in his best German accent, *"**Wie bitte? Es tut mir leid aber ich kenne Sie nicht!**"* (Excuse me, but I don't know you!)

"What the hell is going on?" replied the now irate Ray.

"Oh, nothing really. I just wanted to teach you some manners, and some old-fashioned intelligence know-how. Where on earth did you boys go to school? The Polish Intelligence Service?" replied Jeremy, a small smile now spreading across his lips.

"Don't be such a smart ass! I came here to discuss business! Why don't you get off your high horse, and maybe I'll tell you a thing or two," replied Ray, his chest puffing out like a gamecock.

"Okay, 'Ray' tell me why it was so urgent for you to contact me today," replied Jeremy.

"My sources tell me you have been going all over town asking about Russians. Is that true? If it is, I want you to tell me what you know and why you are so interested," asked Ray in an insolent tone of voice.

"Well my friend, there are ways to approach me, and there are ways to make me want to shove this .45 caliber automatic up your asshole. Sources, sources?! Who are your damn sources?" replied a now pissed-off Jeremy.

"Our sources are confidential, you know that. However, they are very reliable," replied Ray.

Ray could feel the pressing barrel of the large automatic pushing forcefully against his crotch. Ray's palms began to sweat profusely and he suddenly began speaking in a lower octave.

"Now, there is no need for that kind of rough-stuff, Jeremy. We are all friends after all," replied a now subdued Ray.

"Good! I am glad I made my point. If you have any questions, please feel free to ask them. If I can answer them, I will. If not, I'll tell you to hit the road. Do we understand each other?" answered Jeremy, his voice barely above a whisper.

"That sounds fair to me. I need to know why you have such interests in our local Russians, and what is going on? That's all!"

replied Ray, a genuine smile now spreading across his face.

Jeremy explained the situation as best he could, leaving out those details that might jeopardize his position. He told Ray just enough to get him interested, but not enough to give away his position. Ray sat there and listened to Jeremy, knowing that Jeremy was holding something back. However, he was intelligent enough not to push him. Jeremy, on the other hand, demanded to know why the local CIA was so interested in a U.S. Customs operation, and why were they dealing with Russian mobsters? At first, Ray was reluctant to tell Jeremy anything about his "deal", but slowly Jeremy was able to extract information bit by bit.

"Beware, my friend. I have dealt with these guys before, and they lie. You can't trust them!" Jeremy warned.

"Thank you for your advice, but if we can get what they promised it would be a great intelligence coup, and of course a feather in my cap," grinned Ray, as he stood up to leave.

Ray had not come out and told Jeremy the complete truth, but merely skimmed the edges. The word *source* had come up in the past, and recently. Jeremy was extremely interested in this mysterious *source*, but was not quite able to identify him yet. However, Jeremy had been an intelligence officer long enough to deduce some of the information.

"Well my friend, I sincerely hope that 'the feather in your cap' isn't sticking out of a big fat hole in your head! If you are stupid enough to deal with them, you may very well pay the price," replied an angry Jeremy.

The not so clever CIA operative got up and stared down at Jeremy. He nodded his head one last time, and walked out the door. Jeremy remained seated for a few more minutes, and carefully exited the restaurant through the emergency exit. He waved good-bye to his two bodyguards and carefully made his way back to his office. He was careful to use every evasion trick he had ever learned, and managed to reach his office in less than forty-five minutes. His boss, Neal Brown, was waiting for him.

"Glad to see that you made it back in one piece. You have got to stop making enemies all over the place. I received a call from some asshole at the CIA office, and he said you pulled a gun on one of his agents and shoved it up his crotch! Is that true? Don't answer. I don't really care one way or the other. However, please try to be a little more diplomatic next time. Let's remember what our job is and try to stick to it. Okay? You may need these 'friends' someday," stated a rather excited Neal Brown.

"I am sorry, boss, if I caused you undue worry, but that asshole came off like a prick, and I just wanted to let him know who was boss. I promise I won't do it again. One thing I know for sure is those 'boys' are involved with something to do with Russians, and some mysterious 'source' is setting them up. I can't figure out yet what it is, but I am sure it's going to reach up and bite them on the ass," replied Jeremy.

"Okay, but what I really don't understand is why the FBI has not been involved in this matter. I think the CIA is treading on thin ice. They are bound to get in deep trouble! I want you to write a memo to them, informing them in general terms about the possible smuggling, and the possibility of Russian nationals being involved. Be sure to inform them that we are not seeking help, merely informing them as a matter of courtesy," ordered Neal Brown, as he walked out of the room.

Jeremy obeyed Neal's order and sat down and wrote the most generic and boring letter he had ever written. He was not happy about this, but he was following orders.

Jeremy had that funny feeling in the pit of his stomach, the same feeling that he got in combat when he knew the "shit is going to hit the fan", better yet, the feeling you have when you are making love to a beautiful women, and you are right on the edge of an orgasm. You get a tiny squeezing feeling in the pit of your stomach, just before you explode. Jeremy knew he wasn't making love, but that tense feeling was persistent. He decided to go back and check all his sources again for more intelligence updates, and talk to that detective again about Suzanna's homicide.

His first stop was in San Francisco's Chinatown district. He went to have dinner at his favorite restaurant, Wo Fat's Imperial Gardens, The owner was a short and rather fat Oriental by the name of Henry

Wo Fat. Henry had been in this country for over sixty years and still spoke English with a thick Cantonese accent. Jeremy was always amused by his sloppy at pronouncing his name, 'Jelemy.' Jeremy knew that Henry hired and used illegal kitchen help, and that they occasionally imported opium for personal use. Jeremy's office had caught Henry red-handed on a couple of occasions and Henry owed him a favor or two.

"Henry, how are you doing today? How are your wife and children? Well, I hope," asked Jeremy in a joyous mood.

"Vely well, thank you. I am honoled to have you in my lestaulant, Ml. Jelemy. What can I selve you today?" asked an over friendly Henry.

"I will have the house special, and heroin on the side. Can you provide that for me, Henry?" asked Jeremy.

"Oh, no! You must not joke like that. Henly don't selve heloin. I alleady told you last week, No, No, No! Henly is a good citizen of Amelica! Please, don't talk silly like that," replied a frightened Henry.

"Well Henry, I happen to know that you have at least six illegal immigrants working in your kitchen, and don't forget that opium we seized not too long ago," replied a now serious Jeremy.

"Okay, okay! I still don't know nothing conclete. I will tell you evelything I heal about the Lussians. I plomise you. I only heal that maybe ship involved," replied Henry, in a compliant voice.

"Ship, did you say? What ship? When? Can you tell me more?" asked Jeremy.

"No, no! Don't get so excited. My cousin's son, Telly. He wolked as dishwashel in Lussian lestaulant in Saclamento. He undelstand a little bit lussian. When he was young man, he studied in Lussia and he was able heal something. He heal them talk about big shipment coming next month. That all he can undelstand. He tell me mole, and I tell you, okay?" replied a proud Henry.

"Okay, Henry. You did good. I need to know the name of the restaurant. Can you get that for me?" asked Jeremy

"Sule, sule, no ploblem," replied Henry walking away from the table.

Jeremy rushed back to his office and informed Neal of a new

promising intelligence indicator he had just received. Not wanting to wait for Henry, or depending on one source he was going to contact his Sacramento office for help.

"That is great news, Jeremy, but do you know how many ships visit San Francisco each month? Over 3400! Even if we wanted to, we could not search all of them. What we need to do is eliminate as many as we can. Let's call our Sacramento office on Fulton Avenue, and have them try and locate all the Russian restaurants. Second, let's prepare an analysis by tonnage, size, home port, registry and any other pertinent factor. Get Alex to help you, and have Pattie follow up on Henry Wo Fat. You might want to use your other analyst, the Army guy, ahh Stuart; that's it, Stuart, to coordinate all incoming 'Intel', and we should also advise the Special Agent in Charge (SAC) about what is going on, just in case we need outside assistance. Any questions? Good, let's get with it. Remember, stay safe!" stated Neal as he walked out of the room.

Neal walked back into the room and almost shouted at Jeremy.

"Don't forget to attend the monthly law enforcement intelligence meetings and advise our colleagues of what may be happening in the next thirty days. I particularly want the Marine Patrol units advised, Coast Guard, and all Marine Patrol units down the channel all the way to Stockton. Is that understood?" shouted Neal, in an uncivilized manner.

Jeremy called in his staff, and outlined the game plan. Each person was given his mission and told when to report back. Now that they knew how, they needed to find out when. If would be imperative for the Sacramento office to locate all the Russian restaurant and find which one employed Henry's cousin. Jeremy called the Sacramento office and spoke with the SAC directly.

Kitty White was a forty-something, twenty-year veteran of the U.S. Customs Service. Kitty was very anxious to advance up the ladder, and would step over corpses to promote herself. She saw an opportunity like this as God sent. She would do everything in her power to get the information, and if at possible, get herself included in this case.

"Sure Jeremy, I understand, but I think I may have your restaurant.

Right down the block is the Anastasia Restaurant, and I believe there is another restaurant in West Sacramento. We should be able to have an answer for you by this afternoon. I am sure you have already thought of it, Jeremy, but you might want to advise all law enforcement along the river to be on the lookout for anything suspicious," replied Kitty.

"Yes, we have. However, if you would like to advise the locals in your area I really would appreciate it. Be sure to let them know as much as we have, and have them report anything suspicious back to us," replied Jeremy, seeing right through her ploy, but appreciating the enthusiasm.

Jeremy received a call from the homicide detective, and it wasn't very positive. So far everything was negative and no suspects could be positively identified. Jeremy still had no direct proof of a connection between Suzanna's homicide and his troubles and the heroin. Although the bloody message seemed to point in that direction, he needed some more evidence.

One thing he knew for sure, the Russians seemed to be involved in a lot of local criminal activities, Jeremy decided to attend one of the monthly intelligence meetings held at the California Department of Justice's Bureau of Investigation. It had one of those "cutsie" names that no one can ever remember, SOCIT, ROCIT or something like that. This meeting was attended by at least twenty-five different law enforcement agencies. However, after listening to all the agencies, he realized that the ROC had a larger role to play in the criminal statistics of Northern California. They were involved in murder, extortion, robbery, fraud, drugs, car thefts, insurance, welfare fraud, etc.

It was during one of these intelligence meetings that the first connection between the ROC and the Italian Cosa Nostra was made known to Jeremy. Apparently, the FBI had an undercover informer in Las Vegas, and she had stated that her bosses had made a comment about the Vegas group getting some "**Red Snow**" from the Russians. This information was like an atomic bomb going off in Jeremy's head. Las Vegas, he hadn't thought of Las Vegas since his discharge. He wondered if Guido Fontana was still alive, how his cousins Douglas and Danny Lawyer were. He thought to himself, *I must return to that* *crazy Mecca someday.*

Against his better judgment, he stopped the FBI agent after the meeting and tried to solicit more information about the Vegas operation. True to their custom, the FBI agent was vague and uncooperative. "It's Classified" was his answer to every question.

"Okay, buddy. You made a statement in that meeting and I need some information! How about if I give you the answer, and you simply nod your head if I am right?" asked a now angry Jeremy.

"Is it involving Guido Fontana?" asked Jeremy with authority.

The FBI agent slowly looked up and nodded his head. He started to say something, but stopped in mid-sentence. Without allowing any questions, he turned around and walked out of the room. Jeremy was sadly disappointed that his old friend was somehow involved in this mess.

Jeremy went back to WSIN and asked them to do a telephone sort of all the numbers at this restaurant and those belonging to Viktor Varmessy and Guido Fontana. He was hoping that some sort of conspiracy could be established between these two individuals. Maybe, he thought, he might also get a clue as to who the mysterious source was. Unfortunately, these computer printouts took several days to sort and he would not have an answer until at least the following Thursday.

Chapter 25

Loretta

Jeremy woke up one morning at his "safe house" feeling miserable, aching and tired. It was one of those gray San Francisco days. Cold, damp and just plain uncomfortable. Everything hurt, especially his old 'Nam' and Afghanistan wounds. It seemed as if everything was catching up with him. He had always worked out and kept in shape, but he couldn't help noticing that it was more difficult to walk and run lately. His bones ached and he was tired all the time. He expressed his concerns to Neal, who immediately ordered him to go in for a checkup. Jeremy realized that it probably was a good idea. He hadn't seen a doctor since his return from Afghanistan. He probably just needed a little tune-up, he thought.

Jeremy was a federal civil service employee and was entitled to coverage under the blanket policy which was offered by his employer, but when he called for an appointment, they said "nine weeks" is the earliest we can see you. Jeremy was in no mood to wait nine weeks. He realized that as a disabled veteran, he was also entitled to be seen at any of the veteran's hospitals in the area. He called and they promptly offered to see him as a walk-in patient on the following day.

Jeremy woke early the next day and drove southward to the new clinic near Stanford. After filling out the requisite paperwork and receiving the obligatory plastic admissions card, he was asked to take a seat in a brightly lit waiting area. About thirty minutes had passed when a nurse admitted him to a room, after taking his vital signs. He sat there for a few more minutes, then the doctor walked in.

"Well Mr. Grant, what seems to be your problem?" asked the doctor without looking up from her chart.

The voice had not changed. It still had that sweet southern twang to it. However, it had mellowed over the years. Both of them looked and stared at each other in utter disbelief. Slowly, very slowly, a large tear began to well up in Loretta's right eye. She stood there transfixed. Her whole body began to slowly shake like she had done on their last day together. The tears began streaming down her face like great waterfalls. The tears and sobs could not be stopped.

Jeremy was equally paralyzed. For the first time in his life he did not know what to do. He stood up from his chair and put his arms around her. The tears and sobs continued for a few more minutes, but slowly she seemed to regain her composure.

"Jeremy, Jeremy, Jer…! I thought you were dead. You disappeared, my letters were never answered. You just disappeared! Where were you? What happened to you? What…you?" sobbed Loretta, her words coming out like bullets from a machine gun.

"Whoa, there! You are the one who disappeared. I wrote you at least two letters every day for almost a year, and nothing! Nothing at all! What happened? Why didn't you…?" asked an equally excited Jeremy.

They both sat there holding each other. After thirty minutes of jabbering, sobbing and crying they both calmed down enough to explain to each other what had happened. Loretta was first. She took a deep breath and started to tell him a wonderful, but sometimes sad tale. After she had gotten to Vietnam she found out that she was pregnant. Obviously Vietnam was no place for a pregnant doctor. She tried calling Jeremy, but he was already discharged.

"Stop!" he yelled.

"You were pregnant! That means you had a baby?" he asked stupidly.

"Well, yes, that usually happens after you get pregnant," she replied in a mocking tone of voice.

"Stop everything else, and tell me about my kid! I want to know, is it a boy or girl? How old, where…please tell me," replied Jeremy, showing more emotion than he had in a long time.

"Look at the picture on the wall. That is your son, Jeremy Jr. He looks just like you, and he is just about your size, too. Haven't you been following college football? All-American tight end at Stanford, two years ago, and now he is the starting tight-end for the San Francisco Forty-Niners," replied Loretta, with a big grin on her face.

"All-American, Forty-Niners! This is too much to believe. Just like his dad. I could have played professional football. Did you tell him anything about me? Does he know who I am? Does he...?" answered Jeremy, his words spilling out of his mouth like salmon swimming up river.

"Just slow down, and we will get a chance to get reacquainted. You have to give us a chance. After all, we haven't seen you in about twenty-seven years. There is time for everything. Are you married?" asked Loretta, her face blushing like a cherry.

"No, I am not, and I have never been married! You were the only women I ever loved, and I just couldn't get married. What about you? Did you ever get married?" asked Jeremy, his heart hoping that the answer would be negative.

"I thought of marrying several times, but for some reason I could never bring myself to do it. I concentrated on my career and now have a very successful practice in the East Bay area. I stayed in the Army Reserves and retired as a colonel two years ago. I am an orthopedic surgeon, and I volunteer one day a week here, just to repay all the guys who never came home," replied Loretta, her voice trailing off.

"Wow, that is quite a handful for a women without a husband to help out. I am sorry I haven't been around to help you raise our son. But from what you tell me, he's turned out just fine," answered Jeremy, tears of his own welling up, and slowly streaming down his cheeks.

They once more hugged each other, and quietly looked into each other's eyes. Both of them afraid to start the next conversation. They just sat and held each other's hands. Jeremy went on to explain his rather sordid and exciting career, and legitimate reason for never receiving her letters. Both of them were unsure of how to proceed and perhaps rekindle their romance. It was finally Jeremy who broke the ice and said, "Why don't we have dinner tonight, and continue from there. I don't have any plans, do you?" asked Jeremy, lying through his teeth.

"That sounds like a great idea but, I don't get out of here until 17:30 or so. Why don't you pick me up, let's say around seven-thirty and I'll take you to this great Italian restaurant in Fremont. However, before we do anything else, tell me about your ailments and let me, once again, take care of you," stated Loretta with emphasis.

Loretta prodded and poked and generally gave Jeremy a thorough going over. She didn't like what she saw. His body parts were becoming brittle, and she did not like the look of one minor stress fracture on his right leg. His left shoulder was also showing renewed trauma, and he really needed a week or more of bed rest. She wanted to give his injured leg a chance to heal.

"Well, I can tell you haven't had any female care lately. You are a mess! Did you know that you have a stress fracture in your right leg? They are near those steel pins inserted in your foot and ankle. This is a very common occurrence, especially for someone of your stature. I can tell that you still exercise, but you will have to switch to a low-impact aerobics workout, such as swimming. No more long-distance running for you! And that's the doctor's orders! We will also have to put you on a calcium/vitamin supplement immediately, and of course I will insist on regular doctor visits. If the price is right I might even make house calls. How does that sound?" stated Loretta, a wide smile spreading across her face.

"I think you have yourself a deal, especially that part about house calls," answered Jeremy as he put his clothes back on.

"However, I do have one more question. When do I get to see my son? Is he around? When will you tell him about me? I…?" questioned Jeremy, as he stood up.

"That will have to wait a week or so. His team is on the road and they are playing the New Orleans Saints this week, so he won't be home until Monday morning. Please give me some time, I need to slowly bring you back into his life. He's never met you, and I want to do it the right way, okay?" replied Loretta.

"That sounds fair to me," answered Jeremy.

"Why don't we talk more about it during dinner tonight. I am sure Junior will need some time to find out that his father is still alive and kicking. Give me your address and I will pick you up at seven-thirty tonight," stated Jeremy.

Loretta gave him the address, and as she was bending over the table to pick up the scratch paper, he noticed that her figure was still as desirable as in her younger years. Images of a motel flashed in his head. Visions of the last trip to Travis AFB, and that last day kept dancing in front of his eyes. Except for the few patches of gray hair, and an occasional wrinkle, she still was the same ravishing beauty of twenty-seven years ago. At this moment in time he felt like the luckiest man in the world. He kissed her one last time and rushed back to his "safe house." When he got there he had a message from Neal, "Extremely urgent! Contact me immediately!" Jeremy picked up the phone and called him back right a way.

"Hello Neal! I am back from the hospital and with the exception of a few minor problems, I will live. By the way, I am also a father! Can you handle that? I will tell you all about it, when we meet. What is the great urgency?" asked an inquisitive Jeremy, disappointed that he was unable to tell Neal about Loretta right a way.

"I am glad to hear that you will live, but I also have some good news. We have found out which restaurant Henry's cousin works at, and a federal judge has authorized an immediate Title III wiretap authorization. Additionally, your buddy Alexander has discovered that a whole Russian fleet will be visiting San Francisco in the next few weeks! A whole fucking fleet! Can you believe that? How in the hell are we going to watch all of them? Anyway, get back to the office as soon as possible and we will discuss the possibilities," said Neal, without allowing Jeremy to respond.

Jeremy looked at his watch and it was nearly fourteen-thirty. If he really hustled, he would be able to make both appointments. He changed clothes and wore his fancy blue suit, white button-down collar shirt, and a colorful Rush Limbaugh collection tie. He looked at himself in the mirror, and could not help but admire what he saw. For a fifty-something man, he still looked pretty damn good.

He drove the few blocks to his office and ran up the stairs. The meeting was already in progress; his entire staff and Neal Brown were hard at work.

"Hey, don't you look nice," quipped Alexander.

"He sure does. Do you have a hot date tonight?" asked Neal.

"What if I do? It's none of your business, but I just found out I am a papa!" answered Jeremy, jokingly.

"Papa, what do you mean papa? When is it due? Who is the lucky woman." asked everyone almost in unison.

"Whoa, there! It's a long story, but I'll tell you about it some other day. My son is already twenty-six years old, and he plays professional football," answered Jeremy, pride showing in his voice.

"Jeremy Grant Jr. of the Forty-Niners! I can't believe it! I should have put two and two together, but of course he looks just like you," blurted out a now-proud Alexander.

Okay you guys! We are all happy for Jeremy, but we have to get our act together. Let's save the chatter for later!" ordered Neal.

The room suddenly got quiet, and Neal began outlining the assignments for the next few days. They knew which Sacramento restaurant was involved, and there was a great probability that one or more of those Russian naval vessels would be involved in the drug delivery. The problem would be which one.

Jeremy and Alexander teamed up together, and the other two agents did likewise. Jeremy and Alexander were responsible for following the wiretap, and Pattie and Stuart would follow the Russian fleet's movements. Neal would remain in the office and coordinate all the movements.

Jeremy informed Alex of dinner plans, and made arrangements to meet in Sacramento on the following day. Jeremy got back in his car and fought the afternoon bay area traffic on southbound Highway 101. After nearly two hours of bumper-to-bumper traffic, he arrived at 1772 Foxworthy Lane, in the city of Fremont. The home was a beautifully restored Victorian-style three-story home. Jeremy could tell that it had been recently completely restored.

He walked up the eight stairs and rang a very ornate doorbell. He looked at the shiny brass plaque, and it said: "Dr. Loretta Q. DeFaut, MD, Orthopedic Surgeon. Monday-Thursday 08:30 to 17:30, weekends by special appointment only." He felt somewhat strange standing in front of her door. It seemed surrealistic and confusing to him.

The front door was made of beautiful, ornate stained-glass depicting an ancient San Francisco skyline. Jeremy was so engrossed in looking at it, that he did not see Loretta open the door. He was somewhat startled at first, but quickly recovered when he saw Loretta. She had apparently taken a lot of time in preparing herself for this date. She was wearing a beautiful Victorian-lace gown that reached to the floor. It had a high collar, but with just enough see-through lace around her bosom to display her magnificent breasts. It was an off-white color with an occasional burgundy ribbon interwoven at the right places. Her hair was swirled around the top of her head in an almost teasing fashion. He stopped to take a deep breath, and said:

"Whoa! You are about the most beautiful woman I have ever seen. I am speechless! Here, I brought you some roses, but they pale in comparison to your beauty."

"That kind of sweet stuff will get you very far," replied Loretta, as she invited him into the parlor.

"I couldn't help myself; I haven't been on a formal date in a long time, and you are still as beautiful as the last time I saw you," replied an embarrassed Jeremy.

"I hope you don't mind, but I have made a slight change of plans. I asked the restaurant to cater our meal. We will be served right here. I figured it would give us more time together," stated Loretta with firmness.

"Mind? Not at all! It's a great idea. You have a beautiful home, and I would like to spend more time with you," answered Jeremy, as he stepped into the parlor area.

An elderly woman all dressed in white came into the parlor, and with a very heavy Spanish accent said:

"Senora Loretta, should I bring in the wine now?"

"Yes, of course, Conchita. Also bring in the those wonderful little snacks you made up for the occasion."

"Yes, Senora Loretta, I will be right in," replied Conchita as she walked away toward the back of the house.

"In case you are wondering, I do pay her social security taxes. Conchita is over seventy-five years old, and social security is the only retirement she has," stated Loretta in a matter of fact tone.

"Don't be so defensive, Loretta. I don't really care one way or the other. But I do find it admirable that you make the effort to obey the law, when so many of our politicians, including our president, find ways to violate it. Enough about Conchita, tell me what you have been doing for the past twenty-seven years!" replied Jeremy.

Loretta sat on the couch, and reached over for his hands. She sat there for a while and began to speak in a slow monotone voice. She didn't even notice Conchita and her tray full of goodies. She continued for almost an hour, telling Jeremy about her life without him. Every once in a while, she would stop and take a sip of her wine and continue without a further break. She suddenly realized that she had been monopolizing the conversation, and apologized to Jeremy.

"Don't worry, sweetheart, I am fascinated by your life, and I want to hear all of it. Please continue, I am really enjoying myself," replied Jeremy lovingly.

"No! I have been venting for too long, and it's now your turn! Tell me, darling, about your life. I am anxious to hear about the other women in your 'sordid' past," stated Loretta in a laughing way.

"I think 'sordid' is the wrong description. I really did not have too much time for romances. They were basically just carnal affairs. Plain old-fashioned raw sex! I never really got involved with any other woman, because I knew that I would be transferred to another part of the world, and she could not know about it. I just sorted of floated on the sea of sex like a cork, nothing profound and demanding, like our relationship.

"Demanding? What kind of word is that?" replied Loretta, her voice rising in anger.

"I am sorry. *Demanding* is probably not the right word. Shall we say fulfilled? Is that better? I don't want to anger you, now that I have found you again. Please, forgive anything I might say. I am so overjoyed at finding you again that my mouth and my brain are working at different speeds," answered Jeremy, hoping for forgiveness.

"Okay, that sounds better. I know you just can't help yourself; after all, you are from Mars and I am from Venus!" replied Loretta with a smile.

"Yes, I have heard of that doctor who claims all women are Venutians and all men are Martians. Maybe that explains some of our odd behavior. A lot of what he says makes sense," acknowledged

Jeremy with a wink.

"You are not going to get out of it this easy, my friend," replied Loretta as she once more reached over and pulled him into her arms.

The intense kiss grew in passion. Both of their bodies longed for each other, but it seemed as if they were too shy to take the next step. Conchita made up their minds by announcing:

"Senora, the caterer is here with food. Where shall I serve it? The downstairs dining room, or the upstairs one?" asked Conchita with a mischievous smile spreading across her face.

"Well, Conchita, let's have it in the upstairs room," replied Loretta.

Turning to Jeremy she shyly inquired whether that would suit him or not. For the first time in many years, Jeremy just nodded his head and blushed. Conchita took the food upstairs to Loretta's bedroom, and Loretta dragged Jeremy to the awaiting repast.

Jeremy sat there feeling uncomfortable until Loretta broke the ice by taking her bra off. Jeremy just stared at her magnificent breasts. Time and age had not been too unkind to her. They sagged a bit, but after all she was fifty-something, and they were forty-something. Loretta just stared at him, and said:

"Well, haven't you ever seen a naked woman before? Does this shock you? I have lost some of my shyness, and I want you to get motivated! Understand?" stated Loretta with authority.

"Yes, I do. However, it's going to take a little while for me to get use to eating with a naked woman. Uuhh, maybe ten seconds," replied Jeremy, as he stood up and began stripping.

Both of them tore their remaining clothes off and fell into each other's arms. Their lovemaking at first was almost violent and passionate. He could not get enough of her, and she likewise. Jeremy had almost forgotten that he was a fifty-something man, and did not have the same stamina as he did twenty-seven years ago. Loretta was so beautiful and exciting, that he was able to make love to her for several hours without pause.

"Whoa there! Let's save some of this for after dinner, my dear. We have had our dessert before our main course," stated Loretta with an evil smile on her lips.

"I'll vote for that. However, I hope you will give me some time to recoup. I have a long day ahead of me tomorrow, and I need some food, now!" stated Jeremy, as he tore into his delicious Italian dinner.

The rest of the evening was spent in lovemaking between courses. Loretta's intensity had not diminished, and Jeremy finally dozed off on top of her breasts, *what a pair of magnificent pillows*, he thought as he drifted off into a blissful sleep. Loretta fondly looked at him and gently caressed his hair. She looked at his scarred body, and hoped that he was now in less dangerous business.

Chapter 26

Kiev

Jeremy woke up around four-thirty to the smell of brewing coffee, and the noise of a steamy shower running. Loretta walked over and gently kissed his forehead. She was in a striking Victoria's Secret silk-cotton nightgown, and sexy white house slippers. When she bent over to kiss him, he once again had a direct and unobstructed view of her voluptuous figure.

"I hope you don't mind me waking you up so early, but you told me about your important meeting in Sacramento. I didn't want you to be late," stated Loretta in a matter-of-fact voice.

"No, not all. I'm glad you did. Today is a very big day, and I hope things work out. I will be real busy for the next few days, and I hope that you understand. I will probably be on-call almost twenty-four hours a day. I was hoping you would allow me the freedom to come and visit you on my free hours, even if it's real late or early in the morning. I want to see you as much as possible, but right now, it has to be around my crazy schedule. Is that okay?" asked Jeremy in a plaintive voice.

"Of course, darling. I do understand. You can call me or leave a message. Our son will be home on Monday, and I'm sure he is anxious to meet you as well," replied a gentle and cooperative Loretta.

Jeremy finished his breakfast. He dressed quickly, and kissed Loretta good-bye. He got into his car and sped away toward Sacramento. Although it was only 05:30 hours the freeways were already becoming congested. The little red Mustang was heading northward on an already busy Highway 680. By the time he got to the Oakland turn-off, the freeway traffic was down to ten miles an hour. Jeremy called the Sacramento office on his cell phone to advise Alexander of his possible delay. Once he got past the Martinez 'Straights,' traffic sped up, and he was back on schedule. In less than an hour he was in the Sacramento field office. Both men spent the next several hours going over the tapes that were recorded from the tapped Russian restaurant telephones. It was a very boring and tedious affair, hour after hour of mundane conversation, some of it in Russian and some in English. All of sudden Jeremy sat up and yelled at Alex.

"Stop it! Stop it! Rewind it a few feet," screamed Jeremy at the top of his voice. It was so loud that everyone in the office stopped what they were doing, and took notice.

"Okay, okay! Hold on to your pantalones, (Pants) I will rewind it," replied Alexander, somewhat angry at Jeremy's tone of voice.

Jeremy pushed the headphones tighter against his ear and listened to the voice. Yes it was Bolotin! Suddenly it dawned on him. Bolotin had said he had a cousin in Sacramento, and that was back in Switzerland. Of course Bolotin knew some of the facts about the heroin, and Afghanistan. What better goon to run the operation from this end? It made sense, but who was going to run the operation from the other end? When and how? Colonel Perrin had been right after all. The ROC has a long arm, and they could reach out anywhere and anytime and touch you. There was something else in Bolotin's statement that caught Jeremy's attention. He referred to his old friend from the CIA or of the CIA. The tape quality left a lot to be desired, and Jeremy could not make out Bolotin's last statement, but suddenly something horrible crossed his mind. He would have to make some discreet inquiries with Colonel Perrin again.

Jeremy began to reflect on the events of the past few months and wondered if Bolotin had anything to do with Suzanna's death, the shadowy figures following in the dark, and so on. Yes, of course! Who better than Bolotin to recognize him? Coincidence? Probably, but a very dangerous one. Jeremy stopped the tape and explained to Alexander what he thought had happened, and asked him to advise Detective Lopez-Sanchez of the Police Department. It was imperative that Bolotin be picked up right a way.

Jeremy and Alexander resumed listening to the tapes. Somehow they now seemed more important and urgent. Jeremy made his long-distance call to Paris. Luckily, Colonel Perrin was in.

"Colonel? This is Jeremy. Can we talk? Good! Please listen and don't say anything until I am done, okay? I need your help. Do you have some trustworthy contacts with the organization I used to work for? If you do, try to find out what they are doing in San Francisco in the next few days with members of the Russian fleet! Please call my ex-boss in Germany, you have the number, and find out where he is. I am sure his wife will be most cooperative, if you throw in a free visit to Paris. It is very, very important that I find out as soon as possible. Did you understand everything?" asked Jeremy.

"Yes I did, and I do, and I will. I have your cell-phone number and office number. I should be able to get in touch with you in the next few days. Be careful, my friend. ***A bientot.*** " (Until later), replied a very cheery Colonel Perrin.

Jeremy hung up the phone and continued the boring task. After listening to several more hours of tapes, both men decided to take a lunch break. Jeremy used the opportunity to call Loretta at her office.

"Hi Loretta. How are you today? I missed you very much. I don't know how much longer I will be here. What are your plans for the evening?" asked an inquisitive Jeremy.

"I was just waiting for your phone call. Jeremy Jr. has already arrived. His flight was early. We had a long conversation, and he is anxious to meet you right a way. Is that possible? What time will you be done?" asked an excited Loretta.

"I wish I could tell you, but if this case weren't so important I would be there now. No! I will come over now, and return here later when everyone is gone. Tell Junior to expect me in the next two hours. Tell him I love him, and I can't wait to see him," replied Jeremy.

Jeremy excused himself from Alex and told him the circumstances of his departure. Both men agreed to come back at around midnight. Jeremy got in his car and headed west on Highway 80. Traffic was beginning to get heavier, but he managed to drive out of Sacramento before the afternoon rush hour.

Jeremy fought the westbound traffic and arrived in Fremont at around 17:00 hours. Jeremy parked his car in the gravel driveway and walked up to the door. He knocked twice and got no response. Jeremy was standing there waiting for someone to open the door, when suddenly this invisible force tackled him to the ground. A very large and powerful man held his elbow against his larynx, and with his other arm was trying to pin him down on the ground. For the first time in years, Jeremy was taken completely by surprise. After all, this was "friendly country" and the assailant had blind-sided him. Jeremy rolled to his right pushing the powerful man against the door frame and managed to reverse the position by applying a choke hold from behind. Although he had the man in a weakened position, he could tell that the man was a very fit athlete and had extremely well-developed neck muscles. Just when he thought he might have to kick him in the back Loretta screamed at him, "Stop! Stop! What are you two doing to each other? Stop, right now!"

"What do you mean, 'you two'? I did not do anything, but ring the doorbell, and this goon jumped me from behind! Who is he? One of your hired help?" replied Jeremy, in a somewhat indignant manner.

"Oh, you dummy! Don't you even recognize your son? This is Jeremy Junior! Your baby boy!" Shot back Loretta, in her best Cajun accent.

"Boy, hell! He nearly killed me," replied Jeremy, slowly picking himself off the ground.

Jeremy stood up and looked at his son. Junior was a carbon copy of himself thirty years ago, but he had Loretta's eye shape. One could tell that he was a football player; he had "no neck", and a thirty-four inch waist, broad muscular shoulders, and arms the size of a gorilla. *I bet he scares the opponents when he comes down the line on a crack-back block.* Jeremy reached out and pulled this behemoth of a man into his chest. Jeremy could feel the muscular man tense up, but just as quickly he relaxed, and allowed Jeremy to hug him.

"Well, that's better. Let's go inside and have some coffee," stated Loretta, authoritatively.

Jeremy and his son looked at each other, and meekly said, "Yes, ma'am." She escorted both men into the living room, and asked Conchita to bring in some coffee. Jeremy still could not bring himself to believe that he had a son, and what a son he turned out to be. All these years of not knowing was a great tragedy, than having a son and not loving him, thought Jeremy. I will love him and try to make up for all those years. Loretta snapped him out of his daydream.

"For the love of God, what were you thinking of when you jumped him at the door, Junior?" asked Loretta in a scolding motherly tone.

"Well, well. Uuuhh, well," stuttered a now-quiet and docile Junior.

"Quit stuttering, and get to the point! You are too old and intelligent to behave like that," replied a now-angry Loretta.

"I am sorry, Mom. I had all of this frustration boiling in me my entire life, and I just had to let it out. I always dreamed of having a father, but at the same time I was angry at him for not being there when I needed him. I am sorry Dad, Jeremy! What in the hell should I call you?" Finished Junior as he stood up to shake Jeremy's hand.

"You can call me just about anything you want, son! I am so proud of you! I promise to spend as much time with you as I can," replied a now-humble Jeremy.

Jeremy, Loretta and Junior spent the next six hours getting to know each other again, and recalling lost memories. Loretta, of course brought out the family photo album, which made Junior nervous. Jeremy Jr. was forced to endure the hundreds of "and here was Junior when" photos. Although Junior moaned and groaned throughout the experience, Jeremy could sense a feeling of pride and accomplishment emitting from Junior. After all, it wasn't everyone who was graduated as both a scholastic and football All-American from Stanford.

Jeremy took this opportunity to tell Junior how proud he was of his son, and what a honor it was to be the dad of such an accomplished son. Both men looked at each other in silence for a few seconds. No words were exchanged, and none were needed.

Junior was extremely interested in Jeremy's job, and kept asking questions about his past, and his current assignment. Jeremy told his son as much as could, without putting him in jeopardy. Junior expressed genuine interest and expressed amazement at his father's job.

"Hey, Dad! Do you think I could go along, and watch what you do? Do you? Huh? Please don't say no! I have been waiting my whole life for a 'show and tell,' and you just can't deny me! Please?" pleaded Junior in a whining sort of way.

Jeremy looked at Loretta as if to ask for help, but she only shook her shoulders. Jeremy knew that this was highly irregular, and it could get him canned if something went wrong, but he had not seen his son in twenty-seven years and he had some catching up to do. He also began to develop a plan which involved Junior. He looked at both of them and threw up his arms in submission. However, he had one condition.

"Son, I have but one condition. You drive your own car! And if anything starts to go wrong you follow my exact orders, is that understood?" asked an official sounding Jeremy.

"Yes, Sir, yes, Sir! I will follow orders. No problem, Dad! Besides, we have a 'Bye' week this week and I don't have to report back to the training camp until next Friday. I have four entire days off!" answered an enthusiastic Junior.

Both men said good-bye to Loretta, and got in their cars for the drive back to Sacramento. Traffic was very light at this time of night, and they were able to get to Sacramento in less than ninety minutes. Alex was surprised when Jeremy walked in, trailing his son, the famous pro-football player.

"Hey, Alex! This is my son, Junior. I brought him along in case you got out of hand," joked Jeremy as he walked in the office,

Alex was just dumbfounded. He couldn't believe it. Here he was in the company of one of America's top football players. His twelve-year-old son would die for the opportunity.

"I, aawh, dawh. I am sorry for staring, but you guys really look alike, and I am such a big fan of yours. I don't know what to call you," stated a confused Alex, as he extended his hand. I hope you don't mind me asking for an autograph for my son, Kenny. He would kill me if he knew I had spent time with you and not gotten your autograph.

"Junior is fine. Just ignore me. I promised my dad I wouldn't interfere. So just pretend I am a wall, and I will try to stay out of your way. I would be more than glad to help you. Just give me a paper and pen, and I'll sign away," replied a gracious Junior.

Alex and Jeremy resumed the tedious task of listening to the tapes. Junior just sat in the corner and reread old issues of *National*

Geographic. A couple of boring hours went by, then Jeremy yelled, "Hold it, Alex. I think we have something again." Alex rewound that portion and one could clearly hear Bolotin mention the ***Kiev,*** his CIA friend, and Las Vegas. Jeremy was very excited, but he still didn't know how everything tied together.

"Well there it is, Alex. Bolotin said it again. There has to be a connection, but unless we know more details, our hands are tied. I can only hope that Colonel Perrin will be able to dig up something in Paris," stated Jeremy, as he walked over and sat down at the table nearest Junior.

"You got that right! Unless we get some concrete evidence there is nothing we can do, especially if the CIA is somehow involved in this plot.

"Let's analyze our 'indicators' and see what we come up with. The ship ***Kiev*** has been mentioned several times. So has the name Bolotin, and of course let's not forget the CIA. Ooops, I forgot Las Vegas has also popped up several times. We know that the ***Kiev*** won't reach our territorial waters until the next twenty-four to forty-eight hours. We also know that nothing will happen until it gets here. Right? Alex, you and I have worked more overtime in the past three weeks than is legal, right? Why don't we take some time to fly to Vegas, and see an old friend of mine. He might be able to help. If not, we will have some fun for the next thirty-six hours anyway. Everyone can reach us by cell phone or pager. Right?" stated an unusually happy Jeremy.

"That's sounds like a great idea, Jeremy, but don't you think one of us should stay behind, just in case? It might look better. What do think, Jeremy?" replied Alex, hoping that Jeremy would agree with him.

"Okay, I agree. I was hoping you would say that. I did not have the heart to tell you, you could not go! I am sorry, Alex," stated Jeremy, a huge grin spreading across his face.

"You are pretty sneaky, pretty sneaky. One for you," replied Alex, making an "X" in the air with his index finger.

"Hey Junior, you have been very quiet about all of this. How would you like to go to Vegas? After all, I'm your dad and I want to marry your mom, someday soon!" stated Jeremy, slowly turning to face his son.

"Of course I do! I was only following orders. My God! Does she know yet? No, of course not. This is better than winning the "Super Bowl. Let's go back and tell her, right now!" screamed an exuberant Junior Grant.

Chapter 27

Las Vegas

All three of them landed at the modern Las Vegas MacClaren Airport, on the first Southwest Airlines flight out of Oakland. It had been less than eight hours since Jeremy had thought of the idea, and he was well on his way to becoming the husband of Loretta Q. DeFaut.

It seemed that Jeremy Junior was more excited than anyone else. Every stranger was a "new target" for his expressions of joy and happiness. Every passenger on the flight heard about 'his mom and dad finally getting married." It made for some interesting comments and looks from amused passengers. Loretta was overjoyed at the warmth shown by Jeremy and Junior toward each other. Loretta was sure that this sudden decision to fly to Vegas and get married was motivated by love and not convenience.

Jeremy was honest with her when he informed Loretta of his plan to meet a possible "source." He felt it was best to start off their "new" relationship with truthfulness. He also informed her of the necessity of returning home in less than thirty hours. He explained the circumstances, and she understood. Besides Loretta explained:

"I ran off on such short notice I didn't have time to reschedule my surgeries. I, too, have to get back in the next couple of days or my patients will suffer. We can always find time at a later date for a proper honeymoon. By the way, who is going to marry us? Please, don't tell me you have hired an Elvis impersonator priest for the ceremony," replied Loretta.

"No! Actually, I have a surprise for you. You will get to meet some of my family members. My cousin Douglas Lawyer is now a federal district court judge, and he has agreed to perform the ceremony. My other cousin, Danny, is the mayor, and he will also be present," stated a rather bubbly Jeremy.

"That sounds great! When will all of this take place?" asked the bride to be.

"Douglas assures me that everything will be ready around ten o'clock this morning. We have a few hours to kill, so why don't we go and check into our hotel? We will be staying at the MGM," stated Jeremy as they walked out of the airport into the hot Vegas sun.

All three of them, and particularly Jeremy were dazzled by the "New Vegas." All of the new hotels and adult entertainment centers were spectacular sights. Jeremy's last trip to Vegas had been sometime in 1968/69, and things had really changed since then. The taxi dropped them off at the MGM, and they were promptly escorted to two magnificent adjoining suites. Even Jeremy was impressed. These rooms were almost as impressive as the opulent ones he had been in twenty-seven years earlier.

Douglas and Danny arrived promptly at ten a.m., and all around introductions were made. Douglas had put on some weight and lost more hair, but he generally looked like the same "old Douglas", except now he was a respectable judge, and not a shyster. Both cousins had bought flowers for all, and the ceremony went off without a hitch. Of course Douglas was the first one wanting a kiss from the bride. Loretta did not object, and really put on a show for the judge. After he was done kissing her, he nearly fainted in ecstasy. Douglas turned to Loretta and said:

"Do you really want to marry this schmuck when you can have a real man for a husband?"

Jeremy just laughed it off, and forgave Douglas. Douglas was and always would be a "skirt chaser". Douglas had arranged for a special luncheon at a fancy restaurant, and a long white limousine for the newlyweds. During a quiet moment Jeremy pulled Douglas aside, and confided in him about his secondary purpose in visiting Vegas.

"Are you crazy? Do you want to make your wife a widow before she can even enjoy her honeymoon? Guido is the most vicious and dangerous 'Hood' in Vegas. He is one of the last old-style gangsters, and even the law enforcement community is afraid of this lunatic. Are you crazy? I stopped dealing with him over twenty years ago, when I found out about his dark side. Not only that, but he has been a recluse since his incident." replied a now openly agitated Douglas.

"Slow down, 'Cuz,' I know what I am doing. Besides, you forget that Guido and I go back a long way, and he owes me plenty! I will use him for the information he has, and then discard him like a 'cheap whore.' I am not going to take any chances. What incident are you referring to? Don't worry, in and out. However, I would like to use your cell phone as insurance," replied Jeremy in a soft tone of voice.

"Cell phone? Is that all you are worrying about? Half of Vegas tried to gun him down a few months ago!" said an incredulous Douglas.

"Yes, cell phone! I am surprised at you, 'Your Honor'! Cell phones are open communications and anyone can tape record them. I will dial your number prior to going into Guido's office, and you can listen to what is being said, and if your answering machine happens to recording, oh well! If they tried to gun him down and he is still alive, I am sure he has taken care of business," smiled Jeremy.

"Yes, yes indeed! You are very clever. Safe and secure. No one would ever doubt the word of a federal judge. I like it, and I now feel more secure about your going there. I might get a crack at marrying your beautiful bride yet! Have you told your wife and son?

"No, I haven't. I don't think it is a good idea. Loretta would worry and Junior cannot afford to be seen in that neighborhood. Please occupy them until I return," asked Jeremy as he left the room.

Jeremy left Loretta and Junior at the hotel, knowing that Douglas would take care of everything. It was a great relief to Jeremy, and he immediately felt a lot more confident in his actions. Jeremy took a taxi to Guido's hotel. En route his pager was activated. It was Alex calling from their office in San Francisco. Jeremy called back using Douglas's cell phone.

"Hello? It's me, Jeremy. What do you need? What is going on?" asked a concerned Jeremy.

"I have some interesting information I felt you should know about. I just received a complete list of Russian personnel from aboard the ***Kiev.*** It is 'protocol' for the ship's commander to notify the Customs officials and provide them with all the pertinent data, etc. The ***Kiev*** is expected to dock in forty-eight hours, and approximately half of its four-thousand-men crew will be given alternating days off in San

Francisco. In other words, we will have at least two thousand Russian sailors in our neighborhood for at least three days! By the time we check each of them through our Intel and law-enforcement channels it will be time for the next group, and so on!" explained a very desolate Alex.

"That is definitely not good news. But if we have to work all night, and in shifts, we must screen everyone! Understood?" replied an unhappy Jeremy.

"Don't hang up yet, Jeremy! Your French colonel called, but he would not reveal anything to me over the phone. He did not 'trust' me! Can you believe him? Anyway, he said he had some 'URGENT' information for you. Call him right now!" explained Alex in a mocking nasal French accent.

"You have done well, Robin," mocked Jeremy as he hung up the phone.

Yes indeed! Things are increasing in tempo. It looks like the proverbial 'shit' is going to hit the fan. Jeremy hoped that his trip to Guido's would confirm what he already knew. The taxi pulled up in front of the Matador casino, and Jeremy could already tell the difference. Major reconstruction had taken place since his last visit. The old casino had been completely demolished and in its place, a beautiful twenty-seven storied, four-thousand-room palace had been erected. No money had been spared in building Guido's newest casino. It had as many lights as stars in the sky. Jeremy had to admit that it had been tastefully done. The combinations of lights, paint and glass turned it into a shimmering oasis.

Jeremy paid the taxi driver, and walked up to the bell captain. It was almost deja-vu, as a young, snot-nosed kid sat on stool, and said:

"Can I help you, sir?"

"Yes, you can! I need to see Guido Fontana, is he in?" asked Jeremy of the on duty bell captain.

"Uuh! Yes, Sir! Who shall I say is calling?" asked the young man.

"Tell him it's an old friend. Jeremy is my name. Jeremy Grant," he replied.

One thing he had noticed in these new casinos. Although they had even more slot machines, it was definitely quieter than before. The advent of modern electronics had reduced the noise levels in most casinos. Jeremy waited in the front lobby area for approximately ten minutes before a tall silver-haired gentleman approached him and said:

"Good evening, Sir, may I help you?"

"Yes, you can. I would like to speak with Guido Fontana. Is he still the owner of this fine establishment?" inquired Jeremy in his most polite fashion.

"Yes, of course. But my boss, Mr. Fontana, asked me to ask you for some identification. You see, he seems to think that you are dead," stated the "hood" in his best "Brooklyn" accent.

"Of course, I understand! Here is my California driver's license," replied Jeremy by showing his license.

"Good, good! I guess that's okay! I can let you up. Are you carrying heat?" asked the goon.

"Don't worry. I left it at home. I wouldn't think of violating any city ordinances by 'packing heat," replied an amused Jeremy.

The elevator ride to the penthouse was no less exhilarating than it had been the first time, twenty-seven years ago. When the doors opened to the corridor, the mandatory security personnel were visible in the hallway, except this time they were "packing" pump shotguns and .45's. They immediately became visibly alert, and edgy. The escorting gorilla explained to them that Mr. Fortuna was expecting Jeremy. They nodded their heads in unison and opened the door to the penthouse suite.

Jeremy walked into an incredibly beautiful room. It was modeled after an English Tudor-style building. At first Jeremy was shocked to see this type of decorative style in a home owned by a gangster, but had to admit that Guido had taste. Jeremy glanced around the room, but could not immediately see Guido or anyone else for that matter. After a few seconds, a fifty-something woman dressed in a nurse's uniform beckoned to him to come over to the window. Jeremy was surprised by her, but walked over anyway. There lying prone on his back was Guido Fontana. Every known medical instrument, probe, ventilator, and gizmo was visibly attached to him. An audible wheezing sound could be heard from a raspy voice.

"Hi Jeremy! I, I, I thought you were dead? No news in all these years! But I see that except for looking a little older, you are still in one piece," stated the man in the bed, who had obvious difficulty in talking and breathing.

"Well, I can't say the same for you. What on earth happened to you? When and why?" asked a shocked Jeremy.

Guido's appearance had taken Jeremy by surprise. He had always been a specimen of good health, and in extremely good shape. He had now shrunk down to skeleton size, and was obviously dying. At most, he weighed one hundred and twenty pounds, and was shrinking at the rate of a pound a day.

Guido slowly explained that he had been the victim of an ambush by a rival mob family, and had barely survived. Guido went on to explain that his combat experience and will to live had forced him to hold on. He wanted revenge, and by God, he had gotten it. All of the hit men, had been hit in return, and the gang leader was now dead.

Jeremy stared at this wretched man, and almost felt sorry for him. He could not believe that anyone in this condition could still be alive. Jeremy approached Guido and said:

"Guido, I can see your time is soon approaching. How about giving me a few seconds? I need your help! Do you know anything about a large shipment of heroin? We know that it's coming soon, aboard a Russian ship! Why don't you come clean, Guido? You owe me, and I am holding you to your promise. I need to know, and I need to know now. You obviously know that your time on this earth is quite limited, and it would surely serve your cause to come clean. You don't want all those souls on your conscience," demanded an irate Jeremy.

"Yes, I owe you, Jeremy, but you are not going to get anything out of me this way. If I decide to tell you anything it's because I want to, not because I owe you! Remember, we have our own code, and I can't violate it, even for you. This bond is a lot stronger, and my family's reputation is at stake. Even after I die, my family will live on, and I can't worry about anyone except them. I hope you are not too disappointed? We were good friends at one time, but that was out of necessity. That was merely a training ground for my job here. My father wanted me to be hard, and tough. I figured out soon enough that the Army would either toughen me or kill me. It also gave me access to hundreds of weapons, and explosives," replied an ever-weakening Guido.

Jeremy looked upon this hulk of a man, and he knew that Guido's time was nearing an end. *How ironic,* Jeremy thought, *the once indestructible hulk, is now a burned-out wisp of a man.* Jeremy looked down at this carcass, and pleaded one last time.

"Please! I beg you! Tell me anything you can. Why don't you try to meet your Maker with a clean conscience?" pleaded Jeremy.

"Okay Jeremy. A riddle; if you can figure it out you might get a clue that might help you: ***Essem Quam Videri***, Do you speak Latin? You figure it out, Jeremy. Don't let them fool you. That's all I have to say. Please, give me the dignity of dying in peace! Leave me alone! Get out now!" screamed a dying Guido.

Two of Guido's henchmen escorted Jeremy out the door, and down the escalator. Jeremy realized that it would do no good to argue anymore, and he took the next available taxi back to the MGM. On the way back to his hotel Jeremy kept pondering Guido's dying words: "**ESSEM QUAM VIDERI!**" "Don't let them fool you," also stuck in his mind. Was Guido trying in his own way to warn Jeremy? Or was he trying to confuse him? *Enough of this*, he thought. The taxi pulled up to the hotel, and Jeremy went straight for his room. There awaiting him were Douglas, Danny, Junior and Loretta. They had started the party without him, and had consumed several bottles of champagne in his absence.

Jeremy was eager to join the party and catch up on the amusement. His stay with Guido had depressed him, and he was glad to see Loretta again. Although she didn't want to show it, she had anxiously awaited his return. Jeremy grabbed her and gave her a long and passionate kiss.

"Great to have you back, darling. I should have you go away more often, if this is the reward I get upon your return. How were things? Did you get information from this guy?" stated Loretta, as she handed Jeremy a full glass of champagne.

Jeremy went on to explain the events, and how confused he was.

Without giving too much information, he expressed his disappointment.

"I can help you out, Jeremy. I had four years of Latin, and after all I am a doctor and we still use many Latin terms. Okay, let's go over it again. **ESSEM** means 'to be,' **QUAM** means 'rather' and **VIDERI** perhaps means 'to seem.' TO BE RATHER THAN TO SEEM? Do you think that's right, Jeremy? What could this mean? Does it make any sense to you?" asked Loretta, in a rather confused way.

"Well, it could if I knew what he was referring to. Let's worry about it upon returning to San Francisco. Nothing is going to happen anyway until that ship makes port, and that won't be for a day or two. I do have to make one more phone call to Paris, and then we can party!" Replied Jeremy, as he walked over to the phone near the hallway, and dialed France.

"Hello, hello! Is that you, Colonel Perrin? Good! How are you doing? I am glad," inquired a polite Jeremy.

"I am so glad you called. I think you may have a big problem on your hands! I called around to my contacts, and they were very reticent at first to reveal anything. It appears that they seem to think that something big is going to happen in San Francisco," explained a nervous Colonel Perrin.

"What do you mean something big? Yes, we already know that. Explain yourself. Please, tell me all you know," asked an anxious Jeremy.

Colonel Perrin went on to explain that his contacts were reluctant at first to reveal anything. It was only after the offer of giving a suspected dormant "STASI mole" (Former East German Secret Service) that they agreed to talk. The CIA claimed that three Russian officers aboard the ***Kiev*** were defecting and bringing a new type of missile with them! They went on to explain that all details were being co-directed by someone in California!" explained a proud and cheery Colonel Perrin.

"What? What kind of bullshit is this? Are you sure about this? New missile? Defectors? This sounds like something out of a James Bond movie! Are they that stupid? Oh my God! They are surely being led by the nose. Was any word mentioned about the heroin?"

asked a rather excited Jeremy.

"No, not directly. I tried as much as I could, but there was no mention of drugs. However, I tried contacting your ex-boss in Germany, but I was only able to reach his wife. She told me that Bill was in California on business, and would not be back for a few weeks!" replied Colonel Perrin, his voice expressing amazement.

"California? Did you say California? Of course, now I see it all! Damn it! How could I have been so stupid? Billy Bob! Of course! Bolotin, the 'friend', the heroin, and Oleg! Only Billy Bob knew everything. I think we both know what is going on, colonel. Once again, you have been a true friend. I will let you know what happens."

Everyone in the hotel room had been staring at Jeremy. He had unknowingly raised his voice, and he was now mumbling to himself.

"That asshole! That S.O.B! I'll kill him! I'll, I'll…! " muttered Jeremy as he walked around the room in a rage.

"What's wrong darling?" asked a concerned Loretta.

"Oh, I am sorry. I apologize for my manners, but something terrible has just happened, and it is life threatening to a lot of innocent victims. I am devastated. Can I talk to you alone for second, sweetheart?" asked Jeremy, as he pulled Loretta into the bathroom.

Jeremy went on to explain to Loretta the events of the past few years, and the possible involvement of his best friend and former boss. Loretta just sat there and listened quietly. She understood the gravity and consequences of these events. She took Jeremy's hand and asked him to please make reservations to go back home as soon as possible. Jeremy then informed Alex by phone and told him to expect them back in the next five or six hours. Junior was the one most disappointed. He hadn't quite understood Jeremy's predicament, and quite honestly wanted to stay on in Vegas. Jeremy assured him that, as soon as this debacle was over, they would be coming back for a week of fun and amusement.

Douglas escorted them back to the airport, and wished them well. Exactly one hour and twenty-five minutes later they landed in Oakland, California. Jeremy excused himself from Loretta and Junior and returned to his office.

Alex was there to greet him with a stack of crew member listings, and a note to see the boss right a way! Jeremy knew that Neal was probably not very happy to find out about his trip to Vegas.

"How could you? How could you go to Vegas and meet a known mobster, without reporting to me first? That is not your job! You know the rules! The SAC knows about your holiday, and he also wants to know why you violated department policy!" exclaimed an irate Neal Brown.

"Well boss, it was one of those things. I finally got married to Loretta, and I figured I'd take the opportunity to talk to Fontana. As you know, I was his commander in Vietnam," explained Jeremy in the hopes of mollifying his boss.

"You got married, and didn't invite me! Shit, that is even worse! Wait till the SAC hears about this!" yelled a pissed off Neal Brown.

Jeremy had to do a lot of fast talking and pleading to keep his job and his role in the developing case.

Chapter 28

"Shit" Happens

Aboard the ***Kiev*** Oleg, Yuri and Admiral Zurkov were putting the final touches on their bold plan to off-load the heroin in plain view of the world. Oleg had been in touch with Viktor Varmessy in Sacramento, and they and Billy Scarsdale were going to get the CIA to pick up the missile in a warehouse along the waterfront in West Sacramento for the alleged defection and exchange of money. However, in order to ensure security, the CIA would send two or three agents to the ***Kiev*** ahead of time, and escort the cargo to Sacramento. They, in fact, would be the insurance against any interference from curious law enforcement officials.

In order to avoid suspicion from his own men, CPT Chetskiy and LT Nikolayev distracted the men by arranging a ship-wide volleyball contest aboard the ***Kiev.*** Her cavernous aircraft storage bays made for ideal volleyball courts. It was hoped that this boisterous event would occupy their attention for most of the day. CPT Chetskiy offered a rather generous first-prize reward of $500.00. This bountiful gesture ensured 100% participation of the crew, and large quantities of vodka flowed freely throughout the day, numbing those who might get suspicious. Most of the men did not even notice the activities surrounding the movement of the missile, and if they did, they really did not care.

CPT Chetskiy and LT Nikolayev had already repainted and loaded the missile with the heroin. In order to assure safe transportation, it had also been covered with several layers of canvas and secured with heavy chains to facilitate easy handling. When the missile was later off-loaded to the admiral's personal motorized fifty-two-foot boat, no one seemed to notice, or if they did they did not let on.

Oleg and the rest of the off-loading crew had already changed to civilian clothes and were waiting for their final contact with Varmessy and Billy Bob. The rest of the crew remained oblivious to the events and were intensely involved in their game or were preparing for shore liberty. The ***Kiev*** now stood in the outer bay, just outside the Golden Gate Bridge, and awaited final U.S. Customs approval, and the harbor pilot. Due to darkness, Customs had delayed their boarding until the following morning.

Yuri and Oleg both agreed that the sight of a Russian admiral's large motorized boat cruising through San Francisco Bay would arouse unwanted attention. In order to avoid suspicion, the missile would be off-loaded aboard a large yacht somewhere near the Martinez Straights during the hours of darkness. It would then proceed back up the basin toward Sacramento, for its West Sacramento rendezvous. The Varmessy group had a large warehouse in Benicia, right off Lake Herman Road, with waterfront access. They could use the loading dock to switch the missile from the admiral's boat to the yacht. The dock was equipped with a loading crane and it would make the transition an easy matter. The warehouse was only two thousand yards from the Vallejo Bridge, and was naturally hidden from prying eyes, by a large ridge.

The CIA had made veiled notifications to law enforcement and were hoping not to attract a lot of attention, although by now they were aware of the "warning" from Customs. The weather report predicted poor weather, and in its traditional manner San Francisco's famous fog was scheduled to make an appearance that evening and would definitely assist in cloaking this dubious ship to shore exercise.

The CIA felt that the boldness of the plan was their best camouflage. All they were concerned about was getting this new missile on U.S. soil before the Russian government could scream foul, and they would have to give it back. They fully intended to give it back, but only after they had discovered all its secrets. They were like kids with a new toy, and weren't quite ready to believe that it wouldn't function properly.

Billy Bob Scarsdale had duped the CIA into this plan, and he was confident that they would follow his lead without question. After all, he was one of them, or used to be, and was still trusted by them. Only Jeremy and Colonel Perrin suspected the real Billy Bob. Jeremy was at a loss on how to contact or convince the CIA that he already knew of their plot, and that it was a trap. Like so many times in the past, they were blinded by their own agenda and failed to see the truth. Only his agency had a true picture of what was going on. Jeremy spoke to his boss and they both concluded that a multi-jurisdictional task force should be considered. It was hoped that using this approach might "spread out the backlash," should anything go wrong.

Neal agreed to the task force idea, but U.S. Customs was not above being territorial, and wanted to keep this an all-Customs affair. Through some dedicated effort and persuasion, Jeremy was able to convince a Customs official to initiate an immediate task force in the hopes of preventing a disaster from occurring. Jeremy was assigned the task of organizing and coordinating the entire affair. Alex and the remaining members of his staff went about contacting the FBI, ATF, Coast Guard, Naval Intelligence, San Francisco Police Department, etc. Within a few hours a dozen or more officers were involved, and actively participating in the case.

Although the wheels had been set in motion, there was no one driving the train. As long as the CIA believed Scarsdale, and that they were going to get a "genuine article," there wasn't much anyone could do but follow them and try to intercede at the right time. The CIA has no jurisdiction within the borders of the continental U.S. If the opportunity surfaced, Jeremy and his Task Force would swoop down on them "like flies on shit."

Jeremy and his staff continued checking the names of crew members for prior criminal history. They all came up negative, with one exception. Oleg Kolkov's jumped out of the crew's list and hit Jeremy like a ton of bricks. He could not believe that Kolkov would be so brazen as to use his real name. His name was listed under the "officers" column, and had the title of "Chief Translator." Jeremy informed his staff, Neal Brown and the rest of the task force of this new development. This was the final proof that he needed of the connection Oleg to Bolotin, to Billy Bob, to the heroin. Jeremy hoped that this new bit of evidence might convince his ex-colleagues at the CIA that they were falling into a trap.

Jeremy and his crew were convinced by now that the heroin, the

Kiev and the CIA were all working in conjunction with each other, but they were totally ignorant as to the method of entry. The CIA, in fact, did not know yet that the heroin had been hidden in the missile. Jeremy prevailed upon Neal to accompany him to the CIA office at the federal building in San Francisco. Both men were convinced that their efforts would not be appreciated, but Jeremy had to give it one last try.

They arrived at the federal building and showed their credentials to the federal police officer manning the security desk on the ground floor. They were allowed to pass the metal detectors, and proceed to the eleventh floor. A small sign on the door of room 1101 said, “Resident Office, Central Intelligence Agency.” They entered and found themselves in a small gray office waiting area, with an enclosed bullet-proof area to their right. A video camera slowly panned the room and recorded their actions. A young woman sat on the other side of the cubicle and stared at her monitor. After a few seconds she looked up, and asked:

“Can I help you?” Her voice sounding nasal and twangy.

“Yes, you may. We are from the San Francisco field office of the U.S. Customs Bureau, and we need to speak with the Resident Agent in Charge (RAC),” stated Neal Brown, in an official sounding voice.

“Let me see if he is in, and may I tell him what this is all about?” asked the young clerk, without even looking up from her monitor.

“It’s urgent, and many people may die if we don’t see him now!” screamed an irate Jeremy.

The young woman looked at him, and got up from her desk. Neal reached over and put his hand on Jeremy’s shoulder in an effort to calm him. They waited for fifteen minutes and no one showed up. All of a sudden, Neal Brown’s pager buzzed. He looked down at the number, and saw his boss’s private number, and *911 was after it. He knew that was the code for an immediate call back. Neal used his cell phone and called back the special agent in charge, Tim Spooner.

“Hey Tim, what is the emergency? Now, now, slow down. We are only here to prevent bloodshed, not to cause any! I see, okay boss, it’s your call, but you had better tell that CIA ‘dweeb’ that when the shit hits the fan, it will be his neck, and not mine. We tried to warn him, and he wouldn’t even open his fucking door!” replied an irate

Neal Brown.

"Stop before you say anything, these rooms are bugged, and we don't want to tell that PRICK anything that might help him!" screamed a fuming Jeremy.

Jeremy had never seen Neal this angry before. The arteries in his head and neck were bulging to the point of exploding. Neal grabbed Jeremy's arm and pulled him out of the office. When they got out in the hallway, he started to say something, but then put his hand over his mouth, and walked a few more yards before saying anything else.

"Those, those mother-fucking assholes! Those, those…I can't believe them. They called Tim, and said if we didn't leave immediately, they would call Washington, and tell the commissioner that we were interfering with a 'national security' matter, and have us 'arrested'! Can you believe the nerve of those guys!" screamed an extremely irate Neal Brown.

"Look boss, we tried and it failed again. The only thing we have to do is chronicle all of our steps and ensure that our asses our covered when this goes wrong!" replied a less irate Jeremy Grant.

Both men returned to the office, and continued to coordinate their next moves. One thing they wanted to do was ensure that the Sacramento law enforcement agencies were briefed, and put on an alert, and also contact the Coast Guard and ask then to keep an eye on the ***Kiev.***

Jeremy felt at this point that it might even be a good idea to move part of the task force to Sacramento. He spoke with Neal, and they contacted the Sacramento RAC. She was to act as coordinator until they were in place. He was moving his entire staff to Sacramento for the duration.

Jeremy took advantage of this opportunity to stop by Loretta's house in Fremont, and explain the situation to her. She was obviously concerned, but knew that Jeremy had survived many such encounters, and he could take care of himself. *Besides*, she thought, h*e now has a desk job, and won't get in too much trouble.* Junior Grant had overheard the conversation and was pleading to be allowed to go along.

"No, I am very sorry, son, but this time I can't let you come.

However, you can stay glued to your television and watch CNN, they will surely announce what's going on as it happens!" replied a half-joking Jeremy. Junior Grant was not happy, but he knew better than to push the issue.

Jeremy kissed Loretta good-bye, and left the Fremont area, driving northbound toward Sacramento. Alex, meanwhile, called all of Sacramento's law enforcement agencies and spoke to the watch commanders. He advised them of what might be happening on the waterfront in the next twenty-four hours.

Sacramento's Police Department marine unit was the only one scheduled for patrol along the busy Sacramento River that day. They had planned to have two units on the river from dawn to approximately 02:00 hours. However, these units had the discretion to stay longer if the situation warranted it. These units were normally composed of longtime veteran marine officers, who were paid reserve officers. Most of these officers had twenty, thirty years of experience cruising the rivers of Sacramento. It was one of the choice jobs in the Sacramento Police Department, and these veteran officers really liked their work.

The watch commander had instructed them to start their shift a little earlier, and gave them complete instructions. Corporal John Martinez and Sergeant William "Bill" Craiger were assigned the first twelve-hour shift. Both men had a combined law enforcement experience of over thirty-five years.

"Hey, Bill and John. I really appreciate you guys coming in earlier today. We have this B.O.L.O. (Be On the Lookout) from U.S. Customs. They are expecting some trouble with Russians, and a possible large load of heroin. Keep your eyes open for unusual activity, and call in every stop. The only backup you will have is a CHP (California Highway Patrol) helicopter, and perhaps a Coast Guard unit out of Stockton. I really would not count on them; they are too far away. Be safe, and don't take any chances." The watch commander finished his speech taking less than one minute, and he was out the door.

Bill and John sat there for a while and were somewhat perplexed by the B.O.L.O. It was very seldom that the watch commander personally briefed them. It was normally done by one of the sector sergeants, or the administrative sergeant. *Oh well,* they thought, *maybe tonight is the night.*

They loaded up their patrol car with all the extra gear that a marine officer must carry and drove to the Miller Park city boat docks. They carried all of their gear down to the boat, and stowed it aboard. A safety check was made, and they then started up their engine. The blue and white police boat slowly drifted out into the current. Their first stop would take them to the Shell marine station in the marina. Once they were filled up with gas and provisions, they gently eased the throttle forward on their powerful 454-cubic-inch Chevy engine. The boat surged forward into the swift-moving river. The recent rains had made the river extremely muddy and dangerous. Large logs and debris could easily punch a hole in the side of the boat.

The engine responded to the expert throttle commands and before they knew it, they were cruising northward toward the Vietnam Veterans Bridge, which is the dividing line between West Sacramento and Sacramento City. *If anything is going to happen it's going to start here,* thought both men. Although they knew the area by heart, they wanted to cruise the area one more time, just in case. In less than ten minutes, the powerful twenty-six-foot Bayliner passed under the bridge. As the boat cruised the area, campfires from homeless people could be seen along the bank. A thirty-minute cruise through the area revealed only a new sand bank on the south side, and a new large houseboat docked near the jetty. Everything else seemed to be quiet and peaceful.

Bill swung the boat around and headed back south for a patrol along the southern edge of their district.

Chapter 29

Action Stations

Oleg and the rest of the shore party left the carrier. As the admiral's boat pulled away from the large protective shield offered by the ship's side, Oleg had a momentary feeling of insecurity and fear. He looked up and patted the sides of his eight hundred pounds of heroin, and felt somewhat reassured. So far, everything had gone his way, except his hideous Russian imprisonment of course, but that was a small price to pay for what was about to happen. Yuri saw him pat the side of the missile and came walking over to him.

"Hey cousin, we have done it! We are in America! Can you believe it? Everything is going well, isn't it?" questioned a buoyant Yuri.

"Yes, it is! However, that is my worry. I don't believe in so much luck. Something has to go wrong. I will feel much better once the transaction has been completed and we are back on board, and on our way to Tahiti, or Australia or Indonesia, I don't care, as long as we are away from here. Besides, the fog is getting very thick and I hope that this pilot can find our location." answered a worried Oleg.

"Don't you worry, little cousin. Everything will be fine. I am sure that Mr. Scarsdale has thought of everything. The CIA will not know what hit them. Hasn't our operation worked so far? No interference from Coast Guard or Customs, right? He has worked everything out to perfection. Should we have any problems, those two CIA gentlemen who came aboard last night, along with our good Mr. Scarsdale, will part the water, just like Moses," replied a confident Yuri.

As if on cue, Billy Bob Scarsdale came up on deck with a bottle of champagne and three glasses in his hand. Well gentlemen, I think we should celebrate, don't you?" asked an ebullient Scarsdale.

"Yes, yes of course! Let's toast to our success, and to you, Mr. Scarsdale," replied a happy Yuri.

All three men sat silently, sipping champagne, all three reflecting on the past few years and the efforts involved in getting the heroin to this point. They grew strangely silent, and gazed off in different directions. The San Francisco fog slowly engulfed them, and within a few seconds they completely disappeared from sight.

The Coast Guard patrol boat at Treasure Island had been given the task to watch and track anything or anybody getting off that ship. GM2 (Gunner's Mate Petty Officer 2nd Class) David Kaminski was on duty, and he held powerful binoculars in his hands. He reached in his right coat pocket for a cigarette, and lit it. Just when he did, he thought he noticed a dark object glide away from the ***Kiev.*** He was pretty sure it was a boat, but he could not tell if it came from the ***Kiev.*** He shouted down to the radar operator and asked him he saw it, too.

"Hey Jones, did you see that blip moving away from the ***Kiev***?"

"Yes, I did, but the mass of the carrier, made it impossible to tell 100% or not. I am pretty sure thought," he replied, an almost convinced radar operator.

"Okay, thanks! I guess I better contact LT Myers. He gave specific instructions," stated a somewhat nervous Kaminski.

GM2 Kaminski called LT Myers and reported the incident. Myers ordered that the ship be made ready for sailing immediately. By the time "Action Stations" orders were given, and the ship left its mooring, the Russian admiral's launch was a good five to six miles away and slowly blending in with the numerous other radar contacts in the bay. At this time there were over a hundred small boats of that size, and at least twenty of them were moving in all directions at the same time.

"Sparks! Give me a better reading. Can't you tell which direction they went? Oh, man! Someone is going to catch hell for this," shouted an irate LT Myers.

The Coast Guard cutter sped through the inner bay not knowing which direction the Russian launch went. After cruising around for an hour or so, they returned to Treasure Island and reported the incident. The incident was eventually passed up to the task force headquarters. LT CDR. Kelly called Jeremy and reported the incident.

"Shit, shit and double shit! I can't believe we let them off that ship!" screamed an irate Jeremy.

"I am sorry, Jeremy, but those things happen. After all, the weather is pretty miserable, isn't it?" replied LT CDR. Kelly, the Coast Guard liaison officer to the task force.

"Yes, yes it is! Right now was a lousy time for them to screw up! Can you get your boys to continue patrolling until dawn, anyway?" asked an exhausted Jeremy.

"Can do!" answered an embarrassed Kelly.

"What's going on? Has anything happened?" asked Alex.

Jeremy went on to explain the events. Although they had apparently slipped away, at least they knew that they were moving toward Sacramento. Jeremy called Sacramento P.D.'s watch commander and informed him of the incident. LT Sanchez immediately called the dispatcher and had them contact P.D.'s Marine 1 unit again.

"Marine 1? Marine 1? This is control. Do you copy?" called an anxious police dispatcher.

"Marine 1, go ahead, control!" answered Marine 1.

"Be advised that LT Sanchez wants you to know that the B.O.L.O. subject is possibly headed your way. It was possibly seen in the bay area ninety minutes ago. Unknown description, except it was a large ship. Check!"

"Marine 1, copy and thanks. If you get anymore of a description let us know. Do you know if plans have been made for additional marine units?" asked Marine 1.

"Marine 1. No, I don't, but I will inquire for you," replied a sincerely worried dispatcher.

The dispatcher contacted LT Sanchez, and relayed the message from Marine 1. Being a veteran officer, and wishing to cover his ass at the same time, Sanchez called the watch commander at West Sacramento P.D. and advised him of the dilemma. CPT Garcia was well aware of the situation, but had no one available until 06:00 hours. His marine unit officers were currently working regular patrol, and could not be pulled away until then. Garcia agreed to relieve them an hour earlier and have them start at 05:00 instead.

Meanwhile the Russian ship and its precious cargo continued

unimpeded toward the rendezvous in Benecia. The ship's pilot was obviously a local, because he guided them through the harbor and around traffic with the agility of a jet-skier despite the heavy fog. In less than ninety minutes he was moored alongside a large seagoing, seventy-foot-plus yacht. A stealthy crew of hooded men manhandled the missile from one ship to another. In less than thirty minutes the *Sexy Sally* out of San Francisco was heading eastward up the channel toward Sacramento. Oleg, Yuri, Scardale and company also transferred aboard the luxurious yacht.

Varmessy and his gang had prepared an ambush for the CIA, the moment the drugs were off-loaded in West Sacramento. The CIA officials would be executed, and the heroin transferred to a truck. Varmessy had picked this warehouse because of its solitude and location. They knew from experience that West Sacramento P.D. could not respond to any incident in this part of the county in less than eleven minutes. Various assassins had been diligently placed in such a manner as to maximize firepower on the helpless CIA agents, and should any other police officer accidentally stray into the killing zone, they, too, would meet the same fate.

Varmessy and his crew had thought of everything. They would then transport the heroin by truck to another garage in Sacramento. From there, it would be broken down into smaller parcels, and transported to the various clients. On the surface the plan appeared to be foolproof, except Varmessy did not now that Jeremy knew about Scarsdale and Kolkov.

Jeremy and his crew were stuck in their office, anxiously waiting for something to happen. They knew who was doing it now, but they could not figure out exactly where. Suddenly, Jeremy hit upon an idea. U.S. Customs had some of the strongest law enforcement powers of seizure and arrest.

He discussed his plan with his boss, and got approval for deputizing or cross-designating Sacramento P.D.'s marine unit officers, and anyone else involved in the task force. This authority would allow them full Customs powers of search and seizure, and allow them the power to basically search any vessel coming up the river, without the necessity of search warrants or other "probable cause," etc. Jeremy called West Sac. P.D. and offered them the same credentials. It was enthusiastically accepted by CPT Garcia. Jeremy asked both watch commanders and their officers to meet at the ramp of Miller Park in Sacramento for a short conference.

Forty five minutes later, Jeremy, Alex, Neal, West Sacramento P.D., Sacramento P.D., and several other law enforcement agencies met to discuss the upcoming game plan. Jeremy knew that the Russian ship had last been spotted four hours ago in the bay area, and it would take them approximately four or five hours to reach Sacramento. By then, both marine units could patrol the river, and it was hoped that by daylight, the helicopter unit and the second Sacramento P.D. marine unit would be operational. Each of the two marine units took on an additional two officers. Jeremy and Alex went with Sacramento P.D.'s Marine 1, and Neal and another officer went with the West Sacramento marine unit. The remaining task force members were put in motorized-patrol units and given sectors of the river to patrol.

A control element was left behind to coordinate the operation. At approximately 04:25 hours, this control element received a report from the San Francisco Coast Guard cutter that a Russian ship was stopped and boarded near the ***Kiev,*** and thoroughly searched. Nothing suspicious was found aboard, and it was released to return to its mother ship. Although the report, in itself, was disappointing, it proved that the cargo had already been off-loaded and was definitely en route to Sacramento. All marine and motorized units were advised and kept abreast of the situation.

For the next few hours Marine1 patrolled the area from Miller Park westward, and West SAC, patrolled everything eastward. Jeremy hoped that no one could get through the web.

Chapter 30

"The Russian Are Coming"

It was about 0:30 aboard the *Sexy Sally.* The ship's cook had just served breakfast, and everyone was just finishing their coffee. Billy Bob, Oleg, and Yuri were sitting around the lounge talking about what they would do with their share of the money. The CIA guys were outside guarding "their" missile, oblivious to what was really going on. Oleg stood up and looked down at Billy Bob.

"Are you sure these guys don't have a clue? I would hate to come this close and fail," stated a nervous Oleg.

"Look, I have told you ten times already. These guys are like robots. Once you program them, they just keep on going. You know, 'Like the Ever-ready Bunny.' We have nothing to worry about. Not even Jeremy can hurt us now! We are less than fifteen minutes away from Sacramento," smiled, an overconfident Scarsdale.

Okay, okay, I am convinced. What about the money? Is it still going to go to a numbered Swiss Bank account, as agreed?" asked Oleg as he sat back down.

"That's right, for the hundredth time! Look, you just remember your part during the exchange, and everything will be fine."

Just then the ship's captain came running in.

"Mr. Scarsdale, what should I do? What should I do? That police boat wants us to slow down and stop. What should I do?" asked a very nervous captain.

"Ask him what the problem is, but keep moving, don't stop!" barked a very nervous Scarsdale.

As the ship's captain went back topside, Yuri pulled out an AK-47 from underneath the cushions and "racked" a round in the chamber. He told Oleg and the rest of the crew to be prepared to fight their way through this police boat. The two CIA guys came back down into the lounge and looked at Yuri. One could see by the look in their eyes that they were unsure what to do. Yuri made up their minds real fast. He pulled out a silenced automatic and fired two shots into their brains. Both men dropped to the ground without so much as a sound. Oleg walked over, and fired two more rounds from his silenced gun into their already lifeless bodies.

The ship's captain came running back in a few seconds later, a look of horror on his face.

"Yuri! They say that they are US Customs officers and want to board us!" screamed a hysterical captain.

"You listen, and you listen good, dear captain! Do not, I repeat, do not stop until we get to our West Sac. docking area. We will take care of these guys right now," screamed a furious Yuri.

Yuri, Oleg and two others climbed up the stairs holding automatic weapons in their hands. Their plan was to ambush Marine 1 as soon as it got close enough.

"*Sexy Sally, Sexy Sally*! This is the Sacramento Police Department, and the U.S. Customs, we are ordering you to 'heave to' now!" commanded a pissed-off SGT Craiger.

CPL Martinez was on the radio with Control One.

"Control One, This is Marine 1."

"Go ahead, Marine 1," replied the dispatcher.

"Yeah, we are in pursuit of a large seventy-foot cruiser called the *Sexy Sally* out of San Francisco. Her captain is refusing to…Shots fired, shots fired! Code 900, Code 900! Code three back-up now, I…" screamed SGT Craiger. Those were the last words he spoke.

The first burst of Yuri's AK-47 had caught him in the chest, and one round had gone clear through his skull, killing him instantly. His body slumped to the deck and oozed blood all over the place. CPL Martinez grabbed the wheel and swung the wheel hard to starboard. This action got them out of the direct line of fire, and gave them a chance to compose themselves. Martinez asked if either of them could steer a boat, and Alex said yes, he was a former Marine and had learned how. "Good," he replied," you will be my assistant," directed CPL Martinez.

"Control One, Code 900! Code fucking 900!" screamed Martinez as he gave the dispatcher his location.

"I need some help now! My partner is dead! Give me some cover," screamed Martinez again.

"Marine 1, I copy. Help is on the way. Give a description of the weapons and shooter. Any ideas what they look like?" asked a very professional dispatcher, a slight tremble in her voice as she spoke.

"Hell no, it's too dark, but I am sure they were AKs, and a lot of them! I am going to drop back and keep them covered until backup arrives. Call West Sac.," replied Martinez, his actions a little less erratic and more under control.

Under the excitement, Martinez had not noticed that both Jeremy and Alex were returning fire with side-arms and the P.D.'s shotgun. The fire was apparently not very effective, because the ship did not even slow down, but at least it let them know that they were alive.

Aboard ship, the situation was a little more chaotic than it appeared. Several crew members had already slipped overboard, and disappeared into the night. The captain kept screaming that they should "give up" now, before it was too late!" Scarsdale quietly got on his cell phone and called Varmessy and told him of his predicament, and asked him to come and assist immediately. The "*Sexy Sally*" was quickly approaching the West Sacramento loading dock when Yuri instructed the captain to reduce power and coast toward a particular jetty. Varmessy's group had arrived with a large truck and were already waiting for them. The ship glided to a stop; before anyone could even move, a dozen or more men rushed aboard and picked up the precious cargo. The truck backed down the ramp a few feet, and the missile was shoved aboard. Once the missile was loaded, the rest of the men disappeared in fast-moving vehicles.

Martinez was on the radio the whole time giving directions to the dispatcher and relaying information to the other units. In frustration he began firing his sidearm toward the boat. Alex and Jeremy joined in, but everyone realized that these peashooters were not going to stop this boat, or its heavily armed crew. Martinez reached down and pulled out a flare pistol from his emergency kit. He loaded a shell into the chamber and carefully aimed at the ship's fantail. He fired, and the star-shell exploded exactly where he had aimed it. He reloaded the flare pistol and fired once more. The second round smashed through a window and landed in the galley area. His third and final round was quite unnecessary; it landed in the engine area and quickly spread.

Within a few minutes a giant fire spread throughout the ship. Suddenly, a huge fireball leaped into the Sacramento skyline. One of their small arms rounds had cut a fuel line, and the star-shell ignited it. The "*Sexy Sally*" blew up into a million pieces. The explosion was so great that pieces landed on both sides of the river. Witnesses on the east side of the river had to dodge flying debris.

Just before she exploded, Jeremy was able to see Oleg running toward the stern, a briefcase in his hand. The force of the explosion blew him into the water, fifty feet behind the ship, and in the middle of the river. His body slipped under the surface without even making a ripple. The burning fuel spread across the entire river, and it seemed impossible that anyone could survive the conflagration. Jeremy continued staring at the spot where he had last seen Oleg, but only the burning fuel was visible on the river.

Martinez took the wheel, and powered the throttle forward. The bow shot skyward and the police boat rushed forward toward the bank. Just before he was about to crash, he eased off and she glided into the sand bank without so much as a scratch. All three men jumped off the bow, and landed on shore without even getting wet. Several West Sac. PD. units were already on the scene. Jeremy turned around again and looked in the direction of Kolkov, but the river was swift and deadly. All that could be seen now was the flotsam of death and destruction. Jeremy shook his head and walked away, hoping that this nightmare would finally end. However, just to make sure, Jeremy instructed the fire department to conduct a thorough search of the area, and look for any survivors. However, deep in his heart he hoped that Kolkov was at the bottom of the river, already being devoured by the hungry eels and other critters.

The first vestiges of sunlight appeared over the skyline adding an orange twinge to the burning carcass of "*Sexy Sally*". Jeremy, Martinez and Alex all jumped into waiting police units and went off in hot pursuit. Sky One (CHP Helicopter) got on the airwaves and immediately spotted the truck heading westbound on I-80 toward San Francisco. Everyone jumped on the nearest freeway on-ramp and the pursuit started in earnest. Luckily for them, an off-duty CHP LT living in Dixon was having breakfast at the local International House of Pancakes (IHOP). LT Doug Geolog had heard the call for help, and drove down to the westbound lane of I-80 and coordinated the chase from there. He instructed Davis and Dixon PD. units to stop all westbound routine traffic. When he was assured by "Sky One" that the only ones on the freeway were the "Russian truck" and the pursuit units, he carefully placed a "nail strip" across the freeway. This device would ensure that anyone driving across it would not go very far.

The truck came barreling down the freeway at over ninety miles an hour. LT Geolog took a position in the middle of the center divider, and waited for them. The driver of the truck, one of Varmessy's men, did not see the nail strip until it was too late. When the tires hit the "strip", all four of them exploded into a thousand pieces. The explosion jerked the large truck to the right. The driver attempted to regain control of the vehicle, but the heavy load and the missile shifted forward and smashed through the back window.

The force of the missile caused the driver to swerve off the road. Once the truck started rolling, nothing could stop it. The missile broke free and was launched through the front windshield. It flew through the air and landed right in front of "Dixie the dinosaur" at the Chevron gas station in Dixon. Dixie was part of Dixon's charm, it was recently put on display there and quickly became an instant hit. Dixie was a replica of a 36-foot-tall brontosaurus. LT Geolog just stood there and watched this incredible scene. A twenty-foot Russian missile flying through the air and landing right between the front legs of an extinct dinosaur replica. The force of the impact had caused the missile to break in half, and the eight hundred pounds of heroin were being blown everywhere by the gusty wind.

Jeremy arrived on the scene, and immediately looked for survivors. There, mangled in the front seat, but still alive was Billy Bob Scarsdale. Jeremy could see that he was still alive, but had great difficulty in breathing. Jeremy paused and looked down at him. He felt no sentiment or emotions toward this longtime friend, only coldness. Jeremy looked around for any more victims, but could only find the crushed remains of Bolotin and the driver. Bolotin had not survived. He had a large piece of guardrail sticking through his chest; his eyes were bulging like a birthing goldfish. The driver was crushed beyond recognition, and only Billy Bob clung to life.

Jeremy patiently waited for the fire department to arrive on the scene and extract Scarsdale. Jeremy was anxious to talk to him. Jeremy needed to know. It was imperative for him to ask him, why? After ninety torturous minutes, the fire department was able to pry the bloody remains of Scarsdale from the truck. Scarsdale's body was so badly mangled that the firemen had to use the "jaws of life" to extricate him from the wreckage. Scarsdale was barely holding on to life. Jeremy sat in the ambulance as it rushed him toward the hospital.

"Bill, Bill, please tell me, why? I need to know. Please, Bill. I have to know," begged a disheartened Jeremy.

Scarsdale's eyes slowly opened up. His voice was very raspy, and barely audible. He had the look that Jeremy had so often seen before.

"Jeremy, Jeremy. Are you there? I am sorry. It was only money! Only for money. My wife needed it, and I couldn't provide it any other way. I am…" Billy Bob's voice trailed off, and the sentence was never finished. He died in the back of the ambulance, somewhere between Davis and West Sacramento, California.

Jeremy was pleased that they had recovered the heroin, but Oleg's untimely disappearance in the river still haunted him, and probably would for the rest of his life. It somehow seemed unfair to end a major portion of his life in this unresolved way, but circumstances dictated it. It was then and only then that Guido's dying words made sense: "To be rather than to seem."

THE END

About the Author

Sean Ryan Stuart is a southern boy by birth and heritage, however as the only son of a professional military man he traveled extensively throughout the world. His personal military experience includes six years in the Air Force and seventeen in the US Army as a counter-intelligence special agent. Additionally, he worked with various local, state and federal law enforcement agencies in his varied career. This association with civilian law enforcement extended up to and included his last seven years in the military.

Mr. Stuart has had extensive training in the field of security, investigations, narcotics, counter-terrorism and linguistics. He is fluent in five languages and has also been used as a technical advisor in Hollywood. Mr. Stuart is currently living in California and is teaching specialized subjects. He is also the author of dozens of articles on Russian Organized Crime and other related subjects.

www.ingramcontent.com/pod-product-compliance
Lightning Source LLC
Chambersburg PA
CBHW060423030726
47495CB00003B/706